The Only Way

by

Ola Wegner

This book is dedicated to M.K. Baxley and Brenda Webb in thanks for their support, help and encouragement while writing this story.

Chapter One

Fitzwilliam Darcy tightly gripped the rim of his top hat with both hands, as he stood in front of the parsonage. He could hardly believe what he was about to do. Life had surprised him many times, but this was perhaps the most unexpected turn of events for him. He found himself attached to a woman whom he had, from the beginning, perceived as entirely unsuitable for him. Considering her low social standing, her lack of connections, and her family made her the last female he should turn his attention to.

He was well aware of all these facts which spoke against her, and still he craved her. This past winter had been miserable for him – away from her, away from Netherfield, away from that little town full of mediocre people and gossip. He had considered himself almost cured when he met her again at his aunt's house, of all places. The first few days he had even prided himself that she had no effect on him. It had lasted till he had seen her from a distance on one of her long walks. Then, he admired how she stood up to his aunt and played the pianoforte, laughing with his cousin.

Now he was not only thinking about her, he felt a physical pain, some sort of ache in his chest when he did not see her for more than a day. The discomfort was taken away the moment she was in the same room with him. Another complication arose when she was too close, walked past him, or sat by him and he could catch her scent. At such times, her presence created quite different kind of discomfort for him.

He did not deserve such torture, and he could no longer pretend that the problem of Elizabeth Bennet did not exist. There were two solutions, first to leave instantly, run away from her and try to forget her. As he had already tried that before with no results, he was not particularly eager to repeat it. The other option was to propose and make her his, to have her company, her smiles, her attention, and one day, children with her. The warmth enveloped his heart at the thought of Elizabeth as his wife, sitting by his side next to the fireplace, teasing him, touching him, kissing him.

Some other man would perhaps consider the third option of making her his lover, but for Fitzwilliam Darcy, it was out of question. He could never offend and degrade her like that. She would never accept such a proposal from him, he was more than certain. Should he propose it, he would lose her forever, as she would not ever want to see or speak to him after hearing such an insult from his mouth.

He looked down at his hat, battered by his own hands. He would have to buy a new one. This one was unfit to wear.

He walked closer to the small house. There were some tall bushes planted in front of the windows. He stood behind one of them, safely hidden, and looked inside. Elizabeth was curled in an upholstered chair, her feet tucked under her, and she was reading a letter. She looked sad, or at least concerned with a small frown even visible on her forehead. He wondered what could have caused that. She could tell him later and he would try to aid her, or at the very least, improve her spirits. First things first though. He had to propose before he could be granted the right to hear about her worries.

He knocked at the front door, but nobody answered. He let himself in the small foyer. The house was quiet, as if abandoned. With his throat tight, he stood in front of the parlour door, and knocked. There was a moment of hushed sounds, before he heard Elizabeth's bright voice, calling him in.

The expression on her face told him that she was not expecting him. Quickly, she composed herself though, and offered him a seat, explaining that Mr. and Mrs. Collins were not present at the moment, and that she was all alone. She had excellent manners despite the unhappy circumstances of her upbringing, he had to admit. She would not bring shame to him. On the contrary, her intelligence, her lively mind, her charm would earn her respect everywhere.

She kept her eyes lowered, as if expecting him to initiate the conversation. He gathered his courage, and sat down, however not on the chair she had pointed for him, but next to her on the sofa she was occupying.

He could see that she stiffened at his close presence, and gave him a guarded look. He hoped she was not afraid of him; he would never hurt her. Never.

He cleared his throat. "Miss Bennet," he started, "You must have noticed that for some time now, I have developed a very special interest in you. I have struggled with my feelings for a while..."

He paused, thinking whether it was necessary to point out the discrepancies in their social standing, and remind her how her family was beneath him. After a moment of consideration, he decided against it. She must be well aware of that, and his words could only offend her unnecessarily. He did not wish to upset her. Clearing his throat, he continued. "I cannot stay silent on this any longer." He covered her small hand resting on her muslin draped thigh with his much larger one. "Miss Elizabeth Bennet, you must allow me to tell you how much I ardently admire and love you." He shifted to the floor, on one knee, wrapping his fingers around her delicate wrist. "In vain I have struggled. It will not do. Therefore, I ask you to end my suffering and agree to become my wife."

As he said the words, he looked intently into her face, waiting to hear her answer. Would it be too forward to kiss her? No, perhaps he should leave it for later, but surely she would allow him an embrace.

Her pink lips fell slightly open, and her dark brown, cat-like shaped eyes seemed even wider than usual. Her eyes were unquestionably her best feature; making one forget that she was not exceptionally pretty.

"Mr. Darcy, please stand up," she voiced herself at last, swiftly rising to her feet.

He rose together with her, and now towered above her as always. At the beginning of their acquaintance, he had thought her to be much too short for his likening, but now it suited him quite well. He was so enamoured, that he liked everything about her.

"Mr. Darcy," she said, lifting her eyes to him. "I … have no words. I am more than astonished."

Poor dear, he thought, amused with how shocked she appeared. "I understand that you cannot believe your own good fortune, but I assure you of the honesty and steadfastness of my intentions."

She walked away from him to the window. "Mr. Darcy, you must see that marriage between us in not possible," she said, not turning to him.

In two steps, he was next to her. She was such a sweetheart. She wanted the best for him, even by the cost of her own happiness.

"Your low connections and the lack of dowry bothered me as well, but after lengthy consideration, I decided to overlook those. You will adjust quickly to my circle of friends; no one would ever guess your unimpressive origins. I am wealthy enough to marry where I wish. Though you will not bring money, your intelligence and sound mind are of great value, something

I hope you will pass on my... our children. I have no desire to leave Pemberley to some idiot who will ruin it as I have observed many times among my neighbours."

During his speech, she flushed slightly, and her eyes sparkled excitedly. Did she like hearing about their future children? Was she embarrassed thinking what activities would be necessary in order to bring those children to be? He had certainly thought about it many times himself.

"Mr. Darcy," her voice drew his attention from his pleasant musings, "I thank you for your kind offer, I appreciate your honest intentions towards me. However, the union between us is not possible. It was never my intention to injure you by giving rise to expectations that are neither desired nor sought, and I can only hope that you will not suffer long."

He stared down at her with a frown. "You refuse me?" he asked slowly.

"Yes, I do," she answered simply.

He shook his head, not believing his own ears. "May I ask your reasons?"

She sighed, "Sir, I do not want to say something which may not be pleasant for either of us. Let us end this embarrassing conversation and never return to it again."

His hands tightened into fists, and he clenched them so hard that the nails cut painfully into the skin of his palm. "Pray, enlighten me," he murmured.

"Mr. Darcy, please do not make it more difficult than …"

"I will take the risk," he interrupted her. "Your reasons?" he prompted.

She looked him straight in the eye. "I have promised myself I would only marry for love. I have witnessed a loveless union firsthand, and I do not wish it for myself."

"I agree with you in that with all my heart," he assured. "I love you, and we will have a happy, loving marriage."

Elizabeth let out a short laugh. "Mr. Darcy, I know of many of your faults, but I never thought of you as daft. My intention was to be delicate, and considerate of your feelings, but you are making it impossible."

She caught his eyes and spoke slowly. "I do not love you, Mr. Darcy. I do not even like you. I am sorry to cause you pain, but it was unconsciously done. I beg you not to ever return to this conversation again."

She moved away from him, once more walking to the window, her back to him. "Leave me now, please."

"No, I will not go till you explain," he said, walking to her. "I do not understand."

She turned to him, "What do you not understand?"

"You claim not to like me," he reminded her. "Why?"

She cocked an eyebrow with a small smile playing on her lips. "My understanding is that you do not believe that a woman may dislike you."

"I do not care whether other people, women included, like me or dislike me," he spoke impatiently. "I am only interested in your opinion."

Her eyes narrowed. "Do you think that I would ever consider tying myself to a man who has ruined perhaps forever the chances of happiness for my most beloved sister?" she asked, pointing her tiny finger into his chest. "I know that it was you who separated Jane and Mr. Bingley. His sisters were involved as well, to be sure, but it was you who talked him out of making his proposal to Jane. Can you deny it?"

He hung his head low. "No, I cannot deny it, but I had my reasons."

"What reasons?" she cried, and began pacing the room, clearly becoming agitated. "My sister is the sweetest person I know. She did nothing wrong to anyone, and she did not deserve such treatment. Your friend treated her like a toy, broke her heart, and you supported him on that, perhaps even put the idea into his head."

He winced as he saw the tears in her beautiful eyes. He felt as if someone had kicked him in the gut. He had somehow forgotten the matter with Jane. He had hurt his dearest, loveliest Elizabeth, and she was crying now because of him.

"Perhaps I was wrong in my judgment," he acknowledged reluctantly. "I thought I was doing a favour to both of them. It can be repaired; it is not too late. Our marriage will bring Bingley and Jane together."

She shook her head. "No, no, it will not bring them together, because I will not marry you. It is not only the matter of Jane that I hold against you, but your general arrogance and lack of consideration for the feelings of others. You are rude, proud, and I do not enjoy your company. I beg you, sir, to leave me alone. Do me this courtesy, and do not prolong this any longer."

He stood rooted in place. He could not believe how badly this conversation had gone. He could not truly blame her. Her devotion to her sister was one of the qualities he had admired in her from the beginning. It was obvious that Miss Bennet must have harboured deeper feelings for Bingley than he had initially thought. Bingley, too, had been somehow subdued when he had last seen him.

His eyes rested on Elizabeth, who was far from calm. Good God, she was beautiful when angry, especially with her breasts falling and rising so rapidly. They were rather small, but how he wanted to see how they looked bared before him.

She lifted her eyes at him, giving him an angry look. "If you do not wish to leave, then I do," she hissed, storming out of the room.

He turned on his feet and went after her. She ran up the stairs, and he heard the slamming sound of a door.

He was faced with dilemma. He wanted, needed, to talk to her, explain to her, but he began to understand that she was not in the best mood for that. She had a temper, which was obvious. He found it rather attractive. A passionate woman was something to be desired. Once she calmed down and was ready to listen to reason, they would talk again. He could hardly follow her to her room; it was improper and he had no right.

He had no other choice but to leave her alone. He would come tomorrow, or even better, he would rise early the next morning and wait for her in the park. She always took an early morning walk. They would have enough privacy where they could have a sensible conversation, without unnecessary emotions.

He returned to Rosings without delay. Brusquely, he told his cousin to relay to his aunt that he had important correspondence to respond to, and he would not be joining the company in the drawing room.

His night was mostly restless. Elizabeth's words telling him that she did not love, or even like, him cut into his very heart, but he explained to himself that she could not feel it any differently at this very moment. She had witnessed her sister suffering from a broken heart, and faulted him for it. Consequently, she had convinced herself to disliking him. She was loyal to Jane, and she could not admit, even to herself, feeling the attraction to a man who in her opinion was responsible for ruining her sister's happiness.

Darcy was ready to acknowledge that he had been wrong and hypocritical in separating Jane and Bingley. However, as he had told Elizabeth, nothing was yet lost. Once the wedding date was set, he would ask Bingley to stand up for him, and he and Miss Bennet would have the opportunity to see each other again. They could even invite Jane to spend the summer at Pemberley.

He would make sure that Bingley would come too, and this way they would have plentiful opportunities to rekindle their friendship. Elizabeth would be so pleased with him. He could not wait to witness her reaction when he told her about his plans concerning Bingley and Miss Bennet. He wondered how she would show him her gratitude.

Sleep did not come to him easily. All the emotions boiling up prevented him from rest. He felt apprehensive, but hopeful; excited, but fearful about their meeting tomorrow. Had someone told him a year ago that he would be afraid to talk with a slip of girl of no consequence in the world, he would have laughed him off. He still found it unbelievable that he had lost control over himself to such an extent. Once they married and settled together, he would return to his own self. He would be the Fitzwilliam Darcy he had known all his life, only happier.

Having in mind that Elizabeth was an earlier riser, he was up and dressed before six. The house was quiet, and his still sleepy valet let him out. He walked the grounds back and forth for the next few hours, staying longer at the sites that Elizabeth favoured. Around eleven, he was certain that she had not gone on her morning walk that day as she usually did. Was she ill? She walked every single day. He had a niggling feeling that something bad must have happened.

He decided to visit the parsonage.

Mrs. Collins was seated in the parlour, together with her sister, Miss Lucas, but Elizabeth was nowhere to be seen. Now he was almost certain that Elizabeth was ill.

"Oh, Mr. Darcy," Mrs. Collins rose to greet him. "Have you heard the dreadful news?" she asked.

His heart froze. Bad news? Had something happened to Elizabeth? "No, I have not," he managed to say. "Where is Miss Bennet?"

"Poor Elizabeth, I thought you knew ..." She put a painful expression on her face. "My husband went to Rosings some time ago to tell your aunt about it."

"What happened?" he demanded impatiently.

"My friend received a letter late yesterday with such dreadful news. Her father, Mr. Bennet, has died in a tragic circumstance. Apparently two carriages crashed on the road, and he fell out, breaking his neck."

Darcy digested the information for a moment before asking gravely. "Where is Miss Bennet now?"

"On her way to London. Jane is still there, visiting their uncle."

Darcy frowned. "Did my aunt send a carriage with her?"

"No, she left by post two hours ago."

"Alone?" he questioned unbelievably. "You let her?"

Mrs. Collins' eyes widened at his harsh tone. "How could I stop her?" she asked meekly.

Darcy walked out of the room without saying goodbye, nor waiting for further explanation. He took the shortest path to the manor. How Elizabeth must be suffering now! He knew how close she had been to her father, that she had been his favourite. The despair he felt when his own father had passed away was still fresh in his mind.

He understood that she wanted to return home as soon as possible, but travelling alone by post with random strangers, without protection, was unthinkable. He could not allow it. He was not really surprised that she had done that. After all, he remembered well how she had walked three miles across the fields to see her sister when she was ill at Netherfield.

He would take his horse and intercept her in Bromley, where they would stop to change horses. There they would wait together for his carriage to arrive. She would not likely want to travel alone with him, as it would not be proper, so he would have to ask someone to accompany them. Mrs. Jenkinson, Anne's companion, would be the best choice, but he doubted whether his aunt would allow it. One of the maids would have to go. He had no time, nor was he in a mood to explain the situation with Elizabeth to his aunt. He could only imagine how Lady Catherine would react to the news. Today was not a day to listen to her hysterics.

Darcy found his man and ordered him to prepare their carriage without delay, take one of the maids, and drive to Bromley, where he would be waiting for him. His servant seemed surprised, but did not question his orders, and Darcy knew that he would do exactly as instructed.

Half an hour later, he was on his way to meet Elizabeth travelling on horseback.

Chapter Two

The Bell Inn was crowded, which was nothing unusual in the middle of week with so many travellers stopping on their way to London for a rest or a necessary change of horses. Thankfully, Elizabeth managed to find a place for herself in the quiet corner unbothered by anyone. She ducked her head low, hiding behind the wide rim of her bonnet. She did not wish to draw attention with her tear-stricken face.

There was a part of her which still could not accept the truth of the dreadful news she had received yesterday after Mr. Darcy left. Her Papa was not among the living anymore. How could it be? There was still a hope within her that she was dreaming it, or that it was a mistake, a misunderstanding... that it could be explained. The short letter from Mr. Gardiner gave no hope of that, though. Her uncle would never have shared such news with her if it had not been confirmed. The circumstances of the accident sounded tragic to her ears, and her imagination created the worst scenarios of her parent's demise. She dearly hoped that her father had not suffered long, and was not conscious and aware at his last minute. How she wanted to already be with her family, joined together in their grief.

In his message, Mr. Gardiner explained that he was sending the man servant for her earlier than planned, and that the man should arrive within two days in order to escort her to London. Elizabeth did not want to wait, though, and decided to take the early morning post to London. Charlotte and Mr. Collins had attempted to convince her that it was improper and unsafe for her to travel all alone with strangers. She had not listened to them. She could not sit and wait idly by at Hunsford when she could be with her family sooner.

Knowing that she had at least an hour before the post chaise carriage would be ready to start the journey again, she tried to mute the voices around her. It was only when someone's voice called her name close by, she looked up.

"Mr. Darcy?" she whispered hoarsely, marvelling at his presence. She blinked her eyes, but he did not disappear. He stood, leaning above her, a familiar scowl darkening his countenance.

He took a seat beside her, his broad back separating them from the people in the room, giving them a semblance of privacy. His eyes searched her face with intensity. She realized that her first recollection was wrong. He was not displeased; his expression was full of concern and worry.

"I was not aware that you were planning to return to London today, sir," she offered politely, concentrating on controlling her voice and emotions. She was not in any condition to speak with anyone today, Mr. Darcy especially.

"You thought I would not have come after you? I was on my way here half an hour after I spoke to Mrs. Collins, and she told me about what had happened."

She frowned. "You talked to Charlotte?" She was certain that her cousin, Mr. Collins, was going to run to his noble patroness at the first opportunity to chat about their tragedy, but she did not expect that from her friend. Charlotte was always very discreet.

"Yes, I visited the parsonage about two hours after you had left."

She regarded him with a blank expression. "Why did you go to Hunsford?" she asked, not quite understanding him. Surely he had no intention of speaking with her again after her blatant refusal of his proposal the day before.

He leaned closer, lowering his voice. "To see you, of course," his voice laced with impatience. "I planned to meet you during your early morning walk, but when you did not come to the park, I became worried that you might have succumbed to a sudden illness, and decided to call on Hunsford to enquire after your health."

She felt him taking her cold hand into his gloved one. He was wearing strong leather gloves, the ones men usually used while riding. Had he come here horseback?

"My sincere condolences, Miss Bennet," he said, his expression sincere. "I lost both of my parents, and I acutely remember my despair at the time. Even now, years later, I miss them. If I could, if it was in my power, I would take the suffering away from you."

"Thank you, sir," she whispered, so quietly that she was not sure whether he heard her.

A new wave of overwhelming anguish shot through her, tightening her chest and throat.

She choked a sob as the tears started to run quickly down her cheeks. She had succeeded in not shedding too many tears on her way here, but his presence, his kind words and compassion, unlocked something inside of her.

Her control completely broke, and within a minute she was sobbing, her vision blurred, gasping for air.

Darcy touched her arm gently, and said something before he left her alone for a moment. She frantically searched her reticule for a clean handkerchief, but the last one that she had with herself was crumpled and damp.

Soon a large, round man appeared in front of her, looking to be the owner of the place, or at least someone in charge. She attempted to compose herself, as she did not want any questions directed at her as to why she was weeping. The man must be concerned that she was making a spectacle out of herself in the room full of people, disturbing them.

Darcy was next to her again, taking her arm gently. "Miss Bennet, come." She allowed him to lead her across the common area, to a small chamber at the back which looked like a private sitting room designed for more affluent guests.

She heard him ordering tea, and soon they were left alone, for which she was grateful.

"May I?" he asked, tugging at the bow of her bonnet. When she did not protest, he untied the blue ribbon and gently removed her hat. Then he retrieved his own crisp linen handkerchief and dried her cheeks, before leaving it in her open palm.

She took a deep, shaky breath, hoping to calm herself.

Darcy sat on the chair opposite her, leaning forward. One of his hands was lightly touching the sleeve of her jacket.

"I have asked for a cup of strong tea for you," he said, stroking the navy blue velvet of her spenser. "It may help you to feel better."

"Thank you," she whispered, looking at him through her teary eyes, biting her lip hard, determined not to devolve to tears again.

He must have guessed her struggle because he said, "You should cry; I cried too when my father left this world."

"He was sad when I was leaving. I should have stayed..." she choked, erupting into sobs again.

"Shush," he whispered, moving to sit beside her. He put his arm around her, and she supported her forehead against the fine cloth of his coat.

Elizabeth closed her eyes, snuggling against his solid frame. She knew she should not allow it, that it was not right to use him for comfort, but she had no strength to break the embrace. He rocked her gently, stroking her back, murmuring kind words.

There was a knock at the door, and a young girl walked in with a tray full of refreshments.

Darcy broke his hold on her carefully and stood up to take the tray from the servant, ordering her to leave them alone. Elizabeth felt instantly cold without him beside her. She rubbed her arms with her hands to stop the shiver running through her body.

She observed as he prepared tea for her. He added a flat spoon of sugar and a drop of milk, exactly as she liked to take it. Was it an accident, or had he remembered how she preferred her tea?

"Here you are," he handed her the cup.

Her hands were trembling; he assisted her, helping to hold the cup.

She closed her eyes, enjoying the taste and the feeling of the warm liquid spreading down her parched throat.

"Thank you," she said as she finished. He took the empty cup from her, putting it aside.

"Would you care for some more?" he asked.

She shook her head. "No, thank you."

Darcy fell silent, which in her experience was nothing unusual for him, but then she had nothing to say either. She was grateful for his assistance. He had taken her away from the crowded place when she broke down, giving her the comfort of a private room where she could calm herself and gather her thoughts. It was, however, time for her to go. The post carriage would be leaving soon, and she did not want to miss it.

She picked up her bonnet and reticule at the same time remembering she had a small carpet bag with her as well.

"My bag!" she exclaimed worriedly. "I had it with me. I must have left it in the main room."

All her money, apart from a few coins that she kept in her reticule, was in her valise. Why had she not put her money in the reticule? How would she continue her journey if someone had taken her bag? She would need money to hire a hackney in order to get to her uncle's house near Cheapside once they arrived in London.

"What does it look like?" Darcy asked.

"A small carpet bag with wooden handles, a green one." she described.

He was out of the room and back within a short time, carrying her bag. She retrieved it from him quickly and opened it, checking whether anything was missing. She sighed in relief, her hand on her chest, seeing that the small purse, which had been a present from her mother on her last birthday, containing ten pounds, was still tucked neatly in the side pocket.

"It was under the bench you sat on previously," Darcy explained. "I hope that nothing is missing."

She shook her head. "Thankfully, no... I should have put the money into my reticule, and not in this bag. I do not know what I would do in London without it," she said more to herself than to him. She should have been more prudent, and despite her distress, looked after her possessions more closely.

"You should not have chosen to travel on your own in the first place," Darcy spoke, his tone lecturing. "It is dangerous for a young woman to do so."

"I hardly had a choice," she defended. "I need to be with my family as soon as possible."

He took a step closer. "You could have asked me to help you with your travel arrangements." He made a point to look directly into her eyes. "I would do anything for you; you know that."

She blushed under his gaze, remembering yesterday's proposal. Had it not been for the news about her father, she would have surely spent the entire night thinking about Mr. Darcy, and what he had said.

"Mr. Darcy, I thank you for your help today, for your assistance," she said with sincerity. "It was very kind of you to offer me a moment of peace and privacy. I will not forget it. However, I am sure that the post carriage is ready to leave. I should go."

She tried to move past him, but he blocked her way, reaching for her hand. "Stay with me. My men should be here soon, bringing my carriage. I will deliver you safely to your aunt and uncle."

"How would that look, Mr. Darcy?" she asked calmly. "Do you wish to compromise me?"

"A maid from Rosings is coming for reasons of propriety. Let me draw your attention to the fact that travelling without a companion by post is hardly proper for a young woman."

She pressed her lips together, muttering angrily. "I do not care about propriety. My father is dead; I want to be with my mother and sisters as soon as possible." New tears stood in her eyes, but she fought them, not wishing to lose control over herself again.

He sighed, placing both hands on her shoulders. "Elizabeth, my offer stands. Just say yes, say yes, and I will take care of everything." He cupped her cheek, stroking it with his finger. "Please, let me help you."

His gaze was pleading, and he looked sincere. If she was to be honest with herself, she would have to admit that there was a very small part of her which wanted to say yes to him, let him assist her, deal with troubling matters, take some of the burden from her. It was enough, however, to remember the manner of his proposal, the fact that he neither truly loved, nor respected and understood her, to refuse the temptation without regret. She had no patience for analyzing his intentions towards her, nor her own feelings at that very moment. She wanted to be alone with her pain on her way to Jane, her mother and her younger sisters. There was no place for him with her.

The door opened suddenly without a knock, and the familiar, muscular figure of Colonel Fitzwilliam stepped in. Elizabeth jumped away from Darcy, but she was certain that Colonel Fitzwilliam saw them standing close to each other, Darcy touching her face.

Not looking at the two men, she put on her bonnet and gloves, and collected her carpet bag and reticule.

"Colonel Fitzwilliam, Mr. Darcy," she nodded her head at them. "I am afraid it is now time for me to continue my journey."

Hastily, she stepped forward, but was not surprised when Darcy caught her arm.

She gave him a determined look. "Please, unhand me, sir," she whispered icily.

To her relief, he let go of her hand, and she rushed past the two men.

She walked through the room, which seemed less crowded, and continued toward the front of the inn. The post carriage was nowhere to be seen, and she wondered whether it had been moved to wait somewhere other than before.

"Excuse me," she enquired politely of a young lad who looked as if he worked around the stables, "Do you know where the post passengers are awaiting?"

"You missed it, Miss," the boy said.

Her heart sank. How would she reach London now? "Are you sure?"

"Quite sure, Miss."

"I travel to London with them. Why have they not called for me?"

"They were calling for people, and the driver even mentioned a young lady who paid for the whole trip in advance, but Mr. Brewster, the Bell's owner, told them not to wait for you."

"He said that! Why?"

"Don't know, Miss," the boy shrugged, "Something about travelling by private carriage with a betrothed I think."

It took Elizabeth a moment to comprehend what the lad had said. Darcy must have told the owner she was coming with him, and asked his to relay the information to the post chaise driver.

"Is there another post going to London today?" she asked.

"No, Miss. That was the last one today."

Elizabeth nodded and reached into her reticule to give a coin to a lad for his help.

"Thank you, Miss," the boy exclaimed, grinning widely.

The lad ran away as Elizabeth stood alone in front of the inn, thinking frantically what she should do now.

A familiar shiver ran down her back as she felt someone's close presence behind her. Turning around without much surprise, she saw Darcy and his cousin.

***

Darcy's eyes stared after Elizabeth as she hurried through the main room towards the entrance. She clearly intended to continue her journey on her own. He had a feeling that she would not be pleased when she learned that the post chaise had already departed. Her independence was equally admirable and infuriating to him. Why could she not see that he wished only the best for her, that he wanted to spare her hardships and make this difficult time easier for her?

"Darcy, would you care to explain to me," his cousin spoke, following Elizabeth's retreat with his eyes, "what are you doing here with Miss Bennet? Is it true that her father died in tragic circumstances? Collins came with such news earlier today."

"Yes, it is true," Darcy confirmed reluctantly. He was not particularly eager to discuss this matter with his cousin. "What are you doing here, cousin?" he asked coldly.

Colonel Fitzwilliam blinked, obviously surprised with the hostility on Darcy's part. "Must I remind you that you are my sole means of transportation at the moment? How was I to return to London? You brought me to Rosings to visit our dear aunt, and I expected that you would take me back. Was I wrong? When on my return from a ride, I saw your men preparing your carriage. I thought that I had no choice but go with them. I ordered my things to be packed and here I am. You could have informed me about your plans of departure a bit earlier." His cousin's tone was light on the surface as he was regarding him carefully. "It is so unlike you, Darcy, this behaviour. Is something bothering you?"

Darcy nodded, "Yes, but it is private, and I lack time to go into details now."

Colonel Fitzwilliam's blue eyes narrowed, "Is it about Miss Bennet? What were you doing with her earlier?"

"Yes, it concerns her, which reminds me that I have to find her now." Darcy confirmed. He made a move to walk past his cousin but was stopped by a firm grasp on his arm.

"What is your meaning?" the colonel asked sharply. "I knew that you fancied her, but I never thought that there was more to it. Are you following her? Why?"

"Why do you think?" Darcy enquired sarcastically.

Without warning, he was pushed back against the wall of the small room, unable to move, pinned by his cousin's strong hold.

"How dare you?" Colonel Fitzwilliam hissed. "She is someone's daughter, someone's sister, she may be poor, but you have no right to do that to her. Do you think that now, when her father is dead, and she is without protection, you can pursue her in such a manner? I always thought you a better man—a man of honour!"

"I will not allow you to do that," he added, "It was obvious to me that she was not pleased with your company. I myself will deliver her safely to her family if necessary..."

Darcy rolled his eyes, interrupting his cousin. "Do not be so melodramatic, Fitzwilliam. She does not need you to rescue her. My intentions are entirely honourable."

"Honourable," Colonel Fitzwilliam repeated, frowning. He let go of Darcy and stepped back. After a moment, his forehead smoothed and his face lit up. "You proposed?"

"Yes... yesterday," Darcy confirmed, a small smile lifting his lips. "I cannot imagine how you could have thought otherwise," he sounded offended.

"Forgive me, Cousin." Colonel Fitzwilliam's voice boomed, and Darcy received a sound smack on his back. "Congratulations! She is a very charming young woman. I did not know that you had it in yourself, man. I have always thought that you would eventually marry someone more ... predictable. Someone my mother would pick for you."

Darcy made a face at the mention of his other aunt and her matching ways, which caused his cousin to laugh.

"When I saw her so distressed, I just thought that..." Colonel Fitzwilliam continued, his voice apologetic. "I am happy to be wrong," he assured with a wide smile, which faltered a moment later. "She must be truly devastated with her father's demise," he added thoughtfully, "you should not push her now. You should be more patient with her."

"I know," Darcy acknowledged, and then added hesitantly, "We had a little argument, and I was trying to reach an understanding with her when you came in, explain some matters to her, make her see my point."

Colonel Fitzwilliam was nodding his head, but his expression was guarded and confused.

"We will talk later, Cousin," Darcy said. "I truly need to go to her."

They walked together outside the inn where they saw Elizabeth conversing with a young boy. The boy soon ran away, and she stood alone, hugging herself and rocking back and forth.

She turned to them when she must have sensed them approaching. She looked straight at Darcy, ignoring Colonel Fitzwilliam. "I missed my carriage," she said, her tone accusing. "You asked to have the driver told that I was not continuing my journey with them."

Darcy shrugged, stating calmly, "I assumed you would continue with me."

"You had no right," she said, her voice trembling. "I have not given you my consent to do that."

Darcy's expression darkened, his jaw line tightening, but he spoke calmly, "I only want what is best for you. We have already discussed it."

She opened her lips to say something, but then closed them, looking to the side, away from the two men.

Colonel Fitzwilliam looked between his cousin and Elizabeth, before taking a step forward, speaking gently, "Miss Bennet, please accept my sincerest condolences. I cannot imagine how you feel now. I did not have the pleasure of knowing your father, but I am sure that he was a man of rare character and value to be blessed with a daughter like yourself."

Elizabeth looked up at him warmly, "I thank you, sir."

"I understand that you will continue your journey with us," he offered lightly.

"I have no other choice," she agreed quietly. "I want to reach my uncle's house in Cheapside as soon as possible, so my sister and I may return home to Longbourn as soon as may be," she explained.

As she was speaking, she kept her eyes on Colonel Fitzwilliam, as if Darcy was not there with them.

The older man nodded with understanding. "I am afraid that we need to wait some time before Darcy's carriage will again ready to travel. The horses need their rest. Let us return inside, Miss Bennet."

He offered his arm, which Elizabeth accepted without hesitation. They walked past Darcy, and she did not give him a second look.

Once back in the private sitting room at the inn, Elizabeth excused herself so that she might refresh herself. Darcy ordered a late lunch for all of them. He was hungry, and he knew that his cousin would not refuse a meal, but his first thought was for Elizabeth. He doubted that she had eaten much today, if anything. He did not want her to get sick.

"She is furious with you," Colonel Fitzwilliam stated, using the first opportunity when they were alone. "What did you do to her?"

"It is not your business," Darcy responded coldly.

"She does not act as a happy bride to be," the other man pointed out.

"What do you expect? She has just learned that her father, with whom she was very close, died."

"Do not talk to me as if I am an idiot, Darcy," Colonel Fitzwilliam challenged. "You are not telling me everything."

They stared at each other for a moment.

"She refused me," Darcy divulged at last, seeing that his cousin had no intention of stopping the interrogation.

He was met with an unbelievable look. "She what?"

"She refused my offer of marriage," Darcy repeated quietly. Hastily, he added. "She bears certain misapprehensions about me, but once I explain everything to her, she will come to senses, and we will be happy together."

"It must be serious indeed if she refused you. In her situation, you are the best that could ever happen to her."

"I unknowingly did harm to a person close to her, and she holds it against me. However, she knows how much I love her, and once I repair what I did, she will forgive me and all will be well between us."

"I hope so, Cousin," Colonel Fitzwilliam spoke with sincerity. "I like and admire her. She has spirit, and is not boring like so many other ladies. She is a good choice for you. I would consider her myself if my situation was different."

Darcy gave him a dark glare. "You cannot imagine that I wish to hear that."

"Calm down, as a second son I do not have your freedom to choose where I wish, and you know it very well. Moreover, I would never pursue her knowing your intentions. You deserve your happiness, Darcy. You have not had much of it in your life."

Their conversation came to an end when Elizabeth walked in. She looked refreshed, her face freshly scrubbed, with a healthy pink glow to her cheeks. She seemed calmed and more in control of her emotions. She politely refused any food, and only stared out of the window as the two men partook of their meals. Darcy tried to persuade her to eat, but stopped when his cousin gave him a meaningful look, combined with a light kick under the table.

She stayed like that until it was announced that the carriage was waiting and they could go.

Chapter Three

She did not look at him for the entire trip to London. Even though he understood that she was tired, grieving, and displeased with him, he could not help from feeling slightly hurt and rejected with her behaviour. At least she did not cast a second glance at Colonel Fitzwilliam as well. She scooted into the corner by the window, so quiet and motionless that he could swear she was not even breathing.

The carriage box, though spacious, was rather crowded in his opinion. Elizabeth and the maid were seated on one side while his cousin and he were on the other. Darcy purposively took a place opposite Elizabeth so he could stare at her at his pleasure. It was a habit he had started at the very beginning of her acquaintance and he would not break it now.

How he wished to be alone with her now, to be able to draw her in his arms and offer her the comfort of his embrace. She had enjoyed being held by him earlier, in the privacy of the sitting room at the inn. She had calmed considerably, cuddling close to him. His heart had soared at having her in his arms despite the sadness of seeing her in such distress.

Mr. Bennet's unexpected demise had complicated matters considerably. He had had no chance to properly explain his involvement in separating her sister and Bingley. They needed an opportunity to talk, so she could see him in a different light and trust him.

He planned to ask for a private talk with her uncle; Gardiner was his name if he remembered correctly. The man was Mrs. Bennet's brother, and Darcy sincerely hoped that, contrary to his sister, he was not a blathering witless fool as his sister was. He searched his memory for the times when Elizabeth had talked about her uncle, and he realized that she had always done it with a smile on her face—a warmth in her voice and obvious admiration. Moreover, she and Jane seemed to be good friends with the man's wife, Mrs. Gardiner. That was a good sign, as Elizabeth had excellent taste in people, apart from Wickham perhaps, but he was an entirely different matter. That cad could charm the devil himself if he put his mind to it. Darcy all too clearly remembered how his Elizabeth had seemed to enjoy Wickham's company this past autumn.

Taking everything into consideration, the chances were good that Mr. Gardiner was a reasonable man and would support Darcy's cause. He had a feeling that Elizabeth highly respected her uncle's opinion.

Cheapside was not a part of London which he favoured, and he had no acquaintances there. He was pleasantly surprised when they stopped in front of a handsome building. He had expected something much worse. On the other side of the street, there were impressive looking warehouses and a large shop which as he believed were owned by Mr. Gardiner. The house itself was unpretentious, not small by any means, two stories high, built in red brick with large, tall white windows.

A woman in her early thirties flew through the front door as he helped Elizabeth down from the carriage steps. It had to be her aunt, because Elizabeth fell into her arms and they embraced. Darcy gave a discreet appraisal to the lady as she and Elizabeth hugged each other, crying and speaking interchangeably in hushed voices.

He had to admit that Mrs. Gardiner was a pleasant looking, objectively attractive woman if someone fancied round, freckled strawberry blondes. There was nothing crass or vulgar in her outer appearance. She was dressed in light colours, and though he knew little of women's fashion, he could see that her dress was finer than Elizabeth's.

At last, Mrs. Gardiner acknowledged him and his cousin, enquiring after Elizabeth's companions.

"These are Mr. Darcy and his cousin, Colonel Fitzwilliam. They were visiting their aunt, Lady Catherine de Bourgh of Rosings Park, during my stay at Hunsford. They were kind enough to offer me a place in their carriage on their way to London," Elizabeth explained quietly, her eyes downcast, not looking at any of them.

Mrs. Gardiner frowned, gazing intently at her niece. Darcy could see from her expression that she was not sure what to think about Elizabeth travelling alone with two strange men that she probably had never heard of before.

Darcy stepped forward. "Madam, Fitzwilliam Darcy of Pemberley, Derbyshire, at your service," he bowed, introducing himself. Elizabeth had mentioned their names, still he had to be sure that her aunt knew who he was exactly, and that his intentions were honourable.

He had noticed that Mrs. Gardiner's eyes widened in recognition as he said his name. She must have heard about him before; he was almost certain.

Had Elizabeth talked with her about him, or mentioned him in her letters to her aunt? That was possible.

"I assure you that we travelled with a maid so that Miss Bennet would not feel uncomfortable in our company," he continued. "Since she received the tragic news yesterday, she has been adamant to return home as soon as possible. I could not allow her to travel alone by post, especially when she is so distressed."

He noticed that Elizabeth pressed her lips tightly at his words, her body stiffening. Mrs. Gardiner was regarding them with astonished eyes, glancing back and forth between her niece and Darcy.

Soon, however, the woman composed herself, and politely invited them in. Elizabeth interjected instantly, suggesting that the gentlemen had important matters to attend.

Before Mrs. Gardiner could answer anything to that, Darcy spoke.

"We are happy to accept your invitation, Mrs. Gardiner. I was also hoping for the opportunity to speak in private with your husband, madam."

Mrs. Gardiner stared at Elizabeth for a moment before nodding at Darcy and Colonel Fitzwilliam. "Please, gentlemen, let us go inside the house. You must be tired after the journey." She looked over at the driver, the footman and the maid who now stood by the carriage behind them. "Your servants are invited into the kitchen, and I am sure that your horses need their rest too. Our stable is behind the house."

Darcy thanked Mrs. Gardiner, checking quickly with his men whether they had heard and understood her instructions. He decided that he already liked her. She had a pleasant, melodic voice, spoke sensibly, and held herself with grace and refinement. She was nothing like Elizabeth's other aunt, that horrible Philips woman.

They were led into a rather spacious drawing room. Darcy was pleased, impressed even, to see calm, tasteful, almost elegant interiors. There were open books and newspapers lying on the tables, and a new-looking pianoforte stood by the window. It was very similar to the one he had bought Georgiana for Christmas.

Elizabeth excused herself from their company without giving much explanation. Mrs. Gardiner seemed confused with her niece's behaviour, and obviously worried for her.

Darcy could see that this situation was uncomfortable for Elizabeth; it was for him as well, but he had no other choice. He needed to talk to her uncle and the sooner the better, so he could explain his intentions to him. His cousin gave him a few questioning looks, but otherwise was very helpful, using his easy manner to engage Mrs. Gardiner into conversation.

They did not have to wait long before Mr. Gardiner came into the house. He did not look pleased as he heard from his wife that Elizabeth had arrived in the company of not one, but two, strange gentlemen. He was polite, but his voice was cold as he addressed Darcy and Colonel Fitzwilliam. Darcy was not in the least offended by the less than welcoming reception from Mr. Gardiner. He would be hostile too, even more so, if he was in Mr. Gardiner's shoes.

He was about to ask Mr. Gardiner for a private conversation, when the door opened and several children ran inside followed by Jane Bennet.

The smallest of the children was still a baby, and it was wrapped around Miss Jane like a little monkey, clearly sleepy and tired.

Two older ones, which could be twins, but not identical, clung fiercely to their father's legs. From their chatter Darcy understood that they had not seen their Papa for the entire day and they missed him. The oldest girl, looking to be around eight years of age, stood politely on the side, glancing curiously at the guests from time to time.

The children's cheeks were rosy, and they still had their jackets and hats on, so Darcy assumed that they had just returned from their walk.

Mrs. Gardiner took the baby from Jane's arms and gathered the rest of the children, taking them away despite their protests to being separated again from their father.

As they were left alone, only in the company of Mr. Gardiner and Jane, the latter stepped forward. "Mr. Darcy, I did not expect to see you here," she said in her usual calm, controlled voice, but he could see the surprise written in her eyes.

"Miss Bennet," Darcy bowed deeply, having every intention to be polite and engaging in his relations with Jane from this moment on, even if he had not done so in the past. It was clear to him now how much Miss Bennet's happiness and opinions meant to his Elizabeth. Having Jane on his side would undoubtedly improve his own relations with her sister. "We have escorted Miss Elizabeth from Kent after we heard about your tragedy," he explained. "Please accept our condolences."

Jane's blue eyes filled with tears as he referred to Mr. Bennet's demise, but she composed herself quickly. "I thank you, Mr. Darcy. I am sure that my sister is most grateful that you were so thoughtful to ensure so she could reach us so quickly."

Darcy knew very well, whether he wanted it admit or not, that Elizabeth was currently less than pleased with him, but he appreciated Jane's kind words. He had once thought Jane Bennet to be cold and emotionless, but he could see now how wrong he had been. She did not seem to hold a grudge against him, though she could have a legitimate reason not to like him, if Elizabeth had shared her suspicions about his involvement in the matter of Bingley. He felt suddenly ashamed of himself for what he had done. Elizabeth was right, Miss Bennet had done no wrong to him, to anyone, and still he had purposely brought her pain and suffering.

He was awakened from his musings by the not so gentle nudge from his left side where his cousin stood. He glanced at Colonel Fitzwilliam in annoyance, and noticed his raised eyebrows and eyes pointing meaningfully at Jane.

Darcy barely stopped from rolling his eyes, considering it would not be polite in this company, and motioned to his cousin. "Miss Bennet, let me introduce you to my cousin, Colonel Fitzwilliam."

The colonel stepped forward and bowed deeply, murmuring his condolences, combined with ensuring how happy he was to finally meet her, despite the sad circumstances.

Jane was about to answer, her mouth forming words, but Mr. Gardiner cut in, asking her directly, "Jane dear, do you know this gentleman?" He glanced at Darcy.

"Yes, uncle. Mr. Darcy was a guest at the house of our neighbour this past autumn. We met him at several dinners and assemblies," she explained.

"Which neighbour?" Mr. Gardiner asked sharply. "Do I know him?"

Instant sadness appeared on Jane's face, her delicate eyebrows frowning. "It was Mr. Bingley, Uncle, but I do not believe that you met him," Jane acknowledged quietly, her eyes lowered.

Mr. Gardiner looked pointedly from Jane to Darcy. "I do not believe that being Mr. Bingley's friend is the best recommendation for any man."

Darcy swallowed and even felt his face blushing.

The older man was not beating around the bush. He must know how Bingley had treated Jane, that he had hurt her, paying her attention, only to abandon her without a word of goodbye. He did not want his other niece to suffer from the same fate. Darcy was determined to prove, however, how wrong he was.

"Mr. Gardiner," he turned to the man directly, "I wish to talk with you in private. I assure you that the matter is of utmost importance. It concerns Miss Elizabeth, and I believe the future and well being of the entire Bennet family."

Mr. Gardiner said nothing, but only walked across the room, opened the door, and called for Madeline. Darcy assumed that Madeline was his wife, and he frowned slightly at the impropriety of calling Mrs. Gardiner by her first name. It would be understandable when in private, of course, and he had every intention of using Elizabeth's given name when they were alone. Nevertheless, when in company, she would always be Mrs. Darcy, and he certainly would be proud to call her that.

Mrs. Gardiner came quickly, still carrying the baby in her arms. The baby's face was red and tear stricken, and though it was not crying loudly, steady whimpers of distress were coming from it.

They talked quietly for a moment, and though it was not his intention to listen to them, he understood that the baby was fussy, or sick, and Mrs. Gardiner did not want to leave it alone. Darcy wondered where the baby's nanny was. Surely Mrs. Gardiner did not take care of her children by herself.

Mr. Gardiner took the wiggling baby from his wife, and asked her loudly enough for everyone to hear, to keep the company of Jane and Colonel Fitzwilliam in the drawing room.

Still with baby in his arm, Mr. Gardiner stepped to Darcy. "Let us go," he said curtly.

Darcy followed him, being quite certain that on their way to the study, or the library, or whatever room he was being led to, Mr. Gardiner would dispose of the child, giving it to its nanny or the nursemaid.

Nothing like that happened. Mr. Gardiner pushed the door to a small library, filled with books up to the ceiling, and walked in. Darcy closed the door after them, and took the seat in the chair pointed to him.

Mr. Gardiner sat down, settling the baby on his lap. Darcy noticed only then that the child had a piece of bread in its hand, which it put into his mouth, chewing it together with his chubby little fingers.

"He is teething," Mr. Gardiner offered as the explanation of his son's actions, trying to pull the little hand out of the baby's mouth. "Not the most pleasant experience for him, I believe."

"That is unfortunate," Darcy said.

"On the contrary, we were quite worried that he grew no teeth at all for a long time. It is high time for him to get some. His siblings had all cut several teeth by his age."

Darcy nodded politely, not being sure what to say. The man seemed to be very much involved in the child's upbringing. Such behaviour was not something common, Darcy believed. He was quite certain that his own father, though caring deeply for him and Georgiana, had rarely visited the nursery, or played with them when they had been babies. Darcy's first clear memories of interactions with his parents had been from the times when he had been much older, five or six, being taught horse riding by his father.

"So, Mr. Darcy," Mr. Gardiner began to speak, his tone uncompromising, "you wished to speak to me privately. I hope that you will explain this situation to me. I come home to find my dear niece earlier than she was expected, delivered by two men who have, to my knowledge, at least, no relation to our family."

"I perfectly understand your apprehension, sir," Darcy assured.

Mr. Gardiner cocked his eyebrow. "Do you?"

"Certainly. I am a guardian to my sister, who is more than ten years my junior."

The man did not comment on that, but continued, "You are the friend of the infamous Mr. Bingley then?" he enquired.

"Yes, sir, as Miss Bennet has already explained, I was introduced to your nieces last autumn while I was a guest at my friend's house." In short words, he explained how his admiration for Elizabeth had grown from almost the first moments of their acquaintance. He talked about their accidental meeting in Kent and how all his feelings for her had returned with double force.

"I realized then that I could not see my future life without her by my side, and proposed yesterday afternoon, just before she received the news about Mr. Bennet's tragic death," he finished his tale.

Darcy could see that the older man seemed much calmer now, but was still cautious in his attitude.

"As my brother-in-law, Elizabeth's father, is sadly not among the living, I feel entitled to ask this question," Mr. Gardiner paused, his eyes narrowed.

"What can you offer my niece? Can you support her and ensure her safety? You must know that she has no dowry to speak of, and she will not receive any money, especially now, when Longbourn will go to the Bennets' cousin, Mr. Collins."

"I am well aware of that, Mr. Gardiner. I do not care for her dowry. I love her, and wish to marry her," he answered simply.

Mr. Gardiner leaned back into the chair, a thoughtful expression on his face. "What is your occupation, Mr. Darcy? I can see you are a gentleman, but may I know more?" he asked in a lowered voice, clearly because his son looked sleepy, his eyelids drooping.

Darcy knew that Mr. Gardiner was asking specifically about his income, but he was delicate enough not to enquire directly.

"I have an estate in Derbyshire which gives me around ten thousand a year. Moreover, I have savings and some investments which give profit up to five thousand a year."

"Derbyshire, you say?" Mr. Gardiner spoke with sudden interest. "My wife was born and raised there. Have you heard of a small town near Matlock, Lambton?"

Darcy nodded. "Yes, sir. It is but five miles from my home."

"Your home?" Mr. Gardiner's eyebrows lifted high on his forehead. "Are we speaking about Pemberley?" he asked incredulously.

Darcy's chest rightfully swelled with pride. "Yes, sir."

"Darcy... yes, of course. I knew that your name sounded familiar... but I could not remember where I had heard it. I would have never thought that someone like you would..." Mr. Gardiner shook his head, frowning. "Forgive me, Mr. Darcy, but you come from one of the oldest families in the country, you own half of the county, people come to tour your home, and you wish to marry my niece, a girl without a penny to her name and no connections to speak of."

"Yes, sir. I admit that I hesitated for a long time before I made her an offer. I was very attracted to her from the beginning, and even tried to forget about her, distance myself from her, but to no avail. I love her, and I cannot imagine my life without her. Even more now, when she suffers so much from her father's death. I hate to see her in such distress. I believe that she was very close with Mr. Bennet."

"Yes, she was his favourite, in many ways like the son he never had," Mr. Gardiner confirmed.

"I want to help. I have not yet discussed it with Miss Elizabeth, but I plan to secure her mother and sisters."

Mr. Gardiner looked astonished once again. "That is more than generous. Not many would decide to do something like that."

Darcy shrugged his shoulders. "I know that she would not be happy knowing that her closest family lacks comfort and security. I was thinking about buying a house for Mrs. Bennet, and settling Miss Bennet and the younger sisters with suitable settlements to ensure their future. I will ask my solicitor to draw the necessary papers, reviewing them with you, if you allow."

Mr. Gardiner was silent for a longer moment, his expression thoughtful, before he spoke again, "I must say that my niece is very fortunate in securing your devotion, especially now, in her current situation. You have my blessing, and I am sure that my sister, Mrs. Bennet, would also be pleased with Elizabeth's engagement to you."

Darcy breathed out in relief, some of the tension leaving his body at Mr. Gardiner's acceptance of his suit.

"Will you and your cousin stay for the dinner, Mr. Darcy?" Mr. Gardiner asked more cheerfully, standing from his chair, placing the baby on his shoulder, careful not to interrupt his sleep.

"I thank you, sir, but I believe that it would be too much of an imposition. We do not wish to invade your privacy more than we already have. Moreover, it is quite late, and it has been a long and eventful day for all of us I believe."

"As you wish, Mr. Darcy," Mr. Gardiner agreed easily. "I will call for Elizabeth so she may say goodbye to you."

"There is no need for that, sir," Darcy said quickly. "She must be very exhausted. However, I will call round tomorrow, if you will allow it."

His conversation with Mr. Gardiner had gone very well, and he did not wish anything to spoil the good impression he seemed to have given the man. Elizabeth must be tired, grieving, exasperated with him. In summary, not in the mood to see him again today. The best proof was that she had left their company so suddenly, without attempting any kind of explanation. He knew that he would have a better chance to come to an understanding with her tomorrow, when she would be well rested.

"Yes, of course, feel welcome to visit us tomorrow," Mr. Gardiner smiled, holding out his left hand, as the right one was supporting his son. "It was a pleasure to meet you, Mr. Darcy."

Darcy took the man's hand, and returned the firm handshake, replying sincerely, "Likewise, sir."

They returned to the drawing room where they found Mrs. Gardiner, Colonel Fitzwilliam and Jane, having tea. Elizabeth was nowhere in sight, which only convinced Darcy that his decision not to speak to her again tonight was a good one.

Darcy thanked Mrs. Gardiner for her hospitality and apologized for the intrusion. She repeated her husband's invitation for Darcy and Colonel Fitzwilliam to stay for dinner. He refused, as before, but was thankful for her welcoming manner. Both Mr. and Mrs. Gardiner proved to be sensible and kind people. He had great hopes to gain allies in them on his matter. Elizabeth liked and respected them. She obviously relied on their opinions and wished for their approval.

As the front door was closed behind them, and they were waiting on the street for their carriage to arrive, Colonel Fitzwilliam asked a rather unexpected question.

"Is Miss Bennet the lady whom you forbade Bingley from marrying?"

Chapter Four

Seated in one of the guest bedrooms, which Jane had claimed as hers since the beginning of her stay at the Gardiners' house in the first days of January, Jane took her sister's hand in hers. "You cannot be serious, Lizzy." Jane exclaimed, staring at her sister with wide eyes. "Mr. Darcy proposed to you yesterday?"

"Believe me, Jane, I can hardly believe it myself," Elizabeth responded dryly.

The older sister blinked her eyes, a confused expression written over her pretty face. "But how…? He always seemed so cold and distant. You always claimed that he disliked you the same as you disliked him."

"Exactly," Elizabeth cried, standing up from the sofa, and began pacing the room. "He denied my good looks from the first moments of our acquaintance. He made it perfectly clear that he disapproved of me and my ways. He rarely spoke to me, and when he did, it was always to disagree with me."

"Yes, I remember how we talked about his particular behaviour more than once." Jane nodded thoughtfully and then frowned. "I do not comprehend one matter though. From your recent letters, I understood that he was engaged to his cousin, Lady Catherine de Bourgh's daughter. Anne is her name?"

"It was my impression they were engaged," Elizabeth explained. "Mr. Collins talked about it often. It was implied that their union had been arranged by their mothers when they were children. However, neither Mr. Darcy nor his cousin, Colonel Fitzwilliam, ever confirmed it."

Jane was silent for a moment, before asking, "Did Mr. Darcy pay you any special attention while at Kent?"

"No, he did not." Elizabeth answered instantly, but then hesitated. "I thought his behaviour bizarre at times. Charlotte even attempted to suggest that he was interested in me, but I rejected such thoughts at once. I did not believe her. I laughed at the idea of Mr. Darcy having any feelings for me."

"What caused her to think that he was interested in you?"

"He paid me visits at times when he had to be aware I was all alone in the parsonage. He asked some unconnected questions, like for instance whether I would prefer to live close to my family or not in the future, and what was my opinion on Charlotte's marriage. I met him often during my walks. I told him specifically which my favourite spots were so he could avoid them, still he returned to them time and again. He walked me back to parsonage quite often, but he was quiet, not initiating conversation. At the time, I found it all very strange, but I could not come up with a reasonable explanation for his behaviour towards me."

"Mr. Darcy has been in love with you all this time," Jane marveled, shaking her head, "perhaps even since last autumn. We all thought that he did not like you though, even Mama."

"Yes, it is so..." Elizabeth paused, lacking the right words, "unexpected, impossible." She brought her hands to her head and rubbed her temples. "I still cannot wrap my mind around it all."

"Lizzy," Jane directed her blue eyes at her sister, demanding her sole attention. "What did you say to him when he asked you to become his wife?"

"Oh, Jane, do you have to ask?" Elizabeth cried, outraged. "I refused him, naturally. What else could I answer? You know how much I dislike him. His manners, his arrogance, his rudeness, his selfishness... the fact that he did everything in his power to remove Mr. Bingley from Netherfield, not to mention the matter with poor Mr. Wickham, how unfairly he treated him."

Another heavy frown appeared on Jane's forehead. "If you refused him, why did he bring you here in his carriage?"

Elizabeth stepped back to her sister, standing in front of her. "I had no other choice, he forced me to do that," she said simply.

Jane's eyes widened. "Are you implying that he put you in the carriage by force, with him and his cousin? That is horrible! I have always thought him a gentleman."

"No, no, I came willingly, but... oh, Jane, I had no other choice," Elizabeth sat down next to her sister, and in short words she explained what had happened since early morning that day.

"Oh, Lizzy," Jane spoke compassionately. "You indeed had no other choice if it was the last post departing for London."

"I could choose to go with him or spend the night in the inn. I decided to go with him, hoping that the presence of the maid, and good Colonel Fitzwilliam, would guarantee that he would not try to do so something completely against my will, like taking me to Gretna Green for instance."

"You think that he would be able to do something like that?"

Elizabeth leaped from her place to her feet and began pacing again. "I do not know what he could do." She let out an exasperated sound, resembling a growl. "Oh, Jane, I am so angry with him! He does not listen to me!" she exclaimed, gesturing wildly with her hands. "I tell him how I feel, and he disregards it as if I was a child and did not know any better. He gets something in his head, and he does what he wants, not looking at the other people's wants and needs. He all but forcibly invited himself into this house. I left him there with Aunt Madeline alone, because I knew that one minute longer by his side, and I would start screaming at him, or worse, slap him. I had to excuse myself from the company, or I would not be able to control myself."

Jane saw that her sister was extremely agitated, clenching and unclenching her hands, still walking the length of the room back and forth. She waited a moment before saying the next sentence, which she knew would upset Elizabeth even farther.

"Mr. Darcy spoke with uncle for quite a long time."

Elizabeth froze. "He did?" she whispered, pausing, biting her lip. "I should have guessed that. I do not want to think what he told him." She covered her face with her hands.

As soon as she said the words' there was a knock on the door, and their aunt and uncle walked in.

"Lizzy, can we talk?" her uncle asked, holding little Fred to his chest.

Jane rose smoothly, making her way to the tiny boy in her uncle's arms.

The boy smiled widely at her, all his three teeth showing, reaching to her with his pudgy arms.

"I will leave you alone," Jane said, cuddling the baby to her.

"Thank you, Jane," Mrs. Gardiner smiled at her. "Can you please see that the children finish their dinner?"

"Naturally," Jane agreed, and with one warm, reassuring look at her sister, she left the room.

"Lizzy," Mrs. Gardiner was first to speak. "I think that we should talk about what happened today, about Mr. Darcy."

Elizabeth nodded. "I owe you both an explanation," she agreed. She knew how bad it looked, her arrival with not one, but two strange gentlemen.

"Mr. Darcy left not so long ago," the older woman continued gently. "Your uncle tells me that he did not wish to say goodbye to you, claiming that you must be exhausted. You excused yourself from his company as soon as you could. Forgive me for asking, but am I guessing right that you had a misunderstanding and argument?" she enquired gently.

Elizabeth's heart sank in worry; her aunt was speaking in a way as if she was sure that there was something between Darcy and she, some kind of close connection.

"It was more than a misunderstanding," she acknowledged, trying to keep her voice even. "He does not listen to a word I say to him; he only does what he wants to do," she repeated what she had said earlier to Jane.

Mr. Gardiner stepped closer. "Let us sit down, Lizzy." He motioned the woman to the sofa and himself chose a nearby chair. As they all were seated, he started speaking again, leaning forward. "What was your meaning when you said he did not listen to you?"

Elizabeth looked straight at him. "Uncle, can you tell me what Mr. Darcy told you? Jane mentioned that you talked for a long time."

"Mr. Darcy explained the circumstances in which he brought you here. We talked about your engagement and your future together."

"There is no engagement," she interrupted him.

Mr. and Mrs. Gardiner exchanged astonished looks.

"We are not engaged," Elizabeth said firmly.

"He did not propose to you?" her aunt asked. "He said that he did."

"He did, that is true, but I refused him."

"You what?" they cried simultaneously, staring at her as if she had grown another head.

"I said no to his offer of marriage," she repeated firmly.

For a moment, there was a perfect silence in the room, as if all of them had stopped breathing.

"Lizzy, are you out of your mind to refuse this man?" Mr. Gardiner asked first, his voice raised. "You know who he is? It is a miracle that you even had an opportunity to meet him."

Elizabeth blinked her eyes at him, surprised with the man's attitude. Her uncle was usually so calm. "Uncle, you do not know him as well as I do," she defended herself. "He is selfish, arrogant, and prideful. He fancies hurting people who did nothing wrong to him."

"Are you certain that he is all that, Lizzy?" Mrs. Gardiner asked slowly, concern painted all over her face.

"Yes, I am quite certain." she answered, trembling. "I have known him for some time, and I saw how badly he can behave."

She was more than hurt. She had not expected such a reaction from her aunt and uncle. She had never doubted that that they would show an understanding for her decision and support her on that.

"When I was a little girl," Mrs. Gardiner spoke, taking Elizabeth's hand, gazing at her fondly, "I knew Mr. Darcy's parents, not personally, of course, but everyone knew them around our little town. They were exceptional people. My father did business with the Darcys, and he never said a bad word about them. Do you know that Mr. Darcy's mother, Lady Anne, started an orphanage in Lambton?"

Elizabeth shrugged, speaking indifferently. "I do not know much about his family. I know that he has a much younger sister. He did not speak much about his parents, only that he was devastated when his own father died."

Mrs. Gardiner squeezed her hand. "I cannot believe that their son could be as bad as you describe him."

"But I know him better," Elizabeth insisted with fierce conviction, looking at her aunt and uncle. "Do you remember Mr. Wickham? The officer of the militia

Darcy refused him the living that his late father had promised to him. Mr. Wickham could not become a clergyman, and he had to make his own way in the world."

"How do you know about this, Lizzy?" Mr. Gardiner wanted to know.

"Mr. Wickham told me himself. He confided in me about his misfortunes at Mr. Darcy's hand. He suggested that Mr. Darcy was jealous of his father's affection for him, and did this on purpose, as revenge."

Mr. Gardiner's eyes narrowed. "Did someone else confirm this story?"

Elizabeth shook her head. "No, but Mr. Wickham was so sincere about it."

"I heard this story during our last visit at Longbourn a few times, and from several different people," Mrs. Gardiner said, gazing at her husband. "Mr. Wickham must have shared this tale with many in Meryton. I am certain that he would not be so eager to speak about his misfortunes from Darcy's hand if he happened to be serving in Derbyshire."

"You doubt Mr. Wickham's word?" Elizabeth asked.

"I do not know Mr. Wickham that well," her aunt stated. "All I saw was a young officer of great manners and charm. However, my father knew George Darcy, the late father of your Mr. Darcy, and he always spoke of him with the utmost respect. I simply find it hard to believe that old Mr. Darcy would raise his son in such a way that he would break his word once given."

Elizabeth looked between her aunt and uncle, her expression unbelieving. "Why are you taking his side over Mr. Wickham's?" she demanded. "Is it because Mr. Wickham's father was a servant? Do you hold this against him? You choose to believe Mr. Darcy's words because he is from nobility."

"You are unfair, Lizzy," Mr. Gardiner gave her a pointed look, a slight reprimand in his voice.

"I have nothing against Mr. Wickham's father being a servant," Mrs. Gardiner said calmly. "My own dear mother was a servant too, before she married my father."

"Forgive me, Aunt," Elizabeth said, embarrassed. "I just cannot comprehend why you are so against believing that Mr. Darcy might have done anything wrong."

The older woman put her arm around her niece, rubbing her arm. "Lizzy, dear, you have a kind, tender heart, and I perfectly understand why you believed in Mr. Wickham's tale."

"Elizabeth, you have an inclination to form your opinions about people too hastily," Mr. Gardiner spoke with conviction, supporting his wife. "I ask you to trust our judgment, dear. I have lived almost twice as long as you, and in my line of work, I have dealt with many wealthy men, such as Mr. Darcy. I know from my own experience that the ones who have much less tend to invent untrue stories about the more fortunate, because of their pettiness and simple human jealously. I do not believe that Mr. Darcy would have refused a living promised by his father to a servant if he had not had a valid reason for this. It is like pocket money for him."

"I suggest that you should ask Mr. Darcy about this matter so he can explain it to you from his standing. It is only fair," her aunt added.

Elizabeth just huffed, crossing her arms in disapproval.

Mrs. Gardiner shared a long look with her husband before speaking to her niece. "Lizzy, I know how pained you are with your Papa's death, but you must realize your current situation."

"Mr. Darcy told me that he wants to provide for your family," Mr. Gardiner told her. "He has promised to buy a house for your mother and secure your sisters' futures."

Elizabeth stood up abruptly. "He wants to buy me then," she exclaimed. "He knows my situation, my reduced circumstances, and he wishes to purchase me like a horse, so I could breed him children."

"Elizabeth, do not be so vulgar!" Mr. Gardiner interjected, raising his voice slightly.

"Uncle, these are his own words," Elizabeth protested. "Can you guess what he said when he proposed? He told me that his is ready to overlook my lack of connections, and dowry, hoping that I would give him intelligent sons to run his estate in return."

The man rolled his eyes. "Do not be so melodramatic, Lizzy. Sometimes you resemble my sister more than I would wish to see in you. Darcy is a practical man. He values you; that should please you."

"It was not a very romantic thing to say though, Robert," Mrs. Gardiner pointed out softly, looking at her husband steadily. "I can see why Lizzy was offended by it. He could have put it in a more delicate way. He should have said that he admired her high spirits and her bright mind, the fact that she was well read, well mannered and could carry on a polite conversation."

"Women," Mr. Gardiner let out an exasperated sound. "He was only honest with her. He told her the truth—that he knew the differences between them, but still he wanted to marry her, because he cared enough for her to take the risk, probably going against his own family wishes and his common sense. If that is not romantic, I do not know what is."

"Uncle, cannot you see what he is doing to me?" Elizabeth cried, the tone of her voice turning desperate. "Do you not find it wrong? He lied to you by omission, making you believe that I accepted his suit when I did nothing of the kind. Does it not bother you?"

"Lizzy, child, you are not seeing matters as they are," Mr. Gardiner tried to placate her, "I do not say that Mr. Darcy is perfect, or that his conduct is always what it should be, but I have a good feeling about him. You should give him a chance, at least that. Talk to him, allow him to explain himself."

"You wish me to accept him then," she spoke quietly, dropping back on the sofa, her voice defeated.

"That would be very wise in your situation," Mr. Gardiner agreed. "Please remember your mother and your sisters. Darcy is willing to take care of them. Moreover, I am convinced that he loves you. I do not see any other reason why he would have taken so much trouble and been so generous to you if he did not."

"Aunt Madeline?" Elizabeth looked at Mrs. Gardiner with hope still lingering in her eyes.

"I must say that I agree with your uncle, Lizzy," the woman said, leaning closer to her. "I saw how he looked at you. It is as plain as day that he loves you very much and is willing to do everything in his power to make you happy with him. It is almost heart breaking to observe how he wants you to return his affections, how he begs with his eyes for a single look from you."

"You want me to accept him," Elizabeth repeated dully, staring blankly in front of herself.

The Gardiners looked at one another and replied together. "Yes."

Chapter Five

"Brother?"

Darcy heard his sister's surprised voice as he and Colonel Fitzwilliam entered the townhouse. As he looked up, he saw his sister on the landing of the staircase, dressed in her nightclothes, her blonde hair let down in a loose braid.

"Are you not asleep yet, sweetheart?" he asked warmly, smiling up at her.

"Brother!" she exclaimed, flying down the stairs, her long skirt fluttering as she moved.

"I did not expect you today." She lifted on her toes to embrace him.

"I hope you are well," he spoke, returning her hold, stroking her silky hair.

"I am well," she confirmed. "I am happy to see you. I have missed you."

"You could have come with me to visit Aunt Catherine," he reminded her.

Georgiana was very attached to him, which was perfectly understandable, considering how young she was when their father died, and she could not even remember their mother. She had always clung to him, even as a small child. His attempts to make her more independent, more self reliant, had ended badly. A cold shudder ran down his spine as he remembered her trip to Ramsgate last year. He had thought that spending part of the summer without him would be beneficial for her. How he regretted his decision now. How wrong he had been.

He saw her face fall slightly. "You know why I chose not to," she said uneasily, fidgeting her long, slim pianist's fingers. "I am grievously nervous around her."

"Will I not receive a similar welcome?" Colonel Fitzwilliam's merry voice boomed from behind. Darcy had to admit that his cousin always knew how to lift the mood.

"Cousin Richard, I am so pleased to see you," Georgiana beamed as she stepped to the older man, hugging him tightly.

"You look well, Flower," Colonel Fitzwilliam praised, using the nickname which he had called Georgiana when she was little.

"Where is Mrs. Annesley?" Darcy asked, frowning, as he referred to Georgiana's companion.

"She has already retired."

"And why are you not in bed?"

"I did not feel fatigued. I was reading in my room when I heard the carriage stopping in front of the house," she explained.

"It is late, you should return to bed."

"I want to stay with you," she spoke shyly, her eyes pleading. "Please, I am not tired."

Darcy nodded. "Very well, Georgiana. We have yet to have dinner. Could you ask Cook to prepare a meal for us?"

He understood why Georgiana wanted to spend the evening with him; they had not seen each other for many weeks. Moreover, her presence was rather convenient, postponing the inevitable conversation with Colonel Fitzwilliam. The men had not spoken about Jane Bennet in the carriage due to the presence of the maid, but Darcy was aware that his cousin was curious enough about the lady to broach the subject of her and Bingley's relationship again.

"Of course, with pleasure." Georgiana smiled happily, before hastily making her way to the back of the house.

Once Georgiana was clearly out of the earshot, Colonel Fitzwilliam turned to his cousin. "She seems much recovered," he noted as they entered the drawing room.

The servants were hurriedly rebuilding the fire and lighting the candles in the room.

Darcy sighed sadly, his heart heavy at the memory of the pain caused to his baby sister. "Yes, she is, but only with the closest family. She can barely talk when in company of someone she is not familiar with. She has lost her faith in people after what happened last summer."

The other man's face tightened, his lips pressed in thin line as he murmured, "I would kill him with my bare hands, if I could. Do you know what he is doing now?"

"I hear that he joined the militia, as an officer," Darcy said.

He hesitated for a moment whether to tell his cousin that he had seen Wickham last year in Hertfordshire, but then decided against it. Colonel Fitzwilliam did not really need to have the specific knowledge about Wickham's whereabouts, as long as the cad kept his distance from Georgiana. The fact that Wickham had not come to attend the Netherfield Ball, despite all the officers being invited, was enough proof that he had taken Darcy's threats seriously, and had no intention of approaching any member of Darcy's family in the future.

There was also another reason why Darcy did not wish to even mention Wickham's name in the context of Hertfordshire and Meryton. For him personally, it could only bring back the painful memory of how Elizabeth had seemed to defend the bastard while they danced together at Netherfield. He had been so angry with her after that evening, that it had been very easy to make the decision to cut himself off from her, and leave the very next day, never coming back.

He had felt so proud of himself after his return to London from Netherfield. He had been strong enough to fight down the fatal attraction he had felt for Elizabeth Bennet. He had gone to pay a visit to Annette, his mistress, without delay to prove to himself that the little country Miss meant nothing to him. How terrified he had been when in the heat of the moment he heard himself crying Lizzy, strangely seeing dark brown hair instead of his lover's pale blonde.

Annette, always a professional, had been very tactful about his slip, but at the end of his visit, she asked whether she should start looking for another arrangement for herself. He had not seen her since last December, even though he still paid her allowance, keeping her available. He realized that he would have to pay Annette a visit soon to inform her about his upcoming nuptials, so indeed, she would have to search for another supporter.

Georgiana returned, putting the end to any discussion about Wickham. She was dressed again in one of her day dresses, but she had not pinned her hair up, and it was left in a braid.

She kept Darcy and Colonel Fitzwilliam company during their dinner as they ate their hot soup, cold meat and boiled vegetables with gusto.

"How are you doing, Flower?" Colonel Fitzwilliam asked her, as they finished their meal while tea was served in the small parlour.

"I am well, Cousin Richard," Georgiana replied softly. "I am continuing with my studies, and my pianoforte practice. Mrs. Annesley and I go for a walk to the park every day, as long as the weather holds, understandably. I missed Brother though," she finished, looking warmly at Darcy.

"And not me?" Colonel Fitzwilliam asked, feigning hurt.

"Oh, you too, Cousin, you too," she assured quickly.

"Well, not long from now, you will have a new close friend," Colonel Fitzwilliam announced cheekily, glancing at Darcy.

Darcy frowned slightly, but then shrugged and nodded, knowing that his cousin was eager to announce the news to Georgiana. He had intended to tell his sister himself later, but she could very well hear about his marriage now.

"A friend?" Georgiana asked, confused.

"Yes, your brother here asked a certain young lady for her hand in marriage."

The girl set her bluish grey eyes at Darcy. "Truly?" she whispered.

"Yes," he answered simply, not being able to stop the bright smile coming on his face. "I finally found someone I want to share my life with."

Georgiana smiled, but it did not reach her eyes. "Congratulations," she croaked.

Both men gazed at her with worry.

"Is that Miss Caroline Bingley perhaps?" she asked fearfully.

Colonel Fitzwilliam chuckled loudly, while Darcy presented the most horrified expression.

"Certainly not, Georgiana," he spoke haughtily. "Where did you get such an idea?"

Georgiana lowered her eyes to her lap, "When we spoke, she gave such impression..." she murmured uneasily, biting her lip, obviously not willing to continue.

"Who is it then?" she asked after a moment, frowning, before her expression changed into one full of hope. "Is it Miss Elizabeth, the lady you met while visiting Mr. Bingley, the one you talked about last winter?" she exclaimed. "The one you met again in Kent when she was visiting her friend, as I read in one of your recent letters."

"I did not talk about her that much," Darcy defended himself, clearly embarrassed.

"Perhaps not, but you mentioned her at least three times, if I recall correctly, and it is more than you have spoken to me about any other lady ever before," Georgiana reminded him quickly.

"She is right, Darcy," Colonel Fitzwilliam's laugh echoed through the room. "Miss Elizabeth has you wrapped around her little finger."'

"It is her then?" Georgiana beamed at her brother. "You proposed to Miss Elizabeth?"

Darcy felt the blush creeping on his face, and feeling that hotness in his cheeks, he reddened even more. "Yes."

"Oh, brother," Georgiana leaped from her seat, wrapping her arms around him, kissing his cheek. "I am so happy for you. I know how much you like her, your face looks so different when you speak about her."

Darcy cleared his throat, patting the girl on her back. "I am pleased that you approve."

As she sat back on the chair, her enthusiasm seemed to falter and soon she was asking worriedly. "Do you think that she will like me?"

"Of course she will," Darcy assured quickly with force in his voice. "Colonel Fitzwilliam was right that you would have a friend in her. Elizabeth has sisters of her own, and I am certain that she would welcome another one with an open heart."

The girl smiled shyly. "I hope so, brother," she said, before asking with eagerness, "When will I meet her?"

"Not soon, I am afraid," Darcy answered, serious again. "It is an unfortunate time indeed for Miss Elizabeth."

In short words, he explained the circumstanced of Mr. Bennet's sudden death.

"Please repeat my condolences to Miss Elizabeth," Georgiana insisted sincerely. "Tell her that I will pray for her in this difficult time."

"Of course, I am sure that she will appreciate your concern." Darcy smiled at his sister. "But now I think it is time for you to retire. It is quite late, after all, and your pianoforte instructor will be here rather early in the morning, I believe."

"Yes, brother," Georgiana, agreed sweetly, standing up and saying good night to the men.

"Well, I think that we should retire as well," Darcy said, as they were left alone.

"Not so hasty, Cousin," Colonel Fitzwilliam called as he stood up and walked to the small bar. "I think you wished to explain some matters to me, about Miss Bennet and Bingley." He filled two tall glasses of brandy, handing one to Darcy while sipping from the other one.

Darcy shrugged, "I cannot imagine what more you want to know. You asked whether Miss Jane Bennet was the lady I advised Bingley not to marry, and I answered affirmatively."

"I do not understand you," Colonel Fitzwilliam said, sinking into a stuffed armchair, stretching his muscular legs out in front of himself. "You proposed to Miss Elizabeth, but you did not want her sister to marry your best friend. Where is the logic?"

Darcy downed nearly half of his drink at once. "Do we really have to speak about that? It is an old matter."

"Not so old as you want it to be, and I am sure it is the matter that Miss Elizabeth holds against you."

"You guessed then," Darcy commented without surprise.

"That was not particularly hard; it is obvious how close they are, Miss Bennet and Miss Elizabeth. You did yourself an injustice with that thoughtless act," the other man observed.

"I know," Darcy murmured. "I knew that Miss Bennet was in London the whole winter, but I concealed the knowledge from Bingley. It was I, as well, who convinced him to abandon her in the first place. Now I will have to tell him about it and convince him to see her again. Elizabeth will not be happy if I do not bring them back together."

Colonel Fitzwilliam leaned forwards, gazing amusedly at his cousin. "You know, Cousin, I never thought that I would see you in such a situation - playing matchmaker just to please a woman. I rather enjoy it."

"Can you be serious for once?" Darcy muttered, as he walked to the bar to pour himself another drink.

"I have a confession actually, and it is rather serious," Colonel Fitzwilliam spoke.

"Oh," Darcy said distractedly.

"It seems that Miss Elizabeth learned about your intervention with Bingley and her sister from me."

Darcy dropped the glass onto the small table not so gently, spilling some of its contents on the polished surface. "What?"

"Yesterday," Fitzwilliam started hesitantly, wincing visibly, "I met her during her stroll around the grounds and walked a bit with her."

"And?" Darcy demanded.

"She started asking me about Bingley and his sisters. I did not think much about her enquiries, believing it innocent gossip, nothing more. I told her how you were such a good friend to Bingley because you had saved him from most unfortunate marriage. I had no suspicion that I was speaking about her own sister."

"Do you remember how she reacted?"

"Yes, she paled considerably and soon excused herself, saying she had a sudden headache. I am sorry, Darcy; it was not my intention to harm you. If I had known that it was her sister, I would have kept my mouth shut."

Darcy waved his hand with resignation. "It does not matter now. She must have had some suspicions before that, and you only unknowingly confirmed them."

Colonel Fitzwilliam gave his cousin a long, thoughtful look. "Darcy, what do you have against Miss Bennet? She is very beautiful, and seems terribly kind. I would say that she is too good for Bingley. Their family is not as bad as you claimed them to be. Those Gardiners give a very good impression, you must admit. True, they are in trade, but it is hardly a scandal nowadays. I would say that the future of this country belongs to people like them, the entrepreneurs, merchants—certainly not the landed gentry and aristocracy like us."

"I know, I know..." Darcy acknowledged reluctantly. "I dug a hole for myself, and now I have to find my way out of it. I only hope that Elizabeth will forgive me."

Colonel Fitzwilliam put his drink away and stood up, "I am certain that she will marry you. After all, her choices are limited after her father's death. She cares for her family deeply, that is obvious, and I am sure that she will marry you to help them. However, I do not envy you. She seems to hold a lot of resentment towards you."

Darcy shook his head, his heavy frown mirrored on his forehead, "It only a misunderstanding between us. We shall be fine," he insisted with determination, as if he wanted to convince himself to believe his own words.

"If you say so." Colonel Fitzwilliam put his hand on his cousin's arm. "I truly wish you every happiness with her."

***

Darcy awoke quite late the next day. He had a headache and was slightly hung over from his late evening and brandy with Colonel Fitzwilliam. On the other hand, the alcohol had helped him to fall asleep without trouble, and he truly needed his rest.

He took a bath and spent more time than any other day to dress himself and look presentable.

It was almost eleven when his carriage stopped in front of Gardiners'. He was more than uneasy about the visit, not being certain of Elizabeth's behaviour. The apprehension squeezed his throat, tightened his chest, and knotted his stomach. taking one deep, calming breath, he gingerly knocked on the door.

He was let in immediately and led into a drawing room he had seen yesterday. He did not wait long before Mrs. Gardiner appeared.

"Mr. Darcy, we were expecting you," the woman greeted him with pleasant expression.

Darcy allowed himself to relax at Mrs. Gardiner's warm smile. She seemed to favour him, and it was a good sign.

"Madam," he bowed, "I hope that you and your family are well today."

"As well as the sad circumstances can allow us to be, Mr. Darcy. We still find it hard to believe that Mr. Bennet is not among us anymore. He was such a prominent figure in our family."

"I regret that I did not know him better," he said, and he was truthful speaking the words. The few occasions he has been in a company of Mr. Bennet, he had never tried to engage the older man in conversation. Perhaps if he had done so, taken the effort, Elizabeth would have looked at his suit in a more favourable light.

"I believe that you would have grown to like him, Mr. Darcy. He had his own little habits and peculiarities, which greatly affected his wife's nerves, but he was an interesting man, very well read, having well defined opinions on many subjects. He loved his daughters very much, even though he seemed not to be able to show his affection for them in many situations."

"How is Elizabeth feeling today?" he asked cautiously.

"She managed to have a few hours of sleep, as her sister assured me. You must see how devastated she is, Mr. Darcy. Her father meant the world to her, even though they did not always agree on certain matters. She will not be herself for a long time, I am afraid."

"I would wish to… make her suffer less."

"I do not think that is possible, but I am sure that the awareness that her mother and sisters are well taken care of will ease this time of mourning for her," the woman assured him smoothly.

"May I see her?" he asked, his heart nearly jumping out of his chest at the fear that he would hear a negative answer.

Mrs. Gardiner nodded with a smile. "Of course. She is upstairs with Jane, awaiting your visit; however, my husband wanted to talk to you first. He had to go to his office, as he has to settle some matters before our trip to Longbourn tomorrow. Would you mind seeing him there? I shall send the servant to show you the way. It is just across the street."

Despite the nagging feeling that the reason for which Mr. Gardiner wanted to speak to him was not a pleasant one, Darcy agreed to meet him without hesitation. Mrs. Gardiner, on her part, assured him that Elizabeth would be waiting for him once he returned.

Darcy refused the company of a servant when crossing the street to enter Mr. Gardiner's warehouses. He was not a child, and he could find his way. He was rather impressed with the scale of the business. There were many workers employed, all of them looking very busy and preoccupied with their work. The place was loud and full of energy. He gave his name to an older man who looked to be a sort of foreman, asking that he be directed to the office of Mr. Gardiner.

"Come in, come in, Mr. Darcy," Mr. Gardiner invited him with wide gesture, standing from behind his desk strewn with thick account books and many opened letters. "Please take a seat. Forgive me for admitting you here, but there is so much to do before our trip to Hertfordshire."

"I understand, sir. No need to apologize. It is you who should forgive me for taking so much of your time away from your business," Darcy offered, politely taking his seat.

"I will speak briefly, Mr. Darcy, as I believe that you are rather eager to see my niece."

Darcy allowed himself a small smile. "Indeed I am, sir."

"Yes," Mr. Gardiner cleared his throat, leaning over his large desk, his hands folded in front of him. "My wife and I talked with Elizabeth after you left yesterday. She was very... emotional about your proposal, your behaviour, and some of your attitudes."

Darcy suddenly felt his blood run cold. "She was?" he whispered, his voice unusually high.

Mr. Gardiner looked straight into his eyes. "You failed to mention that she refused your offer."

"Sir, I..." Darcy started but was interrupted.

"Mr. Darcy, let us not go into too much detail. I am really not interested in your private conversations with Elizabeth. I want the best for my niece, and I think, my wife supporting me on this, that you are the best that could happen to her. You are not only wealthy, but you seem to like her. My wife thinks you love her, judging the way you look at her. I believe you wish to make her happy and take care of her, which is good enough for me. However, I know how stubborn Lizzy can be, and if she will insist on rejecting you, we will not force her to do otherwise."

"I see," Darcy murmured with heavy heart. It was not quite what he wanted to hear, but at least he knew where he stood. "Thank you for being sincere with me."

"For now, we have convinced her to talk to you. It was all we could do," Mr. Gardiner informed.

"Thank you."

"I am not certain whether you know that she holds certain matters against you. She mentioned some officer... Wickham... It is my understanding that he told her some disturbing story about how you hurt him in the past, refusing him the living left him by your late father, almost leaving him starving on the streets."

Darcy froze, not believing his own ears for a few seconds. That bastard! How dare he turn Elizabeth against him! He would pay for that. His cousin had been right, that they should have ended Wickham long ago.

"That is absolutely not true," he spat, rising from his chair. "Wickham is a despicable liar... I swear I did nothing like that. He refused to take the living and was paid off. Two thousand pounds, which he spent as soon as he got it."

"Mr. Darcy, calm down, please. Sit down." Mr. Gardiner walked over his desk, gesturing him to take his seat. "We believe you," he spoke with force. "Madeline, my wife, told Elizabeth that she did not have faith in Mr. Wickham's history, knowing your outstanding parents and their reputation from the times of her childhood spent in Derbyshire. I think it gave Elizabeth something to think on, but still you have to explain this her."

"I will, sir, be certain of that," he grunted angrily.

Mr. Gardiner glanced at the clock on the wall, his expression apologetic. "Forgive me, Mr. Darcy, but I have a meeting in twenty minutes for which I need to do a bit of preparation."

"Of course," Darcy stood up, extending his hand in the direction of the older man. "Thank you, Mr. Gardiner," he said as they shook hands, "I am more than grateful for your support and for being honest with me."

As Mr. Gardiner walked the guest to the door, he spoke, "One more word of advice, if I may."

Staring into his face with a frown of concentration, Darcy gave the man his full attention.

"Elizabeth is very independent, and she does not appreciate when people tell her to do things in a certain way, or even worse, order her around. You can very well say that she was, to a certain degree, spoiled by her father's attention, and he always encouraged her free thinking. Try to listen to her more, and perhaps ask about her opinions on some matters. Even if you know that you are absolutely right, it is always good to say something in the lines of 'What is your opinion, dear?' or 'Do you have another suggestion?' Let her participate more, and avoid announcing your will to her. She does not react well to that."

Darcy sighed. "I have noticed."

"Good luck." Mr. Gardiner clapped his back lightly. "You will need it in order to convince her."

Chapter Six

As Darcy left Mr. Gardiner's office and was walking through the warehouse back to the Gardiners' house, his emotions were conflicting, but there was one very clear one; he hated Wickham. That bastard was always in his way, trying to destroy the little peace and happiness Darcy had. Deceiving his father and trying to seduce Georgiana was not enough; now he was trying to turn the only woman in whom he had ever taken a serious interest against him.

"I want him finished, no longer walking on the surface of the earth," he muttered fiercely as he passed through the busy street.

Before knocking at the door, he took a few deep, calming breaths. He had to keep his temper in check, and control himself in order to face Elizabeth and hopefully convince her. He must hold his anger in check. Elizabeth was an innocent here; he could not allow himself to take out his resentment on her, or he would further alienate her or worse—lose her completely.

He was let inside by the servant and allowed directly into the drawing room. The whole family sans Mr. Gardiner seemed to have gathered there, including the Bennet sisters.

His eyes swept over the women and children before stopping on Elizabeth. She was not looking at him, but she stood up the same as Jane to greet him.

When she kept avoiding his gaze, Darcy glanced with desperation at Mrs. Gardiner.

The woman seemed to understand his silent plea for help. "Lizzy, I believe that you and Mr. Darcy were supposed to discuss certain matters," she suggested, her tone gentle, but decided.

To his relief, Elizabeth agreed without hesitation, "Yes, Aunt," she spoke evenly. "Do you think that Uncle would mind if we go to his study?"

"No, of course not, dear." Mrs. Gardiner smiled reassuringly. "No one will disturb you there."

Elizabeth nodded. "Thank you, Aunt." She walked to the door, "Shall we go, sir?"

Her voice was neither angry, nor resentful. She seemed sad, but calm.

Elizabeth led them through the house to the same room where he had been the night before. As he closed the door behind them, she walked straight to the tall window, opening it wide. The study was situated at the back of the house, and the window looked into the small but intensely green garden.

He stepped closer, standing near her. Her eyes were closed as she inhaled deeply.

"It is the main disadvantage of London, I believe. The air smells much less appealing than in the country, and you cannot go for a truly long walk," she spoke wistfully. "Will you not agree, Mr. Darcy?" she asked, looking up at him.

He did not answer, but merely drank in her sight, wanting to make sure that she was well. She was paler than usual, without that healthy glow to her skin he liked so much. Her eyes were puffy with dark circles underneath. Her hair was pulled back smoothly, without the usual, curls framing her small face. She looked much younger like that, and so very innocent.

"Mr. Darcy," she said quietly, regarding him carefully.

"Forgive me, Miss Bennet." He came out of his musings. "I only wondered how you are feeling today."

Her eyes met his, and pain shot through him as he saw the heartbreaking sadness in her face.

She shuddered, and he reached to close the window, thinking her to be cold. She was wearing a gown he did not remember ever seeing her wear. It was pale pink, and it was the first time he had seen her in that colour. She usually wore white, yellow, cream, mint green, and she had one deep red dress which he remembered fondly. She had worn it often while nursing Jane at Netherfield. He guessed that the pink dress did not belong to her, as it hung shapelessly from her delicate shoulders.

"I owe you an apology, Mr. Darcy, for my behaviour yesterday. I was rude to you. I understand that you wanted to help me."

"No, no," he assured quickly, surprised with her words as he had expected her to call him on his actions yesterday rather than apologize for her own. He wondered briefly whether he owed this to the Gardiners and their influence on Elizabeth. "That is perfectly understandable. You had every reason to be upset," he continued, wanting to show her that he, too, could be remorseful. "Perhaps I should not have… I might have been too forceful when planning our journey. You are right though, I only wished to help you."

Her eyes searched his face, but she said nothing.

She was looking out the window again, and he was at a loss to what she was thinking.

He gathered his courage and reached for her hand. She allowed him the touch, which he thought to be a good sign.

"Elizabeth, please," he beckoned her closer, pulling her slowly to him. He waited till their eyes met before continuing. "I am aware that matters between us are not as they should be, but I am certain that we should be one, that we do belong together, that..." his voice cracked, "we will be right together."

She stared straight into his face for what felt like an endless moment. He had to fight the urge to avert his eyes, and retreat into the safety of his usual haughtiness.

She lowered her head, and he could see the indecision painted on her face. He cupped her cheek, making her look at him again.

"Trust me," he whispered, his voice low, deep and soothing. "I swear that I will take care of your mother and sisters. I will adore you, worship you. Trust me."

"I would wish to," she responded with sincerity, and even, he hoped, longing, "but I hardly know you. Once married to you, I will have no possibility of going back. I know so little about you, and what I know cannot convince me to trust you."

His hand dropped from her cheek. "You are referring to the matter of Bingley and your sister," he said knowingly. "I admit that I was mistaken in separating them; however you have to believe me that at that time, I was convinced that I was acting in my friend's best interest."

Her eyes narrowed. "His or your best interest?" she demanded harshly.

He froze, feeling as if she had slapped him. "Yes, that is correct, I wanted to remove myself and all the people close to me from you and your family's company. I was confused and terrified with my rapidly developing feelings for you," he admitted.

"You sound as if liking me was a punishment for you, a great misfortune, something which may bring you down, ruin you," she uttered with resentment.

"No, Elizabeth, no." He closed the space between them, putting his hands on her thin shoulders, feeling her delicate, smooth skin against his thumbs. "I want you; I cannot imagine my life without you. You are my happiness, everything I need to be whole, perhaps for the first time since my mother's death. I was not prepared for all those emotions you evoked in me, and it terrified me. I was not certain how to deal with them. I am still not. However, I cannot walk away from you."

She stomped away from him, freeing herself from his touch, frowning. "I do not know what to think about you. My aunt and uncle seem to like you... and I trust their judgment, but..." She put her hand to her mouth, and started to chew on her fingernails. When she realized what she was doing, she removed her hand from her face quickly, embarrassed.

"I know what you are thinking about," he said, not being able to remove the coldness from his voice. "Wickham." He hated to mention his name in her presence, even worse was the necessity of discussing this sad affair with her, but there was no other way. He only hoped that he would say what he needed to say now, and then they would never again return to this subject.

"Uncle mentioned him to you?" she guessed.

"Yes, and I am furious at the lies he told you," Darcy said in a harsh, authoritative voice, that he was not in habit of using when speaking to her. He noticed that he had caught her attention immediately, her eyes widening slightly at his tone.

"Will you allow me to explain this from my standing?" he asked formally.

She nodded, and he began speaking without delay. He was precise, and spoke to the point. He poured out all the resentment he felt for the son of his father's steward. He told her how Wickham had been cruel, even as a little boy when they had been growing up together, how he had wasted his opportunities in the university, how he had refused taking over the parish and had been paid off. The hardest part was telling her about the last summer when Wickham had tried to seduce his sister, who had been only fifteen at the time.

"If you do not believe me, Colonel Fitzwilliam knows all of this, and he can confirm my version of events," he ended his tale. Not waiting for her reaction, and not looking at her, he walked to the window, opening it again.

Soon he felt a careful touch on his arm, and she was standing just next to him. "I do believe you, and I can only be deeply ashamed of my own blindness. You could not have possibly invented such a history about your own sister, of that I am certain. I apologize. I should not have given faith to his words so easily."

He turned his whole body to her. "I do not blame you," he assured warmly. "I know of your kindness. Wickham can be very convincing when he wishes to be."

Her eyes were confused as they searched his face. "Why did he tell such stories about you to perfect strangers? Why does he hate you so much?"

Darcy shrugged. "Trying to decipher the source of his motivation is not something I want to waste my time on. I do not want to see him, or hear about him. Please, promise me that we will not speak about that vile creature ever again."

"Of course," she agreed instantly. "Your poor sister," she whispered. "How is she now?"

"Better, but I doubt whether she will able to trust anyone in the future. She has retreated into her own world in a way. I have hoped that you would help me to bring her out of her shell. You are so good with people, unlike me."

She gave him a pale smile, but then went quiet again for a longer moment, staring away from him. Her bouts of silence and avoiding eye contact drove him almost to insanity.

"I understand that you need time to know me better," he started, trying to sound patient, even though he felt far from that. He was tired; he wanted to hear yes or no from her. To be precise, he wanted to hear yes. The negative answer would mean that he would have to rethink his strategy, but at least he would know where he stood with her. "Perhaps you would be willing to agree to a courtship first, a long engagement? You are in mourning, and it is natural that you are in no disposition for romance at the moment. If you wish to wait, to postpone our union, I will accept it."

She shook her head decidedly, "No, no courtship. If we were to make this happen, the wedding should take place as soon as possible."

He regarded her carefully. "I can wait for you," he stressed. "If only I have your promise, your word that you will marry me one day, I shall wait."

"No, I do not wish to wait. We can marry shortly after the funeral, as soon as you will be able to procure the license."

"Is that a yes?" he asked, not quite believing the sudden turn in their conversation.

"Yes."

He could not help the wide smile which broke across his face.

"Oh, darling," he gathered her into his arms. "Is that truly a yes?"

She nodded, her smile tight, her eyes sad.

She gasped, her eyes widening, as his arms tightened around her, and he picked her up, twirling her around a few times.

At last he put her down gently, loosening his hold, but still keeping her close. "Will you not smile for me?"

She smiled up at him, showing the row of small, white teeth. Soon the smile disappeared though. "I have one condition though," she spoke nervously.

He leaned into her intently, "I am listening."

"You must…" she closed her eyes for a moment, before opening them, her face blushing but determined. "I must have a legal assurance, a document of sorts, signed by you that you will take care of my mother and sisters. I will ask Uncle Gardiner to discuss it with you on my behalf."

She stood stiffly in his arms, her eyes on the floor.

"Of course, Elizabeth, I promised this to Mr. Gardiner, and I am promising this to you. You will have the opportunity to read the settlement, and we will introduce any changes if it is not to your liking."

"No, that will not be necessary," she said quickly. "I trust my uncle. I do not want to see it, read it."

"As you wish," he agreed.

"Thank you," she said, again avoiding looking at him.

He sighed. She was still distant, but overall, he should be pleased. She had said yes. He had their whole life to convince her to accept and love him. He was overjoyed that she did not want a long engagement. How soon could they marry, a month, two? Yes, a month should be enough to deal with all the matters and find a suitable home for the Bennets around Meryton and help them to move there. There was much to do, but it was in his interest to do it quickly.

Slowly, he brought her closer again, so her stiff form could be supported against his body. It was time to start the wooing. He put his arm around her, rubbing her back. "How are you bearing, dearest? May I assist you with anything?" He kissed her forehead.

"No, thank you," she murmured.

"Perhaps there is something I may help you with," he insisted.

"You are doing enough already," she responded.

He walked her to the cushioned bench and motioned both of them to sit on it. "You must know that I enjoy helping you."

"Well…" she started, her voice undecided.

"Yes," he leaned into her eagerly.

"Tis about my trunk... I was forced to leave it at Hunsford. All the seats in the post chaise had been already booked when I decided to go with them. They squeezed me in, but I could not take my trunk. Charlotte promised to send it at the first opportunity. However, it probably will take around two weeks; likely not until Maria, her sister, is about to return to Lucas Lodge from Kent. Mr. Collins may arrive sooner, but I am not certain whether he will wish to deal with my trunk."

"Speak no more," he covered her hand with his. He was pleased that he could do something for her. He liked to be useful, even if it was a small thing like fetching her trunk. "I will deal with it yet today. Your trunk shall be awaiting you at Longbourn in two days time at the latest."

"Thank you," she answered sincerely. "I have most of my gowns packed there."

He reached his hand to touch the back of her graceful neck. "I have noticed that it is not your dress that you are wearing today."

Her cheeks reddened as he stroked her nape with the pads of his fingers. It was an innocent touch, but he was pleased to see that she was responding to him.

"Yes, it belongs to my aunt," she smoothed the material over her knees, her hands shaking slightly. "She was kind enough to lend it. I cannot wear Jane's dresses, as they are much too long for me," she explained. "She is so much taller that I."

They spoke briefly about the plans for their journey to Hertfordshire. Elizabeth told him that they were leaving tomorrow, early in the morning. As they returned to the drawing room, Elizabeth went straight into Mrs. Gardiner's embrace, and soon after, Jane's. The women whispered something to each other, but he could not hear. He was invited to stay for tea, but refused. He sensed that Elizabeth needed her time now away from him and wished to talk with her aunt and sister in private. He also had many matters to see to before tomorrow.

Chapter Seven

All three women, Mrs. Gardiner, Elizabeth and Jane, followed Darcy's tall figure with their eyes as he left the room.

Jane took her sister's hand, giving it a light squeeze. "How was it, Lizzy?" she asked compassionately.

"Better than I expected," Elizabeth smiled bravely. "He was agreeable; he truly tried to be cordial. We explained a great deal to each other. I find it difficult to comprehend all he has told me." A small crease appeared between her eyebrows as she remembered what she had heard about Georgiana Darcy and Mr. Wickham. She shuddered at the thought; poor girl, to be used and deceived at such a young age by someone whom she had considered a family friend.

"Judging by the gentleman's expression, I dare say that you came to an understanding," Mrs. Gardiner spoke, her expression betraying how pleased she was with the turn of the events.

"Yes, Aunt," Elizabeth confirmed. "We are indeed engaged."

Mrs. Gardiner touched her face. "Why so sad, Lizzy? It cannot be that bad."

Elizabeth fisted her palms on her knees growling with frustration. "I do not know, Aunt. A part of me wants to run from him and never see him again."

Mrs. Gardiner was silent for a moment. "We do not wish to force him on you, Lizzy. If you truly feel that you cannot accept him…" the woman's voice trailed.

"No, that was not what I meant," Elizabeth said. "I know that I could never forgive myself should I reject him now in our current situation when with this marriage I can ensure security for Mama and my sisters. It is only…" she sighed, biting her lower lip hard.

"What do you want to say, sister?" Jane encouraged gently.

"I am so angry with him for putting me in this situation. I have always thought him to be a rude, arrogant, proud man, whose company I did not enjoy. I had him classified into the group of people I disliked. Then suddenly he comes to me asking for my hand in marriage. He is so different - kinder –

even the tone of his voice has changed - is so much gentler - when he addresses me."

"You need time, Lizzy," Mrs. Gardiner spoke gently. "Give him a chance and let things happen naturally. As you are in mourning, I believe it only adds to your discontent of the situation."

"You are right, Aunt. I know that you are right. However, it is difficult to do as you say," Elizabeth whispered brokenly.

"All in good time, Lizzy...all in good time." The older woman patted her back.

She smiled ruefully. "I do not have much time at my disposal. The wedding will take place shortly after the funeral. I do not know how soon exactly, but within a month, I believe."

"Did he demand that?" Mrs. Gardiner asked, her much tone sharper.

Elizabeth shook her head. "No, Aunt, it was my condition. He said that he was willing to wait, allow me as much time as I need."

"I am afraid I do not understand, Lizzy." The woman frowned. "Do you not wish for a period of courtship before making your vows? He is offering you the time you so desperately seem to want, time not only to know him better, but to grieve as well."

Elizabeth stood up, and began pacing in front of the fireplace. "It would not change anything! Can you not see?" she cried, wrenching her fingers together. "I still have to marry him to repay his generosity. I prefer to do it sooner rather than later. That way, I will feel more honest with myself, and not so indebted to him. He will have what he wants—what he paid for without delay."

"Oh, Lizzy, you cannot think like this," Mrs. Gardiner reasoned. "You are being overly dramatic about it all. He loves you, wants to marry you and take care of you. It is all perfectly natural, as it should be. You sound as if you believe you are selling yourself."

Elizabeth stopped her pacing and stared at her feet. "That is how I feel about it," she acknowledged quietly.

"Oh, Lizzy," Mrs. Gardiner whispered compassionately. "You cannot think like that; you will only torture yourself."

"I am only glad that I can help my family. It is the only bright point I can see," Elizabeth answered dully. "The thought that Mama and my sisters will be secured brings me happiness and peace. I can live with that thought."

Jane stood up then, and with the tears in her eyes, she hugged Elizabeth. "I wish it could be me, Lizzy. It breaks my heart to see you so miserable."

Mrs. Gardiner reached for Elizabeth's hand, pulling both of her nieces back on the sofa beside her. "There is a happiness to be had for you there too," she spoke with conviction. "I am certain of that."

Elizabeth said nothing, only stared at the fireplace in front of her. The day was unusually cold and rainy for the late April, so the fire was started.

"Lizzy," Jane's sweet voice captured her attention. "I agree with Aunt that you indeed see all this in colours too dark. Mr. Darcy has faults to be sure; however, he has many good traits of character as well. Even you have to admit that indeed he is not Mr. Collins."

Elizabeth smiled despite herself. "No, he is not. He is more pleasing to the eyes and smells much better."

Jane smiled as her sister referred to their cousin's well known disregard of personal hygiene.

"You noticed his smell then?" Mrs. Gardiner asked cheekily, raising her eyebrow.

Elizabeth shot her a confused look, before blushing intensely. "No, of course not," she murmured, frowning. She did not want to give impression that she was sniffing Mr. Darcy. Nevertheless, she had noticed that his scent was comforting - clean and spicy, alluring even. "It is a relief though, that I can stand by his side without fighting the urge to return my last meal, as it is in the case of Mr. Collins. Poor Charlotte, I have wondered more than once how she can stand him."

"Perhaps she should convince her husband to take a bath more often," Jane offered reasonably. "I am certain that it is in her power."

Mrs. Gardiner decided to steer the conversation back to the main point as she spoke lightly, "Well, I believe that we can safely state then that among Mr. Darcy's admirable qualities is the fact that his smell is appealing. I may as well add that he is a very handsome man - so tall too."

Elizabeth glared at her.

"You cannot deny it, Elizabeth," Jane supported their aunt shyly.

"No, I cannot," Elizabeth admitted at last.

"He is a good brother and a good friend," Jane said.

Elizabeth wanted to argue with the last, remembering Darcy's interference with Bingley and Jane, but she remained quiet. It was not her intention to remind Jane of the sad past which still had to be painful to her, even if she stated otherwise.

"I suppose," she said after a moment of hesitation.

At least he was a loving brother who cared for his sister. She could not deny that. The pain in his expression when he had spoken to her about his sister's attempted elopement with Wickham was too tangible, too raw to fake.

"He is rich and independent. He can provide well for you and all the children you will have one day," Mrs. Gardiner pointed out.

"He truly likes you, sister. I believe he cares for you deeply," Jane added sweetly.

Elizabeth nodded, seemingly agreeing with them, but said nothing. Her sister and aunt meant well; she knew they wanted to lift her spirits, but they were not those who were about to marry a man they hardly knew.

"Mistress," the servant's voice brought their attention.

The children's nanny came closer, holding little Fred in her arms. The older children abandoned their activities as well, gathering around the sofa. "I think that Master Fred is warm again."

Mrs. Gardiner took the baby in her arms instantly, touching her lips to its forehead. "Yes, indeed, he is feverish again," she agreed worriedly. "It is the third time this month." She bounced the baby as he whimpered. His little face was scrunched in discomfort, tears shaping in the corner of his eyes, running down his fat cheeks. Glancing down at the rest of their children, she said, "Now the older ones will become sick too. It is only matter of time," she added, resigned.

Little Fred's condition put an end to the discussion about Mr. Darcy for the rest of the day. The women concentrated their efforts on comforting the child, and helping him feel better, hoping that his illness would not turn into something more serious.

***

Darcy nursed his drink in the privacy of the study. It had been a long, emotionally draining day, but he had managed to accomplish everything he had set out to achieve.

The brightest point of his day was understandably Elizabeth's agreement to their engagement. What had come later was considerably less pleasant.

After leaving the Gardiners' home, he had contacted his solicitor so the man could begin preparing the marriage settlement and other necessary documents.

Next he had called on the Bingleys, hoping that his friend would not be home, and that their conversation could be naturally postponed. However, Bingley was present, and Darcy had no choice but to reveal his involvement with Jane. He had confessed that he knew that she had spent the entire winter in London, and that he had kept it from him, or at least omitted to tell him the truth.

His friend was less than pleased; however, Darcy was not certain whether he was more angry with him or his sisters. His mood seemed to improve vastly when Darcy assured him that according to her sister, Miss Bennet had not forgotten him, and still thought about him warmly. Darcy understood that Bingley's intention was to return to Netherfield instantly, pay his respects and condolences to Mrs. Bennet and attend the funeral. Bingley had even suggested visiting the Gardiners yet today so he could see Jane. Darcy convinced him that it was not the best idea. The sisters were surely busy with their preparations for travel to Hertfordshire with their aunt and uncle tomorrow morning.

With Bingley returning to Meryton, Elizabeth should be pleased with him. That thought warmed his heart. Surely, she would not hold the matter with Bingley and her sister against him any longer.

It was dinner time when he said goodbye to Bingley, but he had one matter left to attend. Now, being engaged to his dearest Elizabeth, the presence of Annette in his life did not sit well with him.

He had sent her a note earlier in the day informing her that she should expect his visit. It was a few minutes past seven when he knocked at her door. Annette lived in a small but comfortable house in a respectable, quiet neighbourhood. He had not bought it for her; she had already owned it when they met.

She admitted him in a negligee, all smiles, saying how happy she was to see him after such a long time and how she had missed him. Her gown was more see-through than dressed, her long hair let free as he liked. He turned his eyes away from her, not wishing to look. She did not seem to notice, and approached him bodily, putting her lips on his neck, her hand stroking him through the lap of his trousers. He cleared his throat and pushed her away, asking her to put on a robe before they could talk.

She had instantly done as he asked. She had always agreed with everything he said and asked from her. She had never argued with him. It had been boring, but it was what he paid her for, after all.

In short words, he had announced his current situation, that he was happily engaged, planning to be married within a month, and that he had to terminate their agreement from this day on. Before she could respond, he assured her that he was aware how sudden the news must be for her. He promised that he would pay her allowance, and accept her bills for the next six months so she have time to adjust to her new situation.

Her reaction angered him. She had said that she was willing to maintain their contacts even after his marriage.

"Absolutely not," he declared before standing up and directing himself to the door.

She had walked after him, and touched his arm before he managed to leave, drawing his attention. Then she looked him in the eye.

"Forgive me," she said. Her face looked so different, older and wiser. It was as if she had always worn a mask of pleasant contentment before, and only now could he see her true self. "I did not want to offend you."

He nodded, accepting her apology. "I wish you all the best," he answered stiffly. "Goodbye."

He was more than astonished when she stepped to him, locking her arms around his neck, hugging him tightly. Before he could push her away from him, she whispered. "She is a very lucky woman your fiancée, your Lizzy. I do hope that she is aware of that, but if she is not, you know my address."

"No. That will not be necessary, I assure you," he said and then abruptly left, desiring to be away as quickly as possible.

The visit had made him very uneasy. He felt discomfort even now and was relieved to end this chapter in his life. Now, as a married man, he would not need to look for physical fulfilment elsewhere. He had never felt entirely comfortable with the fact that he had kept the mistress in the first place.

He was not entirely certain whether Elizabeth would allow him in her bed right from the beginning, but surprisingly, it did not bother him. He could wait a few months till she would be ready to accept him. He did not want to force her into intimacy that she was not ready for, even if he was more than ready, eager even.

There had been a time when he had cursed the fact that passion for physical release ran rather strong in him. He had tried to restrain for longer periods of time, but prolonged abstinence seemed to bring out the worst in him; he was short with the people around him and in a constantly foul mood. Keeping himself under good regulation was a challenge indeed when it came to matters of the flesh.

He remembered that when he had been a lad of fifteen or sixteen, he had spent every single night pleasuring himself. Now, as he thought of that, he marveled that his manhood had not fallen off, nor had his hand become permanently deformed with his actions.

His father had been too ill at that time to notice what bothered him. Darcy had refused to follow Wickham's way of dealing with a problem, which was cornering maids and tenant daughters. Such conduct was beneath Darcy men. His pride in his family name had fought down his lust in that case.

It was his cousin, Richard, not yet a colonel then, who had helped him. It had been when he reached eighteen, the year he had gone to university. Richard brought him to one of his lady friends in Matlock. She must have been in her thirties, a widow, owning her own store, which she had inherited after her husband had passed. Darcy had remembered that first time to be such an immense relief for him. It had not even bothered him that his cousin had been sitting in the next room, reading a book about ancient war tactics, throughout the whole act.

She had been a pleasant looking woman, and very kind to him, and thus he had visited her several times more.

His thoughts were interrupted with a knock at the door. He frowned, putting his half emptied drink away and called to enter. He could not imagine what business someone might have with him at such a late hour.

The butler walked in, his expression exasperated.

"Is something the matter, Stewart?"

"Yes, sir, there is a lad here, demanding to see you," the man explained.

"Did he explain why he wants to see me?" he asked calmly.

"Yes, Master. He says that he has a letter for you, but he would not give it to me," the man huffed. "He insists on giving it to you personally. He says that it is a message from a Miss Elizabeth."

Darcy bolted from his chair, starting the servant. "Why did you not tell me this in the first place?" he cried. "Bring him here immediately, or no, I will go myself."

His butler gaped. "Yes, Master. The boy is at the door."

Darcy strode through the house, straight to the main entrance. He tore the door open to see a lad around fifteen years old, standing by his horse.

"Hello there," he cried.

The boy looked up. "Are you Mr. Darcy, sir?" he asked, coming closer.

"I am. Do you have a message from Miss Elizabeth for me?"

"Yes, sir. She told me to give it to your hands only." He reached behind his jacket, procuring what looked like a small sealed note.

Darcy took it, trying to read the name of the top in the semi darkness. Mr. Fitzwilliam Darcy was written in a pretty, tight feminine script.

"Miss Elizabeth said I should wait for your answer."

"Is she well?" Darcy asked worriedly. Something must have happened if she had a need to contact him at ten in the evening.

"She is well, sir," the boy assured.

"Come inside the house, you will wait in the kitchen for my answer. I am sure that the cook has something for you there."

The lad's face brightened. "Thank you, sir."

Darcy turned to Stewart and the other servant who stood behind him, "Take the boy to the kitchen, feed him, his horse goes to stable so it may rest," he ordered.

He hurried back inside, opening the seal on the note under the light of the nearest candle.

Dear Sir,

Forgive me disturbing you at such a late hour, but the sudden illness in the family forces me to do so.

Illness? She seemed perfectly well when he had seen her in the morning. The lad, too, claimed that she was well.

With fear creeping in his chest he returned to reading.

The youngest Gardiner child, little Fred, became feverish just as you left us earlier today. My dear aunt hoped it was nothing too serious, however, his temperature has risen steadily since the afternoon, now accompanied with very unpleasant cough.

My aunt is afraid to allow him to travel tomorrow. Understandably, she does not wish to leave him in London alone with the nanny. It has been just decided that only my uncle will accompany Jane and me to Hertfordshire while my aunt will stay with the children in town. She fears that the other children may become ill as well in the next few days.

My uncle is unwilling to leave his family in London without the carriage at their disposal. It is our understanding that you plan to travel to Longbourn tomorrow yourself. Would you mind if Jane, my uncle, and I go with you in your carriage? We hoped to depart early in the morning, no later than eight.

The boy with will await your reply.

I thank you in advance,

Elizabeth Bennet.

Darcy marched to his study where he hastily pulled out a fresh sheet of letter-paper. The little man he remembered so well from his conversation in Mr. Gardiner's study was sick then. Well, the little chap had no luck, first the teeth, now a fever. He understood how worried his parents must have been. His sister, too, had been sick often as a young child.

My dearest Elizabeth,

He began his answer. The tone of Elizabeth's note was polite, but rather cold. He reminded himself that it was too early to expect endearments on her part, especially in their current situation, but it still hurt him that she had been so abrupt.

I am immensely sorry to hear about the illness in the Gardiner house. I can recommend an excellent physician. He cared for Georgiana when she was ill as a little girl. She was quite prone to catching colds as we stayed in London during winter months, and he always managed to help her. I can arrange for him to visit the Gardiners and see the child. Please pass my offer to your aunt.

I would be more than happy to offer my carriage to your disposal. It is only sound that we should all travel together, especially in the current situation when the child is ill.

You can expect me at seven o'clock sharp, so that we may depart before eight, as was your wish.

I wish you a good night's rest, my love.

Faithfully yours,

Fitzwilliam Darcy

He sealed the letter and called the servant, asking him to summon the lad.

The boy entered his study within a few minutes.

"Here is my response to Miss Elizabeth," he said, giving him the note. "You did well." He smiled down at the lad, handing him a few coins. He knew well that it probably equalled what the child made for three months at the Gardiner's household.

"Oh, thank you, sir!" the boy exclaimed, beaming in awe at the money in his hand. Hastily, he hid his pay and the note inside his jacket.

Darcy walked the boy to the entrance, making sure that he got on his horse and rode away in the right direction.

He turned to the butler, eyeing him solemnly. "You will always inform me without delay if there is a message from Miss Elizabeth Bennet."

"Of course, sir," Stewart nodded. "I was not aware that… it is a priority."

"It is indeed," he answered calmly. "Miss Bennet is your future Mistress."

With these words, he turned on his heel, and climbed the stairs. It was high time to retire. It was late, and he had promised Elizabeth to be at the Gardiners' early tomorrow morning. He needed a good night's sleep.

Chapter Eight

Elizabeth raised her gaze carefully, looking from behind her eyelashes at the man sitting in front of her. Yes, nothing had changed; he was still looking at her. Could she ask him to stop? Was he not aware that it was rude to stare at people in such a manner? She truly did not understand why he looked at her like that. She was not a beauty, he had said it himself, and she was tolerable in his opinion.

She glanced across the carriage to see Jane and her uncle sleeping soundly. Mr. Darcy's grand carriage certainly offered the best condition to take a nap. They must have been exhausted; the last couple of days had been taxing, especially the previous night with little Fred screaming his little lungs out. Poor little one; he could only cry, he could not tell them what hurt him. Elizabeth sincerely hoped that the baby would get better soon. Her aunt was so worried about her boy. Mrs. Gardiner had not slept the entire night, carrying Fred in her arms, trying to calm him down.

Elizabeth was both eager and afraid of going home. Without Papa, Longbourn was not her home anymore. Never again would she see him through an open window on her return from a walk, reading in the library.

The tightening in her throat and the new tears prickling in her eyes were signs that she was close to weeping again. It was no time or place for that. She needed to direct her attention to something different.

"Mr. Darcy," she whispered, leaning slightly forward.

He looked her right in the eye, his expression confused, as if he did not believe that she had actually spoken to him.

"Yes, love," he answered in the same hushed tone.

She felt her face glow hot. She was not certain how she felt about Mr. Darcy calling her endearments. It was very unsettling.

"I must thank you for giving my aunt the address and the letter to the doctor. I know how much she appreciates it."

"Anyone would do that," he shrugged. "Dr Graves is a good physician, and I am saying this from my own experience. He does not take on new patients often, and that is why I wrote him the letter. He took care of Georgiana a few times. She always managed to develop nasty colds during our stays in London. I think that the air in town does not suit her well."

"I am not entirely certain whether anyone would do such a thing to help a stranger," she opposed. "It was very thoughtful of you."

"I would not say that the Gardiners are strangers to me, not anymore," he offered. "Helping them in such a small way seems natural, even expected."

She frowned, not understanding his denial. "You do not enjoy when someone praises your kindness?"

"I simply do not see anything unusual in my deed."

"May I disagree with you on that?" she asked.

He smiled. "Of course you may."

His deep set eyes stared into hers with intensity, and she felt the heat creeping on her cheeks. She had never before blushed in the presence of a man so often, not even when she had thought herself being infatuated with Wickham. Insufferable man, why did he evoke such emotions in her?

She broke their eye contact and looked outside the window. It was a rainy day, and the road was becoming more muddy with every mile. She suspected that they would reach Meryton later than expected.

A warm, large, gloved hand was placed on her knee, and she froze. Slowly she looked up at him. His gaze was concentrated on her face, and he was leaning forward from his seat.

She glanced quickly to the right to make sure that her uncle and her sister were not paying them any attention. Thankfully, Jane was still dozing, her plump lips half open, shaping into a small 'o.' Mr. Gardiner was stretched across nearly half of the spacious carriage, snoring lightly.

"I truly like the Gardiners," Darcy whispered, making her look at him again.

"They like you too," she whispered back.

His hand moved from her knee to touch the side of her face.

"Perhaps we could invite them to Pemberley for the summer."

Her eyes widened with surprise. "Truly? What about the children?"

"With the children, of course," he answered without hesitation. "I believe that the little ones could only benefit from the fresh air in the country."

She gaped at him unbelievably, her heart fluttering quickly as he stroked her cheek. Was this the same cold, unfeeling, rude man whom she had known last year?

"That would be very agreeable indeed," she rasped, not trusting her voice anymore.

"Then it is settled," he smiled, dropping his hand from her face, retreating back to his seat.

Elizabeth shifted towards the window, and closed her eyes, hoping that sleep would come. Surprisingly, it did, because the next thing she felt was someone shaking her.

"Elizabeth, love, wake up. We have arrived at Longbourn."

She blinked her eyes and saw Darcy's face in front of her.

"So soon?" she murmured, stretching her arms, yawning.

He chuckled. "It actually took longer than I expected because of the weather."

She looked to the side. "Where are Jane and my uncle?"

"They have already gone inside. I believe that they are upstairs with your mother. We tried to wake you, well, your sister tried, but you only elbowed her, murmuring something in protest."

He was grinning at her, clearly amused.

"I was tired," she murmured defensively.

His eyes caressed her. "Of course you were, but now as you are conscious again, I think we should follow Jane and Mr. Gardiner."

She yawned into her hand and moved her hands to her head to check whether her bonnet was in the right place. Darcy moved swiftly out of the carriage and waited for her outside.

It was pouring rain, and as she looked down from the step of the carriage, she noticed that the usually neatly gravelled path leading to the main entrance was now one big puddle. Well, a little rain had never harmed her before.

Before, however, she could step down on the ground, a dark coat was put around her, covering her completely, and a secure hold was placed around her waist.

In no time, she was inside, her feet never touching the wet ground. Mr. Darcy had actually carried her, keeping her to him with only one arm. He was strong. She remembered how her father had done the same when she and Jane were little girls. He would pin each of them under one of his arms, and run around the garden. Poor Papa, to end his life so young, and in such tragic circumstances.

"What it the matter?" Darcy asked, lifting her chin up.

She touched her face, finding new tears. Hastily, she dried her cheeks with the back of her sleeve. "I only remembered how Papa carried Jane and me in the same fashion as you just did, when we were little. Our mother would run after him, crying to put us down, afraid that we would vomit, ruining our pretty dresses.

He stepped closer, putting his arms around her, bringing her to him gently so she could support herself on him.

As she placed her head on his chest, he spoke.

"I remember my father teaching me to ride a horse when I was five years old. My dear mother was beside herself with worry and was following the pony every step, despite the fact that my father was just beside me."

She smiled into his coat. "Did you fall?"

"Yes, but only a few times. Father always said that I was a natural on a horse."

She could hear the pride in his voice, but this time, she could not hold it against him.

"Cousin Elizabeth! What are you doing here with Mr. Darcy?!"

She turned to see Mr. Collins coming out of the library. His eyes were round, bulging out of his plump face.

Elizabeth's heart squeezed painfully in instant worry. What was he doing here so soon? He must have left Kent right after her.

"Dear Cousin!" the man exclaimed, approaching them. "Have you no decency in the face of your father's death? Mr. Darcy is engaged to the daughter of my noble patroness, Lady Catherine. It is shameful of you to stand here, grasping on him like some common…"

He did not finish, as Darcy abruptly moved forward, interrupting him in a low, menacing tone. "One more word, and I will order the servants to throw you out of this house."

Mr. Collins gaped at him, closing and opening his mouth.

"You cannot do that," Mr. Collins spoke meekly, in a high pitched voice. "I am the Master here now. My noble patroness, Lady Catherine, your aunt, told me to come here without delay, in order to take over my new possessions."

As Elizabeth looked up at Darcy, she saw him grinding his teeth, his jaw line tense, his face set in an ugly grimace.

"Go back to the library and wait for me there, Collins." he growled.

Mr. Collins opened his mouth to say something, but Darcy seemed to change his mind with a hard stare. The parson turned on his heels, obediently making his way to the pointed room.

Elizabeth bit her lip to prevent herself from bursting into tears. "He will throw us out," she choked. "Perhaps even before the funeral. Mama will not survive this."

"Nothing like that will happen, love," Darcy said calmly, placing his hands on her shaking shoulders. "I shall talk to him; do not worry."

She lifted her eyes full of tears. "Your aunt told him to come here. He listens to everything she says. He will not even allow us to take our personal things, I am certain. What are we going to do now?"

"You will go upstairs to your mother," he spoke slowly. "I will talk with that creature of a cousin of yours. I promise you that he will be gone from here before evening."

"But…" she started to speak, stopping when he put a gloved finger on her lips.

"Have a little faith in me, love."

A sob broke through her tight throat, and she began to cry in earnest.

"Shush," he wiped the tears from her cheeks with his handkerchief. "There is no need to cry." He pulled her to him, wrapping his arms around her.

She closed her eyes, taking comfort in his embrace as his hand stroked her back in soothing touches.

She took a deep breath, trying to calm her racing heart as she pulled away from him. "Perhaps I should talk to him?" she suggested.

"No, love," he disagreed, his voice gentle but firm. He turned her by the arms towards the staircase, and pushed her gently.

Elizabeth climbed a few steps before she turned to look at him. He was standing by the library door, clearly waiting for her to disappear from his view.

As she reached the landing, she was tempted to go back quietly and wait at the library door, hoping to hear something.

The door to her mother's room opened and Mr. Gardiner stepped out.

"Lizzy, your mother has been asking for you," he said. "She is awaiting you."

"Oh, uncle," she rushed to him. "Mr. Collins is here."

He nodded. "Yes, I am aware of that. My sister has already told me the news. He came the day before yesterday, late at night. It put your mother into hysterics, and this time I honestly cannot blame her for reacting as she is. She has not left her room since then, I understand."

"Oh, uncle, I fear that he will simply throw us out without any consideration."

Mr. Gardiner's expression turned troubled, his eyebrows drawn together. "I do not wish to scare you, but from what your mother and younger sisters told me about his behaviour since he arrived here almost two days ago, I believe that you may be right on that, niece. He may try. I will go now and talk with him."

"Mr. Darcy is there already, talking with him."

"He is?" her uncle asked, his face instantly more relaxed.

She nodded. "Mr. Collins saw us together, standing close, as Mr. Darcy touched me..." she blushed. "He began to call me names... and Mr. Darcy stopped him, ordering him to go to the library."

"And Collins did?"

"Yes, he did. Then Mr. Darcy sent me here, going to the library himself."

"Well, Lizzy, I think that you are a very lucky girl. Things might become very ugly without Darcy's presence here with us. His name alone is enough to protect you, your mother, and your sisters. You do as your betrothed asked you and greet your mother. I will join Mr. Darcy in the library."

Elizabeth wanted to go with her uncle and witness the conversation with Mr. Collins, but she knew that neither Mr. Gardiner nor Mr. Darcy would welcome her there.

She knocked on the door to her mother's room and walked in.

As she expected, her mother was half lying in the bed with all her sisters except Lydia gathered around her.

"Lizzy!" she cried out as soon as she saw her, opening her arms.

"Mama!"Elizabeth ran to her, sat on the edge of the bed, and returned the embrace.

Before she could say anything, her mother surrounded her with questions. "Oh, Lizzy, is it true what I hear from my brother and Jane? Are you engaged to Mr. Darcy? Is he truly here? Has he brought you in his carriage?"

"He is here, Mama," Lydia who just entered the room replied instead of her. "I listened at the library door. Mr. Darcy is there talking with Mr. Collins and Uncle Gardiner. I heard raised voices, but I could not hear exactly what they were saying." She glanced at Elizabeth. "However, earlier, I heard as Mr. Darcy told Mr. Collins that he would throw him out of the house if he did not stop making rude remarks to Lizzy."

Mrs. Bennet's eyes moved from Lydia to Elizabeth, who understood that her youngest sister had been hiding downstairs the entire time, witnessing everything, including her interaction with Darcy. She was not in the least surprised with Lydia's behaviour. Moreover, she was almost certain that it was their mother who had asked her sister to do that.

"Is it true, Lizzy? I must hear it from you," the woman insisted.

Elizabeth gave her a pale smile. "Yes, Mama. I am engaged to Mr. Darcy. He came here with me to help us."

Mrs. Bennet sat speechless for a good minute before she began to cry and laugh interchangeably. She loudly thanked the heavens several times for rescuing all of them.

"Now, Lizzy," her mother spoke as she calmed herself. "You must tell me everything. Where did you meet him?"

"In Kent, Mama. We met again in Kent," Elizabeth answered evenly.

"Kent? What was he doing there? Did he come to see you?"

"No, Mama. He came to visit his aunt Lady Catherine de Bourgh of Rosings Park."

Mrs. Bennet's eyes widened. "That horrible woman who told Mr. Collins to come here is his aunt?!"

"Mama, Mr. Collins mentioned that Lady Catherine is Mr. Darcy's aunt during his previous visit," Jane reminded.

The older woman frowned. "I do not recall him saying that. It is of no importance now. Lizzy," she turned to her second daughter, patting her hand. "You met in Kent and then what happened? How did you manage to catch him?"

Elizabeth barely stopped herself from rolling her eyes. With a resigned sigh, she began telling in short words the tale of their unusual courtship. She confessed that she had not expected the proposal, but she did not mention that she had refused when Darcy asked for the first time. It was a personal matter between Darcy and herself, and her mother and younger sisters did not have to know everything. The Gardiners were not gossipers, and they would never betray her confidence; nor would Jane, naturally.

"He promised to help us?" Her mother reached for her hand, squeezing it.

"Yes, Mama. He promised to buy a house for you, and ensure my sisters' future."

"He did." Mrs. Bennet smiled blissfully. "He did. Thank you, God." She closed her eyes, bringing her hands together like in a prayer.

"I must say that I am very proud of you, Lizzy," Mrs. Bennet spoke after a moment. "You are such a smart girl. I always knew that you were not so smart for nothing."

"I think I should return downstairs, Mama," Elizabeth stood up.

"Oh, yes, go Lizzy, go," Mrs. Bennet encouraged her. "I will dress myself to greet him. Before that, I need to talk with Hill about dinner. Jane, Jane, send Hill to me. We must make sure that the guest bedroom is prepared for him and that the best bed clothes are placed. I am certain that Mr. Darcy is hungry after such a long journey and talking with that horrible Mr. Collins. Lizzy, what is Mr. Darcy's favourite dish?"

"I do not know, Mama," Elizabeth answered.

"Then go and ask him, girl, so we may cook it for him for dinner!"

Elizabeth left the room quietly, listening to her mother ordering her sisters around. Mama seemed her old self. It pained her that she had not mentioned Papa even once.

She walked to the library doors and listened. It was quiet. Lydia had mentioned raised voices, but now no sound was heard.

As she knocked, she heard her uncle's voice calling to enter.

Mr. Darcy and Mr. Gardiner were standing by the window. Mr. Collins was nowhere in sight.

"Elizabeth," her uncle spoke first. "You may thank this gentleman here, as Mr. Collins shall not bother us for the time being."

She walked to Darcy, standing by him. "Truly?"

He smiled down at her. "He is gone. He will stay at the inn in Meryton, I believe, or return to Kent."

"How did you accomplish that?" she asked in curiosity.

"I threatened him," he answered flatly.

She heard her uncle's retreating steps. As she glanced behind, she saw Mr. Gardiner closing the door carefully behind him, leaving them alone.

"Threatened him?" she repeated, her attention on Darcy again. "I do not understand."

"I told him that my friend, the archbishop, would gladly hear how he treated his relatives in the face of family tragedy. Throwing away a mother with five children, a few days after her husband's death is not something that a clergyman should do, after all."

"He believed you? Are you truly the archbishop's friend?"

Darcy gave her a half smile. "Not exactly, however my father befriended him in Oxford, and he is my godfather. I have not seen him since my father's death, but I am certain that he remembers me, and would not refuse me a small favour if I asked him."

Elizabeth took her eyes from his face, staring in front of herself. She had no idea that Mr. Darcy had such connections.

"I negotiated with Collins that you have three months to leave Longbourn. I am sure that we shall find something suitable for your mother and sisters within this time. I have also announced to him that he is not welcome during the funeral."

"Mr. Darcy," she started with emotion. "I truly do not know what to say. I feel humbled by your goodness. I do not want to think what would have happened, had you not been here. Thank you."

Impulsively, she reached for his hand, lifting it to her lips. He stopped her, before she could kiss it.

"Do not ever do that, Elizabeth," he ordered harshly, placing his hands on her arms. "It is not necessary," he added in a gentler tone.

"Thank you," she said again. She wanted to show him her gratitude, but she was not certain how to do that.

"Speak no more about it," he hushed her, bringing her closer.

With trust, she went into his arms, placing her head on his chest.

She felt his chest rising and falling, before he let out a quiet sigh. She raised up on her toes and wrapped her arms tightly around his neck. "Thank you," she whispered one more time. She hoped that he would understand how grateful she was.

"You are welcome," she heard, feeling a kiss on the side of her neck. He had one hand wrapped around her waist, and the other placed higher on her back, stroking her nape.

She had to admit that she liked the way his touch felt on her body. He was very gentle, never forceful, but he seemed to carry some hard object in the pocket of his coat. It was poking at her upper leg.

Slowly, she pushed away from his embrace and looked up at him with smile. "Mama asks about your favourite dish. She wants the cook to prepare it for dinner."

He frowned. "I think I should go. It would be better if I stay at the inn."

"No, you cannot," she protested with energy. "Mama will never allow that. She is already preparing the guest room for you. It is much more comfortable than the rooms at the inn."

He seemed unconvinced. "Will I not impose? You are grieving."

She shook her head vehemently. "Please stay. You will have company in Uncle Gardiner."

He smiled in agreement. "As you wish, if it pleases you."

"It does," she smiled back. "What about your favourite dish? Mama will demand an answer from me, and if she does not receive it, she will bother you."

Darcy presented an exaggerated, terrified expression. "I like everything well enough except carrots. I like fish."

She blinked at him. "Carrots?"

"Yes. I do not eat carrots," he informed her.

She nodded. "No carrots for Mr. Darcy."

"My mother forced me to eat them when I was a child," he offered as an explanation. "Nasty orange things."

"Do you wish to refresh yourself and rest before dinner perhaps?" she asked, taking his hand in hers. "I will show you to your room."

He smiled shyly. "Yes, please."

She led him out of the library, thinking what a contradiction this man was. One moment he was haughty and arrogant only to become sweet and boyish the next one. Perhaps she should trust him when he claimed to love her? What could be another explanation for everything he had done for her and her family today?

Chapter Nine

Darcy's first night in Longbourn passed peacefully. He chose to retire early, feeling considerably awkward in the room full of women. Elizabeth was kind to keep his company, staying close to him, as if she sensed his discomfort. Regretfully, he could hardly talk with her freely with her mother and sisters listening to his every word. Mr. Gardiner was quiet and lost deep in thought. Darcy guessed that he was worried for his wife and sick child whom he had left in London.

Mrs. Bennet asked Darcy some questions, visibly attempting to engage him into conversation. He offered polite answers; however, in general, he found talking with her bothersome. There was one vast similarity between Elizabeth's mother, and Darcy's aunt Lady Catherine, despite the obvious differences between them. A man could never expect what new idiocy would fall out of their mouths.

Darcy praised the dinner to Mrs. Bennet, which indeed was very tasty. Elizabeth must have repeated exactly what he had told her about his favourite dish, because there was fish prepared in three different ways on the table, cooked, fried, and in jelly. Moreover, no carrots were present, not even in the soup.

As he had gone to sleep before nine, almost like a baby, he woke up early, at five. He was shaved and dressed by six, and decided to take a morning walk. He considered going to Netherfield to see whether Bingley had indeed arrived yesterday, as he had planned to do when they had talked last time. It was only a three-mile walk, and as Elizabeth had once travelled the distance on foot, he could do it as well.

As he came downstairs, he thought to hear Elizabeth's voice. He followed the sound, finding her in the small room at the back of the house. She and Jane, dressed entirely in black, were kneeling in front of the open cabinet, looking through some linens.

Shuffling his feet, hoping to be noticed, he cleared his throat.

Both women turned simultaneously to look at him.

"Mr. Darcy, you are awake so early," Elizabeth noted, rising to her feet.

Jane stood as well, her arms full of what looked like tablecloths to him. Darcy bowed his head in her direction. She answered him with a warm smile and nod of her own.

"You are up early as well, ladies," he spoke conversationally.

Elizabeth's face saddened visibly, and he was at loss what caused this.

"We do not rise so early on a daily basis," Jane explained kindly. "However, as the funeral is tomorrow, we must make preparations and plan the meal for the guests. Later today, Mama expects possible callers, so it was decided that we should began our day as early soon as possible. Uncle Gardiner will be absent for most of the day, taking care of the arrangements concerning the burial itself."

Darcy did not respond to Jane's words, only looked away, berating himself inwardly. Naturally, they would start their day earlier than usual, needing to prepare the house for the funeral. He had a rare talent for saying things which offended, or saddened others. Usually he did not care, but not in this case.

Jane , her arms full, made her way to the door. "I will bring these to Mama, Lizzy," she said, leaving them alone.

He was both surprised and relieved when Elizabeth stepped up to him, smiling.

"Good morning, sir."

"Good morning, dearest," he said, grinning back at her.

Her beautiful eyes were looking into his, and he sensed that she was still pleased with him today. He more than liked that. She had never before gazed at him like this, with admiration. Who knew that the idiot Collins would have turned out to be so useful to him? She was obviously impressed with how he had managed the situation with the parson yesterday. He could bask in her warm eyes like in the summer sun the entire day and night, especially night. He wondered what the expression in her eyes would be when she was well loved after he had pleased her.

He took his time to appraise her appearance. She looked impossibly small and delicate in her black dress. Her hair was drawn into a tight, heavy looking braid, laid over her shoulder, the end tied with a black ribbon resting against the top of her bosom. He marvelled that the braid must be almost as thick as his hand. He craved to see her hair let free, strewn around her shoulders, down her back and scarcely covering her bare breasts.

"Are you done, sir?"

He blinked rapidly, focusing his eyes on her face again. "Excuse me?"

She smirked, ducking her head. "Forgive me, it was rude of me. I noticed you gazing at me, so I wished to ask whether you were finished with your staring."

He gaped at her for a moment, not sure how to react. "You are teasing me," he stated, frowning.

Her dark eyes met his. "Do you mind?"

"No, not at all," he murmured quietly, leaning to her, searching her face.

He noticed with pleasure that her pale cheeks flushed a delicate pink. The fact that he was able to affect her made this already pleasant morning even better. Only a few days had passed since he had professed his feelings to her, and despite her denial, he could see that she was not indifferent to him. He had high hopes for the future, becoming even higher with the every new blush he elicited from her.

Her thick, black eyelashes fluttered, and she took a step away from him, straightening her back. "I am afraid, sir, that the breakfast is not yet ready. It will be served in two hours. However, I will ask cook to prepare some eggs and tea for you."

"No, that is not necessary," he assured hastily. "I thought that I would go for a walk before breakfast."

She tilted her head to him, resembling a curious little bird. "Perhaps you would prefer taking one of my father's horses?"

He hesitated, not wanting to upset her by riding an animal which belonged to her father. "I am not certain whether I should…"

She shrugged. "They are only horses. Papa had several stallions. He liked to ride daily."

As he could not see any new distress in her face, he nodded. "I would like that."

"I shall show you to the stables then." She stepped out of the room first, and he followed her.

They were near the staircase when she turned to him. "I will run upstairs for my shawl, the mornings are still chilly."

Waiting for her to get back, Darcy pushed the main door open, allowing light and fresh morning air into the darkened foyer.

"Mr. Darcy!" he heard a faint shriek and stiffened.

Mrs. Bennet approached him with one of the younger girls in tow. It must be Kitty, he realized, the one who most resembled Elizabeth in appearance, with her slight build and dark brown hair. Mary was the one with glasses, and

Lydia was the large, buxom blonde with red cheeks.

"Oh, my goodness, Mr. Darcy, what are you doing up so early?" his future mother in law questioned.

He bowed. "Good morning, Mrs. Bennet, Miss Catherine. I was about to go for a morning ride."

The woman seemed to digest his answer for a moment. "Have you had breakfast?"

"No, I have not, however…"

He did not finish, as he was interrupted. "You cannot go without breakfast, Mr. Darcy!" the woman announced with energy. "You may faint in the saddle."

"I assure you that I have ridden before breakfast many times before, and I have never felt unwell."

Mrs. Bennet looked unconvinced. Thankfully, Elizabeth's light steps were heard on the stairs.

"Mama, I will show Mr. Darcy to the stables. He wants to have a morning ride."

Mrs. Bennet turned to her older daughter. "He says that he does not want breakfast."

"I have already proposed eggs and tea to him, but he claims that he will eat later with everyone."

"It is not healthy. He should eat, such a big man."

Darcy frowned, not enjoying that they were speaking about him as if he was not present, or was a child.

He cleared his throat, extending his arm. "Shall we, Miss Elizabeth?"

Elizabeth came to him quickly, taking his arm. A warm woolen shawl was draped around her shoulders. Her braid was twisted and pinned low at the back of her head.

"I will be back soon to help you, Mama," Elizabeth assured.

"Stay away from Devil," he heard Mrs. Bennet exclaiming as they were outside the house.

"Who is Devil?" Darcy asked as Elizabeth directed them across the front lawn to the smaller side buildings.

"One of my father's horses," she explained. "Mama hates him. She called him Devil when Papa brought him to the house for the first time. Papa decided it was a very fitting name, taking into consideration the animal's temper and the fact that he is entirely black. Mama is of opinion that Papa bought him just to spite her."

Darcy raised his eyebrow. "Did he indeed?"

She shook her head. "I do not think so. He previously belonged to Sir William Lucas, but he was so wild and unrestrained that no one at Lucas Lodge was brave enough to mount him. Papa said that the horse was still young and could be trained. He bought him rather cheaply, I believe. "

Darcy's interest was instantly piqued. He enjoyed spirited animals. "Had your father succeeded in his training?" he wanted to know.

"Yes, I believe so, to an extent. He was able to ride him himself, but prohibited any of us from even coming close to him."

As they entered the stables, Darcy found without trouble a tall, glossy black horse.

"This is Devil," he more stated than asked.

"Yes."

Darcy opened the stall, and confidently, but calmly, approached the horse.

"Be careful, he can bite and kick," he heard Elizabeth's voice behind him.

Darcy put the harness gently on Devil, and led him out of his stall.

"Beautiful," Darcy murmured, stroking the animal's neck. "I will ask Collins if he would mind selling him to me."

"Are you certain you wish to ride him?" she questioned quietly, glancing nervously at the black beast. "There are other horses. Calmer ones."

He turned to her, his attention taken away from the horse for the first time since they had entered the stable.

"I like spirited animals. I shall be fine." He touched her chin. *And spirited women. They are both a challenge to ride.* He added in his thoughts only.

She sighed in resignation, but pointed to one of the stalls. "The saddles should be there."

A few minutes later, Devil was saddled, and Darcy led him outside. Elizabeth followed them, but kept at a safe distance.

Darcy turned to say goodbye. "I should be back before nine. I may bring Bingley with me," he mentioned casually. "I hope that your mother will not mind me inviting him for breakfast."

Her eyes widened, and she stood speechless for a longer moment. "Mr. Bingley is here? At Netherfield?"

"When I talked with him the day before yesterday, he planned to travel to Meryton the same day as us."

"How?" She shook her head. "You saw Mr. Bingley? Talked to him?"

He nodded. "The day after we returned to London. I confessed everything to him, meaning my involvement in separating him and your sister. He was not pleased. However, he seemed to forgive me when I told him that Miss Bennet still thought warmly of him."

Her face lit up. "Why have you not mentioned anything before now?"

He shrugged. "There was no time or opportunity."

His breath was momentarily taken when she crushed herself against him, her arms locked around his neck, kissing his cheek. "Thank you!" she exclaimed, her entire face lit up. Her first real smile since the news about her father had come, he noted.

He laughed, fully using the chance to keep her in his arms. "I think that I like the manner in which you thank me."

She smiled, and regretfully stepped away from him. "Please be careful," she motioned her head towards the horse that was standing calmly nearby. "He was named Devil for a reason."

"You have nothing to be worried about. I can manage him," he assured, and before he could lose his courage, he cupped her cheek, bowed his head, and lightly touched her lips with his. It was a quick and chaste kiss, but still an audible gasp escaped her lips.

He mounted Devil and kicked his sides, setting him into an immediate gallop, and rode away.

***

The abundant breakfast was getting cold, and still there was no sight of Mr. Darcy. Elizabeth glanced nervously at the clock on the mantelpiece. It was almost half past nine. He had been gone for three hours. What could have delayed him for so long? She prayed that it was not Devil's fault. She ordered herself to remain calm. Mr. Darcy was an excellent rider. As she had observed him galloping away, and she could see that he was in full control of the animal.

"Mama!" Lydia exclaimed, her nose glued to the glass of the window. "Someone is coming. Two riders."

Mrs. Bennet hurried to her side. "Mr. Darcy and…" she narrowed her eyes, craning her neck to see better, "and… Mr. Bingley… Can it be?"

Elizabeth felt that the time for some explanation came. "Yes, Mama," she said, glancing at Jane. She did not mention to Jane the possibility of Mr. Bingley's visit. She was afraid of raising her sister's hopes, only to have her disappointed if Mr. Bingley did not come after all. "Mr. Darcy mentioned to me today that he saw Mr. Bingley in London a few days ago, and informed him about our... about Papa. I think that Mr. Bingley wishes to pay his respects."

"Of course!" Mrs. Bennet clapped her hands, laughing. "Mr. Bingley is Mr. Darcy's dear friend, after all. Your marriage, Lizzy, shall benefit us in so many ways! Matters are going so well."

"How can you say so, Mama?" Elizabeth cried sharply, rising abruptly from her chair. "Papa has just died, and you laugh and clap? How can you? How can you keep saying that matters are going well? Not even once have you mentioned him! Not even once!"

Tears in her eyes, Elizabeth stared at her mother, who only gaped at her, mouth wide open. She expected her to say something, but she waited in vain.

With a sob, she turned on her heel, tripping over the chair, which fell to the carpeted floor with soft thud. In her rush, she bumped into Mr. Bingley in the entrance to the room.

"Miss Elizabeth," Mr. Bingley spoke with visible concern, steadying her with one hand on her elbow.

Not lifting her eyes, she pushed past him, and ran forward. This time she crashed into Darcy.

"Lizzy, love, what is the matter?" he questioned frantically, taking in her pained expression.

"What happened?" He shook her gently.

She took a deep breath, trying to calm herself. "I simply need a few moments to myself. I will go for a walk to clear my head."

"Allow me to accompany you."

"No," she shook her head. "I want to be alone."

"Please, I will be sick with worry," he insisted. "You are distressed. You should not go on your own."

"Very well," she agreed, knowing too well that he was too stubborn to give in.

He would have followed her anyway even if she had insisted on going alone. She needed to go out desperately. She could not stay in the same house with her mother in her present state.

She sprinted out of the house towards the gardens and small park, and soon she was out in the open pasture. As she glanced over her arm, she saw that Darcy was only one step behind her.

He did not attempt again to ask her what had happened to put her in such a state, for which she was grateful.

At last, exhausted with her almost running pace, she lowered herself to the ground, sitting under a tree growing at the border between two fields.

"You must forgive me, Mr. Darcy, for dragging you here," she said after a long moment of silence.

He was seated against a low tree branch, not far from her spot.

"You must think me wild and unstable," she commented.

"I would only wish to know what put you in such a state. Perhaps I could help." His voice sounded both concerned and reassuring, but not judging.

She stared down, pulling out blades of grass with her fingers, uprooting them from the soft ground. "Mama has not even once mentioned Papa since I came home. She behaves as if nothing has happened. She is enraptured because I caught a rich man, as she puts it... Now, when she heard about Mr. Bingley's return... she forgot completely that we are to bury Papa tomorrow. I understand that she did not love him, that their union was not blessed with happiness, but she was married to him for over twenty years. Should she not feel a hint of sadness? Some regret over his death, especially in such tragic circumstances? He was not perfect, but he never mistreated her, as it is heard with other husbands. I cannot comprehend it."

He came closer, blocking the sun. As she looked up, she saw him kneeling next to her.

"It is out of my experience, I am afraid. My parents greatly loved each other," he shared. "I remember that they touched and kissed in front of me when I was little. When my mother died... my father went almost mad with sorrow. He was never the same."

"You were fortunate indeed to be born into such a family, even if you had both of your parents beside you for such a short time."

"Do you wish to return?" he asked, rubbing her back.

She shook her head. "Not yet, but you should go back."

"I will stay with you as long as you wish me to."

"You do not have to feel obliged to stay here with me," she murmured.

"I wish to be with you when you are happy, and when you are sad, like now," he acknowledged quietly.

She met his eyes, taken aback with the sincerity of his expression. Over the last few days, this man whom she had considered almost her enemy, seemed to transform into her best friend. How could this be?

Chapter Ten

If Elizabeth expected that her mother would wish to have a conversation with her about what had happened between them, she was met with disappointment. Mrs. Bennet pretended as if nothing had happened. As Elizabeth and Darcy returned from their prolonged walk, Mrs. Bennet behaved as usual. The only difference was that she avoided looking directly into Elizabeth's eyes.

Elizabeth considered whether she should ask her mother for a private conversation. Eventually she decided against it. She found no strength in herself to do that. She was afraid of what she might hear from her mother, and she was not at all certain whether or not she wanted to hear it. Such a conversation between them would probably change nothing. She doubted whether they would ever understand one another. Her only hope was that her mother possessed enough sense to behave with moderation in front of their neighbours during their mourning period.

The bitter truth was that she was in no place to judge her mother. She herself had agreed to marry a man whom she did not care for only to secure herself a life of comfort. Would she become her mother in thirty years? Would she feel nothing if Darcy was to die first? Would she be relieved, feeling no connection to him on the day of his funeral? It was the last thing that she wanted for herself.

Darcy seemed so convinced that they would be happy together. He did not fear their future. On the contrary, he anticipated it, he was filled with hope. He certainly did not wish for them to be strangers living under the same roof. He was so affectionate with her, open, attentive, kind, considerate. He was wrong about many matters, but she could not deny that he was more than eager to repair his mistakes in order that he might please her. She had never remembered her father acting in such a manner towards her mother.

On the day of the funeral, Elizabeth was busy, along with her sisters, preparing the house for the mourners. She was relieved that women did not attend the funeral, as she doubted whether she could maintain a polite, indifferent façade. Hearing from her uncle that her father's body was in such a state that the coffin could not have been opened to anyone's view, was quite enough for her. She did not want to watch as it was lowered into the grave.

As the guests were filling the drawing room, she observed with relief that her mother and younger sisters behaved appropriately. Her mother was perhaps a bit theatrical in her gestures, pretending to dry her eyes with a lace handkerchief every second minute. However, Mrs. Bennet did refrain from informing everyone of her great fortune in procuring such as a son-in-law as Mr. Darcy.

As for Elizabeth's betrothed, he sought her eyes from the moment he entered the house with Mr. Gardiner and Mr. Bingley. She instantly felt comforted and calmed with the sheer sight of him. She wished to lean into him, and feel his arms around her, which was hardly possible in the room full of people.

The guests were in the middle of consuming a late lunch, seated at the long table which had been brought out from the dining room especially for the occasion. Sir William was just raising his voice to remind everyone what a good neighbour and honourable man Mr. Bennet had been, when there was a commotion heard outside the main entrance of the house.

Mrs. Bennet hurried to the window to see who had arrived. She was not expecting any new additions to the party. Silently, she gestured to Elizabeth and Jane, who came to her side.

"Who is that?" Mrs. Bennet wondered. "What a grand carriage," she observed. "It must be someone important."

"Oh, no…" Elizabeth whispered, her eyes widening as she recognized the woman stepping out of the carriage.

"Do you know her, Lizzy?"

"I do, Mama," she said, and without saying more, she walked directly to Darcy, who was seated beside Mr. Bingley.

As she stood by his chair, and leaned to him, she instantly had his full attention.

"Is something the matter, dearest?" he asked, not minding that his best friend was listening.

"Your aunt is here," she whispered into his ear. "She has just arrived. She is outside the main entrance."

It took him a moment to register her words. "I shall deal with her," he whispered back, discreetly rising from his seat, making his way through the crowded room.

"Where is she? Where is that insolent girl?" the loud, feminine voice hollered through the house.

Darcy hastened his pace, almost running towards the door. Elizabeth had never seen him move in such a hurry.

The door was pushed open, their butler unceremoniously shoved aside, and Lady Catherine de Bourgh stood there in all her glory, dressed in a wine coloured dress with three green feathers protruding of her bonnet. The representatives of all the four and twenty families which the Bennets had relations with craned their necks from their places at the table to see what the commotion was about.

Darcy blocked his aunt's way, not entirely politely, but effectively removing her from the entrance to the drawing room.

The guests remained perfectly silent as everyone listened to the woman's words. "I must speak with her this instant! You cannot forbid me, nephew!"

She was quiet for a moment, and Elizabeth guessed that Darcy was trying to explain the situation to her, because soon another wave of furious bellowing was heard.

"I do not care whether you love her or not! You could have taken her as a mistress if you had to have her!"

Elizabeth did not dare to look at the people around her; she could only feel the heat rising in her cheeks, though her hands were icy cold and shaking violently.

"Ladies and gentleman, let us go out to the garden for some fresh air," Mr. Bingley spoke in his rich voice, standing abruptly from his chair. "It is such a lovely day, and we all know how Mr. Bennet enjoyed the outdoors. Miss Bennet," he turned to Jane, "shall we have tea on the terrace?"

Elizabeth lifted her eyes slowly to Mr. Bingley as he energetically led the stunned guests out of the room. Gradually, the room emptied. The servants, directed by Mrs. Bennet and Jane, moved a few smaller tables and the chairs, along with the refreshments, to the terrace.

Elizabeth did not join the others, but she followed the sounds of a heated argument coming from the library. As she stood by the door to the room which had once been her father's sanctuary, she could clearly hear Lady Catherine's voice again.

"Your poor mother is rolling in her grave! She wanted you to marry Anne."

"She never said anything of the kind to me, neither she nor my father," Darcy responded, his voice raised, but not as loud as his aunt's. "They wanted me to have a happy life. They were a love match, and I do not see why I should not follow in their footsteps."

"You think she loves you! Ha, ha! She wants you for your fortune and position! Do you think I did not notice how you stared after her every time she came to Rosings with the Collinses? But she never gave you a second look. She laughed and talked with Richard, but never with you. You fool. Are you blind? She is using you."

Darcy answered something, but Elizabeth could not hear the exact words.

"Tell me," Lady Catherine demanded. "Is she with child? I would not be surprised if you have already bedded her. If that is the case, you can send her away quietly, and even visit her and her little bastard from time to time. And should it be a boy, he could be raised as a gentleman, and if it is your wish, even given a small estate in the future. You do not need to abandon them, but marrying her is out of question."

Suddenly the door opened with such a force that Elizabeth thought that it would surely fall off the hinges.

She stepped back in the shadows.

"Get out," Darcy hissed, in a voice she had never heard from him. "There will be no relationship between us till you apologize to me and my future wife."

"Is that your final word?"

There was only silence in response, and soon Lady Catherine marched out of the library, down the hall towards the main entrance. She did not look back, nor speak to anyone, only got into her carriage, ordering her people to leave without delay.

"You heard everything," Darcy stated from behind her back, as she stood by the window, looking after Lady Catherine's carriage as it disappeared from sight.

She did not respond. He put his hand on her shoulder. His hands were always warm, contrary to hers.

"I apologize. I am deeply ashamed for my relative's behaviour. There is no excuse for her. I did not think she would come here, interrupting the funeral so rudely. You must believe me. Collins must have written to her. I knew that Lady Catherine would not be pleased with our engagement, however this… I did not expect. Where is everyone? The house is so quiet." He was speaking quickly, nervously.

He gave her shoulder a squeeze. "Elizabeth, pray say something."

She turned to him, her eyes downcast. "Mr. Bingley rescued the situation. He proposed that the company take tea on the terrace."

"That is good," Darcy nodded, relieved. "I only hope they did not hear too much."

"The library is on the other side of the house, so I think that should be the case."

He touched her chin with his finger. "Please look at me."

She did as he asked. He must have not liked her expression, because he took her hands in his, stroking her palms with his thumbs, squeezing her cold fingers.

"I cannot even imagine how humiliating it was for you. I swear that I would have tried to prevent it, had I known... I should have guessed. It is my fault."

"No, no," she shook her head, freeing her hands from his hold, "Lady Catherine can be called rude; her arrival here on the day of the funeral insensitive, however, she was right in what she said to you about me."

His brow furrowed, a dark scowl darkening his countenance. "No, she is not."

"Yes, she is," she insisted. "You know that she said nothing untrue. I agreed to marry you because of your fortune and position. Your family will hate me. In time, you will begin to dislike me too, regretting this union. You will be unhappy. We will be like my parents or worse."

"That is very far from the truth," he contradicted at once, speaking with energy, even enthusiasm. "Colonel Fitzwilliam likes you, even too much for my taste. Georgiana will love you, she already does. As for Lord and Lady Matlock, they may have some reservations at first, but once they know you, I am sure they will accept you. They are not like Lady Catherine. She was so furious because she convinced herself that I would marry her daughter."

"Perhaps you should marry your cousin."

"No, I definitely should not," he argued, his tone laced with irritation. "I want a companion, someone I can share my life with, someone I would want to take to my bed without abhorrence and have children with. My cousin Anne is the last person to fit that role."

She closed her eyes, before opening them, looking up at him. "You are a worthy man, a good man, I can see it now. Let us put an end to this before it is too late. You deserve someone who loves you. Lady Catherine is right, I am only using you."

"No, no..." he protested, looking around. They stood in the darkened corner of the foyer; however someone could pass by any moment. "Come," he took her elbow, pulling her with him.

He led them into the library and closed the door firmly.

"We will not be like your parents," he said.

"How can you be so certain?" she asked, searching his handsome features. "I do not wish to hurt you. I was selfish for myself and for my family, but this is not right. We can part our ways discreetly..."

She was taken aback when he grasped her forearms with force. "You will not speak about our parting ways any more," he ordered. His hold on her was not painful, but much stronger than ever before. "There is no such possibility. You gave me your word that you would marry me. Are you taking it back?"

"I do not wish to hurt you," she repeated with feeling what she had already said before.

"Then pray stop speaking about leaving me," he spat out.

He was silent for a moment, and she felt his grip on her arms loosening. When he motioned her to take a seat on the small sofa, she did not protest.

"Can you not see how similar we are in our attitudes, in our perception of the world and people?" he asked, sitting next to her. "We are both stubborn; however, we are able to acknowledge our mistakes and improve ourselves when pointed in the right direction. We will never be like your parents."

"I do not know," she whispered, unconvinced. She could not help but see everything in the darkest colours.

He placed her hand again in both of his. "Can you honestly say that you feel nothing for me?"

"I am confused," she acknowledged.

A pleasant shiver ran through her body, as he kissed the side of her neck, "You cannot deny that you react when I touch you, when I am close."

He cupped her face in his hands. The kiss which came was nothing like the light peck he had given her the day before. His lips tugged insistently, till she opened her mouth and let him inside. She would have never guessed that having someone's tongue inside her mouth would create such intensely pleasurable sensations.

He ran his hand from her waist up, brushing the side of her bosom, which caused an instant reaction in her as she jerked in his arms. She could feel that his lips shaped into a smile against hers, as his hand moved down her side, curving around her hip. "You see, you are so responsive," he murmured, nuzzling her neck with his nose. "You do not want me to stop."

She closed her eyes, her head lolling against his chest. She felt tingly and uncomfortable all over her body. Her bosom, especially, ached, and there was an embarrassing, unexpected wetness, between her legs in her private place. He tucked her against him, her back to his chest.

"No more talk about putting an end to anything," he murmured, placing kisses on the path from her neck to shoulder. "Do we understand each other?" His hands wrapped around her midsection, squeezing her to him.

She sighed. "I am not certain whether you know what you are doing."

"Trust me."

She turned in his arms to look into his face. "I am so grateful for your help, for assisting my family. I hope that you will not regret it. I will try to be a good wife to you; and give you happiness if it is in my power."

He stroked her face with the back of his palm, "It is."

"What should I do?"

He grinned. "So far you are doing everything right."

She lowered her eyes. "Do you expect me to be more forthcoming?" she asked quietly. "Touch you more?"

He leaned to place a small kiss on her lips. "Do not fret about this; we have time. There is no hurry. Whenever you are ready."

She swallowed, searching his face. "What about the wedding night?"

His expression did not change, and he did not hesitate a second before answering. "As I said, whenever you are ready."

Before she could begin pondering on his words anew, he stood up, pulling her to his feet as well.

"I think that we should join the company."

She nodded. "Mama must be wondering about our whereabouts."

"Stay close to me. I will answer all the questions if they ask about the unexpected guest."

"Thank you," she replied gratefully.

She took his arm, and together they walked out of the room. Elizabeth hoped that their neighbours would leave the house soon. She wished to visit her father's grave yet today.

Chapter Eleven

As Darcy and Elizabeth returned to the company, they received numerous curious glances, but no direct questions were posed. Elizabeth acknowledged that it was due to Darcy's cold and discouraging manner. As promised, he did not leave her side. His scowl was priceless to observe, and soon, she wondered whether he practiced in front of a mirror to achieve such an effect. He could be very intimidating when he put some effort to it. She slowly began to understand that it was only a façade for strangers, and that in his relations with close family and friends he was entirely different.

Within only an hour after the incident with Lady Catherine, the last of the guests were gone. Mr. Gardiner also set off to London, even though Mrs. Bennet tried to convince him that it would be much safer to leave tomorrow, early in the morning. However, the man was determined to be joined with his family yet this night. Everyone guessed that he was concerned about them, his youngest son especially.

After they waved away Mr. Gardiner, Mrs. Bennet pulled Elizabeth aside. It was not difficult to guess what Mrs. Bennet wanted to talk about. Elizabeth attempted to be patient as she explained what had transpired between Darcy and his aunt. She did not include the finer details though.

"Are you sure, Lizzy, that he will keep his word and marry you?" Mrs. Bennet whispered fearfully. "Will he go against his family? Lady Catherine was so displeased."

"He assured me that nothing has changed. He still wants to marry me."

Mrs. Bennet seemed doubtful, pressing her lips together, twisting a handkerchief in her pretty, white hands. "Oh, child, perhaps you should encourage him."

Elizabeth frowned, at first not understanding her mother's point. "Encourage him?" she repeated.

Mrs. Bennet shifted her weight from one foot to the other. "You know what I mean to say." The woman's eyes rounded in exaggeration. "I will certainly not check whether you spend the nights in your room in your bed, alone."

Finally, her mother's meaning dawned on her. "Mama!" Elizabeth cried, truly outraged. "How can you suggest that?"

"Oh, shush, girl!" Her mother waved her hand before Elizabeth's face. "I am not blind. I can see how he stares at you. Be clever about it. That would bind him to you even more."

"On the contrary, Mama. He would lose any respect he holds for me," she spoke with conviction.

She was hurt, and shaken; she wanted to cry. She could not believe that her own mother had suggested that.

"If you were to become with child before the wedding…" Mrs. Bennet continued obliviously.

"No, I will not do it!" she exclaimed.

"Do not be so selfish, Lizzy," Mrs. Bennet scolded her. "Think about your family. You should go to him tonight. He will not hurt you. You may even like it." Mrs. Bennet winked at her knowingly.

Elizabeth gaped at the woman in front of her, wondering how they could be mother and daughter. They would never understand one another.

"Mama, I cannot help you with putting the house into order now," she spoke coldly. "I will go to visit Papa's grave, and I want to be alone. You will have to deal on your own with the help of the girls and Jane."

She walked away without giving her mother a second glance. She did not want to say something she would regret later. She was about to turn in the direction of her room to fetch her bonnet and change her shoes to more sturdy ones, when she remembered about Darcy and his whereabouts. She had not seen him for some time, since he had been saying goodbye to her uncle. Now with Mr. Gardiner gone, poor Darcy had no sensible company in this house apart from Jane and herself. She could not leave him for the rest of the afternoon, alone on her mother's mercy. Heaven only knew what she would tell him. She shuddered at the thought. Mr. Darcy and her mother alone. She could easily see her mother advising him to pay her a visit at night, giving him a free hand. She should find him, and perhaps convince him to visit Mr. Bingley, or go for a ride.

She knocked on the door to his room, but he was not there.

The next place she decided to check was a library, and indeed she found him there.

"Are you well?" she asked, concerned, as she saw him sitting at the desk with his forehead placed against the smooth wooden surface.

He looked up instantly on hearing her voice.

"Perfectly well, thank you," he replied.

However, she was not convicted of that. He was pale, his face without the usual healthy glow to it, and she could see the lines around his eyes and on his forehead were more pronounced than usual.

"Does your head hurt?" she asked

He tried to shrug off her question and stood up, but she pushed him back in the chair. "It started after your aunt's visit," she guessed.

"What started?"

She rolled her eyes. "Your headache. I can see that you suffer." She touched his face, her hand clasping his forehead which was cool to touch.

"I have felt the onset since the morning, but yes, it intensified after my aunt's visit," he acknowledged at last.

"You should lie down; take a nap," she suggested.

He straightened up. "I will not sleep during the day. I am not a baby. I have some letters to write."

"I do not think that you will write a lot, with your head on the desk, refusing to have a true rest. You should be resting in a darkened room. It is the best for a migraine."

"I do not have a migraine." He scowled. "It is only a slight headache."

"I am not listening to you, as you are not being reasonable."

He gaped at her, unblinking.

She took his hand in hers and pulled him up from the chair.

"Where are we going?" he murmured.

"To your room, so you can have a nap," she explained calmly.

He rooted his feet into the floor, refusing to move. "I said that I would not sleep during a day. It is a waste of time."

She counted to three, praying for patience. She considered arguing back, but then decided against it.

Lifting on her toes, she cupped his face, her other hand placed on his arm for a balance, and said. "Do it for me. I will be worried."

He frowned, staring down at her.

"Please," she smiled, giving him the look she always treated her family with when she wanted something badly as a little girl. "For me."

"Very well," he murmured, still scowling, but she could see the warmth and amusement in his eyes. He allowed her to lead him upstairs. As they walked into his room, she closed the door firmly, and pushed him to sit on the bed.

He seemed bewildered as she removed his coat.

"This cannot be comfortable to sleep in," she justified, unbuttoning his elegant waistcoat and loosening his pristinely white neck cloth.

"Take these off," she ordered, looking down at his feet. Thankfully, he was not wearing his long riding boots, because she would have to call his man to remove them. He kicked off his shoes obediently, and she pushed him down so he lay down. Reaching for the light, loosely knit blanket, she pulled it over him.

She made her way to the window, leaving it open, but closing the curtains, darkening the room. This way he would have an abundance of fresh air, without direct sunlight to hurt his eyes.

As she returned to the bed, his eyes were closed. She leaned over to pull the blanket higher over his arms, when he caught her hand, opening his eyes.

"Stay with me," he asked.

"I wanted to go to Papa's grave," she reminded him.

He gave her a pleading look. "Just till I fall asleep."

"Very well," she pulled herself on the edge of the high bed, her back to the headboard. There was a proper distance between their bodies. She reached her hand to comb the hair falling on his forehead.

"Sleep," she whispered. More than once, she had put one of the Gardiners' children to sleep, and they enjoyed when she sat by them, stroking their hair. True, Darcy was not a child, but he did not protest in the least.

He had something different in mind, however, as he sat up, hooking his arm around her waist and effortlessly pulling her to lie next to him. She stared in shock as he reached down to remove her slippers, throwing them dismissively on the floor. Then he draped blanket over both of them.

They were lying facing one another, and soon Darcy's eyelids dropped. He had his arm draped loosely around her waist, and although there was a very little space between their bodies, they were not touching directly.

Elizabeth never went to visit her father's grave that afternoon. When she woke up from her deep slumber, she realized that it must be almost evening, as very little light was coming through the drawn curtains. She was on her back, feeling hot, with a heavy weight upon her.

Darcy's dark head was tucked firmly below her chin, resting on her chest, and one arm was thrown over her body. Surprisingly, she could not find anything inappropriate about it. She was not scared. On the contrary, it felt right.

Carefully, she began moving away from him, hoping not to rouse him. Jane knew about her plans of visiting Papa's grave, so she was not worried that she was gone. However, it was dinner time, and she should have been back some time ago.

"No," Darcy whispered, his arm curling firmly around her waist.

"I should go," she whispered back, looking into his sleepy, blinking eyes.

"No," he murmured again, burying his face into her neck.

She tried to push his arm away from her, using all her strength, but it did not budge even an inch. The only response was him kissing her neck.

"Mr. Darcy, let me go, sir," she responded with authority. "I have stayed much too long as it is. Jane must be looking for me. She must be worried." She wanted to say that she should not be found in his room, lying together with him in his bed, but then she bit her tongue. Her mother would undoubtedly be more than pleased with such a development.

Suddenly his weight was taken off her, and he lifted up, supporting his frame on his elbow. "I would wish you to call me by my given name when we are alone," he spoke straightforwardly. "You still refer to me as Mr. Darcy, even when we are like this." His eyes raked over her body sprawled along his.

She smiled. "How is your headache, Fitzwilliam?" she asked, sitting up.

Sometime during their nap, they must have kicked the blanket down, as it was on the foot of the bed. Her skirt and petticoats hitched up, showing her stocking-clad feet and lower calves.

She noticed that he stared down at her feet with intensity. She glanced down at them, hoping the there was no tear in her stocking, as it was her second best pair. Her legs looked the same as usual; she could not guess why he found them so interesting. She reached to push her skirts down, and this, at last, brought his attention back to her face.

"Your headache?" she repeated.

"Much better, love. I think that your way of healing it was the best possible. You must promise me to always treat me like this."

The warmth filled her chest at his affectionate words, his kind expression.

"I am glad that you feel better," she said, moving to the edge of the bed.

Before her feet touched the floor, he was behind her, his arm wrapped around her waist. "Stay," he whispered, nuzzling the nape of her neck.

She stiffened instantly. "You said whenever I was ready…" she reminded him.

He moved around her, cupping her face. "You misunderstood me. I meant to ask you to stay a bit longer with me. I would never force you into anything you are not ready for."

She searched his face for a longer moment, but as his expression was sincere, she calmed down. "I stayed longer than I should have in the first place. You know that we should not be alone like this."

He lay back on the bed with exasperated sigh. "We are not doing anything wrong," he groaned. "I wish to be at Pemberley already, not asking anyone whether I can spend time with you or not."

She smiled, shaking her head. "Where is the very proper Mr. Darcy I know?"

He leaned back to her. "Who said that I was proper?" he questioned softly. "Do I give you such an impression?"

His eyes bore into her face and she could not break the eye contact.

"I am not at all that proper as you may think, Miss Bennet," he whispered into her ear.

Before she knew what was happening, she was lying on her back, with him hovering over her.

He kissed her forehead, her nose and captured her mouth. As he was supported on his arm, his free hand moved down her body. He did not touch her bosom, but traced his fingers close by it.

Blinking her eyes, she stared at the ceiling, concentrating on the sensation of his mouth on her neck, and shoulder, and his hand splayed on her lower stomach. She knew that she should end this, but she could not summon a force to ask him to stop. She felt dizzy, and so good with his attentions. What was she doing? It was the day of her father's funeral, and she was allowing this man to do such intimate things to her.

"Mr. Darcy, are you there, sir?" Jane's faint voice was heard from the corridor. "I am looking for Elizabeth."

He lifted up, responding in his usual tone. "I will be right with you, Miss Bennet."

He kissed her mouth one more time, a short sweet kiss, his hand running down her body one last time, making her shudder violently as it skimmed over her breast.

She was still on her back, not able to move as he walked across the room.

"Forgive me for interrupting your rest, Mr. Darcy," Jane spoke as Darcy opened the door. "Lizzy has not yet returned from her walk. I have been to Papa's grave, but she was not there. I thought to ask you before alarming Mama and the girls. She is never back from her walks so late."

Jane was speaking quietly, but quickly, and Elizabeth could hear the fear in her sister's voice.

Elizabeth walked from behind Darcy. "I have been here with Mr. Darcy, Jane."

Jane's pretty mouth fell open, and she stared at her with round eyes. It lasted only a few moments before she composed herself. "Of course. Forgive me." She turned on her heel, and hastily scurried down the hall.

Darcy closed the door.

"Are you afraid of what she will think?" he asked.

Elizabeth shook her head. "Jane will understand once I explain to her that you did not feel well, and that is the reason why I stayed with you. She is not one to judge others easily." She smiled ruefully. "Not like me."

He pulled her to him, wrapping his arms around her. "Thank you; that was a wonderful afternoon."

She frowned.

"Forgive me. I should not have said that, especially today, the day of your father's funeral."

"And the day of your aunt's visit," she remarked.

He nodded. "That too. I simply cannot help feeling overjoyed when we seem to be growing closer."

She smiled, not being sure how to answer him. "Will you go downstairs for dinner?" she changed the subject.

He hesitated. "Can I eat here?"

"Naturally, I shall send the tray." She lifted on her toes to kiss his cheek. "Goodnight."

"Goodnight, love," she heard, as she was closing the door.

Chapter Twelve

The week after Mr. Bennet's funeral turned out to be very busy for both the Bennet women and Mr. Darcy. Elizabeth did not know what to think about the fact that her mother had no wish to linger in Longbourn. When Darcy asked whether or not she was ready to look at the available houses in the neighborhood, she was more than eager to begin the search.

After a few days, it was decided that the Bennets would move to Purvis Lodge, with the house being refreshed for the new inhabitants. Elizabeth felt ill in her stomach every time she heard her mother speaking about the move. Her mother was much too demanding, in her opinion. When Mrs. Bennet announced that she wanted new wallpaper in all the downstairs rooms of her new home, Elizabeth thought that she was about to lose control over herself and physically harm her. It was the first time ever, when she had a strong urge to do something violent to the woman who was her mother in order to stop her from speaking. It bothered her to the core and shamed her deeply that Darcy paid for every single thing. She cringed inwardly, her cheeks flaming, every time Darcy discussed the new expenses with her mother or Uncle Philips who dealt with the legal side of all the arrangements.

Darcy was delicate enough to never mention financial matters directly to her. They talked about everything but the current situation. She often asked him about his sister and Pemberley, as he was always happy to talk about it. She learned a lot about his childhood, his youth, about his university years and how he had formed his friendship with Mr. Bingley. Her impression was that he was a very private person, very thoughtful, controlled, well organized and sensible.

She agreed readily when he tentatively proposed the wedding date for the last Sunday of May. She wished to fulfill her part of the bargain and have it done with. Once she was his wife, she would not feel so indebted to him. She would miss Jane and her younger sisters, being so far away from them in Derbyshire. However, she was relieved to be soon separated from her mother. It pained her that they had grown even more apart since Mr. Bennet's death. She doubted whether it would ever change.

One day, just before his scheduled trip to London, Darcy asked her to accompany him to Meryton. He had one last appointment with Uncle Phillips concerning legal matters, and wanted to buy a present for his sister. He claimed that he brought her a present from his every trip since she had been a baby.

Without surprise, her mother acclaimed the idea of them going together to Meryton, and they left shortly after breakfast. Elizabeth felt guilty about leaving Jane alone with all the packing. Her mother liked to direct others, giving instructions how things should be done, but she was not much real help, the same as the younger girls. Jane could really count only on Mary.

"My sister wants to meet you," Darcy informed her as they stepped on the road leading directly to Meryton.

She looked up at him. "She does?"

"Oh, yes," he assured with enthusiasm. "I received a letter from her yesterday. I will show it to you later if you wish."

"The wedding is in little more than two weeks," she reminded him. "We will meet soon."

She had thought about inviting Darcy's sister here; however, she was not certain how Darcy felt about it. Despite his generally polite behaviour towards everyone, she knew that he looked down on the society in Meryton. Perhaps he did not wish to expose his sister to such company. Moreover, as they were in the middle of the move, admitting any guests was rather troublesome at the moment.

He stopped, looking down at her. "I was thinking about you two meeting sooner."

"Oh," she responded, waiting him to say more.

"As you know, I am going to London tomorrow, planning to return a day before the wedding." He closed the space between them. "Come with me. I cannot bear to think that we would be separated for two long weeks."

"Fitzwilliam, I am not certain whether it is the best idea," she said slowly. "Jane needs me. There is so much to do."

"I am sure that your mother and sister will manage with the move. They have friends and family here, they can count on them. There is Bingley too, if they need more assistance."

"I would have to stay with the Gardiners," she said more to herself than to him, considering his words.

"They will welcome you."

"I would have to ask Mama," she murmured, knowing very well that her mother would not protest such plans. On the contrary, she would probably allow her to live with Darcy at his house even before the wedding.

"You could ask your aunt to help you complete your new wardrobe while in Town."

She blanched at his suggestion. "I do not need anything."

"Elizabeth, you are expected to dress in a certain way as my wife. You need more dresses than you have now. Everyone in Derbyshire must know from the first glance that you are the mistress of Pemberley."

His voice was neutral, and she did not think that he tried to purposively offend her with his words; still, she felt as if he was ashamed of her because of her wardrobe. She glanced down at the dress she was wearing. It was one of her older ones which had recently been dyed black. She thought it did not look that bad with the new black one-inch ribbons attached along the hem, sleeves and the décolletage.

"I do not know much about women's fashion, but it will take time to make all the things you need. When Georgiana orders her dresses, it always takes a few weeks to have them made, and there are always several adjustments needed in the process. The sooner the process begins, the faster we can set out for Derbyshire for the summer. I have not been home in a long time. I am needed there. Moreover, I cannot wait to show my home to you."

Elizabeth gazed at the ground with a heavy heart. He wanted to spend even more money on her. She did not like it. She was in no particular mood for shopping either. On the other hand, she had promised herself that she would be a good wife to him so that she might repay him for his generosity. If he thought that she needed new clothes so that she did not to bring shame to him, then she would not argue on that point.

Leaving tomorrow only to return a day before the wedding would mean that she would be separated from her family sooner than planned. Although she would miss Jane, she knew that her sister was happier now with Mr. Bingley returned to Netherfield; but still, Jane was the closest friend Elizabeth had in the world. However, if she did Mr. Darcy's bidding, making him pleased with her, then perhaps he would be willing to invite Jane to Pemberley in the future for a prolonged stay.

"Very well," she smiled at him. "I will go with you tomorrow."

His face broke into a wide smile, "Thank you, dearest." Quickly, he looked around, surely to check whether the road was empty, and bent his head to place a sweet, short kiss on her lips.

As they walked, Darcy seemed perfectly at ease, being silent and as usual, it was Elizabeth who started the conversation first.

"From what you told me, I understand you and your sister must be very close. I wonder whether she is not apprehensive about your marriage, about another woman taking your attentions."

"That is not the case, I assure you," he responded spiritedly. "She wants me to be happy. I think that she was concerned over my loneliness. She looks forward to meeting you."

"What did you tell her about me?"

"Not much, but those few times I mentioned you, was more than I ever spoke before about any other woman to her. Her conclusion was that I was in love with you."

"I can hardly believe that I was the first woman you mentioned to her," she responded lightly.

He seemed confused. "Why?"

"You are a man who has lived in the world. I am certain have you met at least a few women who drew your interest enough to mention them casually to your sister."

"Yes, it is true. You were the first lady worth mentioning."

She narrowed her eyes as she glanced up at him. He sounded so self assured, and yet she found his words hard to believe. He was walking, looking straight ahead, in this confident fluid stride, so characteristic to him.

"In that case, you must have most particular tastes as far as women are concerned," she remarked, using her most playful tone. "May I guess that you do not like those who are claimed classically beautiful?"

He gazed down at her, his eyebrows drawn together in obvious confusion. "Huh?"

"Because you would have taken interest in Jane, and not me," she answered his unspoken question. "I remember being only tolerable in your opinion, but not handsome enough to be danced with, when we first met."

He paled visibly. "How do you...?" he mumbled, and then he hung his head down. "You overheard me. I apologize; you should not have taken it personally. I was in a foul mood that evening. I hate when Bingley drags me to those social functions. I dislike balls, meeting new people, especially dancing with women I know little about," he confessed.

She smiled brightly at him, wanting to show that she was not angry. "I think that you have changed your mind about my person."

He smiled back, relieved. "Indeed, I have. I think that you are one of the most handsome women of my acquaintance."

Handsome was not beautiful, but as she knew that she could be called only pretty on her good days, she did not mind his honesty.

"I dare say that you like women who never agree with you, who like to contradict you."

He smirked. "You may say so; it certainly drew my attention to you in the first place. However, I quite enjoy the moments when you are compliant and allow me to lead the way."

She blushed, remembering the recent kisses and embraces they had shared. He certainly had led the way those times, as she had no experience on her hands.

"Summing it up, I am the first woman of your acquaintance who ever dared to contradict you?" she asked archly.

He frowned, thinking for a moment. "Yes, I believe so."

"The first young single woman of your acquaintance whom you mentioned to your sister?"

He nodded. "Yes."

She took a deep breath before asking the next question. "The first woman whom you desired?"

He stopped, rooted in place and turned with his body to her. She had his full attention. "You know that I desire you," he murmured, his eyes burning holes into her face.

She decided not to be intimidated and responded lively. "As I have given some thought to it, I realized that the hard object you frequently press against me indeed is not a large carrot you carry around for your horse's benefit."

He laughed out loud, throwing his head back. "You are a delightful, woman. I shall never be bored with you at my side, to be sure." He reached his hand to cup her face. "I wish we were not in the middle of the road. No convenient trees to hide behind." He shook his head, his eyes gleaming with excitement. "I would think you more shy about these matters, Miss Bennet."

She cocked her brow. "Do you object?"

He shook his head in slow motion. "Not at all."

"As you are aware, I was brought up in the country," she reminded him as they started walking again. "I have seen many examples of life creation, both in animals and humans even."

"Truly? Even humans," he teased.

"Yes, the quick roll in the hay is something rather popular around here."

"It is quite popular in the north too. We may try it one time at Pemberley, we have excellent haystacks," he said with straight face.

She bit her lip. "It is rather difficult to imagine you so unrestrained, Mr. Darcy."

"I cannot understand why," he spoke slowly. "You mentioned something similar before, claiming that I was proper."

"Because you are. You seem rather uptight."

"Do I?"

She nodded. "However, you failed to answer my initial question, or rather assumption, whether I am the first woman you desired."

"What are you asking me exactly?" he asked, his voice changed, without the playful note to it.

She looked up at him, hoping to see the expression in his eyes, but he was stubbornly staring at the fields above her head. "You do not know? Should I use more specific words?"

He faltered with an answer for a longer moment, only to come up with another question. "Why do you want to know about it?" He seemed very uneasy.

"I am about to marry you, in less than a month," she said evenly. "You think I have no right to know about your past?"

They walked for some time before he spoke.

"There is nothing for you to know. You are the first woman I have loved; I have never had such feelings for anyone before. I think that this novelty is the reason I was so frightened at the beginning, why I tried to run away from you."

"I see, we can safely state that you are indeed an innocent in the matters of the heart."

"I am."

"But not in the matters of flesh?"

Her words made him stop, and look down at her with a heavy gaze. "Where do these enquires lead?" he asked, his tone reminded him how he had spoken with her at the times when they had argued in the past, before his proposal.

"My enquiries bother you then?" she guessed.

He hesitated before answering. "Yes."

She lowered her eyes, peeking at him from behind her eyelashes.

"How many?" she asked at last.

He straightened up. "Excuse me?"

"How many women have you desired in purely physical terms before meeting me?" she clarified.

"I do not understand, Elizabeth," he offered, his voice cold. "Why do you need to know about such matters? It is all in the past. It does not concern you."

She noticed at once, that she was called Elizabeth, not love, dearest or Lizzy. She would not allow him to intimidate her. She had gone this far, and she would not back down now. "Would you not like to know how many men I…"

"What men?" he barked.

"I understand that you would like to know about the men, if there were any." She looked into his eyes, which were wide and furious. "There were none. You are the first to touch me the way you touch me, kiss me. My point is that you would like to know whether—"

She did not finish because he interrupted her. "I would not want you in such a case for a wife, a mistress perhaps, but not a beloved wife," he announced bluntly. "I owe it not only to myself, but to Pemberley as well. I could not bear it if you belonged to another before me."

Proud Mr. Darcy was back full force it seemed.

"What if I was a widow?" she questioned contractively.

He scowled again. "What is the point of this discussion?" he asked tiredly.

"Well, you have not answered my initial question," she reminded him, her lips setting in a stubborn pout.

He observed her through narrowed eyes. "You will not let it go?"

She lifted her shoulders, only to drop them a moment later. "I do not understand why you do not wish to be sincere with me on that subject."

"Do you want an exact number?" he asked angrily.

She nodded.

"Are you certain?"

"Yes."

"Ten," he answered, his voice indifferent, no emotion visible in his face.

"That many?" she gasped.

"You think that it qualifies as many?" he sounded doubtful.

"It certainly does," she murmured, not looking at him, only thinking frantically.

He had been with ten women before he met her. Ten! She never thought him an innocent. Even when they first met, she had known that he had to be an experienced man. There had been something in his eyes, his moves, his voice. His recent kisses and caresses only confirmed that. Obviously, he was not a fumbling youth. He knew exactly what he was doing with her, how to touch her to elicit the response he wanted. She had suspected that there had been two or three women in his past. But ten? He was not even thirty years old. Was he a rake? Who was this man she had agreed to marry?"

Would he settle with only her in the future? She could not imagine how she would bear the humiliation of her husband keeping a lover. Perhaps it was the way things were accepted in the higher circles. She recalled some gossip and stories about Georgiana Cavendish, the Duchess of Devonshire, whose husband had openly kept a lover for years and had several illegitimate children, even with the servants. Darcy's uncle was an earl, his family was not simply gentry like her father; they were aristocrats.

Why had she not thought about such a possibility earlier? What had she agreed to? Would he send her down to the country once she had given him the token heir and a spare so that he might have his freedom to enjoy his lovers? She knew so little of him. Was it too late for her to rescue herself from the disgrace? No, she cold not turn back. Everything had been arranged and paid for.

"Do not," he spoke forcefully, lifting her chin up so she would look at him. "I should have not told you that. I should have known better. I can only imagine what is going now through your head." He let out a troubled sigh then stared straight into her eyes. "You are the only woman in my life."

"What about the future? I have heard that rich men from the aristocracy like to keep mistresses after their wives give them an heir and a spare."

"I am not that kind of man, Elizabeth. Have I ever given you reason to doubt me in such a way?"

"You have been with ten women," she reminded him, still horrified with the information.

"Elizabeth, we will not speak about this any more," he commanded harshly. "You have nothing to worry about," he added more gently. "I love you, and I will always be faithful to you and our wedding vows. *Always*. I would never dishonour you or myself, my family name for that matter, in such a way by betraying my promise before God and man to love and cherish you always. It is not the Darcy way. My father did not teach me that."

"Now come," he took her arm again, setting a quick pace. "Mr. Phillips expects me in half an hour. I do not wish to be late."

Chapter Thirteen

They did not speak for the rest of the walk to Meryton. Elizabeth wanted to ask more questions, but at the same time she dreaded to hear the answers. Her imagination was working, as usual, to her disadvantage. Perhaps she should show more trust in him? He said that he would stay faithful to her. He spoke with such sentiment about his parents' marriage, how they had loved each other. Surely, if he wanted a respectable, happy marriage for himself, he would not entertain the possibility of keeping a mistress.

No matter how hard she tried to convince herself not to make a big affair out it, the thought of those ten women bothered her. Who were they? Where had he met them? Were all men like him? In her view, ten lovers seemed a very high number for a man of eight and twenty. He seemed so busy, had so many responsibilities, his sister, his estate. How had he found time? Had he loved them? No, surely he had not. After all, he had said himself that she was his first and only love.

She could not imagine him visiting a brothel - he was too proper, too fastidious for that. On the other hand, he had told her that he was not as proper as she perceived him to be. She shook with abhorrence as she visualised him with one of them. She wanted to cry, scream, and claw those unnamed women's eyes out.

Only then, the shocking realization dawned upon her. She stopped, rooted in place, staring blankly in front of herself. She felt possessive of him. She was simply jealous of those ten women with whom he had been before her. How could that be? She did not have those kind of feelings for him which could justify jealously.

"Elizabeth, are you well?" he shook her gently, his head bent down, so he could see her face.

Slowly her vision focused on him. "Yes, I am well. I am well."

He sighed. "Please do not tell me that you are still thinking about what we discussed before." He cupped her face, despite them standing in the main street of Meryton. "You have nothing to be concerned about," he spoke with quiet intensity. "You are the only one in my heart."

She gave him a pale smile. He seemed so sincere, and she wanted to believe him. "I was thinking about what present you should buy for your sister."

Judging his expression, he did not seem entirely convinced that it was the only matter which she was thinking about.

"I shall look around the shops, and you go to your appointment with Uncle Phillips," she proposed.

He shifted his weight from one leg to the other, hesitating, but then nodded and said. "Very well. I shall not be long."

Elizabeth took her time, walking from one shop window to the next, looking at the displayed products. She concentrated her thoughts on the perfect gift for Georgiana to keep them away from the person of her brother and his colourful past.

She had no idea what Georgiana Darcy would like to receive. Surely the girl like her lacked for nothing, and it was difficult to find something for her which she did not already own. Selecting a gift for her own younger sisters, Lydia and Kitty, would be easy for Elizabeth. They always craved new ribbons and bonnets in bright colours. Georgiana, however, was a challenge.

As she came to stand before one of the favourite shops of her younger sisters, the one which carried the wide selection of hats, parasols, gloves, stockings and other smaller articles of clothing, she felt someone's presence behind her back.

"Miss Elizabeth," she heard all too familiar voice.

She turned. "Mr. Wickham." She thought he had already left Meryton, as the militia was to be stationed in Brighton for the summer.

He began speaking hastily, apologizing for his absence during the funeral. She looked at him without emotion. She did not wish to respond to his polite enquires. His presence reminded her how immature and judgmental she had been. She had fallen too easily for his cheap charm and good, pretty-boy looks. She had a feeling that he would turn fat and bald in ten years.

Rudely, she stepped back from him, turning on her feet, without even nodding in his direction.

She thought that she would simply walk away from him, leaving him alone there in front of the shop, but she was not so fortunate. He blocked her away.

"Are you not speaking with me now, Miss Elizabeth?" he asked, his expression still pleasant.

8

"I am Miss Bennet to you," she spoke coldly. "You are correct that I am not speaking to you. You should not be allowed among polite society."

She noted with satisfaction that Wickham paled, his eyes widening. Soon though, he composed himself, a smiling expression plastered back on his pretty face. "I do not understand, Miss Elizabeth," he smiled, stressing her name.

She narrowed her eyes, "You understand very well. I will not waste my time talking to you. Excuse me."

She was about to walk away, when he grasped her elbow.

She looked down at his hand touching her arm. "I advise you not to touch me, and let me pass."

"You were much more accepting of my company in the past," he reminded her. "Did Darcy forbid you to socialize with me? He bought you, after all. He is in a position to tell you what you can do, who you can speak to," he goaded her, still holding her arm.

She gave him a polite smile, responding in low voice. "Mr. Darcy is now across the street in my uncle's office. Should I inform him that you bothered me?"

He let go of her arm instantly, and stepped back. With satisfaction, she noted that he was glancing anxiously around.

Without a second glance at him, she turned on her heel with the intention of walking away, only to see Darcy hastily making his way in her direction. He looked furious.

"Did he try anything?" he questioned as they met in the middle of the road. "I saw him touching you."

"Nothing happened, calm down, please," she said, making sure she held his gaze. "He wanted to speak with me. I refused, but he attempted to stop me from leaving his company and grasped my arm."

Darcy stepped forward, his face twisted in an ugly grimace. She stopped him with her body. She did not need another public scene caused on behalf of her person.

"Nothing happened," she repeated firmly. "He thought I was alone here. However, when I said that I was waiting for you and that I would tell you that he was bothering me; he instantly let me go."

Darcy stared over her head with a deep scowl, and she could only guess that he was looking at Wickham. She gazed back, to see Wickham disappearing into one of the side streets. She could not allow Darcy to go after him. What was now visible on his face could only be described as pure hatred. Nothing good could come out of those two talking now.

She wrapped her hand over his arm, saying, "Let us go, Fitzwilliam. He is not worth this."

"I should have guessed that he might accost you here," he spoke after a moment, his voice still tense.

"It was enough to mention your name to get rid of him," she assured. "Now, I was thinking about the present for your sister," she started with enthusiasm, hoping to draw his attention to the task in hand. "Does she have a journal?"

This seemed to bring his attention. "A journal?"

"Yes, my father always bought me one. We can find them in the shop nearby. They are quiet large, and look like any leather bound book, only the pages are blank," she explained. "You can write in them, or draw pictures. You mentioned that your sister liked to draw."

"That is a sound idea. I do not think that she has one."

She smiled in agreement and led him in the direction of the mentioned shop.

"You said that your father bought journals for you?"

"Yes, he did," she smiled fondly at the memory. "Once I finished one, the new one was already waiting for me."

"Finished? You mean that you write a diary?"

"No, I do not write a diary."

"What do you need them for then?" he wanted to know.

She hesitated. "It is too silly to be mentioned, to be honest."

"What exactly is silly?" he persisted.

She shook her head. "'Tis nothing important."

They reached the front of the spacious shop which sold books, newspapers, stationery, tobacco, and writing utensils. Elizabeth had developed a custom of visiting it at least once a week.

"Why do you not want to share this with me?" he asked, his voice laced with hurt.

She looked at him and rolled her eyes. "There is nothing to share. They are only silly stories."

"You write?" he cried enthusiastically. "Why have you never said anything?"

"Because it is not something worth mentioning, and it is personal," she almost growled at him in her irritation. "No one apart from Jane and Papa know about it, and you will not tell anyone."

"Of course I will not tell anyone, "he agreed readily. "May I read your stories?"

She frowned. "No, you cannot."

His face fell. "Why?"

She blew out some air before responding. "They are children's stories, about fairies."

His eyebrows rose high on his forehead. "Fairies?"

"Yes, fairies who live in a forest." She pointed her finger at him. "Do not dare laugh at me."

He lifted his hands in a defensive gesture. "I am not laughing. I think it is most delightful. I cannot wait to read them."

"You will not read them."

"Your sister and father read them, I am guessing?"

"Yes."

"Why not me? I will be your husband, the closest person to you. I have the right to read them too."

"They are only mine," she spoke fiercely, curling her fist on her chest. "I write them for myself. Papa read some of them, only the ones I decided to show him," she stressed. "Jane read some too, because she was very curious."

"I am very curious too."

She glared at him. "Can you not respect my decision? Leave this alone, please."

"What was your father's opinion about your stories?" he asked, as if not hearing what she had just said.

She shrugged. "He liked them, encouraged me to write more."

"They must be very good then."

"Can we stop this conversation?" She turned on her feet, making her way to the entrance of the shop.

Inside, there was only a young girl behind the counter, no older than fifteen, whom Elizabeth greeted with enthusiasm.

"Lizzy," the girl exclaimed, bringing Darcy's attention. Elizabeth winced. She could only guess what he was thinking; his future wife being on the first name basis with the girl working in the shop.

He did not know, of course, that Anne was the daughter of the owner of the shop and the Gardiners' cousin.

"You are alone here today, Anne?" Elizabeth asked pleasantly, taking a step closer to the girl. She noted that Darcy walked away towards the shelves with books, clearly intending to give them some privacy to talk.

"Yes, everyone is with Cassie this morning," the girl explained. "They should be back soon."

Elizabeth gasped in recognition. "I entirely forgot that it is her time."

Anne produced a big smile. "She had boy and a girl three days ago."

"Twins? Truly?"

"Yes, Mama suspected it, because she was so big."

"How is she feeling?"

"Still resting. Everything went well, but she is very tired."

Elizabeth glanced quickly at Darcy, but he seemed oblivious to their conversation. She lowered her voice. "Was it very hard on her?"

Anne leaned in, whispering. "Very hard, she was in agony. First time for her, and already two babies at once. It lasted almost two whole days from when the pains started, till the second baby came out. Mama was with her the entire time."

"Well, I am glad that she is well now. Are the babies healthy?"

The girl grinned. "Yes, and so beautiful." Her face sobered then, as if she remembered something. "We were so sorry to hear about Mr. Bennet, Lizzy."

"Thank you," Elizabeth smiled sadly. "I know that your father and brother attended the funeral. We do appreciate it."

"Papa always says what a noble man Mr. Bennet was."

"I would wish to visit Cassie and see the babies," Elizabeth said, wishing to change the subject. "However, I am not sure whether I would be able to do so."

"Oh, I am sure that she understands. You are in mourning." Anne quickly glanced at Darcy's imposing figure in the background before lowering her eyes.

"I would wish to see the leather-bound journals," Elizabeth said, thinking it was high time to finish the small talk. They had come here with a very specific reason, after all.

"The ones that Mr. Bennet always bought for you?" Anne wanted to make sure.

"Yes, the same ones."

"We have recently received new ones in different colours, straight from

London."

With quick efficiency, Anne placed half a dozen different leather-bound books on the counter. Instantly, Elizabeth's eyes caught the one with a lavender coloured cover. It was beautiful, and the pages inside were of good quality.

"It smells of lavender when you open it," Anne offered.

Elizabeth stuck her nose into inside the pages and inhaled. "Yes, indeed it does."

"Shall we take it?" Darcy asked, suddenly appearing behind her.

Anne glanced at Elizabeth, who did not even dare to look at the man.

"Do you think that Georgiana would like it?" she asked.

"I believe so," he answered. "It suits her. She likes the colour, I believe."

Elizabeth closed the journal and pushed it towards Anne. "Can you wrap it as a present?"

"Of course," Anne stuttered nervously, reaching under the counter for the decorative paper.

"We will take two," Darcy said, looking at Elizabeth. "One for you."

"I do not need one," she protested instantly.

Darcy looked at Anne. "Two please, but only one wrapped as a gift."

Elizabeth felt her face going hot. She did not want him to buy her anything, but she did not want to make a scene either.

She tugged at his sleeve, whispering. "I truly do not need one. My old one is only half filled."

"I can see that you like it. Allow me to buy you one."

"Very well," she relented. "Thank you."

Darcy paid for the books and they left the store.

"You know the girl from the shop well," he stated.

She hesitated for a moment, considering how much to tell him, but then she decided it would be the best to be truthful. She was not ashamed of her friends.

"She is my second cousin actually. She is my mother's cousin's daughter exactly."

She watched his reaction. His face told her nothing.

"Really?"

"Yes, her elder sister is Jane's age, and we sometimes played together as children."

"The one who had twins?"

Elizabeth glanced sharply at him. He had been listening to their conversation. "Yes, Cassandra was married last year to a farmer near Netherfield."

She observed him carefully, curious how he would react to the information that her cousin was married to a farmer.

"Would you like to pay her a visit to see the babies?" he asked.

"Yes, but... we are leaving tomorrow, so..."

"You will have no time to do it later though," he pointed out. "We can go today. It is still early enough for the visit."

"We?" she asked cautiously.

"We will return to Longbourn, and take a carriage from there. Miss Bennet could go with us if that is her wish."

"You would accompany us?" she wanted to make sure that she understood his intention right.

"If you do not wish me to..." he started hesitantly.

"No, no, of course not. I would wish you to go with us, it is only unexpected. You realize that they are farmers, quite well off, but still..."

He looked offended. "I have been on a farm before, Elizabeth. I visit my tenants from time to time. I have even worked in the fields and with animals as a young lad. My father thought that some manual labour would do me good."

She gaped at him in astonishment. She certainly did not expect something like that from him.

"I would be more than happy to visit Cassandra and see the babies."

"Excellent, it is settled then. However, first we need to think about some gifts for the babies."

She stared at him as if she had seen him for the first time.

"It would be rude to go empty handed, I believe," he continued. "I have little experience with such matters, though." He looked around. "Is there a shop here where we could find something appropriate?"

She still looked at him as if he had grown another head, but managed to close her mouth and say. "Yes, there is."

"Let us go then," he offered her his arm. "We have little time. We must yet return to Longbourn."

Elizabeth and Jane were overjoyed to spend the late afternoon with their cousin and the infants. They were cooing over the two perfect little beings as they carried them around the nursery. The young mother was delighted with the unexpected company and touched with the beautiful gifts that the Bennet girls brought with them.

However, the most astonished person in the room was Elizabeth, as she observed her betrothed conversing animatedly with the babies' father. They talked about cows, and Darcy seemed surprisingly knowledgeable on the subject. He seemed more at ease talking with the farmer than with anyone in Meryton before.

As Elizabeth's head touched the pillow that evening, she could not fall asleep for a long time. To say that she was confused with Darcy after today was a gross understatement. She doubted whether she would ever understand him.

Chapter Fourteen

"Alone at last," Darcy breathed as the door to the carriage closed, and Longbourn began disappearing from sight.

"It must be a very different experience for you, living in a house full of people," Elizabeth noted.

For the last few days, it had been obvious that Darcy had had enough of the company of her mother and younger sisters. He was either locked in the library, visiting with Mr. Bingley, or riding the fields on Devil. At mealtimes, he strove to be polite; however, he just barely managed that. Unfortunately, Mrs. Bennet faulted Elizabeth for Darcy's low spirits, constantly attempting to give her advice on how to improve his mood.

"Yes, indeed," he responded. "As far as I remember, it was only my parents and me. My mother passed away soon after Georgiana was born, and I was sent away to school."

"Can I ask what caused your mother's death?"

"Pneumonia. She had a cold, but I think that no one, including herself, treated it seriously. It was June, the weather held well, and she did not even stay in bed. Then her state suddenly worsened. I returned from school for the summer on the day of her funeral."

"How old was Georgiana?"

"Not even two."

She moved to sit next to him. She was not sure what to say, so she snuggled closer, placing her hand on his chest. He covered her hand with his.

"You mentioned that your father was not himself."

"Yes, he closed himself in their rooms for a month, and did not even attend the funeral. When he came out, he was not the same. He lost interest in life, I mean Georgiana and me. He seemed to be more at ease with strangers, than his own children. He never looked me in the eye. Later I realized that it was because I have my mother's eyes. As Georgiana grew older, she resembled our mother more and more, so he avoided her. I returned to school and she was left alone. If not for Mrs. Reynolds, our housekeeper, I do not know what would have happened with Georgiana. She raised her as her own."

She reached her hand to touch his cheek, feeling wetness under his eyes. He kissed the inside of her palm, and she slowly climbed on his lap, hugging him to her with all her might.

After a long moment, he pushed her gently away, speaking gruffly. "All right, all right, enough of this. With God as my witness, I never thought a woman would have me crying like a baby. You are a very bad influence on me, madam."

"Am I?" she asked playfully, at the same time attempting to move away from his lap, but he prevented it.

"You can stay here."

She raised a doubtful eyebrow at him. "The whole ride to London? Your legs will go numb."

His hands closed on both sides of her waist. "Do not offend me. You weigh is next to nothing." His expression changed from teasing to serious. "I noticed that you have lost weight," he spoke with concern, one of his hands moving to her hipbone, the other resting on her rib cage. "I can feel all your bones, even through your clothes."

She pushed his hands away from her body, climbing off his lap, blushing. "I eat as much as I need."

"That is clearly not enough to sustain you, especially when we take into consideration your daily walks," he lectured. "You must eat, Elizabeth. You have lost at least five to ten pounds in the last few weeks. I do not wish for you to become sick."

She crossed her arms across her chest in defiance. "I am not a child. I eat as much as I need," she repeated her earlier words.

"That is not childish behaviour, in your opinion?" Darcy gestured to her folded arms and pouting.

Slowly, self consciously, she uncrossed her arms. "I have no appetite."

"Sweetheart, promise me that you will try to eat more."

"I cannot." She bent forward, hands on her middle. "My stomach is in knots, twisted. I feel that if I eat more, I will lose it later. Food makes me sick."

He placed his hand on her back, rubbing it. "Elizabeth, it is all because you fret too much about matters. You should allow yourself to calm down, and not take everything to your heart. All will be well."

"That is easy for you to say," she interrupted him bitterly. "You do not know how I feel."

Darcy searched her face, concerned. "Lizzy..." he tried to bring her closer to him, into his arms, but she shook her head, whispering a small no.

As she sat far away from him, facing the other window, the silent tears began running down her cheeks.

All he could do was gaze at her helplessly.

***

"Lizzy, we did not expect to see you before your wedding," Mrs. Gardiner exclaimed as Elizabeth entered the Gardiners' London home with Darcy in tow.

"Can I stay with you for a few days?" Elizabeth asked, kissing her aunt's cheek.

"Of course you can, dear girl." She eyed Darcy who stood silently behind them. "Has something happened?" she asked uncertainly, taking in Elizabeth's pale cheeks and red eyes.

"Mrs. Gardiner." Darcy bowed deeply. "It is a pleasure to see you again. I had to come to London on business, and I asked Elizabeth to come with me. I want her to meet my sister before our wedding. We assumed that you would not refuse your hospitability."

Mrs. Gardiner glanced warmly at her niece. "Elizabeth knows that she is always welcome here."

Elizabeth smiled. "Thank you, Aunt."

"May I enquire after the baby's health?" Darcy asked politely.

Mrs. Gardiner's face lit up instantly. "He has been healthy for almost a week now. Your doctor is a very wise man, Mr. Darcy. He advised changes in Fred's diet, and now he is like a different baby, so happy, active, cut two new teeth and his poo is..." she flushed, realizing what she has just said in front of the guest. "I mean that his digestion is much improved," she finished awkwardly. "We are so grateful to you for recommending him to us. I was at my wits end with my baby boy being ill so often."

Darcy listened politely to the woman's speech, nodding his head with understanding from time to time.

"Let us not stand in the foyer." Mrs. Gardiner made an inviting gesture. "Mr. Darcy, you must join us for a dinner. My husband should be back from his office any minute."

Darcy shook his head. "Forgive me, madam, but I long to see my sister."

Mrs. Gardiner did not argue with him on that, only made him promise that he would dine with them soon. Discreetly, she gathered her children, who were peeking curiously from behind the corner at the newcomers, and left, giving the couple some privacy.

"Have a good night, Fitzwilliam." Elizabeth said, stepping to him.

Darcy cupped her cheek, and walked her a few steps so her back touched the wall.

"I will send the carriage tomorrow around one in the afternoon. Would that be agreeable?"

"Yes, I truly look forward to meeting your sister," she answered sincerely.

"Feeling better?" he stared at her with concern.

"Much better, thank you," she answered brightly, smiling. "Forgive me for my earlier... behaviour, my weeping."

He sighed heavily, his breath fanning her forehead. "There is nothing to forgive. I only wish to know how to help. I am worried about you."

"I am well," she assured him, smiling again. She closed her eyes. "I only need some time to come to terms with..."she shuddered, "with everything."

He did not respond to that, only lowered his head and captured her lips. He could feel her response almost instantly, and his heart soared in joy. She wanted him.

Just as he was about to deepen the kiss, a current ran down his spine, telling him that they were observed. Breaking the contact with Elizabeth's sweet lips, but still keeping his hands on her waist, he looked to the side, expecting to see a servant spying on them. However, the narrow foyer was empty.

"What are you doing to cousin Lizzy?" a small voice called from the floor.

He glanced down to see a small girl staring at them with wide eyes.

"Who are you?" The child asked the next question, not waiting for the answer to the first one. "Are you Lizzy's husband? Papa is Mama's husband, and he does the same to her."

He looked at Elizabeth, who was biting her lip, trying not to burst out in laughter.

Darcy graced the child with his attention. "I will be Lizzy's husband soon. My name is Mr. Darcy," he explained calmly.

The little girl gaped at him, awed. "You are like a tree in a park."

Darcy frowned, not being quite sure why the child used such a comparison.

"Emily, you were supposed to play with you sister," Mrs. Gardiner appeared, glaring at the child, at the same time sending apologetic glances at Darcy and Elizabeth.

The child pouted. "I was curious, Mama. I wanted to see him better." She pointed one pudgy finger into Darcy's leg

"She was no bother," Elizabeth assured.

"Come on, Missy," Mrs. Gardiner gestured to her daughter, holding out her hand. "It is time high to wash your hands before dinner."

"My hands are very clean," Emily showed the insides of her palms for everyone to see.

"No discussion, Emily," Mrs. Gardiner warned her, narrowing her eyes. "Come. You are interrupting Lizzy and Mr. Darcy."

The girl lowered her head with an audible sigh. Elizabeth reached to stroke her head with compassion. "Go with Mama, Emily. I will tell you a story later."

The girl's face lit up. "Really?"

Elizabeth nodded. "Really."

The child skipped happily to Mrs. Gardiner, taking her hand.

"Will you come back soon, Mr. Darcy?" Emily asked before disappearing from their sight.

Darcy was again surprised to have the honour of being addressed by the little lady. "I will." He cleared his throat. "Of course I will, Miss Emily. Thank you for the invitation."

The girl giggled, and letting go of her mother's hand, bounded in the direction of Darcy and Elizabeth.

"I like you," she confessed, hugging Darcy's leg fiercely. "Will you marry me?" she asked, stretching to look up at him.

Darcy glanced in panic at Mrs. Gardiner. What was he supposed to say to that?

"What about me?" Elizabeth questioned, kneeling in front of her little cousin. "Mr. Darcy said that he would marry me."

The child shrugged. "I do not mind. He can marry both of us. I can share with you."

"Emily Gardiner, you will come here this second!" Mrs. Gardiner ordered harshly, but Darcy could see that she was fighting a smile.

Emily ducked her head, and quickly ran to her mother without further discussion.

"Why am I like a tree?" Darcy wanted to know as they were left alone.

Elizabeth giggled. "I think that she meant to say that you are very tall."

"Interesting young lady, a bit frightening to be truthful," Darcy noted. "How old is she?"

"She just turned five."

Darcy feigned the horror on his face. "Only five. I wonder how she will strike up conversation when she is twenty."

Elizabeth chuckled. "Actually, my uncle always says that she behaves just like I did when I was her age."

The front door was pushed open, welcoming Mr. Gardiner. He was understandably surprised to see Darcy and his niece. Consequently, the entire situation had to be explained one more time. After refusing another dinner invitation, Darcy said a final goodbye to the Gardiners and Elizabeth, and left their home.

***

They had spent a pleasant evening with Mr. Gardiner and all the children, who were allowed to go to bed later than was their usual routine. Little Fred presented the family with his new found ability of walking, which he had been mastering for the last two days. Elizabeth had clapped and cheered her youngest cousin as it was expected. Then, she told the children the promised story.

"I can see that relations between you and Mr. Darcy have improved," Mrs. Gardiner noted as she followed Elizabeth into her room.

Elizabeth could not prevent the blush on her cheeks. "Yes, Aunt."

"You seem so much more at ease in his company."

"Yes, I think that I truly like and respect him," Elizabeth acknowledged, pausing, trying to find the right words. "I do not mind his presence."

"I see," Mrs. Gardiner sat on the edge of the bed, obviously eager to hear more.

Elizabeth joined her, sitting closely. "I must admit that Uncle and you were right about him from the beginning. He has proved many times in the last weeks that he is a man of his word, and that I can rely on him."

The older woman leaned over and hugged her niece. "I am so happy for you. You deserve it, Elizabeth"

"Thank you, Aunt."

Mrs. Gardiner wished her goodnight and moved to the door, when Elizabeth spoke hesitantly.

"If you have a little time, there is something I would wish to talk about with you."

Mrs. Gardiner instantly returned to her side, watching her with an earnest expression. "Yes, dear."

Elizabeth lowered her head, twisting her hands nervously. "I thought to talk about it with Jane, but then I thought that perhaps she might not have enough of life's experience to help me. You are married... and older than us so..."

"Of course, Lizzy," Mrs. Gardiner smiled, her tone neutral. "I hope that I can help you."

They went to sit down on a cushioned bench under the window.

"Well, it is about Mr. Darcy," Elizabeth started with determination written on her face.

Mrs. Gardiner nodded encouragingly. "I guessed as much."

Elizabeth looked at the ceiling before glancing back at her hands folded in her lap. "He confuses me."

"Your uncle confuses me too, even after ten years of marriage," the older woman offered. "Men can have a different outlook on certain matters. In time you will learn to read him better."

"I meant to say that... when we are alone," she cleared her throat. "Oh, it is so difficult to talk about, so embarrassing," she groaned, covering her face with her fingers.

"I see... You do not like when he tries to touch you perhaps? You are worried about your wedding night?" Mrs. Gardiner tried to guess.

"No, no, I am not afraid of him," she assured quickly, blushing. "He is very ... gentle, and never insists on doing something I do not wish him to do. It is all very... pleasant."

"That is good then, I do not think that he will pressure you. He is a gentleman. He wants you to feel comfortable with him, especially taking into consideration your unusual courtship. As for the wedding night you know that you can always ask me questions if you are confused about something. In general, there is truly nothing to fear."

"I am not afraid, but..."

"Yes," Mrs. Gardiner prompted gently.

"I am concerned about his past experiences with....," she paused, "other women."

"Ah, I see," Mrs. Gardiner nodded. "Have you heard some rumours perhaps? Someone told you something about his past from the time before he met you?"

"No, but I noticed how adept he is...," she blushed harder. "I mean when he kisses me... oh, Aunt, he knows exactly what he is doing. He is not a fumbling youth."

"How old is he exactly, surely older than five and twenty?"

"Eight and twenty."

"You expect a man of eight and twenty, with his social position and financial independence to have no experience at all?" Mrs. Gardiner asked dryly. "Is this not a bit naive?"

"No, I always knew him to be a man of the world in every sense. Still, I thought that there were perhaps one or two women in his past."

"You mean that there were more than one or two," the other woman said quietly.

Elizabeth nodded.

"How did you come to that knowledge?"

"He told me."

"He did?" the incredulity rang in Mrs. Gardiner's voice. "Just like that?"

"I was curious, and I pressed him for information."

"And he simply revealed it to you?"

"Well, he did not want to talk about it at first, but I nagged him long enough and..."

"And?"

"He said that he had been with ten women," Elizabeth confessed with a heavy heart.

Mrs. Gardiner was silent for a long moment. "You think that it is too many?"

"Yes," she answered with honesty. Then giving her aunt a worried look, asked, "What do you think?"

The older woman hesitated. "Are you afraid that he will not be faithful to you?"

"Yes... you have heard the stories about aristocrats, the many lovers they keep and illegitimate children they have."

"I think that you must be careful here, Elizabeth," Mrs. Gardiner said at last. "Very careful. I would not try to return to that subject, being in your place. No man is comfortable talking about such things with his wife. Remember that you have already misjudged him more than once in the past.

On the other hand, I would not be pleased hearing what you heard from your uncle at the beginning of our life together."

Elizabeth looked at her trustingly. "What should I do?"

"You cannot do much now. I presume that he has a strong need to be with a woman, which explains the number of his..." she made a gesture with her hand, not finishing.

"He said he had no feelings for them. He claims that I am the first woman of his acquaintance he paid any attention to, whom he loved."

"You do not believe him?"

"I want to believe him," she said with force. "Nevertheless, how I can explain those ten women? He had to have liked them to be with them."

"Lizzy, it is different for men. They can be intimate with a woman without having true feelings for her. They can separate these two matters. Do you understand?"

She shook her head. "No, Aunt, I do not. It does not make much sense to me. It seems so insensitive."

"Do you find Mr. Darcy insensitive then?"

"No, he is far from that, I believe."

"Lizzy, I understand your concern. I truly do," Mrs. Gardiner assured. "I think that you have valid point here, but you worry too much about it. He loves you; anyone can see that."

"Yes, but I cannot stop thinking about it," she insisted.

"You are jealous," the other woman stated, smiling.

"More like possessive," Elizabeth acknowledged. "What would you do in my place? You have been married for ten years, have experience in these matters. What do you think?"

Mrs. Gardiner put a hand on her arm. "Well, I would keep an eye on him, discreetly, of course. You are smart enough to do that without him noticing something. Observe him carefully; see how he behaves in his home and outside it. I would also advise you not to banish him from your bed for prolonged periods of time. He may not deal with a withdrawal very well. That should not be hard for you though, he is very handsome, after all. I do not know what more you can do."

Elizabeth embraced her. "Thank you, Aunt. I do appreciate your advice."

"You are welcome, dear," Mrs. Gardiner patted her back. "Now, you should go to bed and have a good rest. Tomorrow is an exciting day for you, meeting your new sister. I will order a bath for you. It will be ready when you get up in the morning."

"Thank you," Elizabeth repeated.

"Good night," Mrs. Gardiner spoke before closing the door after herself.

"Good night," Elizabeth whispered, deep in thought.

Chapter Fifteen

The next day Elizabeth woke up later than her usual custom and had breakfast in her room. She took a long bath and dressed with care. Mrs. Gardiner helped her with pinning her hair in a more elaborate style, curling it around her face. Lately she had simply pulled the heavy mass smoothly off her face in a simple bun, low above her neck. Today, however, she wished to look her best, more for Georgiana's benefit than for Darcy's, truth to be told.

Once married to Darcy and living in far away Derbyshire, she could only benefit from having a female friend. She was very much aware that Darcy would not spend his days with her - nights and evening perhaps - but not days. He would be busy with the estate and his own matters. If she and Georgiana formed a friendship and she gained an amicable companion in the girl, she would feel less lonely there. Understandably, when she had children, she would have someone to love and occupy her time with.

Darcy spoke with love and adoration about his sister, describing her as very kind, accomplished, and tender hearted, but at the same time painfully shy. Elizabeth was determined to make the girl feel at ease in her company.

Before she knew it, it was a quarter to one, and Darcy's carriage was waiting for her in front of the house. Her aunt must have sensed her apprehension, because she squeezed her hand in a reassuring gesture.

"You look lovely, dear. I am sure all will go smoothly today."

Elizabeth took a deep breath before responding. "I hope she will like me."

"Most people like you, Elizabeth," Mrs. Gardiner assured her. "You have an easy manner, which makes you very likeable. Why should Miss Darcy be different?"

Darcy's town house was a handsome building situated on a fashionable street across from a small square. Elizabeth wondered shortly what his country house looked like. Aunt Gardiner claimed it to be one of the most beautiful places she had ever seen, a perfect combination of wild nature and refined architecture. She knew that people came to Derbyshire with the sole purpose of touring Pemberley. It must be impressive, and she found herself looking forward to seeing it.

Darcy greeted her warmly, helping her out of the carriage. He stared at her intensely as she removed her bonnet.

"You look lovely," he blurted as they were left alone for a moment in a foyer.

"Thank you," she smiled at his compliment. "I wanted to make a good impression on your sister."

"You have made a good impression on me, too."

Taking a step closer, she stood on her toes. "Good afternoon," she whispered, kissing his cheek, before lightly touching his lips with her own, which was difficult for her if he did not bend his head down.

"You minx," he half groaned, half whispered. "You owe me some time alone later," he urged, nuzzling her temple.

She cocked an eyebrow. "Do I?"

His face fell instantly. "You do not wish to…?" he started, but she interrupted him.

"No, it was not what I meant," she placed her hands on his chest. "I was only teasing." She made a point to look into his eyes. "My aunt clearly said that she was not expecting me before supper. We have some time till then, I believe."

He stroked her shoulders, his thumbs grazing her collarbones. "Let us go. Georgiana is awaiting us."

Elizabeth's first impression of Georgiana was that she and Darcy looked little alike. There was a slight similarity in their features, and they were both tall and well built. Georgiana, however, was blonde, and her eyes were blue, not dark hazel like her brother's. Though shorter than Darcy, she could be called tall for a woman, and her figure was fully formed. She reminded her of Jane, comparing their postures and height. Her face retained much of the baby roundness, puffiness, and innocence, but she had the body of a grown woman. From what Darcy had told Elizabeth about his sister, she had more imagined her as a little girl, and he probably still saw her as such.

Georgiana had a sweet, quiet voice, and she spoke slowly, as if carefully considering her every word. A few times she went silent in the middle of a sentence, biting down on her lower lip before speaking again. She twice repeated how she liked the lavender journal which she had received from her brother and that her new sister, as she put it, had chosen for her. Elizabeth could see that this behaviour resulted from nerves, as the girl desperately wanted to make a good impression. They were both apprehensive about their first meeting, and that awareness helped Elizabeth to relax.

Gradually, in the course of their conversation, Georgiana calmed down, stopped twisting and wrinkling the skirt of her silk gown, and began responding more coherently. Elizabeth asked her about her music and other things which she was studying. Georgiana began asking shy questions, mainly how it was to live in a house with four sisters. Elizabeth indulged her by telling silly stories from her childhood. By their third cup of tea, Georgiana was laughing animatedly.

"Georgiana, dear, I think that it is time for your piano lesson," Darcy said, bringing the women's attention to him.

Both Elizabeth and Georgiana stared at him slightly confused. It was the first time he had actually spoken since introducing them. They had forgotten about his presence.

"I believe that your teacher will be here in a quarter of an hour," he prompted, when Georgiana did not respond immediately.

Georgiana glanced over at the decorative clock over the mantelpiece. "I have entirely forgotten," she gasped.

Elizabeth's followed her gaze. It was nearly four in the afternoon. The two hours of the visit had passed more like half an hour. It was a good sign in her opinion. It bode well for the future. Georgiana would make a wonderful companion. She was nothing like the Bingley sisters, which secretly Elizabeth had feared. Her only true fault seemed to be shyness, insecurity and perhaps a self-deprecating attitude.

Both ladies stood, and Elizabeth was both surprised and pleased when Georgiana stepped closer to give her a timid embrace.

"Remember that you are invited tomorrow to dine at my aunt and uncle's house," Elizabeth reminded her, returning the hug with enthusiasm.

"Thank you. I am truly happy that we are going to be sisters," Georgiana said slowly, giving her a guarded look.

"I feel exactly the same," Elizabeth assured, smiling warmly. "We must keep a steady alliance against your brother."

Georgiana opened her mouth, clearly not certain how to respond to the last sentence. However, when she saw that there was a contented smile on Darcy's face, she visibly relaxed.

As Georgiana left the room, Elizabeth turned to her betrothed. "She is such a kind hearted, genuine person," she spoke with sincerity. "You approve?"

Elizabeth nodded. "I truly do. I think I made a new friend today. I do not have many of them, only Jane, Charlotte, and Aunt Gardiner."

"What about me?"

"It is different with you. You are not a woman."

"I cannot be your friend then?" he questioned with the edge to his voice.

"I think that you are my friend," she answered earnestly. "The way we talk, well… I have never been so sincere with anyone, apart from Jane perhaps, and even with her, not when certain matters are concerned. You are so much more than my friend."

"More?"

"Yes," she acknowledged. "You are to be my husband, and I cannot compare the relationship I have with you to any other in my life."

"I like the sound of that." He stepped closer, pulling her into his arms. "Now, my time alone with you has come, I do believe."

"I cannot stay too long. The Gardiners dine at seven. I should be back before then."

"Let us not waste a minute," he said, taking her hand, confidently leading her out of the drawing room.

"What do you wish us to do?" she asked innocently.

"Oh, I have some ideas," he said lightly.

She followed him obediently, till they reached the staircase.

She frowned. "What is up there?" she hesitated on the first step.

He shrugged. "Bedrooms. My room."

She looked around. "What if someone should see us?" she asked timidly.

"We must hurry then," he said, and then without a word of warning, bent down, and put her over his shoulder.

She was too shocked too protest as he ran upstairs, taking two steps at once. He reached the floor in no time and soon was opening the door to one of the bedrooms.

He put her down gently.

"What was that?" she demanded with a frown, putting her hands on her hips, her foot tapping.

He took a step closer, mimicking her pose. "I told you that I was not as proper as you accused me of being."

She burst out in laughter, shaking her head. "You are silly."

"Am I?"

"You can be silly if you want to," she corrected.

He touched the curls around her face. "I am happy with you, which I guess makes me silly on occasion. We are fools in love."

"May I..." she started.

"Yes?" he enquired, breathing into her face.

"May I refresh myself? I drank too much tea with Georgiana, I am afraid."

He guided her to the small adjacent room, which seemed to be his personal bathing room.

As she returned to the bedroom, he was standing casually by the window, with his coat and neck cloth removed.

She came closer, standing next to him. "The garden is quite big for a townhouse," she noted.

"Yes, it is," he agreed. "My great grandfather bought this plot, but my father built the house. My mother enjoyed London much more than he. She wanted to have a place to stay here. If it had depended on my father, however, they would never have left Pemberley, I believe."

"I see," Elizabeth said.

She looked around the room, taking in all the details. It looked more like a guest bedroom. There were not many personal things there.

 She strode to the window to admire the garden once again. Then she walked to the bed, and perched herself on the edge of it.

"Do you wish to take a nap?"

He shook his head. "No."

She locked her eyes with his. "What do you wish to do then?"

He sat on the bed next to her. "It depends on you."

"I do not wish to anticipate our vows," she admitted, staring down at her hands placed neatly on her lap.

He cupped her face so she looked at him. "Neither do I," he assured. "It should not be done in a hurry. I wish to have all time needed to love you the first time."

She nodded, swallowing.

He took her hand in his. "There are other things we can do, though."

"Very well," she lay down compliantly on her back, and then she remembered herself and sat up to remove her shoes, putting them neatly next to the bed.

Darcy removed his shoes as well and stretched out beside her.

For a long moment, he only stared at her, before he pulled her closer.

"You smell so good today," he whispered, putting his nose into her hair.

She wanted to explain that it was a special brand of soap which her uncle imported, a combination of vanilla and lavender, but then she decided not to divulge this information. It was unnecessary, and hardly romantic.

"Thank you," she whispered.

She gasped when he rolled on his back and pulled her over him, so she was spread flat over his body.

"Can you let your hair free?" he asked.

"I will not be able to put it back the same later on my own. My aunt will notice…"

"Does it matter?" he asked.

He was right. It was such a little thing he was asking of her, and he had done so much for her

She sat up on his stomach, her knees bent on his sides. "Am I not heavy?"

His hands wandered on the top of her thighs, keeping her firmly in place. "Perfect."

With quick fingers, she removed all the pins from her hair, putting them on the bedside table. The heavy mass of dark hair fell down her torso, around her shoulders, and down her back. Before he could take time to admire it, she leaned forward and kissed him.

He returned the kiss instantly, one of his hands in her hair, the other stroking her back. She was so concentrated on the kiss, that only after a minute or so, did she notice that he had begun opening the buttons down the back of her dress.

"Fitzwilliam," she whispered with warning in her voice, as the top of her dress began falling loose, and he tugged down at her sleeves.

"I only want to see more of you," he whispered soothingly. He lifted up himself, supporting his back against the headboard. She was still astride him, only now they were both sitting up.

Not taking his eyes from her face, he pushed the top of her dress down as far as it would go, revealing her stays and under clothes. Her chemise was thin and transparent, showing her skin, but it was not enough for him, because without hesitation, he lowered the straps down her arms.

Instinctively, she placed her arm against her now bare bosom.

"Do not hide," he chided, taking her hand away.

She could not look at him; she was too embarrassed. She shuddered when his hands covered her breasts, his thumbs tugging at the nipples gently.

"Beautiful, perfect," he whispered.

She remembered well how her mother said once that she would not find a husband as she was too flat, especially in comparison to Jane and Lydia. She dared to glance at Darcy's face. He did not look displeased; quite the contrary, in fact.

"Open my shirt," he blurted.

It sounded more like an order, but she did not mind. If she was naked from the waist up, he should be as well. Unbuttoning his shirt took only a few seconds. She placed her hands on his chest, and stroked it shyly. He sighed quietly, and then pulled her forward, so her bosom touched his hard chest, the hair he had there, tickling her sensitive skin in a most pleasant way.

"Perfect," he murmured again, gathering her hair to the side to kiss her neck.

The next moment, she was on her back, and he was kissing the path from her neck to the tips of her breasts. It was a feeling like nothing she'd ever felt before. There seemed to be a direct connection between her bosom and her feminine parts. The more he pulled, kissed and suckled on her, the more she had an urge to rub her thighs together.

He did not stop paying attention to her chest when his hand moved confidently under her dress. He first touched her knee, traced with his finger the end of her stocking and her garter, before placing his warm hands on the inside of her thigh. Her back lifted from the bed. She knew she needed him to do more, and she did not care how he would do it. She wanted more - a completion of sorts.

"Patience," he murmured in her ear. Suddenly the place beside her was empty and he was kneeling next to her, lifting her skirt farther up.

"What are you doing?" she exclaimed, her eyes wide.

"I told you I wanted to see more of you," he answered, distractedly, pulling her skirt and petticoats over her knees, his head bending down.

It dawned on her that he had every intention of looking at her private parts.

"No," she sat up abruptly, trying to cover herself below, forgetting that her breasts were swaying in the process. His attention was occupied with her bosom for a moment, and she managed to push her skirts past her knees.

He placed his hand on her calf. "I only wished to look."

"Why?" she asked, scandalized. "There is nothing to look at there."

"Of course there is," he pushed her on her back, covering her with his body. "Let me, Lizzy. Just one look."

She kept shaking her head. "No, it is not right to look there."

"You realize that I will have to touch you there to consummate the marriage."

"Yes, but you do not have to look," she argued.

"I will look when we are married," he informed her.

"Why?"

He looked her in the eye. "I want to. It makes me want you even more, if that is possible. My blood boils when I think about this part of you." He demonstrated what he referred to by sneaking his hand under her skirts again, and placing his hand low on her stomach where her pubic hair started and her stays ended.

She frowned. "Do other men do that as well?" she asked slowly. "Do they look between their wife's legs?"

"Yes," he answered with a straight face, even though she could see that the corners of his mouth were twitching.

"Are you certain?"

"Yes."

After another minute of coaxing, kisses, and embraces, Elizabeth lay down again, and allowed him to kneel between her legs, her skirts bunched around her waist. Not wanting to feel entirely exposed, she tugged her petticoats over her upper self. To her further mortification, he turned her on the bed so that more light could fall on her from the window. She covered her whole upper self, including her face, with her petticoat, and waited till he finished examining her, the cool air and his hot breath fawning over her privates.

"You are small," she heard him, before he murmured something quietly, clearly to himself. "…will have to be careful."

At last he allowed her to close her legs. Still embarrassed beyond any measure, she curled against his chest as he lay next to her again.

"You are perfect all over," he informed her. "I have never seen such a pretty, little…" he started, but she slapped his chest, speaking harshly. "I truly do not wish to hear that."

"Of course," he agreed quickly.

She was relieved when he returned to what she already knew well, kissing, stroking her arms and back. She again relaxed in his embrace, but did not protest as he placed his hand between her legs and began gently stroking and probing. She hid her face in his chest as he touched her.

In no time, he seemed to find what brought the most response from her. There was no discomfort, only pleasure. She expected pain on her wedding night, once he would enter her, but so far it was all very pleasurable, no matter how embarrassing.

As she trembled in his arms, she did not care about anything. For that short moment, she did not even think about those women he had been with before her. All reason abandoned her, and she could only cling to him, hoping to prolong the pleasure.

"You liked it, sweetheart?" he asked, putting his arm around her.

She nodded into his chest, waiting for her racing heart to slow down.

"Do you wish me to do it more often?" he crooned, cupping her face, looking in her eyes.

"Yes," she agreed quietly.

He chuckled and kissed her forehead. She did not protest when he took her hand by the wrist and directed it down his body. Only after a few second did she realize what she was touching.

Her fingers stilled, but she did not take her hand back. She was not sure what he expected her to do.

"Touch me the way I touched you," he instructed gently.

Her unsure eyes met his. "I do not know how."

"Everything will feel good to me."

He laid back as she sat up next to him. She tugged her dress up, just to cover her bosom, as she was not comfortable being so exposed in front of him. She reached to the front of his trousers. She began to palm the hard bulge, keeping in mind to be gentle and not use too much force. She felt inadequate, as truly she did not know what she was doing.

She glanced at him, as she continued with her stroking, judging his reaction. His head was thrown back, eyes closed, jaw line tense. He did not look particularly pleased, more like he was in pain.

"Am I hurting you?" she hesitated, stopping the movement of her hand.

"God, no," he breathed. With wide eyes, she observed as he reached down, impatiently tugging at the opening of his trousers.

She did not look away when he took this part of himself out. She was curious what it would look like. She expected it be ugly, but it was not. It looked oddly attractive, tall and large, just like the rest of him. She briefly wondered how this would fit inside of her. Then she remembered that a newborn baby was much bigger than this. She hoped that when the time came, and he would push inside her, it would hurt less than childbirth.

His chuckle brought her attention to his face.

"You are taking a good look," he noted.

"I have seen pictures in my father's books, but they were all black and white," she explained her staring. "It looks strange, but handsome," she decided, touching the plump, pink head with the tip of her finger.

As he hissed at her touch, she took her hand back.

"No, do not stop, please." He brought her hand back.

She shot him a doubtful look. "You look as if you are in agony."

"Oh, believe me, dearest. I am." He wrapped her fingers around his manhood. "Like this." He directed her hand up and down.

Elizabeth moved her hand up and down and soon discovered what sort of pressure seemed to please him most. His breathing changed, and at one moment, he tugged her dress down, baring her breasts again, cupping one with his hand.

She continued with her stroking, happy to be pleasing him. She sensed that the end was nearing, and he would feel the same pleasure she had experienced before from his hand.

Suddenly he pushed her hands away, shoving her on her back, so she leaned back on her elbows. Then he did something she would never have expected him to do. He took himself in his hand, tugged firmly a few times, and with what could only be his seed, emptied himself on her bare bosom.

That, she did not like. She was more than certain that it was something which he had learned at one of the brothels he must have visited in the past. Tears stood in her eyes. Would he demand such things from her? She felt degraded.

It took him a moment to notice her reaction.

"God, Lizzy… forgive me," he cupped her cheek, brushing away her tears.

She shook her head, not looking at him. She tried to readjust her dress, but her chest was still covered in his… in what he poured all over her. At least her clothes had stayed clean.

She started looking around for something to wipe herself with, and he must have guessed her intention, because he ran to the bathing room, returning shortly with the wet towel.

She took it from him without a word and cleaned herself hastily, before righting her dress. He tried to help her with buttoning the back of her gown, but she jumped away from him, doing it herself.

He stood behind her as she tried to pin her hair up with shaky fingers. She remembered that there was a mirror in the bathing room, so she walked there, and he followed her.

Silently, he handed her a comb, which she accepted. She brushed her hair, untying the knots he had made tugging at it with his fingers, and section by section, she pinned up the heavy mane. She was not able to achieve the same result as before, but it did not matter. She just wanted to leave this place as soon as possible.

"Lizzy, please." She felt his hand on her shoulder. "I apologize. I got carried away. I was in the moment. You have this effect on me."

She did not want to listen to him. What he had done felt horrible. She could not imagine enjoying such antics, ever. Would their marital relations be like that? Him making her do things she felt uncomfortable with? She shuddered. What had happened to him? He had been so gentle and considerate before.

When she finished with her hair, she turned to him, still not looking into his eyes.

"Say something," he whispered.

"I wish to return to my uncle's house."

He sighed heavily. "Of course, if it is your wish."

She moved to the door, but he stopped her, blocking her way. "Please say something. What I did... I should have not done it, especially not with a maiden like you. Perhaps later in our marriage..."

"No," she stopped him, lifting her hand. "I am not one of your whores. I did not enjoy it, and I cannot imagine I ever will."

"Of course," he looked chastised, his hand hanging down.

"I understand my duties as your wife, and I wish to fulfil them, but it was too much."

"You minded only the last part?" he wanted to know, looking intently into her face.

She nodded curtly. "Yes, only the end."

He looked so relieved with her admission that she had to fight the urge to laugh. This lifted her mood considerably.

"I want to touch you and please you," she explained, "but that... was degrading and humiliating for me."

"I will not do it again, I swear. I beg you to believe me, trust me. I do not wish to part with you in anger," he spoke quickly.

She took a calming breath. "I do believe you. I wish to make you happy but that... was too much for my comfort."

"Sweetheart, it is my last wish for you to fear me or avoid me."

She nodded, allowing herself to step into his arms.

"Am I forgiven?" he whispered in her hair, stroking her back.

"Only if you do not do it ever again," she pleaded.

"I will not," he ensured, squeezing her tightly to him.

Chapter Sixteen

Darcy finished reading the letter from his uncle, Lord Matlock, and put it in the drawer of his desk. He moved closer to the fireplace and sank into his favourite armchair, stretching out his long legs. The content of the letter was not a surprise to him. To be truthful, he had expected that the Matlocks' reaction to the news of his upcoming nuptials would be much worse. The tone of the letter was clear – they would have wished a better match for their nephew. However, as he was of age, independent, and his very own man, they had no intention of swaying him in his desire to marry whom he had chosen for himself.

He realized that to some degree, at least, he must have to thank Colonel Fitzwilliam for that unexpected leniency towards his marriage. His uncle mentioned how Richard had ensured them that Darcy's bride, though without dowry and connections, was an admirable young lady, and would not bring shame to their family. His aunt even added a few lines at the bottom of the letter, asking him to bring his wife to Matlock so they could properly meet her.

Darcy presumed that his aunt and uncle were somewhat relieved that he had finally found someone he wanted to take for a wife, especially after he had dismissed countless young women that Lady Matlock had introduced to him over the years. Her understanding was that, as his parents were deceased, it was her duty to recommend the right kind of candidates to fill the role of Mistress of Pemberley.

As he glanced at the clock, he saw that it was almost four in the afternoon. He expected Georgiana and Elizabeth any moment. They were to return from their shopping trip. The wedding was to take place in five days, and he was giddy with anticipation at the surprise he had for Elizabeth. She thought that they would travel to Pemberley directly, but he had planned something entirely different. Elizabeth knew nothing of it. Sensing that she felt overwhelmed with the events of the last few weeks, he wished to grant her a short holiday before she would take on the duties of Mistress of Pemberley. He had never doubted that she would do admirably, but from his own experience, he knew how long it had taken him to adjust to the role of a Master.

She was still not eating as she should, but he did not dare bring the topic back up for discussion. The last thing he wanted was to have her weeping and pushing away from him like the last time he had mentioned her lack of appetite. He would see to it himself that she ate properly once they were married, starting on their honeymoon.

They would go to the seaside, staying at the cottage he had rented, just two of them. The servants would come from the nearest village to prepare their meals and clean, but apart from that, they would be left all alone - hopefully taking long strolls, talking, sea bathing, and loving. He was not opposed to spending all day in bed with her, in addition to the nights.

At the beginning of their engagement, he had been certain that he would start his married life with separate bedrooms. He had even told her that he would wait until she was ready. His intention was sincere when he had spoken those words, even though in truth he did not want to wait a moment longer than his wedding day. However, he knew that she would be more receptive to him if she had the opportunity to make her own choice.

Elizabeth was a passionate woman. She enjoyed his touch, accepted his kisses and caresses. He prided himself that he had played his cards well. He had been very careful at first, not pushing her too hard, taking what she had been ready to give him as he slowly led her towards the marriage bed. As a result, he now had her trusting and clinging to him, whenever they had a few minutes of privacy, which was not often enough for him.

The only mistake he had made, which admittedly had taken him a step back in the relationship, was the afternoon when she had met Georgiana for the first time. In the heat of the moment, he had forgotten himself. She was a maiden, sheltered, innocent; such behaviour on his part was inexcusable and without a doubt very unwise. She had immediately associated what he had done with his past experiences with other women, and she had been right.

She was jealous, which warmed his heart, but there was more to it. He could see disgust in her eyes. He could not change his past, but surely in the future, he would direct and advise his own sons differently. He did not wish for them to repeat his mistakes, being in a situation like he had placed himself in. He craved Elizabeth's respect. He wanted her to admire him, and he knew that she was less than impressed with his amorous past. He did not want her to be disappointed with him ever again. Nor did he wish to see that look in her eyes again.

To his great displeasure, he barely saw her these days. She was always with

Mrs. Gardiner and Georgiana, shopping, or spending the day with Gardiners' children. He did not mind the little Gardiners; they were well behaved, if not a little loud. Still, he preferred to keep a safe distance from them. Emily Gardiner always made a point to climb on his lap, studying him with an earnest expression. Moreover, one time when he had held little Fred, the baby had drooled all over the shoulder of his coat. It was ruined after that, and he could not wear it anymore. It was one of his favourite coats, and he had needed to order another one to replace it. Thankfully his tailor assured him he could make a similar one.

Despite being abandoned far too many times by Elizabeth for the company of his little sister, he was delighted that Georgiana and Elizabeth were forming such a close friendship, understanding each other so well. Georgiana looked up to Elizabeth as a role model, starting her every second sentence with 'Lizzy said this,' or 'Lizzy liked that,' or 'Lizzy laughed about such and such.' He even noticed that Georgiana had begun rolling her eyes at him, as well as mimicking many other of Elizabeth's mannerisms.

Darcy had talked with Mrs. Gardiner personally, asking her to accompany Elizabeth and Georgiana to the dressmaker, to see that Elizabeth had everything she would need for the next year or so, including post mourning clothes. Mrs. Gardiner seemed to be knowledgeable about fashion, at least Georgiana thought so. Elizabeth's new wardrobe would be sent directly to Pemberley once everything was completed, but her presence was needed almost every day to make necessary fittings to the many dresses that were being made for her.

He heard noises in the foyer, indicating that his ladies had returned from their outing.

"Have you had a pleasant day?" he asked, coming to greet them.

"Oh, yes, Brother, it was most delightful. Elizabeth's dresses will be perfect."

"I am glad," he assured, taking note that Elizabeth looked paler than usual. "Are you well?" he asked.

She smiled. "I am pleased that tomorrow is the very last fitting," she said.

"They promised to have four dresses finished for tomorrow," Georgiana added excitedly, "including the wedding dress, of course."

"I cannot imagine how they have managed it," Elizabeth noted. "So many gowns sewn in a little over a week," she marvelled.

Darcy did not comment, even though he had pretty good idea how much this miracle was costing him.

Georgiana looked between both of them, smiled and excused herself from their company.

"You are tired," he stated as the door closed after Georgiana and they were left alone.

"A little," she breathed. She stepped closer and placed her head against his chest. He sat back into the armchair, pulling her onto his lap.

"Close your eyes, rest," he murmured, kissing her forehead.

She shook her head. "I must go soon. I promised my aunt I would look after the children. She and uncle are going to a concert in the evening."

"There is a nanny, I believe." Darcy reminded.

"It is not the same. I have already told them that I would play with them. "

His arms tightened around her. "At least you have practice before our own will come."

She stilled in his arms for a moment, but soon relaxed. "How many children you would like to have?" she asked, playing with the buttons of his waistcoat.

"Three, two boys and a girl would be perfect," he answered without a second thought. It was not that he had considered it earlier in detail, but two sons and baby girl sounded just right to him.

She leaned back to look at him. "Only three?"

He smiled. "Do you wish for more?"

"Do I have choice in that?" she questioned softly. "From my experience, a woman can have a child every year or two till the end of her childbearing years, unless she keeps separate bedroom from her husband."

"I do not plan for us to keep separate bedrooms, not ever," he assured her. "Still, there are ways to prevent conception. They are not always effective, but when the couple is careful, it can be planned. You mother never talked to you about that?"

"No, and I doubt that she has any knowledge of what you are speaking," Elizabeth snorted. "She had five children in less than eight years. The birth of Lydia was very difficult. She could not give birth any more after that. I think that it is the only reason why I have not more siblings. On the other hand, I presume that my parents wanted to try as long as it took for a boy to be born."

Darcy chose not to place his comment on his mother-in-law. He had already learned that Elizabeth did not like to discuss her mother in greater detail. "I see. You should talk with Mrs. Gardiner about it. She seems more knowledgeable."

"Do you think that aunt and uncle..." she mused. "But they share one bedroom."

"How long have they been married?" Darcy asked.

"Ten years this summer."

"They have four children, but there are twins, so your aunt was with child only three times. There is three- four years of age difference between their children. I think that it is not a coincidence."

"I have never thought about that."

"You had no reason to occupy yourself with such matters. Now, as a married woman, you should be aware of them. I want us to enjoy our life together, and when we have children, to be able to devote our time to every one of them. I cannot imagine, doing it properly, having more than five."

"You wish to postpone having children then?" she asked, searching his eyes for the answer.

"I would not mind enjoying you for a year or two without the burden of a child so soon in the marriage," he admitted.

"The baby will not be a burden," she protested, frowning.

"It will take so much of your time and attention though. I am not quite ready to share you. However, it will be expected at Pemberley for us to have a baby right away, preferably a boy and heir. It will calm the people. Their lives depend on the prosperity of the estate, its future."

"I would wish to have a baby," she said. "I do not want to wait."

"You are very young. You have time. We can travel first."

"I want someone to love," she confessed.

He stiffened involuntarily, a searing pain cutting into his chest, right to his gut. "I see."

"Forgive me," she murmured, lowering her head.

"It is said that one should never apologize for honesty."

She clamped her arms tightly around his neck. "I truly like you," she whispered.

He tried to brush off her words, explaining to himself that in such a short time, she could not develop deeper feelings for him. Not even two months ago, she had claimed to dislike him. Now she liked him. It hurt still that what she wanted most from him was a baby so she could have someone to love.

Still her words touched him deeply, more than he was ready to acknowledge.

"I like you too," he whispered back.

She lifted herself from his lap. "I should go."

He nodded, standing up as well. "I will call for the carriage."

She gazed into his eyes. "Only five days."

He cupped her cheek. "There is nothing to fear."

"I do not fear it. I anticipate it," she said evenly.

He searched her face.

"Truly," she nodded, serious.

He was not certain what she meant, but he hoped for the best. It was his own fault that she was so hesitant. Through his pride, he had alienated her from the very beginning. Now he had to win her back. They were making progress. Every day they were getting closer to each other.

***

It was a beautiful, sunny day as Georgiana and Elizabeth travelled in an open carriage. They were alone today, with only Darcy's servants accompanying them. Georgiana's companion, Mrs. Annesley, had asked to terminate her contract a few days ago. Her daughter was expecting her first child, and she planned to live with her. Darcy agreed to that, seeing how well his sister and future wife interacted with each other, knowing that Georgiana would have an excellent companion in Elizabeth.

"I am so curious how your dresses came out," Georgiana spoke with eagerness, a grin splitting her round face.

Elizabeth smiled. Her new sister was so excited about the new gowns, as if they were being made for her. She talked at length of how well Elizabeth would look in them. Elizabeth was no stranger to fashion, and she enjoyed pretty clothes like any other young woman; however, spending most of the day in the shops was tiresome and a boring experience for her.

Georgiana seemed to never tire of it. She was always most enthusiastic, foregoing even her shyness. It was obvious that the girl had no hesitation when it came to spending money. She never asked about the price. When she liked something, she asked to have it sent home, the bill going to her brother. It was quite a different attitude to that which Elizabeth had been used to all her life.

"I am sure that we will not be disappointed." She turned to Georgiana, taking her hand to give it a squeeze. "I must thank you for that. You put so much effort into choosing the right cuts and materials. I do not know how I would have managed without your help," she spoke with sincerity.

Georgiana blushed at the praise. "Mrs. Gardiner was of great help as well."

Elizabeth nodded, fully agreeing with Georgiana. Her aunt had gone to the shop with them the first several times, speaking directly with the owner, Madame la Fleur, about what exactly the future Mrs. Darcy would need. Elizabeth had been amazed at the number of the dresses that her aunt found necessary for her to own. When she questioned her on that, Mrs. Gardiner shushed her, saying that her new station in life required it. Elizabeth said no more, and allowed Georgiana and Mrs. Gardiner to take the lead. There was such a wide selection of materials at the elegant shop where Georgiana had taken her, that she was most grateful for her advice.

As they entered the shop, Elizabeth's eyes fell on the woman who was standing in front of the hat rack. She knew that it was rude to stare, but this lady drew attention. She was tall and statuesque, having the kind of figure Elizabeth knew she would never have. As the woman turned her head, so she could see her face, Elizabeth's eyes widened. She was even more beautiful than Jane, though till that moment, Elizabeth was convinced that no one could be prettier than her sister.

She was so engrossed in observing the stranger, that only after a moment did she notice that the woman was keenly watching her as well.

She heard a soft gasp beside her, and felt Georgiana's hand on her arm.

"Perhaps we should come another time, Lizzy," the girl suggested, glancing nervously at the beautiful lady.

"We have only just arrived," Elizabeth reasoned, not understanding the girl's mood.

"Yes, but..." the girl pressed her lips tightly, her brow furrowed. "I am not feeling well," she spoke hastily.

"You were in such high spirits before."

"Sudden headache. I sometimes have such sudden headaches. I... I think that we should come back tomorrow."

Elizabeth searched her sister's face with worry. Something must have upset Georgiana deeply, as she had returned to her stuttering.

"If you wish."

"Thank you," Georgiana turned towards the door, almost dragging her along.

Elizabeth stopped her though. "We should tell Madame la Fleur that we cannot stay."

Georgiana shook her head vehemently. "That is not necessary. We should go."

Elizabeth shot her a confused look. "Georgiana, you said yourself that Madame has many clients. She may be busy with someone else tomorrow."

She freed her arm from Georgiana's grasp, and made her way to one of the shop assistants. As she walked, she noticed that the beautiful stranger picked one of the hats, and brought it to the counter.

"I want to have it packed and send to my home yet today," the woman ordered. Elizabeth wondered whether she was someone important. The tone of her voice suggested that she thought very highly of herself. She was dressed beautifully.

The shop assistant glanced at the woman, before her eyes rested on Elizabeth. A shiver ran down Elizabeth's back. There was something strange happening here, she could feel it.

The beautiful woman turned and looked directly at Elizabeth, catching her eye. "Send the bill to Mr. Darcy. As always," she spoke loudly, before leaving the shop.

The shop went completely silent. Elizabeth stared at the floor, the woman's last words replaying in her head. Send the bill to Mr. Darcy. As always. As always. To Mr. Darcy.

"Miss Bennet, Miss Darcy, good morning. Everything is ready," the owner waltzed to her with a fake smile plastered on her face. "Would you care for a cup of tea before we start?"

She was pale, and her French accent was much more pronounced than usual.

"Madame la Fleur," Elizabeth started slowly. "The woman who has just left asked to send the bill to Mr. Darcy. Is it her custom to do that?"

"I am truly in not a position to divulge such information..." the woman started uneasily.

"I see. Well, please remember, that from now on, Mr. Darcy will not pay for that lady's purchases. Including this bonnet." She glanced at the counter.

Madame la Fleur was silent for a long moment. "Miss Bennet, with all due respect, I am not certain whether you should..."

She was interrupted, when Georgiana's voice was heard from behind. "There are many other shops in London. We can always go somewhere else if my sister is not satisfied with your service."

Elizabeth turned her head to look at the girl. Where was the shy Georgiana she knew? That cold, haughty tone, that condescending look. She looked so much like Darcy when he had his mind set on intimidating someone.

The woman's eyes darted to Georgiana, and after a moment of hesitation, she nodded, a smile plastered back on her face.

"Of course. That lady is not our client anymore."

"Excellent," Georgiana spoke confidently. "We wish to see the dresses that were to be finished for today. We will take them with us."

The owner walked away, and Elizabeth whispered frantically. "I cannot stay here, not now, not after that."

The girl nodded, her expression sympathetic. "Wait for me in the carriage. I will be back in a few minutes. I will excuse us."

Elizabeth stormed out of the shop. Darcy's servants were next to her instantly, helping her into the carriage. As she waited for Georgiana, she concentrated on keeping her composure. She was in the open carriage, and anyone could see her. She could not cry here, no matter how much she wanted.

Thankfully, Georgiana returned soon, a shop assistant following her with arms full of parcels. They were taken from her by the servant, while Georgiana climbed into carriage, sitting opposite Elizabeth.

The girl touched her hand with her own. "Oh, Lizzy," she said only.

Elizabeth took a shaky breath, and dared to look up. "She is not your relative."

"No, she is not," the girl whispered, biting down her lip, "but, it is in the past; I am certain of that. Brother loves you so much. She does not mean anything to him."

"Means nothing to him, but he pays for her clothes?" she exclaimed with pain.

"I am certain that there is a way to explain this. It must all be a misunderstanding. It must be. He loves you so much," she repeated.

Elizabeth looked her right in the eye. "You recognized her from the beginning, as soon as we entered. That is why you did not wish for us to stay there."

The girl nodded.

"How did you learn who she was?"

Georgiana shrugged. "I am not as naive as my brother likes to perceive me.

I saw her for the first time over a year ago in this very shop. I noticed that she was looking at me strangely. My companion at that time, Mrs. Younge, thought nothing of that though. Then I accidently listened to the conversation between the Madame's assistants. They gossiped and laughed, finding it very amusing that a sister and a lover were in the shop at the same time. I met her one more time when I came for fittings a few weeks later. She looked at me again and smiled, but said nothing. I have never seen her since then, though I remembered her well."

"I am not surprised. Such a face is hard to forget. She is strikingly beautiful," Elizabeth spoke, seemingly without emotion. "Did you tell your brother about that encounter?"

Georgiana shook her head. "There was no need. Nor did I find it necessary to shop somewhere else to avoid her. Madame la Fleur offers all the latest fashions and has delightful ideas when it comes to cut and colour. Her hats are the best in London."

Elizabeth only nodded. She stared in front of herself with unseeing eyes.

"I was so relieved when Brother fell in love with you. You are so different than that woman. He loves only you," Georgiana assured ardently.

Elizabeth noticed that the carriage was approaching the street where Darcy House was situated. The driver must have assumed that they wished to return home.

"Georgiana, please tell the driver that I want to return to my aunt and uncle's house."

The girl was silent for a moment. "Are you certain, Lizzy?"

"Yes. I cannot see him now."

Chapter Seventeen

Darcy had been closed in his study since the early morning, diligently penning responses to the correspondence which had come yesterday from Pemberley. As he was not to return home for the next three weeks or so, he needed to give his detailed opinion about the matters which his steward was asking about in his letter.

He hoped to finish early, just as Elizabeth and Georgiana were to return from their last planned shopping trip before the wedding. He anticipated a pleasant afternoon spent in the company of his ladies. Perhaps they could walk to a park after tea. Elizabeth had little opportunity nowadays to take the long strolls she enjoyed so much.

Out of nowhere, the door fell open and Georgiana barged into the room. Her violent entrance made his hand shake, causing him to make a large ink blot in the middle of the page. The letter was ruined, and he would have to start it all over again.

He stood up, giving his sister his best frown. "What is the meaning of this, Georgiana?" he demanded in a harsh voice. "You should have knocked. You never behave in such a manner."

She seemed not to hear what he said and ran to his desk. "Oh, brother, you must go and see Elizabeth!" she cried. "Now!"

He instantly felt a painful squeeze in his chest, rising to his throat. "Good God, what happened?" he exclaimed. "Where is she? Is she well?"

"She is not well. She had us take her to the Gardiners."

"Is she hurt? Was there an accident?" He looked his sister up and down. "Are you hurt? You were supposed to be together the whole time."

Georgiana shook her head. "Not physically hurt, but she is very upset." She took his arm and began pulling him in the direction of the door. "Come, you must go and see her. I have already asked the stable boy to ready your horse."

"I will go. Of course I will go. However, first you need to tell me what has happened," he stared down at her.

She bit down on her lip. "It is difficult to explain."

"Try."

"I do not know how." Her eyes pleaded him. "It is rather embarrassing."

"Georgiana," he warned, his voice going flat. "Can you tell me what has happened?"

The girl lowered her head, avoiding his eyes.

"What has happened, Georgiana? Speak!" Darcy pressed.

"We met your... your.... mistress in the shop," she murmured, stuttering.

"Excuse me?" He bent his head, thinking he had surely misheard.

She lifted her gaze at him, acute embarrassment written all over her face. "We met your mistress in the shop," she repeated slowly. "She was buying a hat."

"What are you speaking about?"

"We saw your mistress."

He blinked rapidly. "That is not possible. You cannot possibly know who my...." he started, and then silenced himself, realizing it was his baby sister he was talking to.

"I do not know her name; still I know who she is. Tall, very beautiful, pale blonde hair. I met her a year ago."

"What do you mean, met her? Where?"

"I was shopping with Mrs. Younge about a year ago," she explained. "We were at Madame la Fleur's shop. I noticed a very beautiful lady who was staring at me, smiling. Later, I overheard a conversation between the Madame's assistants; they were gossiping, amused, laughing that a lover and a sister met in the same shop at the same time."

"Why did you not tell me about it?" he asked gently.

She lifted her shoulders only to drop them down. "I was mortified. I would not know how to even begin such a conversation. I only saw her one more time after that, again in the shop. She smiled, but said nothing to me."

Darcy ran his hand over his face. He could not believe that Annette could have done such a thing, that she had actually attempted to come close to his sister. Two meetings could not be an accident. Moreover, Georgiana noticed her interest. Even if Annette and Georgiana had happened by accident to be in the same place at the same time, Annette should have left instantly. She knew the rules.

"So, what happened today?" he asked, already dreading the answer.

Georgiana took a long breath. "I noticed her as soon as we entered the shop. I told Elizabeth that I had a sudden headache and asked her to leave. She agreed, but insisted on speaking with the owner, informing her that we would come another time. Then..." Georgiana bit her lip, frowning.

"Finish, please."

She stared at her feet. "That woman took one of the hats, and threw it on the counter. She asked to deliver it to her house, and send the bill to Mr. Darcy, as always. Elizabeth heard every word, because that woman said all of this looking into her face."

"That bitch," Darcy hissed, hitting the desk with his fist. "I will kill her for that."

Angry could not even remotely describe what he felt at that moment. He was furious. It could only be compared to the last summer, when he had discovered Wickham's vile intentions towards Georgiana.

"What was Elizabeth's reaction?" he asked quietly, once he was able to control his voice again.

"She was calm while we were in the shop. In the carriage, she asked me what I knew, and I told her exactly what I have just told you. She did not wish to return here with me. She began to weep as we were approaching her uncle's house."

He placed his hand on her shoulder. "Thank you. I knew you did everything in your power to prevent it. We will talk later, but now I must go."

He hurried through the house, Georgiana following him. Only in the foyer, he noticed the many large boxes placed on the side tables.

"What are these?" he asked.

"Elizabeth's new dresses and hats. She refused to take them with her."

Darcy stared for a long moment at the parcels, before storming out of the house. Thankfully, his horse was waiting for him, saddled. She did not want the clothes he paid for. He feared to consider what this could mean.

***

"Miss Bennet is home?" he barked, rushing into the Gardiners' house, nearly tripping over the servant who had opened the door for him.

"Yes, sir, but she said she admits no calls today," the young maid explained, looking at him with round eyes.

Darcy walked towards the narrow staircase, looking up.

"Is she in her room?" he demanded.

"Yes, sir, but she said that she was unwell."

He glanced at the girl. "Is Mrs. Gardiner home?"

"No, sir, she had just gone to the park with children."

It was all Darcy needed to hear, as he ran up the stairs. He heard the maid's voice from behind him, protesting, but he ignored her. He knew that Elizabeth's room was somewhere in the second floor, next to the children's room, but he had no idea which one it was. He opened the first two doors, finding the nursery, and what looked like an unused guest bedroom. At last he pushed the third door open to find Elizabeth's slight form curled on a bed.

"Sir!" the maid cried from the door, out of breath.

"You can leave us alone, Jenny," Elizabeth spoke quietly.

"Yes, Miss Elizabeth." Obviously relieved, the maid stepped back, closing the door.

Darcy stepped closer. "Georgiana told me everything."

She slipped from the bed, standing in front of him. A sound slap on his cheek echoed through the room.

"I deserve that," he acknowledged gravely.

She shook her head, looking at him as if she had seen him for the first time. "I cannot believe how someone can be so deceitful. I should have listened to my heart and mind, as I see clearly now that my first impression of you was correct. There is only one matter which I cannot understand… why you lied to me, why you pretended to love me. You wanted a toy to play with? If that was your wish, you certainly succeeded."

"I did not lie, and I pretended nothing when I spoke about my feelings for you. Allow me to explain." He tried to take her hand, but she did not allow it, stepping back.

"You could have told me that you needed a wife to bear you a legal heir, who you would leave in the country so she could raise your children while you enjoy yourself in London. My family is in such a desperate situation that I would have agreed to that. At least I would have known from the beginning what I was consenting to."

"Do not say such things," he moaned. "It is a gross untruth."

"Is it? You made no secret you want me in your bed! For what else would you have picked me? I have nothing, no money, no connections, no father to protect me!" she exclaimed, tears brimming her eyes. "You wanted a quiet little wife who would sit home at Pemberley with your sister and say nothing as you whore about London. Admit it. What I cannot comprehend is why you tried to delude me into thinking that you loved me. If it is to be a business arrangement, let us be honest with one another.

"And what about poor Georgiana? Have you ever thought how she would feel? She loves you so much, and yet you parade that woman right in front of her."

He came to her, gripping her forearms, to keep her in place. "You are being unreasonable. Let me explain as this is all a misunderstanding."

"No, I do not wish to speak to you, listen to you or look at you," she spat out. "I want you to leave."

"No, I am not leaving—not until this is settled between us. Elizabeth, you must allow me to explain. I knew nothing about any of this. Annette did it all behind my back, I have not seen her since…"

She gave a short, bitter laugh, interrupting him. "Annette. Is that her name? How delightful. She is so beautiful, it fits her perfectly, I dare say," she spoke mockingly, but was unsuccessful in removing the hurt lacing her voice.

"Elizabeth, please," he shook her gently. "Just listen to me…"

She looked into his face. "Leave. I do not wish to speak to you."

He shook his head, not loosening his hold on her.

"Go away or I will scream so loud that my uncle will hear in his office on the other side of the street," she threatened.

"Lizzy, it is all misunderstanding. I ended it six months ago, sweetheart… as soon as I realized how much I loved…" he tried to sooth her.

He did not finish, because she opened her mouth and a high pitched screech came out of it. It rang in his ears - he could not believe that such a small person could scream so loud.

Without second thought, in attempt to silence her, he put his hand gently across her mouth. It only angered her more. A second later he felt a piercing pain in his groin, like he had never felt before in his life. He had no choice but to let her go, lowering on his knees in agony. She must have kicked him with her knee. He could not believe it! He was aware that she had a temper, but to be so violent… and strong too. God, how that hurt. He sincerely hoped that he would be able to father children after that.

As he was trying to regain his breath, she marched past him to the door, opening it wide. "Goodbye, sir."

Panting quietly, he lifted himself up, trying to somehow regain his dignity. She walked a wide circle, making a point to avoid him, and stood by the window.

"I will come tomorrow so we may talk once you have calmed down," he

assured when he was by the door, wanting her to know that this conversation was not over.

A small vase full of flowers flew right by his temple and crashed against the doorframe. Had she aimed an inch closer, his head would have been cracked in half. He began to fear her.

He took it as a sign that it was best to leave her alone for now. He knew that her temper ran hot but was usually short lived. He would return tomorrow.

***

"Annette!" Darcy roared, banging with his fist at the front door of her house in Hammersmith. "Open this door!"

A short moment later, the door let go and she welcomed him with wide smile. "I knew you would come!" she exclaimed, trying to wind her arms around his neck. He pushed her aside without ceremony, roughly, and stepped inside, shutting the door behind them.

He strode into the small parlor, waiting for her to follow him. He could barely look at her. He had never raised his hand to a woman, but he was very close to doing that just now.

"Are you out of your mind?" he asked, trying to keep his voice calm. "What were you thinking? How did you know that they would be there in the first place?"

She stared at him, seemingly unperturbed by his enquiries.

"Answer me!"

"I paid one of the girls at the store to let me know when they would be coming."

"Why? What were you counting on?"

"I wanted to see her." She narrowed her eyes. "Your Lizzy." She spat with contempt in her voice.

"You had absolutely no right to interfere in my private life. We were finished a long time ago; you know that. I have not been with you since last December, and even then it was a grave mistake."

A slight frown appeared between her elegantly drawn eyebrows, but she said nothing.

"Why are you doing this to me?" he questioned, running his hand over his face. "I was always fair to you."

"You will not be happy with her. She is small, thin and mousy. She will not be able to please you. I know women like her. She will allow you to raise her gown to her waist, and will be laying like the dead beneath you. You will be bored with her after half a year, if not sooner."

"How dare you? Do not speak of her!"

She stared into his eyes, stepping closer. "I love you."

He laughed. "You love me, and yet you want to destroy me?"

"I wish you no harm. On the contrary, she is no good for you. I can give you a child; you can marry me…"

He lowered on the nearby chair, and began to laugh in earnest. "Marry you? You are mad! Do you truly think that I would bring a whore to my ancestral house, making her the Mistress of Pemberley?"

"Do not say that!" she exclaimed. "I had no choice in where I came from, that my father abandoned my mother even before I was born. Not everyone has such luck like your Lizzy, or your sister, to be born a gentlewoman in a perfect little family, with an estate, pianoforte lessons, balls and tea parties. I worked hard for everything I have now in my life."

He raised an eyebrow. "Indeed, you work very hard, on your back mostly," he remarked coldly.

With interest, he noticed that she actually blushed at his last words. He would have never thought that she could be capable of showing even a hint of embarrassment.

"Such things happened before. Do not laugh at me," she argued. "What about Emma Hamilton? Her father was only a blacksmith. She was an actress and a mistress to some wealthy gentlemen before Sir William Hamilton married her. Now she is said to be the love interest of Admiral Nelson himself."

Darcy examined Annette's face, the sincerity written in her expression, becoming more and more convinced that she truly came to believe in what she was saying. "I will not even grant that a comment. I will only say that I am marrying Elizabeth not because of her family, or connection, but because I love her."

"What can she know about love? She is but a child. Sickly and pale. What do you see in her? She looks younger than your sister."

He lifted his hand at her. "Not a word about my wife."

"She is not your wife *yet*."

"I said, not a word about her," he bellowed, hitting his fist against the polished surface of the small table.

She looked down, her features twisted in an ugly grimace.

"Do you even realize how much trouble you have caused for me?"

She smiled with obvious satisfaction. "I can imagine. Did she end the engagement?" she questioned with hope.

"That was your intention?" he asked, his eyes narrowing. "You are indeed stupid. You do not understand that I will not allow her to break with me. I will grovel at her feet as long as necessary till she takes me back. And you, you are finished. One word from me to my acquaintances about what you did, and no sane man will take you. You will end up on the street, or as a kitchen maid."

"Fitzwilliam," she ran to him, kneeling by the chair he was seated on. "I did it because I wanted you back. I needed her to know about me. Now, even if she marries you, she will secretly dislike you. You will be unhappy with a moody wife and coming back to me in no time."

He stood up, walking away from her. "You cannot have me back, because I was never yours. I do not know what kind of delusion you created in your head. If I ever see you again, or hear from my family that you tried to approach them again, you will pay dearly. Understood?"

"I am not afraid," she spoke with conviction, as she lifted to her feet, and joined his side. "You are a kind man. I knew that you liked me more than the others. You are only hesitant to admit it."

"If my sister or wife as much as sees you across the street, I will hire someone, and they will make sure that your beauty is gone forever."

Her eyes widened, but she shook her head. "You would not do that."

He took her hand, twisting it painfully, before unceremoniously shoved her to the floor, so she slid against the wall, hitting it.

"Stay away from me and my loved ones, or you will regret it for the rest of your life." He lashed out before walking out.

He heard her crying his name, but he did not turn around to look at her.

***

It was late evening when Darcy finally returned home that day. After leaving Hammersmith, he went straight to White's. He was not a big enthusiast of sitting in a club, finding it rather tiresome and boring; but still he visited regularly when he was in London. His father had been a member of White's, and his wish had been for his son to join as well. It allowed Darcy to keep relations with his university friends and strengthen the social bonds with some influential people. He was not a fool, knowing well that a man could never guess when the friends in high places might be needed in life.

The club was relatively empty, but he met a few of his closer acquaintances. They loudly congratulated him on his upcoming wedding, asking where he was hiding his lovely bride. He explained that as Elizabeth had lost her father a short time ago and was in deep mourning, the wedding would be a quiet one, including only the closest family.

He was not one to divulge his private matters to those men or anyone else, for that matter, but today he purposively spoke about what happened to his sister and wife to be. They listened eagerly perhaps because it was such a rare occurrence that Darcy spoke about his private life. After a few hours, the small crowd gathered around him, and his story was repeated several times to the newcomers, being even enriched by new details.

Darcy made a point to warn everyone against entering into any relations with Annette. They all nodded their heads, agreeing that there was no future for her in London after what she had done. They were all extremely compassionate about his predicament, and this act of male solidarity, with a few glasses of a good wine, made him feel slightly less miserable. He had even received some advice on how to return into his lady's good graces. He knew that they would be useless though, as Elizabeth was not one to be placated with jewels or a house in Bath.

All the present men came to the agreement that in the current situation, sadly he would be starting his married life with separate bedrooms. Darcy, however, was the least concerned about it. All he wished for was Elizabeth's forgiveness. She could not break the engagement, she would not do that.

It was after ten when Darcy stumbled into his house. He was glad that his horse knew the way home so well; because he was more asleep than alert during the ride. The servant who opened the door gave him only one look, and took him under his arm, dragging him upstairs. He doubted whether it was necessary. He was not that drunk.

He lay on the bed as his valet pulled off his long riding boots. He waved him away when the man wanted to help to remove his clothes.

He was dozing off, filled with a pleasant half dream of Elizabeth resting by his side, stroking his forehead like the time when he had a headache.

"Where have you been?" he heard an angry voice above him.

With an effort, he lifted to a sitting position. Georgiana stood in front of him in her white nightclothes, her hands placed on her hips.

"I have been to see Elizabeth," he answered.

Her eyes narrowed. "For so long? The Gardiners retire early."

He stared at her. "How can you know that?"

She rolled her eyes. "Because they have small children."

"I had some business to attend later on," he acknowledged.

"Have you visited that woman?"

He nodded. "I had a conversation with her before I went to the club. It is finished." he murmured.

"Good."

He frowned, realizing that he was answering to his baby sister as if she was his parent. "I do not see any reason why I should explain myself to you," he spoke with as much dignity as he could manage in his present state.

Georgiana ignored his words. "Has Elizabeth forgiven you?"

He shook his head no.

Georgiana sighed. "Will you go to see her tomorrow?"

"Yes."

"I hope that you will convince her to take you back. If not, I will go to live with Aunt Eleanor in Matlock. She has offered many times to let me stay with them. Cousin Richard is my guardian too, after all. They will not refuse me."

With these words, she turned on her heel, and without as much as a good night, she left him alone, closing the door loudly after herself.

He laid back and stared at the canopy. He could not understand why matters had gone so badly for him. Where had he made a mistake?

He knew how bad the situation looked from Elizabeth's perspective. If someone had done something like that to Georgiana, he would have torn him apart.

He had thought that he could trust Annette. He was gravely mistaken. She seemed so controlled and reasonable.

It was surely his fault that he had not taken a closer look at the source of the bills Annette had been sending to his solicitor. He should have noticed that she had used the same shop as his sister.

Elizabeth thought that he had betrayed her in the worst way. He was stupid. He should have explained to her the situation with Annette in greater detail when she had asked. At that time, though, he had been of the opinion there was no need to bother her with the details of his less than glorious past.

She would have been disappointed with him, perhaps, but she would not have hated him, like he surely did now.

With great effort, he rolled himself to the edge of the large bed, and made his limbs move in the direction of the chest of drawers. He retrieved Elizabeth's shawl from it. She had left it here yesterday, and he had intended to return it to her today.

He took off his coat, and after some struggle, and without strangling himself, he managed to remove his neck cloth. He took a large pillow from the bed, draping Elizabeth's shawl over it. Then he hugged the pillow, burying his nose in it, and lay down on the bed, curling into a fetal position.

Tomorrow he would talk to her and convince her to take him back.

Chapter Eighteen

"Are you feeling better today?" Mrs. Gardiner enquired, sitting on the edge of the bed.

Elizabeth was wrapped in a blanket, still in her nightclothes, even though it was early afternoon. "I am simply tired. I want to stay in my room."

Mrs. Gardiner reached her hand to move away the long, now uncurled fringe which fell over Elizabeth's face. "You may stay here, of course you may. God knows that you had so little time to yourself over the last weeks."

"Thank you," Elizabeth whispered, before fixating her eyes on the unknown point in front of her.

Mrs. Gardiner stroked her arm, "Dear girl, I respect your privacy, and I understand you do not wish to speak about it - still, I need to know one thing."

Elizabeth looked at her expectantly, waiting for the question.

"Jenny told me that she heard raised voices when Mr. Darcy came here yesterday. Did he hurt you?"

Elizabeth sighed. "As I told you, we had an argument, but I really do not wish to talk about it."

"I must ask, Lizzy, though your uncle thinks I am being silly to think this." Mrs. Gardiner bit down on her lip. "Did he mistreat you?" She paused. "Did he force himself on you? Hit you?"

Elizabeth stared at her unblinkingly for a moment. "No, of course not! No, God no!" she exclaimed. "It is not what you are thinking. To be truthful, it was I who...," she shook her head, closing her eyes. "He has his faults, but I do not believe that he would ever raise his hand to me. I have tasted his temper more than once, and he never... He can be stubborn, but never violent. Please, do not ask me more. Please."

Mrs. Gardiner nodded. "Very well. As you wish." She gave her a small smile. "The children have been asking about you. Can they come here?"

"Of course. I am always happy to see them," Elizabeth assured.

"I will send them to you. Do not fret though; they will not bother you for too long."

Mrs. Gardiner left, and not five minutes later, the little Gardiners came in. The twins, Emily and Robert, were the first to run in, while the eldest, Anne, walked calmly behind them, carrying Fred in her arms.

"Are you sick, Lizzy?" Emily asked.

Elizabeth smiled at the girl. "No, I am well, only tired."

"Papa said that you were overwhelmed," Robbie informed. "What does it mean, overwhelmed, Lizzy?"

"It means that I am sad and tired," she explained.

"Why are you sad?" Emily wanted to know.

"You should not be asking Lizzy about that," Anne interjected. "Uncle Bennet, Lizzy's papa, died not a long time ago, and 'tis why she is sad."

Peter nodded. "We would be sad too if our papa died."

"Do not even say such things, Robert Gardiner," his elder sister scolded him, causing the boy to hang his head.

Little Fred chose this moment to mark his presence. "Da..., da..., dada...," he grunted, reaching tiny hands in the direction of Elizabeth.

Elizabeth laughed. "What is he saying?"

"We are not certain. He started saying it yesterday," Anne explained as she stepped closer, placing the baby on the foot of the bed. Fred did not waste any time and crawled busily to Elizabeth.

He sat himself next to her and patted her arm with energy. "Dada... dada. Da!" the boy exclaimed.

"What do you wish little one?" Elizabeth cooed, taking his pudgy fingers to her face and kissing them.

The baby laughed and rolled on his back. She brought the warm, small body to herself, inhaling the sweet baby's scent.

"It is time for his nap," Anne noted, as her brother was nestling against Elizabeth's side, his eyelids drooping.

"Leave him with me. I will watch him as he sleeps," she said, stroking the boy's mostly bald head. He had only a small tuft of hair above the forehead. The Gardiners' children were all blond, like their parents.

"Very well, Lizzy," Anne spoke, taking Emily's and Robbie's hands, indicating that it was time for them to go.

Emily dragged her feet though. "Can I stay?" she whined.

"Mama said that we should not bother Lizzy," the older girl reminded her.

"I will be very quiet. I will not be a bother," Emily promised.

Anne gave her a doubtful look, but let go of her hand. Before she and Robbie left, she wished Elizabeth a good rest. Elizabeth was always amazed at how mature and polite Anne was, especially for her age. She was only nine, but she always behaved like a little lady. She reminded her so much of

Jane, not only because of her behaviour, but in looks as well. She was already a beauty.

At the remembrance of her beloved sister, a new feeling of sadness came over Elizabeth. Oh, how she wished for Jane to be here. She did not tell her aunt what had transpired between Mr. Darcy and herself. She could not bear pity, and she did not wish to worry her aunt and uncle even more than they already were. They were so good to her and Jane, but they could not help her now. No one could.

Emily removed her shoes, and Elizabeth helped her to climb on the bed, on the other side of her. Fred was already fast asleep, his thumb stuck in his mouth.

"Will you not sleep?" Elizabeth asked, tugging at one of the Emily's thin pigtails, as the little girl stared at her with wide, shining eyes.

Elizabeth knew that expression well and wondered what her young cousin was up to this time.

"I do not sleep during the day, because I am a big girl now," Emily announced.

"Your brother sleeps during the day."

"Fred is a baby, and he has to sleep."

"I am talking about Robbie."

Emily pursed her lips. "He is a baby too."

"Is he?" Elizabeth smiled. "He is older than you."

Emily frowned. "We are twins, we are both five."

"Yes, but he was born fifteen minutes earlier than you."

"How do you know?"

"I was here the day you were born."

"You were? What did I look like?"

"Pink and wrinkled." Elizabeth tickled her tummy.

Emily laughed out loud, which made Elizabeth put a finger to her lips. "Shush, remember that Fred is asleep."

"Lizzy, can I tell you a secret?" Emily whispered.

"Of course."

"Mama told us that we should not tell you this."

"Well, then you should not."

Elizabeth watched with interest the obvious conflict written on little girl's face.

"But he is so sad, Lizzy."

"Who?"

"Mr. Darcy."

Elizabeth's heart froze for a moment. "Mr. Darcy? Have you seen him?"

"He was here when I got up. Mama said he came first thing in the morning, but she did not allow him to see you. She said that you need peace and quiet and that he cannot see you."

"Is he still here?"

The child nodded eagerly. "Outside."

"In the garden?"

"No, outside your room, sitting on a chair."

"Emily, dear, can you do me a favour? Can you ask Mr. Darcy to come here? Only make sure no one sees you."

Emily grinned and slipped from the bed onto the floor, running to the door, forgetting her shoes in the process.

Elizabeth shook her head with a smile, sliding from the bed, careful not to disturb Fred. She picked two large pillows, placing them on the both sides of the child, so he would not accidently roll across the bed to the floor.

She had not even managed to smooth her robe, when Emily was back, dragging Darcy with her.

Elizabeth did not look at him, but bent down, picking up Emily's abandoned slippers.

"Have you not forgotten something, Missy?" she asked playfully, kneeling in front of the girl, helping her into the pale blue shoes.

"Will you not run to Mama?" she asked, standing up. "I am sure you could help her with something, or play with Robbie."

Emily nodded, grinned and bounced out of the room, closing the door after herself with a quiet click.

Only then did Elizabeth look up.

"Good afternoon," she said.

He swallowed visibly before answering, "Good afternoon."

Elizabeth walked to the window, and he followed her.

"I do not wish to wake the baby," she whispered, nodding in the direction of Fred, cocooned safely in the middle of the bed.

"Of course," he agreed, his eyes not leaving hers.

"I wanted to apologize," she spoke quickly.

Apparent surprise was written all over his face. "You?"

She blushed in embarrassment. "I should have not screamed or thrown the vase at you; not to mention that kicking you was for certain... the most unladylike deed I have ever allowed myself to do."

"It was nothing. I would gladly take a beating from your hand one more time."

She raised a doubtful eyebrow at him. "When I am angry, I stop thinking rationally," she explained. "I speak what comes to my mind without any kind of consideration of what I am saying and behave in a way I usually do not. It never lasts long, and I always regret it later. It is best to leave me alone at such times, and you insisted on staying."

"'Tis nothing," he repeated.

"You must think me to be some wild creature from the deepest darkest jungle of India."

He smiled. "No, I think that you are honest. You speak your mind. It is a rare quality, I assure you."

There was a long moment of silence before she felt his hand touching hers. "Please, may we speak? I beg you to let me explain."

She nodded. "Let us sit." There was a comfortable armchair near the window, in which she liked to read. It was too small for both of them to sit, unless she sat on his lap, which she would have objected to only two days ago, but certainly not today.

She walked across the room, to fetch a chair from under the vanity, but before she could pick up the heavy chair, he took it from her, carrying it effortlessly across the room.

As she took a seat, she gestured for him to sit on the chair opposite her.

She placed her hands in her lap and waited for him to start. He did not speak though, only stared at her as usual. His eyes lingered below her face, and as she followed his gaze, she noticed that the opening of her robe had loosened itself, and the top of her lacy nightgown was showing.

With a frown, she pulled the robe tighter over her front. He had already seen most of her, but after everything that had happened, she did not feel comfortable enough to let him look again. Why would he want to look at her in the first place, having such a beauty like Annette at his disposal? To make fun of her deficiencies perhaps? She wondered whether he had lied that afternoon in his bedroom when he had disrobed her. His eyes on her had been admiring, enamoured. Could he pretend this? Could this be only an act on his part?

That woman, his lover, had been so much more beautiful than Elizabeth could ever become - blonde, tall and voluptuous. Her mother claimed that she looked like a little dark boy, asking whether the Gypsies had changed her in the crib because of her brown hair and eyes. She tanned easily, and as a child, she had had to wear a bonnet every time she was outside, even though she hated it.

She was used to being compared to Jane. Elizabeth was never jealous of her sister. On the contrary, she admired Jane's beauty, and was very proud of how handsome her elder sister was. Her mother's words hurt her though, especially when she had been younger. Elizabeth had inherited her father's dark colouring and her mother's slight height. However, where her mother was round and curvy, she was slim and light.

At last he started to speak. She refused to look at him, and stared out of the window, but she listened carefully.

"Annette, the woman you and Georgiana saw yesterday, was my mistress for over a year, but it all ended a long time ago. The last time I visited her was early in December, after I returned from Netherfield. I wanted to forget about you. I spent one night with her, but did not return after that. I could not stop thinking about you, even when I was with her."

Elizabeth felt a wave of sickness rising in her throat. He had been thinking of her, while being with the other? She truly did not wish to hear that.

"The day you agreed to marry me, I went to her," he continued. "I told her that we were finished, that I was happily in love and about to be married. I promised to pay her allowance and bills for another six months so she had time to find a new... arrangement with someone else. As you know, she used it against me. I had no idea that she would be in that shop, nor did I know that she had attempted to approach Georgiana in the past. I thought that I could trust her, that she knew what I expected from her."

He did not say anything more. She glanced up at him, and seeing his expectant expression, she guessed he wished her to make some comment. She had no desire to speak. She felt disgusted.

"I went to her yesterday," he spoke again. "She admitted she had done what she did on purpose, to separate us. She hoped that you would break with me after her revelation. I told her in no uncertain terms that there is no such possibility for me to come back to her. She will not bother you or Georgiana anymore."

She kept silent and stubbornly looked out the window. It hurt too much to even speak of it, especially to him.

"Say something," he pleaded, reaching for her hand. She allowed him to keep her cold hand in his.

"She must love you if she risked so much," she whispered, surprised how hoarse her voice sounded.

"I do not care about her. If she cares for me, it is no concern of mine. She knows the terms of a mistress's contract. I paid for services which she agreed to deliver. Affection is not—was not—an option. Whatever she felt for me is her problem. I felt nothing for her."

She looked him straight in the eye, perhaps for the first time today. "Are you certain?" she asked, surprised with the coldness in her voice. "You have been with her for quite a long time. I do understand that you would not wish to marry someone like her, as it would bring shame to your family name. We both know how much it means to you."

He brought her hand to his cheek, kissing the inside of her palm. "Do not say that. I love only you."

She hunched her shoulders and looked down. She wished to stop feeling, if only for a short moment, to feel indifferent, numb to everything and everyone around her.

"Love, please, look at me."

She shook her head, tears running down her cheeks. He grasped her chin between his thumb and forefinger, forcing her to look at him.

"I swear on my mother's grave, I have not been with her since last December. I will never be with her again—not ever—even if…if you were to leave me," he said in a faint whisper.

She could see the sincerity in his eyes, his handsome face. Could she trust him? Her heart and mind answered no, but perhaps she expected too much. She would be able to build a good life for herself in Derbyshire. She would be a mistress of a beautiful estate, feel needed there. She would have children and enjoy the company of Georgiana, who proved her loyalty to her and was a good friend. Should she really wish for more? Was it realistic? Darcy was not wholly bad. She would never have what aunt Madeline had; that was for sure. However, he was generous and responsible; he would take care of her. He would never hurt her physically, what her aunt feared for her. He had had the opportunity yesterday when she had slapped and kicked him, and still he had never lost his temper with her. He did not seem to like children very much, but she doubted that he would neglect them. She would love their children for both of them, so they would never feel unwanted.

She nodded slightly, and it was enough to bring an expression of enormous relief to his face.

"Thank you, love." He moved to his knees in front of her, placing his head on her lap. "I will make this up to you, I promise."

She placed her hands over his shoulder, and he pushed farther into her body. They sat like that for a long time, till a whimper from the bed caught Elizabeth's attention.

She pushed Darcy away, and he looked up at her, disoriented.

She stood while Darcy was still on his knees, and hurried to the bed. Fred's blue eyes were open, and he was looking around for a familiar face.

He smiled instantly as he saw Elizabeth, reaching to him. She picked the baby up in her arms, swaying him gently. "You are awake, are you not? Yes, you are. Have you had a pleasant nap?" she cooed.

"Did we wake him?" Darcy asked, standing next to them.

"No, he just wanted a small reassurance that he was not alone," she said, smiling at the boy, kissing his hand.

"You seem attached to him," Darcy noted.

"He is my Godson," she explained.

"I did not know."

Elizabeth walked around the room with the baby, till she sat with him in the armchair. "Could you pass me that woollen blanket?" She pointed to the bed.

He fetched it instantly, and she wrapped it around the boy, whose eyelids were once again falling.

"Is he not beautiful?" she asked as Fred fell asleep for a second time, rooting his head against her chest.

"A handsome boy to be sure."

She leaned down and inhaled. "Babies have the most delightful scent." She looked up. "I have a favour to ask of you. It concerns the wedding."

He nodded, watching her with an earnest expression, and she could see fear in his eyes.

"I was wondering whether the wedding can take place here, in London."

"You wish to postpone?" he asked quickly.

She shook her head. "No, no, I do not. However, I do not feel the strength to face my mother, my younger sisters, and the entire neighbourhood. I want a quiet wedding, just my aunt and uncle, and your sister."

"What about Jane?"

"Jane," she sighed, "yes, I will miss her, but I will write her a long letter, explaining everything to her. She will understand."

"Everything you want," he said, leaning forward to kiss her forehead, "I will provide. I purchased a license some time ago; we can marry whenever we wish."

"Thank you," she nodded. "I will carry Fred to his crib," she said, standing up. "He should wake soon, and he will be hungry."

As she left Darcy alone in her room, she prayed that she was making the right decision for herself. She knew that she had to be strong, and fight for her future happiness or at least her peace of mind and emotional stability.

Chapter Nineteen

"Let us see, as for the first course... roast beef ribs with boiled vegetables, but only if we do not find good, fat chickens tomorrow... I would prefer chickens, naturally, much more elegant. Then baked pudding, two soups, white soup and pease-pottage, and fish of course, salmon sounds good. While for the second course, something lighter perhaps... fruit cakes, lemon tarts, cheesecakes, oysters and shellfish," Mrs. Gardiner mused, frowning over a menu, scribbling quickly with a small pencil. "What do you think, Lizzy? Will Mr. Darcy approve?"

Elizabeth did not give an instant answer, causing her aunt to ask. "You consider pease soup too common? We may replace it with Hartshorn Jelly served in my new crystal glasses."

Elizabeth shrugged her arms dismissively. "This dinner is so much trouble for you and uncle, as well as so much expense. There is truly no need for it."

Mrs. Gardiner regarded her niece for a long moment with a frown.

"Elizabeth, I do understand that the circumstances of your wedding are not what one would wish them to be, however, the attitude you displayed in the last days... is so unlike you. It is what I would expect from Lydia perhaps, or even Kitty, but not you. You refused having a wedding breakfast, very well, you do not want your mother to be present, I can understand that as well. Nevertheless, let me at least throw a dinner for Mr. Darcy's family - his sister and cousin. It is only right."

A single tear rolled down Elizabeth's cheek. "I want Jane to be here," she whispered.

"May I remind you that it was your idea to have the wedding in London, away from your sisters?"

"I never wanted to be away from Jane," Elizabeth sniffed, her voice croaking.

Mrs. Gardiner moved her chair closer to Elizabeth's. "Lizzy, what is the matter? What is happening to you?"

Elizabeth put her head on the table on her folded arms, hiding her face from view. "I am so unhappy."

Her aunt rubbed her back in a soothing motion. "These are just bridal nerves."

Elizabeth looked up, her cheeks wet from tears. "He has a lover," she blurted.

"Mr. Darcy?" Mrs. Gardiner whispered unbelievably. "That cannot be. He is so enamoured of you."

"It is the truth," Elizabeth whispered brokenly.

"'Tis why you were so upset and put yourself to bed for two days," the older woman guessed. "I wondered what had happened to put you in such a state. I simply thought that the two of you had had an argument. He was so contrite, asking to see you that day, desperate almost, now I can see why."

Elizabeth bit her lower lip, tears running steadily down her face. "I saw her in the shop that day. She asked to have the bill for her hat sent to Mr. Darcy as always."

"What did he say about it?" Mrs. Gardiner asked with a grim expression.

Elizabeth blew out a puff of air and dried her cheeks with the back of her palm. "He denied it, saying that the romance was finished months ago, long before he proposed to me."

"You do not believe him?"

"I do not know whether I should believe him. I am so confused. Everything has happened so fast."

"Oh, dear. Dear, dear." Mrs. Gardiner patted her back. "I think that we should tell your uncle and postpone the wedding."

"No!" Elizabeth protested. "You cannot."

"Elizabeth," the woman placed a calming hand on Elizabeth's shoulder, "your uncle will talk to him. You still have a family to protect you. He should answer some questions. He cannot think that he can do whatever he wishes."

"No, aunt, please, promise me that you will not tell anything to uncle," Elizabeth begged. "I am so ashamed of this."

"It is not you who should be ashamed," Mrs. Gardiner spoke firmly. "It is Mr. Darcy who should be embarrassed by his actions."

Elizabeth stared at her with teary eyes. "Please do not mention anything to uncle."

Mrs. Gardiner hesitated for a minute before nodding. "Very well... I will not talk to him about it for now, however, I want you tell me in greater detail what exactly happened."

"I will," she nodded, touching her forehead. "I cannot wrap my mind around it on my own."

"Your uncle should return home soon, but I will come to your room later after I put the children to bed."

Elizabeth nodded again, taking a handkerchief out of her pocket.

"Perhaps, you should wash your face with cold water," Mrs. Gardiner suggested. "I do not wish your uncle to see that you have been crying again. It worries him."

Elizabeth stood up and moved to the door with the intention of going upstairs to refresh herself. She was passing through the foyer when the doorbell rang. The hour was late, and she could not guess who the visitor might be. Surely it was not her uncle, for he would have simply walked in. She was not expecting Darcy either, because he assured her he would be very busy today, and that they would not see him till tomorrow's dinner.

Elizabeth waited till the servant opened the door, and to her great surprise, her sister Jane was standing in the doorway, with a small trunk behind her.

"Jane?!" Elizabeth ran to her. "What are you doing here?"

"Could you imagine me not attending the wedding of my most beloved sister?" Jane asked, laughing.

"I am so happy to have you here!" Elizabeth exclaimed, hugging her tightly. "However, what are you doing here? How?"

"Mr. Darcy, together with Colonel Fitzwilliam, brought me," Jane explained simply.

Elizabeth lifted on her toes to gaze past her sister. "Where is he?"

"He did not wish to interrupt."

"Jane!" Mrs. Gardiner's voice was heard behind them. "What a surprise!"

Elizabeth pushed past her sister and ran to the pavement outside the front door. She saw Darcy's carriage slowly pulling away.

"Ay!" she cried impulsively, running a few yards.

The driver must have heard her, because he turned his head, and seeing her, stopped the carriage. As Elizabeth caught up with the vehicle, the door opened and Darcy stepped out.

"Thank you!" she cried impulsively.

He laughed. "You are very welcome."

"You did not have to," she added.

He took a step closer, touching her cheek. "I knew you could not imagine your wedding day without Jane."

She smiled, nodding, then lifted on her toes to kiss his cheek. "Thank you."

He frowned and pulled her away from him to inspect her face in the early evening light. "You have been crying again," he murmured worriedly.

She shook her head, smiling. "Tis only bridal nerves, as my aunt says. I am well."

"Miss Bennet!" Colonel Fitzwilliam's voice boomed near them, bringing their attention. "It is a pleasure to see you in such high spirits."

Elizabeth grinned. "The pleasure is all mine, Colonel Fitzwilliam. I assure you."

"Go back to carriage. I wish a word in private with my lady," Darcy spoke brusquely, scowling.

Elizabeth blanched at Darcy's obvious rudeness. "Will I see you at the dinner tomorrow evening, Colonel Fitzwilliam?" she asked pleasantly, trying to cover Darcy's blunder.

The man bowed. "With great pleasure. Please give my thanks to Mrs. Gardiner for inviting me."

She nodded, smiling. "I will."

Darcy kept glaring at his cousin till he turned on his feet, returning to the carriage. Elizabeth chuckled, hearing colonel murmuring to himself about where he could find a girl running after his horse, wanting to thank him.

"You were so rude to him," Elizabeth whispered, once she was sure that colonel was out of earshot.

Darcy did not look even a bit remorseful. "He should have stayed in the carriage. It is not his business."

"He only wished to say hello."

Darcy shrugged, "I do not care." He put his arms around her. "I will see you tomorrow evening."

"Yes." She nodded. "We have just been discussing the menu. My aunt is very excited about the dinner."

He pulled her closer, so their bodies touched. "The day after tomorrow, before this hour, you will be my wife," he murmured in a low voice, before he caught her lips in a gentle kiss. "I am so happy," he whispered near her ear, before kissing her neck.

She shivered, more from the touch of his lips on her skin than the coolness of the early evening air.

"You should go back before you catch a cold," he spoke with authority, running his hands over her bare arms as her dress was short sleeved.

Elizabeth whispered good night, and after one more kiss, she walked away. As she turned her head, just before entering the house, she saw that he was still standing on the street beside the open carriage doors, looking after her.

***

"I feel responsible for all that mess," Colonel Fitzwilliam said.

Darcy shook his head. "Not your fault."

The cousins sat in the darkened study, with the only light coming from the fireplace.

"You found Annette through me, after all."

"I said that it was not your fault. I have only myself to blame," Darcy murmured, putting another log to the fire.

"You could not have known she would act in such a way," his cousin pointed reasonably. "Annette appeared reliable, smart about matters."

Darcy sank into an armchair, stretching out his long legs. "I should have been more careful in my dealings with women and trusted no one."

"What do you mean? You were always very circumspect, very discreet."

"I tell you one thing only, if in some twenty years, my son comes to me asking to raise his allowance because he wants to take a mistress, I will tell him to keep it in his breeches till he finds someone he wants to marry."

Colonel Fitzwilliam gave him a long, searching, slightly confused look. "Are you not too harsh with yourself?"

"Too harsh? No! You should have seen Elizabeth's face... Georgiana's too." Darcy grimaced. "Annette attempted to approach her for over a year. Can you believe that? What a fool I was not to see her true character. I have already had a talk with the shop owner. I sincerely hope Elizabeth and Georgiana will choose to patronize some other shop."

"I understand how upset you must be about this situation, but you are hardly a rake," the other man pointed out calmly.

"That is not the point. Elizabeth is disgusted with me. I can see it in her eyes."

"But you explained what happened. She believed you."

"She has no other choice but to believe me, Richard. Her mother and sisters are at my mercy, so she plays accordingly to show me her gratitude. I do not even wish to guess her true opinion of me. She understands our union as a duty, and all the warm gestures on her part belong to her inborn kindness and not her feelings for me."

"I think you are too impatient. You have been engaged for such a short time, and she still knows little of you."

Darcy curled his hand into a fist, striking his thigh with force. "I am simply furious with myself, my own stupidity. I have bought women all my adult life, and I want to buy her. I am not worthy of her. She is a far better person than I."

"Darcy, Darcy, calm down. You worry too much. Yes, the situation with Annette was unpleasant, but after you two are married for some time, Elizabeth will see the true you. She will learn to trust you, respect you, and eventually love you."

"I am not so certain of it," Darcy murmured darkly. "You know what she told me? She said that she could not wait to have a child so she could have someone to love."

"Well, you should be glad!" Colonel laughed jovially. "You two will be busy making little Darcys. I can think of many less pleasant activities."

"Glad?" Darcy stared at his cousin with incredulity. "She sees me as some kind of stud."

"And I am certain you will meet her expectations admirably."

"Richard, be serious for once! You do not understand what I am saying at all," Darcy cried with irritation.

Colonel Fitzwilliam was silent for a longer moment, only watching Darcy with thoughtful expression. "I do comprehend," he said in a quiet, suddenly serious voice. "You actually want her to love you and respect you for yourself, and not for who you are in the eyes of the world. I never thought you to be such a romantic at heart. You never spoke about your... well..." He made a wide gesture with his hands. "...feelings."

"I am surprised myself with this newly emerged trait of my character," Darcy admitted dryly.

"Elizabeth must be truly a most interesting woman," the colonel mused, "A few months ago, you thought that you were making her a great honour by proposing, and you could not believe that she might actually not want you. Now you are delivering to me the speech on how unworthy you are of her."

An unpleasant scowl twisted Darcy's handsome features. "I can see that I serve as a source of great amusement to you."

Colonel Fitzwilliam reached to slap his arm soundly. "No need to agonize yourself over this. You should simply tell her."

Darcy frowned. "Tell her what?"

"What you told me, that you are ashamed of your past, but you cannot change it, that you will make sure your children will not repeat your mistakes, and that you want her to love the real you."

"No."

"Why not?"

Darcy crossed his arms over his chest. "I will not make a fool of myself in front of her. Again."

"I think that she would appreciate your sincerity."

Darcy shook his head. "No."

"Then you have to be patient and attentive, and she will repay you with the same... in time," his cousin advised.

"I feel as if I am stepping on very thin ice around her," Darcy spoke with a sigh. "I am never certain how she will react to some matters, and Georgiana..."

"What about her?"

"She gave me an ultimatum. Can you believe that? When the whole affair with Annette came to light, my sweet baby sister threatened to leave me and move in with your parents if I do not make my peace with Elizabeth."

"Well... well," Colonel Fitzwilliam chuckled.

"What?"

"Do you realize what it means for you? You will have nothing to say in your own household with Georgiana and Elizabeth cavorting and conspiring together."

Darcy hesitated before answering. "I wanted them to become friends; I wished for it. I simply did not expect it to happen so quickly."

"All in all, I think you should be glad Georgiana has taken such a strong liking to Elizabeth. Imagine the alternative - my mother and sister-in-law for example. They dislike each other strongly, and that will never change. There is no such thing as a pleasant evening at Matlock when they are both in residence. You can cut the air with a knife because of the tension these two create. I feel for my father and brother."

Darcy nodded. "True, true. They are better fast friends than otherwise, even if it means them plotting against me."

Suddenly Colonel Fitzwilliam exclaimed. "Cheer up, Darcy! Your innocent bride to be and your baby sister crossed paths with your ex mistress, which resulted in some trouble to you, but in the end, you will have exactly what you wished for. You will be married to a woman you picked for yourself. Not everyone has such a luxury, if I may remind you. Every girl I fancy is too poor to take her into consideration. First Elizabeth and now her sister."

Darcy went all rigid. "What do you mean Elizabeth?"

Colonel Fitzwilliam shrugged. "I am only saying that if I were in your shoes, I would not be dragging my feet for months before proposing to her, inventing poor excuses."

"My doubts concerning our union were perfectly justifiable, at least I saw them as such at that time," Darcy offered proudly. "As for yourself, even if you had the means to make Elizabeth an offer, you have no guarantee that she would have accepted you," Darcy answered spitefully.

"Neither do you," the other man spoke with a calm smile. "If not for a tragic situation in her family, if her father was still living, would she have agreed? You said it yourself; she is doing her duty to her mother and younger sisters.

Darcy's eyes narrowed. "Thank you for reminding me."

"Do not worry," the colonel said in a gentler voice. "I would never have pursued Elizabeth knowing how much you care for her. Her sister, Jane, is a different matter though."

"You cannot afford to marry Jane. You two could live a modest, still comfortable life, but your children? What future would they have? You would have to marry your daughters to farmers, and sons... you would not be able to afford introducing them in the right professions."

"I am aware of that; however... there would be a chance, perhaps, for improving my financial status."

"I am glad to hear it," Darcy assured with sincerity. "May I ask how you plan to achieve it?"

Colonel smiled. "Were you not surprised that my parents were so accepting of your marriage?"

Darcy hesitated. "Yes, still I do not see the connection."

"You do not? My father is secretly glad that you antagonised Aunt Catherine so much. Are you aware that she changed her will?"

Darcy gave him a blank stare. "She did?"

"Yes. Until recently, you were to inherit Rosings Park in case of her and Anne's deaths."

"I was?"

"Of course. You did not know?"

Darcy shook his head and asked, "Aunt Catherine wants you to marry Anne?"

"No, I doubt that Anne is fit to marry anyone. Father said that she would probably not survive the next winter."

"Is she really that ill? I have always thought that her numerous ailments were just her mother's invention."

"It is confirmed. Anne is in the last stage of tuberculosis. Father thinks that our aunt will be willing to give Rosings to me. She has no other living relatives than us. It is said, as well, that the estate is not in the very best state, that under the right management, it could run at a much higher profit."

"Poor Anne. She was not my favourite relative; still, to die so young, before her life has even begun. Although I must say that I am quite happy for you."

"Yes, but the whole matter may take years. I am not certain whether Jane would wish to wait that long," Colonel Fitzwilliam wondered worriedly.

"You truly fancy Jane that much?" Darcy marvelled. "You barely know her. You have seen her twice."

"I am one and thirty. I know what I want. She is perfect for me: kind, beautiful. I have known enough women to recognize a jewel when I have one in front of me. Tell me, did you ever doubt Elizabeth's character, integrity and intelligence when you first met her?"

"Never."

"You have your answer. There is a matter of Bingley too... I have no way of knowing how close they are. Could you ask Elizabeth about it?"

"Elizabeth thinks that Jane cares deeply for Bingley," Darcy explained. "Still, I always found Jane very difficult to read. They are not engaged, and even if they were, the wedding would not take place soon because of their mourning. Jane seems very proper, and she puts a great deal to such matters. I would say that you have time. I would also advise you to have an honest conversation with Jane about your intentions. She is a very sensible and reasonable woman, as far as I have observed. Plus Elizabeth thinks highly of you and likes you," he grimaced visibly saying the last words. "I believe that she would encourage a union between you too. Sisters are very close. They rely on each other's opinions."

"I will try to talk to Jane tomorrow at the dinner."

"I think it is a good idea. If there is no hope, Jane will tell you so. She is not one to play games. What will you do next?"

"Father says that I should take a leave from the army and go to Rosings. Aunt plans to go with Anne to Bath, hoping to repair her health. She will need some help with the estate during her absence. As soon as I deliver Georgiana to Matlock after your wedding, I will travel to Kent."

"You should go. Such an occasion does not happen twice in a lifetime. I am more than happy to play the role of the ungrateful nephew. I will not even write to Aunt Catherine asking about Anne's health. Let her think the very worst of me."

"Thank you, Darcy," Colonel Fitzwilliam said with sincerity.

"To be truthful, I cannot see you marrying Jane. I think she will agree to Bingley's proposal. It is a safer option for her. Bingley seems quite taken with her. Nevertheless, I would wish for us to have sisters for wives." Darcy looked his cousin in the eye. "You are a brother to me, Richard, the one I never had."

The other man, taken aback with the confession, did not answer immediately. "Thank you. I dare say that Elizabeth has changed you, softened you."

Darcy flashed him a small smile. "Do not dare tell anyone."

***

"How horrible, Lizzy." Jane spoke with feeling as Elizabeth finished her tale of how she and Georgiana had encountered Annette in the shop.

"I have never suffered such humiliation in my life," Elizabeth admitted, closing her eyes. "I do not wish to even remember that day."

Mrs. Gardiner, who was seated at her other side, rubbed her back reassuringly. "Poor child. It is truly too much to bear in your situation."

"I will never return to that shop. Never!" Elizabeth swore. "They are still sending things for me from there, and I do not wish to even look at them, not to mention wear them." She smoothed the skirt of her old gown.

"They are only clothes, sister," Jane pointed out.

"I must agree with Jane," Mrs. Gardiner supported. "They are all very beautiful, the gowns, hats, gloves, shoes and underclothes... everything."

Elizabeth shook her head stubbornly. "I will not even touch them. They will remind me of that... that woman."

"Lizzy, I can only imagine how you feel, but please give this a second thought," Mrs. Gardiner reasoned. "You cannot go down the aisle in one of your old dresses, dyed black at home. Your wedding dress is perfect for the occasion."

Elizabeth stared at the offending garment, hanging on the hook on the door to her room. Her aunt was right, the dress was a modest grey-lilac adorned with black lace, with matching hat, spenser, gloves and shoes. The cut was the latest fashion with the shockingly high waist starting just under the bosom line. She was sure that no one in Meryton wore anything like that. Even in London, she had seen only a few similar dresses.

"Mr. Darcy spent a great deal of money on your new wardrobe," her aunt continued. "Not to mention the effort and time that Georgiana and I put into choosing the right materials and patterns which would suit you the best."

Elizabeth looked down at her hands, saying nothing.

"You cannot allow that cunning woman to influence your life, and if you refuse to wear those gowns, you will give her that privilege." Jane said.

"I cannot agree more with that," Mrs. Gardiner supported in a strong voice. "Mr. Darcy loves you, and he chose you, not her, and not any other. You should raise your head high, and concentrate on building a happy life for yourself as well as him."

Chapter Twenty

The night before her wedding day, Elizabeth slept for two hours only. She retired early enough to allow herself eight hours of good rest; however, she tossed and turned in bed for most of the night. As a result, she fell asleep shortly before dawn.

In the morning, she looked far from a radiant bride. The few pounds she had lost after her father's funeral, she had not gained back, and her usually slim frame was even thinner. It worried her, because Darcy had made himself clear that he would like to see more flesh on her body. She was pale and had dark circles under her eyes. Aunt Gardiner had attempted to cover them with rice powder, but it was to no avail.

Since she had risen at seven, all seemed to be a blur of small events: bathing, dressing, pinning up her long hair in an elaborate style, trying to swallow some breakfast with little success. Before she knew it, she was in front of the church and walking down the aisle supported on her uncle's arm.

As they were announced man and wife, Darcy leaned over to kiss her mouth gently, his hand on her cheek. Then she was outside, Darcy's strong hold on her arm keeping her close to him. She received congratulations and embraces from Jane, Georgiana and her aunt. Next Uncle Gardiner hugged her, whispering into her ear that she would always have a home with them.

From the corner of her eye, she registered Darcy vigorously shaking hands with Colonel Fitzwilliam and Mr. Gardiner, a wide grin gracing his face. Soon she was in the carriage, opposite her husband.

"Elizabeth, my love," he spoke softly, and she looked at him, perhaps for the first time that day.

"Yes," she answered in a voice which sounded as though it did not belonging to her.

He moved to sit next to her, his arm coming around her. "You are so pale, love."

"I could not sleep the entire night," she explained.

"You can sleep now," he said. "We have many miles to cover today."

She nodded, supporting her forehead against his arm.

He removed her bonnet and gloves, kissing her hands and then her forehead.

"Lean against me and close your eyes," he spoke soothingly, pulling her closer.

She did as he asked. She was not sure whether she was in a state to carry a meaningful conversation.

She did not remember the exact moment she fell asleep; however, all too soon he was shaking her gently, telling her to wake up.

"We need to stop for the change of horses," he explained the obvious as he waited for her to put her bonnet and gloves back on before leaving the coach. Even though it was sunny in London, here the sky was drawn with heavy clouds.

They entered the large, crowded inn where they were told that all the private rooms were taken. An unpleasant scowl appeared instantly on Darcy's face, and he was nothing but rude to the owner.

She tugged at the sleeve of his coat as they were being led to a quiet corner at the back of the large common area. "I do not mind staying here."

His jaw line turned sharp as he answered loudly enough for others to hear him, "I reserved a private room in advance. It is outrageous how we are treated."

As they sat at the table, she reached to take his hand. His expression softened as he raised her hand to his lips, kissing her knuckles. "There is no reason to be upset about this. I prefer to stay in the common room; it is much more interesting, so many people to watch."

He attempted a smile. "You are very gracious."

A very flustered girl appeared by the table, ready to take their order. Elizabeth had no appetite. Still, knowing that Darcy would be displeased with her not eating, she asked for tea and a slice of pie.

"Perhaps you would wish for something else, some soup, or meat?"

She shook her head. "I never eat much when travelling," she explained quietly, and to her relief he did not try to convince her to order more.

She drank her tea and ate her apple pie, while he attacked what he had on his plate; cold ham with sauce, some vegetables and pudding. He added soup and some tarts to it. He had always had an unchangeable voracious appetite, and usually devoured during one meal what she could eat through the entire day.

They were back on the road in an hour. Darcy was pleased with their progress, being certain that they would be at the inn where they were to spend the night well before dark. He tried to start the conversation several times, but she was too nervous to talk.

She was so distracted with her own thoughts, that only when they reached the inn where they were to spend the night, did she realize that they were not on the road north but to the south. She waited till they were left alone in their rooms before she asked for an explanation.

"Where are we going?" she questioned him, alarmed.

He smiled. "It is a surprise."

"Where are we going?" she repeated harshly.

"To Hove, a mile from Hove actually."

Her eyes widened. "Hove? Near Brighton?"

He pulled her closer to him. "For our honeymoon. I rented a small cottage outside Hove for two weeks."

"I thought we were to go to Pemberley," she said slowly, looking up at him, trying to decipher his expression.

"It is my wedding present for you. I thought you needed rest in some peaceful place, just the two of us, without family, without servants."

He was giving her an expectant look, obviously waiting for the praise; however, he was met only with a frown.

"You have not mentioned a word of it to me. You led me believe we were to go to Pemberley right after the wedding."

He shrugged his arms defensively. "It was supposed to be a surprise. How could I mention it to you?"

Her eyes narrowed. "Will our future life look like that? With you making decisions behind my back, expecting me to calmly accept them without any concern for my wishes and desires?" she questioned angrily.

"I do not understand…" He blinked repeatedly. "I wished to please you. You mentioned you never had been to the seaside. Therefore I thought you would be pleased with my gift."

Elizabeth closed her eyes, taking a long breath. "I appreciate your concern. Still, I would prefer, in the future, to be at least informed about your plans, especially when you include me in them. I think that I deserve that, at least, as your wife."

"You deserve nothing less." He nodded. "I see that you do not favour surprises though."

"It is not about me not liking surprises," she protested, striving to remain calm. "I understand that you have made all decisions by yourself from the early age, but I ask you to take me into consideration from this point on."

It was his turn to frown. "I do take you into consideration. I do everything with you in mind," he murmured defensively.

"Like taking me to the other end of England without a word of warning, not to mention asking my opinion?" she cried fiercely.

A familiar scowl graced his features. "It was supposed to be a surprise."

Elizabeth lowered her head, clenching her hands together. "I only ask you not to decide on behalf of me when it comes to matters which concern my person," she said quietly.

"Of course," he agreed stiffly. "As you wish."

An awkward silence fell between them. Elizabeth was upset for upsetting him, but she felt wronged by him. She was not a child to be delivered to places and occasions. She wanted him to discuss matters with her, not just tell her what to do and where to go. She was not a doll he could dress, feed or order around.

"Shall we have dinner here?" she gestured to the round table placed near the large window.

"Yes, I will see to the arrangements," he said, and with a formal bow, left the room.

She shook her head, trying to stop the tears from coming to her eyes again. She needed to get a handle of herself. After all, her wedding night was yet before her.

Slowly, she removed her bonnet, gloves and jacket. Two servants walked in, carrying her smaller trunk, as well as Darcy's. She asked them to put them into the second room, which was the bedroom, containing a large four poster bed.

Left alone, and not being sure whether a maid would be sent to help her, she began to undress. Growing up with four sisters had made her more than capable of taking care of herself in that respect.

She hung her pretty wedding dress neatly over the back of one of the chairs. Wearing only her petticoats and chemise, as she disposed of the stays as soon as she took off the dress, she opened the trunk to retrieve one of her every day dresses. She considered abandoning the stays completely for tomorrow. Her clothes fit well without them, and it would be much more

comfortable to sit for long hours in the carriage without the restricting garment hugging her midsection.

She put the fresh dress on the bed. Her mother called it a home dress, and it was something between a robe and a typical morning dress. She, her mother and her sisters had always worn similar ones whenever they stayed indoors in their own company due to bad weather or illness. It had a very simple design, lacked buttons at the back and was tied at the side with small ribbons. She hoped that Darcy would not mind her casual appearance; after all he had already seen her in much less.

She went behind the small screen to refresh herself. There was still warm water in the bowl, and scented soap beside it. She lowered the straps of her chemise, and naked from the waist up, she washed her face, neck, arms and chest. She was drying herself when she heard the heavy steps and commotion in the sitting room. She heard Darcy calling her name loudly in alarm.

"Elizabeth!" he cried, bolting inside the bedroom.

"I am here," she answered nervously. Clutching the towel to her chest, she stepped from behind the partition so he could see her.

"Thank God," he breathed, and in two large steps he was in front of her. "Why did you not answer when I was calling you?"

"I was lost in thought, I did not hear you," she explained. "I only wished to refresh myself."

He wrapped his arms around her, leaning down till she felt his nose against her neck. "I thought you were gone."

She pushed away from him, giving him a confused look. "Gone where?"

He shook his head with a smile. "Nothing, nothing."

One of his hands cupped her shoulder, the other went around her to stroke her naked back. "Our dinner should be served soon. I came to ask whether you need the help of a maid."

She stared into his eyes. "Thank you, but I do not need help. If you will allow me a few minutes, I shall join you in the sitting room."

"Of course." His hands dropped from her body.

She sighed in relief as he left her alone. With haste, she finished dressing. She brushed her hair and tied it loosely with a ribbon in a low ponytail. Her scalp itched from wearing the heavy mass up all day long.

When she joined Darcy at the table in the sitting room, he gaped at her for long moment.

"You look lovely," he murmured.

"Thank you," she whispered. "What do we have for dinner?" she asked with forced enthusiasm.

"Everything you like," he assured, taking the lids off the dishes.

***

"Are you certain?" Darcy asked, as he loomed over her supported on one arm.

Elizabeth was on her back, her legs spread so she could accommodate her husband. She was still dressed in her nightgown, but it was very thin, so she could feel his warmth through it.

"I am," she answered staring into his eyes.

"We can wait. I will not mind," he whispered, stroking her cheek.

In response, she bent and lifted her legs, pressing them shyly to his sides.

He kissed her lips, his hand on her breast. She closed her eyes, silently allowing him to touch her.

As he nuzzled her neck, his hand went to her knee, lifting her nightgown slowly.

"You are so tense," he murmured, touching her leg. "There is no need for this. I will not harm you." He punctuated his words by stroking the inside of her thigh.

"I know," she spoke in small voice. "I am well."

It seemed to appease him, as soon she felt him touch her private place. She closed here eyes again, concentrating on the gentle caress of his fingers. It took him some time to arouse her, but after a few minutes of devoted stroking, combined with kisses on her neck and face, she felt hints of pleasure shimmering between her legs.

She sighed in content, straining against his searching fingers. He opened her gown, pushing it to her navel, and began kissing all over her bosom, his hand never abandoning her private place. She arched her back, biting on her lower lip, her eyes squeezed tight as she tugged at his hair.

A moment later, he was hovering above her again, settling himself firmly between her legs. He arranged one of his arms above her head for support, while with the other guided himself into her. When she felt him against her, she turned her head to the side not wishing to look.

"Lizzy, love, you need to relax," he murmured, pressing her farther into the mattress.

She tried to listen to his words, but she was terrified and felt suffocated by him. Only now did she realize how much bigger he was than she. She took a few calming breaths, but it helped little to calm her racing heart.

He pushed a little, and her eyes widened at the feeling of the unfamiliar fullness.

"Love," he panted, his eyes darkened and blazing. "You must open up and allow me to come inside."

She had no idea how she could accommodate him on that. She gasped as he pulled her right leg up, hooking it with his arm. Then with one swift move he was inside of her.

The cry died in her throat, and she was certain that she might have fainted from the sharp pain inflicted on her. Her aunt had mentioned discomfort, but this was beyond anything she imagined, or ever experienced. It had hurt much less when she had broken her arm falling from the elm tree in her father's garden when she was ten years old.

Tears pricked out of her eyes as she bit back a sob and silently prayed for him to finish as soon as possible. Incoherently, amidst her own pain, she noted his low voice murmuring, telling her how good she felt, and how tight she was.

At last, after what seemed an eternity, but in truth was only a few shorts minutes, he grunted above her, and dropped heavily on top of her. She was afraid that he would truly suffocate her, but thankfully he rolled on his back, his eyes closed.

Elizabeth stared at the canopy trying to assess the damage done to her. Hesitantly she sat up, feeling the shooting pain in all her lower body. Her back hurt, as did her legs, while her privates burned, both on the inside and outside.

She tugged her gown up, tying the ribbon at her bosom with shaking hands.

"Are you well?" he asked, causing a cold shiver to run down her back. He sat behind her, gathering her hair to the side, kissing her neck.

She was not able to respond, nor hide her face as he took her chin to make her look at him.

He saw her tear stricken face. "What is the matter?" he cried in alarm.

"It hurt so much," she admitted.

He ran a hand over his face, before pulling the nightgown up, revealing her slim thighs. "Good God," he said, seeing the blood smeared on her skin.

He jumped out of bed without another word, picking his breeches and shirt from the floor and pulling them on hastily. Soon he was out of the room.

Elizabeth curled in a ball on the edge of the bed, weeping in her misery.

She did not know how much time passed, but the next thing she felt was his hand, shaking her arm gently. She turned her head to look at him through tears.

"I have some warm water," he explained, a washcloth in his hand. "It should soothe you."

She allowed him to raise her gown again and open her legs. She was beyond any shame by then. She winced as the warm cloth touched her torn flesh. Thankfully, after a moment of his ministrations, she began to feel a little better. He left the cloth between her legs, and went to search through her trunk, coming with a fresh gown to replace the blood stained one.

"Thank you," she whispered as she put on the fresh garment.

"How are you feeling?" he asked, great concern written all over her face.

She lowered her head, staring at her hands. She was propped against the pillows, the bed covering pulled up to her chest. "Better," she whispered, not looking at him.

He took her hands in his, kissing her fingers. "Forgive me for causing you pain. I would rather cut my hand off than hurt you."

She managed a pale smile. "I heard it was expected to feel some pain the first time."

He stood up and began pacing the room, running his hand repeatedly over his face and tugging at his hair. "I am an idiot," he murmured over and over again.

She did not know what more she could say, so she turned on her side with her back to him, whispering. "I am exhausted. Good night." She closed her eyes, and attempted to regulate her breathing as well as her racing heart, to simulate a peaceful rest.

However, she truly calmed down only when she heard him leaving the room. She did not know how long he was gone, but she was fast asleep when he returned.

Her eyelids fluttered as she felt him pulling her into his arms. She closed them quickly, not wanting him to notice that she was awake. He kissed her temple, and as his breath fanned over her face, she smelled alcohol on it. She had no strength to wonder what to think of it. She allowed him to cradle her to his chest, and slowly fell into deep sleep.

Chapter Twenty-One

Darcy stepped quietly into the bedroom for perhaps the fifth time that morning. It was after nine, and she was still in deep slumber, not making the slightest sound. Her small frame was very still, buried under the bed covers so that only her dark brown curls were peeking out. He surmised that she must have fallen asleep around ten o'clock last night, so she had been out for almost twelve hours. He did not know what to think about this, as he had learned long ago that she was an early riser.

He perched on the edge of the bed, considering whether he should wake her. A hot bath had been drawn, the tub sitting in the next room. He had ordered it, thinking it would help to soothe her soreness.

He cringed every time his mind returned to the night before. They should have waited. He was an inconsiderate brute. He knew that she was not ready; he had felt it deep down in his heart, and yet still he had done that to her. It was his role to be wiser as he was the older and more experienced one. He should have kissed her on the forehead and order her to sleep.

He had tried to be gentle, prepare her the best he could, and she had been wet for him, she truly had been. Nevertheless, he had hurt her—hurt her in more ways than one. God forgive him!

Bedding an innocent, sheltered girl was nothing like his past experiences. He had no idea that everything would feel so different. It was so much better, deeper, more real; but at the same time frightening and intimidating. The overwhelming responsibility he felt for her shook his very being, making him weak and defenceless.

The women of his past had not been virgins. They had known what to expect. They had usually been more knowledgeable than him when it came to intimate relations. Elizabeth was like day to night when compared to them.

He had no friends he could have talked to about the marriage bed experience, as Bingley and Richard were bachelors. There was Henry, Richard's older brother, who had been married for some time. However, they had never been close enough to make that kind of conversation comfortable between them.

He tugged at his hair roughly, the pain in his scalp bringing his battered soul odd relief. His only hope was that she would not hate him again after last night. He was not eager to make love to her any time soon, definitely not before she was completely healed and in better spirits. He prayed she would allow him to touch her again in the future.

So lost in his thoughts was he that at first he did not notice when she began to stir. Her eyes opened, then closed, before her eyelids fluttered again. At last she sat up, looking disoriented around the room.

"Good morning," she whispered, her voice hoarse.

He swallowed. She was speaking to him. Thank heavens!

"What time is it?" she wanted to know.

"Past nine."

Her big eyes widened even more and she sat up. "Why have you not woken me before now? We were supposed to be on the road over an hour ago."

He moved closer to her. "Tis not important. You need to rest today. You are not fit to travel."

"I am well," she protested.

"Like you were well yesterday?" he asked more sharply than was his intention.

She gave him another one of her round eyed glances, staring at him like a small animal caught by a hunter.

"You have to be honest with me," he spoke evenly, pinning her with his gaze.

She frowned. "I am."

"You were not last night. You were not ready to be with me, even though you insisted that you were. I do not read minds, Elizabeth. You must be more forward with me about these matters - more sincere. I hurt you, and this could have been avoided, at least to some degree, had we waited. You were far from ready; still you told me to proceed."

She answered something, but so quietly that he did not catch it.

"Say again," he prompted.

"I thought you expected it," she whispered.

"I told you that I would not mind waiting till you are ready."

"I thought that you were telling me that out of kindness only."

He ran his hand over his face. "Good God, Elizabeth! Try to listen to me sometimes and believe what I say! I do not speak falsehoods."

"I thought you wanted it, and I wanted to please you." She paused, biting down on her lip with her small white teeth. "That afternoon when you took me to your room... and all those women in your life. I guessed you needed to do this often. I wanted to accommodate you. I feared you would go back to her if I did not..." She twisted her slim fingers, tears watering her eyes again.

He cupped her cheek, making her look at him. "I love you. I want you to feel safe with me - happy. I will not become upset if you are not willing to be with me every single night. It truly offends me when you say you believe I would be willing to break my wedding vows to go to some other woman..." He gripped her delicate shoulders, hoping to pour some reason into her. "I love you. Do you hear me? Whether you sleep with me or not, I love you."

She stared at him with dark, tearful eyes for a moment, before she produced a loud sob and moved to him, wrapping her arms around his neck. He pulled her on his lap, cradling her tightly.

"No more of this. You must trust me a little for your own peace of mind," he murmured, rubbing her back.

She nodded vigorously into his chest, her weeping slowly subsiding.

"Come." He stood up with her in his arms. "Your bath is ready."

She did not protest when he carried her to the sitting room where the portable tub was sitting

The water was just right by now, not too hot, but still decently warm.

He turned around when she removed her gown and climbed naked into the water. He stood by the window with his back to her as she washed herself, judging by the sound of the water splashing.

"Can you help me with my hair?" she asked after some time.

He turned to see that she sat with her legs drawn to her chest, her hair sticking in various directions, the white soap suds covering the dark mane.

Silently he helped her rinse her hair, later wrapping a large towel around her head. He helped her out, making sure not to stare too much at her naked form. His heart tugged, however, when he noticed how thin she was.

Soon he had her dressed warmly, sitting in an armchair by the blazing fireplace.

"How are you feeling?" he asked.

She smiled brightly, energetically drying her long hair with a towel. "Much better, thank you."

"Are you very sore?" He put his hand on the top of her thigh to indicate his meaning.

She blushed. "Not so much after the bath."

"I never wanted to hurt you."

She looked him in the eye. "It was not your fault. It could not be avoided. You tried to spare me discomfort."

He let a heavy sigh. "You are very gracious. I can only think with abhorrence of what I did."

She reached to take his hand. "There is no need for that. I truly feel better, and we can still travel today."

"No, today is for you to rest," he insisted. "We will go tomorrow, early in the morning."

She did not protest any more to his plans. He was pleased to see that she ate more for breakfast than usual. He proposed a nap, expecting her to dismiss the idea, but she agreed. He winced as he observed her walking awkwardly towards the bed, her usual graceful gait replaced with the slow trudging. He wanted to shoot himself seeing this, knowing he had caused it.

He was surprised but pleased, a warm sensation filling his chest when she reached for him, making him lay by her side, asking him to stay till she fell asleep.

He stayed with her for an hour before he left to speak with his servants. When he returned, she was still in deep slumber. She must be very exhausted, he thought, if she needed so much sleep.

As he sat down next to the bed, looking at her, he wondered where they were going.

***

"There is no one there," the footman said as he peered inside one of the windows.

It was close to eight in the evening; the sun was setting as they arrived at the cottage Darcy had rented for their two-week stay.

"The servants were supposed to wait for us yesterday evening with dinner," Darcy mentioned.

"Perhaps they reached the conclusion that you had changed your plans when we did not come yesterday, and resigned from the stay," Elizabeth suggested.

Darcy nodded. "That is possible. Thankfully, I have a key. The owner sent it to me in the letter last week."

"Are you certain that it is the right cottage?" Elizabeth asked apprehensively, worrying they were about to invade someone else's property.

"Oh, yes, I vacationed here once with my parents and Georgiana when she was still a baby," he assured. "I remember it well."

Darcy produced the key from the inner pocket of his coat and proceeded to open the front door. His wife followed him closely.

"It is lovely," Elizabeth said as she glanced around the interiors. "So light and spacious, though it looks so small on the outside."

Darcy gave a thoughtful expression. "I must send the driver to Brighton to contact the owner. I have his address written down somewhere."

"It is quite late, and the horses are tired, the same as the driver and the footman," she pointed out. "Would it not be wiser to wait till tomorrow?"

"The owner must send servants, a cook and a maid at the very least," he insisted. "Who will make dinner?"

She fought hard not to laugh at the low prolonged rumble coming from his stomach. Someone must be hungry.

"There must be something left in the pantry," she replied calmly. "We shall be fine for one night."

He stepped from one foot to the other, obviously undecided.

"We shall be fine," she repeated with force. "I will look through the pantry. You go see to our trunks being unloaded, and see which room above stairs is suitable for us."

He seemed taken aback by her ordering, but after a short moment of hesitation, he nodded his head silently, and stepped out of the house.

Elizabeth found the kitchen and was pleased to see that the pantry was well stocked. She found bread, a bit of ham, cheese, eggs and even cake. She decided to make sandwiches, and if she managed to start the fire in the stove, perhaps even tea and scrambled eggs. There was a large, clean apron on a hook, which she had to wrap around herself several times. Still, it protected her pretty dress.

When she had the sandwiches and tea on the table, and two dozen eggs were sizzling on the large frying pan, she called in a raised voice. "Dinner is ready."

Heavy steps were heard and soon Darcy appeared.

He stood frozen in the middle of the kitchen with his mouth agape.

"You made all this by yourself?" he asked unbelievably. "And in such a short time?"

She smiled modestly. "I only cut the bread, ham and cheese into sandwiches."

He sniffed, stepping to the stove. "You fried eggs," he cried, wide eyed, as she moved the pan off the fire.

She shrugged. "It was not that difficult. I observed our cook making scrambled eggs for the servants many times as Jane and I prepared tea. It was rather tricky to start the fire in the stove, but I managed somehow."

He pulled her into a hug. "You are one in a kind. I lack the words."

A warm feeling filled her at his praise. He kissed her rosy cheek, warmed from the heat, and sat himself behind the table, clearly expecting to be served his food.

She gave him a pointed look.

"What about your men? They must be hungry too."

"We will give them the leftovers," he dismissed her concern.

"They need to eat something warm. They have not had a warm meal since breakfast early in the morning."

His bushy eyebrows rose almost to his hair line. "You expect them to eat with us?"

"Please call them here," she insisted.

He shook his head no, eagerly eyeing the pan with hot eggs.

Elizabeth put the pan back on the stove and came to the window.

Opening it wide, she called out. "Ay, can you come here? I need your assistance."

A minute later, the driver and footman appeared in the door to the kitchen. Elizabeth asked them to sit down. She filled the four plates with eggs, setting the smallest portion for herself.

The servants seemed unsure how to behave, but as Darcy said nothing, they thanked her for the food and began to eat.

Twenty minutes later, there were only sparse crumbs left on the table. It was obvious that the footman and driver had similar appetites to their Master.

As soon as they finished, the men stood up and thanked Elizabeth once again, quite profusely, bowing in front of her. They called her Mistress, and somehow the title pleased her immensely.

"Where are they going to sleep?" she wanted to know when they left.

"There are some rooms next to the stables," he explained. "They shall be fine."

"More tea?" she asked.

"No, thank you." He pulled her onto his lap, nuzzling her neck. "It was all delicious."

"You have a French cook at Pemberley, as Georgiana told me. I am certain you usually eat much more sophisticated dishes than bread, cold ham and fried eggs."

"You underestimate yourself, as always. You must accept the truth: that I have an intelligent, beautiful, and very capable wife." He lifted her hands to his lips, kissing her slim fingers.

Her expression fell visibly. "You do not have to say that," she murmured, trying to lift from his lap.

He frowned, keeping her firmly to himself. "I do not understand."

"I am not beautiful," she clarified, avoiding his gaze. "I know what I look like. I can be called pretty on my good days, but nothing more."

"You are beautiful to me." He squeezed her to him, his gaze earnest. "You think I would lie to you?"

She hesitated with an answer before shaking her head no.

He captured her lips in a gentle kiss. She responded, opening her mouth to his tongue, locking her arms around his neck, her fingers tugging at his hair.

Darcy grunted softly, breaking the kiss.

"You certainly gained the approval of my servants," he changed the subject.

"Truly?"

He nodded. "Yesterday, when I explained that we had to delay our trip because you felt unwell, I thought that Black, the driver, would kill me with his gaze, as it was so disapproving. He drove my parents, and I think he considers himself a father figure to me. He said nothing, but must have guessed what I did to you."

"You did nothing to me," she protested.

"I should have been gentler," he said regretfully.

"I told you many times that it could not have been helped." She stroked his cheek. "I feel so much better today. There is no need for you to torture yourself about this matter any longer."

He did not seem particularly convinced with her reasoning, but let it go, asking whether she wished to retire for night.

"Can we see the sea?" she asked animatedly. "I can smell the salt and hear the gulls in the air, crying. I want to see them."

"Now?"

"It is not yet completely dark. Is it far from here?"

"Not very far, not more than a hundred yards behind the garden."

The walk to the shore was indeed short, and Elizabeth was delighted with the view of a small beach, guarded from both sides by the bushes and tall grass. The birds circled in the air and occasionally dove for whatever they had spied. She knew soon they would nest for the night. Well pleased with all she saw, she stopped to retrieve a small seashell.

"We will have privacy here. No one should come here but us," Darcy assured.

Elizabeth tossed her treasure in the surf and ran to the very edge of the water. Bending down, she splashed water with her fingers and laughed.

Darcy stood behind her, watching her reaction.

"I owe you an apology," she said, looking up at him with sincerity. "I should have been more appreciative about your surprise." She raised her hand to her brow for a better view and stared at the sea, inhaling the sharp air. "I feel that I will like it here." She reached for his hand. "And very much so," she said with a smile.

He returned her smile with one of his own. The touch of her small hand in his and the soft look in her eyes warmed his heart as he began to think—to hope—there just might be a happily ever after for them after all.

They walked hand in hand up the sloped sandy dune past the tall grass to their honeymoon cottage.

Chapter Twenty-Two

Elizabeth smiled in contentment at the sensation of the sea breeze combined with the sun rays sweeping over her face. On opening her eyes, she saw the bluest sky she had ever encountered. It was the tenth day of their stay at the cottage near Hove, and she was sad to think that in a few days, they would have to return to reality.

She sat up, brushing the sand from the tartan blanket spread beneath her, and from her bare feet. She wore no stockings or garters, as she had not bothered to put them on in the morning. They had never left the cottage and its surroundings since they had arrived here; neither had they admitted guests. It allowed her to abandon her footwear completely. Darcy did not seem to mind, only smirking from time when he caught the sight of her feet. As a child, she had loved running barefoot, even though she had been vehemently denied it. Her mother had disapproved of the habit very strongly, and always made sure that her second daughter had put on silky stockings and pretty leather shoes, even on the hottest of summer days.

There were times when Elizabeth had succeeded in abandoning her shoes, hiding them in some safe place (like her father's library, which was excellent for the purpose) to be able run barefoot to Lucas Lodge to play with Charlotte and her siblings. Her mother had always discovered the truth though, usually learning it from an equally scandalized Lady Lucas. The woman had never failed to comment how Elizabeth had again come for a visit wearing nothing on her legs.

Tilting her head, she put a hand over her eyes to create a shadow against the sharp sunlight, hoping to catch a glimpse of her husband, who had been in the water for the last half hour. Darcy was an excellent swimmer, but still she worried whenever he disappeared in the waves for a long time.

Her eyes narrowed as they focused on the tall, lean form emerging from the water.

He never bothered with clothes, swimming naked. It was quite a shock when she had caught sight of his bare bum disappearing in the waves.

She was certain he did not notice her watching him, and she laid down on her side, pretending to sleep.

Soon a shadow came over her. She cracked one eye slightly open, and observed through her eyelashes as he dried himself with a towel before pulling on his breeches. His manhood looked so small, probably shrivelled from the coldness of the water. It was impossible to believe that it was the very same thing which had caused her such discomfort.

"Have you not been in the sun for too long?" he asked, dropping to his knees next to her.

She stilled her body, shutting her eyes, fighting hard to prevent the giggle emerging from inside.

"Perhaps you should have brought a parasol," he offered. "I do not wish you to suffer from a heat stroke."

"I am in deep slumber, taking a nap," she murmured in a low voice, not opening her eyes. "That is why I cannot hear you."

She sensed him stretching beside her, the substantial weight of his arm resting on her waist.

"You have not been in deep slumber for some time now."

Opening her eyes, she smiled up at him. "How perceptive of you, Mr. Darcy. Will you teach me to swim?" she asked, changing the subject.

He seemed surprised with her request, giving her a searching, confused look. "You have never before said that you want to learn."

She shrugged. "I want to now. Can I? Will you teach me?"

She did not mention that her monthly bleeding had ended only two days ago, which prevented her from asking for a swimming lesson previously. She could not help but feel some disappointment when a few days after her wedding, like every month, her courses had come.

She was obviously not with child, which would have been the only pleasant thing derived from her wedding night. She frowned inwardly, thinking how unjust she was. Not everything she had experienced that night deserved such a harsh evaluation. The kisses and caresses which had come at the beginning had been most enjoyable. The conversation which had come the next morning had been both enlightening and freeing, allowing her to understand Darcy better and trust him more.

Becoming a mother was still her wish, though she was less than eager to participate in the activities necessary to beget the child. Her husband was very accommodating in that aspect, and did not pressure her into rekindling their marital relations. They shared a bed, even though there were two more spare bedrooms in the cottage. He was a perfect gentleman when it came to respecting her personal space. He touched her every day and night, but innocently. He kissed and embraced her, but still he kept his hands as a respectable distance, never touching her bosom or lower body.

She was aware that such a state would not last forever. The soreness between her legs had abated completely and her spirits were much improved. There was no point in delaying what was unavoidable. Perhaps she should allow him closer this evening? She would not conceive any time soon if all they did was kiss, embrace, and hold hands.

"Are you certain?" His question brought her back from her musings to the present moment. "You wish to learn how to swim?"

"Quite certain."

"You had such a serious expression painted on your face a moment ago," he noted.

"I was thinking…" she hesitated, before admitting shyly. "My soreness is gone."

He frowned. "Your soreness…" His eyes widened in understanding after a moment. "Elizabeth, dearest, we have time. You do not have to feel pressured."

"My courses have just ended. I am not with child," she confessed bluntly.

"This worries you?" he asked, his expression unreadable to her.

"We could try again," she said, avoiding the direct answer and his eyes.

"You want a child so much?" She sensed sadness in his tone.

"You do not?"

He was thoughtful for a moment before speaking, his voice and expression cautious. "I have not changed my opinion since our last conversation about children. Would it not be better to wait till you settle into your new life? There is no hurry. We have been married for less than two weeks. We are young. The children will come one day, sooner or later. Let us not fret about it now, hmmm?" He gave her an easy smile, but it did not reach his eyes.

She nodded, not quite convinced with his reasoning, but choosing not to speak of it more for now. Tonight, she decided, she would put on the nightgown which she had received as a gift from her aunt. It was, for the lack of the better words, indecent, and she hoped it would break his resolve to wait.

"What about my swimming lessons?" she asked, hoping to distract him from the previous subject.

"Today perhaps?" He smiled, brushing the wisp of hair falling over her eyes. "The sea is calm enough, but I think that we should wait till later in the afternoon, when the water is warmer, or even closer to the evening."

He turned to lie on his back, pulling her with him. She followed eagerly, placing her head on chest, her arm draped over his waist. His skin was pleasantly cool from his swim.

"This is how I think an afterlife will be for me, if I am fortunate enough to reach Heaven," he said after a moment of silence between them.

She lifted on her elbow, staring down at him with a small frown. "An afterlife? Is it not a little too soon to be thinking about that?"

His eyes met hers with serious intensity. "I cannot imagine anything more perfect after I die."

An army of butterflies invaded her stomach, a sensation she had often felt lately when in his presence. Many times she was unable to break eye contact with him, as if he had some kind of power over her.

"Do you believe that we will meet our loved ones there; your parents, my father?" she asked as she sat up cross-legged on the blanket.

"I want to believe in that. I want them to be happy, and I know that they are, because they are together again. I would like to see my mother, so she could embrace me once more." He looked straight in front of himself, his voice even, but laced with underlying emotion. "My father, too, so we could explain all the misunderstandings we had in the years before he died."

"If you need an embrace, I am always here," she spoke quietly.

He sat up too, placing one hand on her knee, the other cupping her cheek. "I know."

Shyly, she wrapped her arms around him, hugging him to her with all her might, his head placed over her shoulder.

"I would wish to believe that Papa is looking over us, over me, Jane and our younger sisters," she confessed when he pulled away from her.

"I would like my parents to be proud of me."

"They are," she assured fervently.

"I have my doubts about that," he spoke slowly. "They were exceptional people, both of them. They taught me how to be a good man, all the right principles, and I know that I failed them."

She took his hand in her much smaller hands, giving it a firm squeeze. "You did not."

"I did." He looked her right in the eye. "I am not the man they wanted me to grow into. I can feel it deep down in my heart. I failed Georgiana when I allowed Wickham near her last summer. I did not protect her. I can be selfish and self concerned. What is worse is that most of the time, I do not see myself as being such. I do not even want to mention what I did to you."

She rolled her eyes. She was fed up with hearing him agonizing himself about their wedding night. "I am well. I have assured you so many times. You are too hard on yourself. There is always a room for improvement when someone is aware of one's imperfections."

He pulled her down on the blanket then for a long, sweet kiss.

"Can we stay here forever?" she asked dreamily as she settled back against his chest, mirroring their earlier pose.

"No, not forever. Nevertheless, we can prolong our stay for a few days."

"You need to return to Pemberley," she stated the obvious.

"You will love Pemberley."

"Oh, I am certain that it is most lovely. Aunt Gardiner said that it was the most charming place she had ever had pleasure of seeing, a perfect balance of nature and human creation."

"I cannot argue with that," he said as he brought her closer and kissed the top of her head.

She hesitated for a moment before she spoke again. "I am apprehensive about…"

"Yes?" he encouraged, his voice deep and soft.

"Will I be a good Mistress?"

"Oh, it is guaranteed," he answered instantly. "Without a shadow of a doubt, you will be the best Mistress Pemberley may wish for. I will be there to help you, as will Mrs. Reynolds. However, I do not believe you will need our assistance. You will manage brilliantly on your own."

She lifted on her elbow to look into his face. "You seem to have much faith in me."

"Why should I not?" he asked, burying his hand in her thick hair.

At his insistence, she had worn her hair down since they had come here. He admitted to preferring it like that, and she was happy to please him with such a small gesture. It was a nightmare, however, to brush the knots out of it by the end of the day.

"You are compassionate and kind, more so than I. Moreover, it was my impression that your mother had taught you well about household matters."

Her spirits dropped instantly at the mention of her mother. Lately, a feeling of overwhelming guilt had built in her, growing stronger and stronger with every day. Despite all the differences between them, she should have allowed her mother to participate in the wedding. She knew how much Mrs. Bennet cared for such matters, if only so she could talk about it to all her friends for the rest of her life.

"Can we go to Brighton later today, or tomorrow perhaps?" she asked, changing the subject.

She could see that he was surprised with her request. Still, he agreed without hesitation. "Of course, my love, if you wish it."

"I do wish it. I would like to buy some gifts for Mama and the girls," she explained.

He gave her a searching look. "You wish to stop by Hertfordshire on our way to Pemberley?" he guessed.

"Can we? I feel that I should."

He reached his other hand to stroke her back reassuringly. "Naturally. We will need to make at least three stops on our way to Derbyshire, one of them can be Meryton."

"I do not want to stay at Purvis Lodge though."

"Neither do I," he admitted. "We will sleep at Netherfield. Bingley will be happy to host us. It is always better than the best of inns."

She nodded, imaging what the meeting with her mother would be like. To be truthful, she dreaded it. As she raised her eyes to him, she noticed that he was also lost in thought.

"Did Jane mention something to you last time you spoke, the night before our wedding?"

She blinked, taken aback with his question. "What do you mean? We talked about a few matters that evening, but we both retired early."

"I see. I did not manage to speak with Richard either," he murmured more to himself than to her.

"Richard? Colonel Fitzwilliam, your cousin?" she questioned, her eyes narrowed. "What is there with him and Jane?"

"I am not sure whether we should discuss this between us," he tried to dismiss her. "It is their personal business."

"Personal business? What personal business may Colonel Fitzwilliam have with my sister?" she cried in alarm.

He seemed reluctant to answer, but her stare was unwavering.

"He sought my advice," Darcy admitted at last. "It seems that he would wish to court her. He wondered how serious the relationship between her and Bingley is, and whether he may have a chance with her."

"Colonel Fitzwilliam wishes to marry Jane?" she exclaimed unbelievably. "That is most astonishing! How can this be? She is too poor for him to consider! He told me himself that he could not marry where he wished to."

It was Darcy's turn to frown. "He told you that? Why? When?"

"Back in Kent," she answered.

He sat up abruptly, making her do the same. "Why should he confess such intimate matters to you?"

She lifted her shoulders in a defensive gesture. "We talked a few times as he joined me during my daily walks, and one time he explained his life situation to me. I do not remember the exact words, or how we came to this subject. Still, I am certain I understood him correctly. He said that as a second son he would need to marry a woman of considerable means; and my sister certainly has little to offer in that regard. I do not wish her to build hopes over someone who may never consider her as a serious match, especially when she can have a home and a safe future with Mr. Bingley," she fretted.

Darcy stood up and began pulling on his shirt.

"What is the matter?" she asked, observing him warily. "Are you not pleased with your cousin showing attention to Jane?"

He shook his head no, bending down to pick up their belongings. Elizabeth helped him to fold the blanket before clearing it from the sand and grass.

"I must write to Jane, warning her that she should be careful when meeting Colonel Fitzwilliam the next time," she spoke more to herself than to him as they walked towards the cottage, Darcy carrying their blanket and food basket. "Is your cousin in London now?"

"No, he is in Kent," Darcy answered, his tone clipped, hostile almost.

Elizabeth grabbed his arm, stopping him in place. "What has changed your mood so much? What did I say?"

"Nothing," he murmured, avoiding her gaze.

She lifted her hand, cupping his cheek, making him look at her. "Is it about your cousin?"

"Was there something between you two? he spat out. "You sounded hurt when I mentioned him being interested in Jane." He eyed her speculatively.

She opened and closed her mouth, before she whispered. "You are jealous?"

"You think I have no reason to be? It was obvious to me that you favored him when we were in Kent. You were all smiles every time you were in his company. He spoke to you about his life situation, as if he was explaining himself why he could not make you an offer." His tone was laced with accusation which instantly made her angry.

"Even if that was the case, that is not your business."

"Not my business? I disagree. My wife admits to me that another man showed his interest in her, and she reciprocated it. *That* is *certainly* my business."

"I had no relationship with you at that time. I was free to bestow my attentions on other men."

His jaw line clenched. "What?" he hissed.

She raised her chin high. "I do not believe that I ever acted against the rules of propriety before our engagement. You are in no place to be displeased over the few conversations and walks I enjoyed with your cousin. I liked his company very well, and that has not changed since then."

She took his glaring at her person calmly, before he stomped away from her, marching towards the entrance of the house.

"You have no right to say a word to me about my past behaviour with men, you with your ten whores!" she cried, before clasping her hand over her mouth. As soon as the words had fallen from her lips, she knew that she had gone too far.

He froze in place, but did not turn around to look at her. After a moment, he began moving again, rushing towards the house without a second glance in her direction.

Chapter Twenty-Three

He had not spoken a single word to her since they had returned from the beach. Neither had he looked at her.

Closed in their bedroom upstairs, she decided that she would not go to him first. He had no right to be upset about her friendship with Colonel Fitzwilliam. Nothing improper had ever occurred between them. How dare he to judge her? She had been forced to endure the humiliation of meeting one of his ex-mistresses, and he was not able to bear that she had had a few friendly conversations with his cousin?

Her husband seemed to think that she was unsupportive of Colonel Fitzwilliam's interest in Jane because she herself had feelings for him. That could not be farther from the truth. Even though she genuinely liked the colonel and enjoyed his company and easy manner, there was nothing more to it. She was a married woman now. Those few men which had caught her attention when she had still been a Miss Bennet were irreversibly left in the past. Her husband, his words and actions, her physical attraction to him, his kisses and embraces, occupied her mind and heart to such an extent that there was truly no place there for anyone else.

The fact that Darcy's cousin found Jane appealing was natural, expected even. However, the fact that he had discussed the matter with Darcy was most alarming. Elizabeth was certain that she had understood Colonel Fitzwilliam correctly back in Kent. He had no means to marry as he wished, then what he was looking for with Jane?

Jane's happiness meant the world to Elizabeth. Jane deserved all the best, she could not bear to see her sister suffer at the man's hands as his toy once again. Mr. Bingley seemed such a secure option - he was close, and this time he appeared to be genuinely invested both with his feelings and intentions. Colonel Fitzwilliam was the unknown. He might never have the means to marry Jane, no matter how honest and honourable his intentions were.

A light knock on the door brought her to the present moment.

"Enter," she called, expecting it to be Darcy.

To her surprise, the driver, Mr. Black, appeared in the opening.

He bowed. "Master has asked to take you for a shopping trip to Brighton. All is ready, Mistress. We can go when it is convenient to you."

Her first impulse was to tell him to go to hell, together with his Master, but she quickly composed herself.

"Thank you. Allow me a few minutes to prepare myself," she responded politely. "I should be ready in a quarter of an hour."

The man bowed again, leaving the room quickly. Darcy was speaking with her through the servants now. Very well; if that was his wish, she would respect his decision.

She picked an elegant grey–lilac, short sleeved gown, adorned with black ribbons. It was designed with the thought of later mourning. However, as it was such a hot day, she despised the thought of wearing the perhaps more appropriate black satin with long sleeves.

Darcy was nowhere to be seen as she walked downstairs and outside the house to the awaiting carriage. Obviously, he had no intention of accompanying her.

As she was about to enter the box, the door opened for her, and she felt the weight of a familiar, warm hand on her waist.

"Do you have money?" he asked.

She turned to him, but was careful not to look up. She was still too angry to make an eye contact.

"Yes," she murmured, clenching the reticule in her gloved hands.

"Do you need more? Brighton is a very expensive town, even more so than London and Bath."

She shook her head vehemently. "No, thank you." She stepped away, climbing into the carriage on her own, ignoring his outstretched hand.

As the door shut, she observed through the lowered window as he walked to the footman. They talked for a moment, before she saw Darcy passing what looked like a small purse with money. She rolled her eyes. Of course he always had to know better.

In her present state of mind, she did not expect to enjoy the trip. However, on the first glimpse of the elaborate shop window displays, she temporarily forgot about her current worries. She had never seen such an abundance of beautiful things, even in London. Her lips curled into a soft smile as she imagined her younger sisters and mother here with her. There would be no end to their excitement. Wide eyed, she walked from one shop window to another, admiring the tastefully arranged articles.

While the driver stayed back with the carriage, the footman followed her, never staying farther than a few feet behind her. Knowing Darcy's protectiveness, she did not have to guess that the man had received a direct order not to leave her alone for even a moment. She did not find it necessary, but with his presence, she felt safer being in a place that was foreign to her.

Darcy's remark on the expensiveness of Brighton proved more than right. In one of the shop, she eyed items which would make excellent presents for Kitty, Lydia and Georgiana, but she was more than disappointed to note that their combined price covered almost all the funds she had with herself. Yet, she had to find gifts for her mother, Jane, and the Gardiners' children.

She pondered for a moment, before she turned on her feet to look for the servant who waited for her in front of the shop. He had no trouble with guessing what she needed; without a word, he handed her the same purse with money which he had received from Darcy earlier. Not much was left in it when she had purchased everything she wanted.

It was nearly five in the afternoon when they returned to cottage. She took her time in Brighton, thinking that some time apart would do Darcy and her good. She even spent some time in a tea shop, where she had tried delicious biscuits. She noticed some militia officers in the crowd of people strolling down the main street, but thankfully there were no familiar faces between them. All she needed today was a run-in with Mr. Wickham.

To her quiet relief, Darcy did not come out of the house to greet her. She left the numerous parcels to the footman and went directly upstairs.

She looked through the purchased items spread all over the white bed coverlet. She felt pleased with herself for her choices of gifts for her sisters, mother and little cousins, when there was a knock on the door.

"Enter," she called, certain that it was a servant to announce dinner.

She stilled, recognizing her husband's footsteps, she but she did not turn around.

"Did you get everything you wanted?" he asked, standing behind her.

She nodded. "Thank you for the additional funds. Brighton is indeed a rather expensive place to shop," she admitted.

She did not wish to be ungrateful. He thought of her, about her safety and needs, even when they were not on their best terms. She should appreciate that.

"Lizzy," he murmured, pulling her into his embrace, her back to his front.

"I cannot stand it when you are upset with me."

Putting her hands on his arms, wrapped around her midsection, she tried to pry them away, which only caused him to bring her more firmly to himself. "Then perhaps you should not..." She did not finish, because he cupped her face, capturing her lips firmly with his.

Her attempted protest died in her mouth as one of his hands slid up, cupping her breast, while the other made its journey down, stopping just above the apex of her legs.

He swept the things which she had bought from the bed on the floor, where they fell with a soft thud. Thankfully, there was nothing breakable among them. He pushed her on the bed, face down, as he hovered behind her.

"Fitzwilliam," she whispered as he let go of her lips, now placing warm kisses to the nape of her neck.

"You will not think of another," he ordered softly.

"I am not..." she began, but her words turned into a shocked gasp as he pulled her skirts up, cool air sweeping over her lower body.

"I cannot abide the thought of you with another," he murmured, his hand caressing the back of her thighs, just above the garter.

"You are most unfair," she said, turning her head to look up at him. "There was no one before you. How much more proof do you need?"

He did not answer, but hid his face in her neck. She felt his weight on her, his chest to her back, as if he wanted to curl around her.

The ability of any coherent speech abandoned her, as she felt him pulling her dress and petticoats even higher, to her waist.

With wide eyes, she observed as he took a large pillow from the head of the bed, and tucked it under her, elevating her backside.

"What are you...?" She did not finish as he closed her lips with his.

His large hand splayed over her skin below her spine, squeezing one cheek.

"Your thighs are so slim, but I have always thought that you have a most deliciously rounded bottom," he praised.

She gave a small cry as he bit lightly into that part of her body. It was surely indecent what he was doing, but she had no will to ask him to stop, and in truth, she did not want to. Despite the acute embarrassment, she felt too good with his new attentions to utter any protest.

He seemed to be done with touching her backside, because he pushed her legs apart, caressing the inside of her thigh.

She had a pretty good idea what his intention was. She hid her face in her enfolded arms, but arched herself up, wordlessly allowing him to continue.

He had no trouble reading her body language, as seconds later she felt his fingers on her most intimate place. He was kissing the base of her spine, his hand buried firmly between her thighs.

Her sighs and pants were silenced by the bed coverlet she buried her face into as he brought her to pleasure. There was no pain this time; he only stroked over her flesh, not trying to open her up with his fingers.

As she calmed down, he pulled the pillow from under her so she could roll over onto her back.

Shyly, she smoothed her skirts, looking up into his smiling eyes.

"You seem very pleased with yourself, Mr. Darcy," she noted unable to stop her own smile.

He grinned, placing his hand on her hip. "You are correct, Mrs. Darcy."

Gathering all her courage, and with her earlier resolution about the baby on her mind, she moved her hand down between their bodies, placing it on the front of his breeches, feeling his prominent hardness.

He did not allow it though, as he took her hand and brought to his lips, before placing it back on his chest.

"If you had had a choice, would you have chosen my cousin?" he asked out of nowhere. "Had he proposed to you back in Kent, would you have accepted him instead of me?"

"No, I would not," she replied without a hint of hesitation in her voice. "I knew him barely a few weeks, how could I entrust my life to his hands?"

"But you liked him," he insisted, his expression sad.

She sighed, praying for patience. "I like many people, both men and women. Colonel Fitzwilliam was kind to me, treated me like an equal." she stressed. "Nevertheless, I had never had deeper feelings for any man, including your cousin. There was only one man whose presence and manners affected me strongly from the beginning of our acquaintance."

He paled visibly, his face turning into unreadable mask. "Who?"

She cupped his cheek. "You. All the hours I spent thinking about my dislike for you and how disagreeable you were…" She shook her head, smiling. "I was never indifferent to you, far from it."

"It is good then?" he asked slowly, searching her face.

"Well, I had met some rude and arrogant men before, and not one of them captured so much of my attention." She smirked. "I was drawn to you when I saw you for the first time at the assembly, but you hurt my pride by refusing to dance with me, finding me not good enough for you. That is a capital offence for any woman, sir. It was easy to convince myself about my dislike for you, and you certainly fuelled my resolution with your later behaviour."

He lowered his head, touching her forehead with his. "I ruined everything from the beginning. Forgive me," he whispered, before kissing her.

"If you forgive me." She looked down. "I should not have said what I did earlier today. It was unnecessary and spiteful."

He wrapped an arm around her, pulling her closer. "All is well," he whispered, rubbing her back.

"I was worried about Jane," she explained. "I respect your cousin. I am certain that he is a good man, but Jane has suffered enough. I do not wish for her to be toyed with again. If he cannot make her an offer, he should not raise her hopes. He should keep his distance."

"There may be a possibility that Aunt Catherine will allow Richard to inherit Rosings. Anne is very ill. The doctors say that there is little hope for her. Since there is no other immediate family, and my aunt will certainly not leave the estate to me. Hence Richard's chance."

"I am sorry to hear about Miss de Bourge's condition. I cannot say I liked her, but to die so young... I do not wish that on anyone."

He nodded. "My feelings are the same."

Elizabeth bit her lip, thinking intensely. "Even if Colonel Fitzwilliam inherits Rosings Park one day, it may take years before it is all legalized. By then, Jane may be happily married to Mr. Bingley with a family of her own."

"I do understand your point, but to be completely honest, I would prefer Jane to marry Richard. He deserves someone like your sister, so good and beautiful. We would be brothers at last, having sisters for wives."

Elizabeth placed her head on his chest, thinking about Jane, Colonel Fitzwilliam and Mr. Bingley. She could not decide which gentleman she liked better, and who would suit her sister more.

"What about the swimming lesson?" he asked, bringing her from her thoughts.

She stretched lazily beside him. "Not today perhaps. It has been a long day and quite emotional too. I am tired and hungry."

He sat up, pulling her with him. "Let us go downstairs then. Dinner is ready by now."

"If it is not cold," she noted.

He shrugged. "The cook will reheat it then."

"You go first. I need to refresh myself," she said, blushing as she referred to the sticky mess left in her undergarments.

"Hurry," he asked, kissing her forehead before he left the room.

***

"May we move under the covers?" she asked as he removed her nightgown. She felt shy, sitting on the bed naked. The sun was setting, but the light coming from the window was still strong enough that he could see everything.

Silently, he stripped the bed down from the coverlet, uncovering the crisp white sheets beneath it.

"We do not have to do anything more than earlier today," he assured her, bringing her closer. They laid down, and he pulled the covers over them.

"You do not wish to?" she asked, clenching the sheet to her front.

With one swift movement, he pulled her leg over his middle so she could feel his hardened manhood rubbing against her thigh.

Following his lead, she climbed over him. His capable hands on her hips helped her to straddle him.

His eyes roamed over her face and lower as he tugged the sheet down, his view of her body unobstructed. He cupped her breasts, covering them with his hands.

"I could stare at you for hours," he murmured. "You have put on weight," he noted with a bit of a smile. "I am glad. I was worried you would become ill from not eating."

"The air here agrees with my appetite," she admitted.

He rolled them so he was above her. First he kissed her face, before his lips descended down her body. His caresses were most pleasant, and she sighed and writhed under his touch, especially when he found sensitive spots on her body. However, she could not give in to the sensation entirely, as at the back of her mind there was the memory of the pain of the first time.

She stiffened involuntarily when his hand wandered between her legs. He seemed to sense her fear, because he shifted his body up, so they were able to see each other's faces. His hand was still placed between her thighs, as if allowing her to accustom herself to its presence there.

His fingers began stroking her tender flesh, his eyes focused on her face as he touched her.

Slowly she opened her legs shyly. He wasted no time before rolling on top of her, still mindful not to crush her.

"Love, you are so tense," he whispered worriedly, stroking the path from the inside of her thigh to her lower belly. "It should not hurt so much this time, as we are past your maidenhead."

She nodded, ordering her body to obey, but to no avail. As his hard manhood touched her private place, she could feel her inner muscles tightening when she should be opening herself for him.

"I love you," he whispered, kissing below her ear. "My dearest, loveliest, Elizabeth, I love you."

At last he pushed inside but as she guessed not entirely.

The deep line appeared between his eyebrows as he cupped her hip, trying to manoeuvre himself farther inside.

"Lizzy, love, you must relax, you are not letting me in," he grunted.

"I am trying," she whimpered on the verge of tears.

The pain was becoming unbearable, as Darcy was panting over her supported on his arms, his eyes squeezed. It felt different than before, more like burning rather than tearing.

"Please, stop," she cried miserably, pushing at his arms with all her might. "Hurts."

He listened instantly, pulling out of her which made her wince in discomfort.

As soon as he was out of her, the pain was gone, and she could feel her inner muscles relaxing of their own. Clenching the sheet to herself, she curled into a tight ball, allowing the deep sob to overcome her.

"Are you still in pain?" he cried frantically, combing the hair away from her face.

She shook her head no.

"Shush." His hands smooth over her back. "All is well."

"How can you say that?!" she cried. "I am useless to you!"

"What are you saying? Do not ever think such a thing!" he ordered grimly.

"I cannot even... accommodate you," she choked. "There must be something wrong with me, 'tis the only explanation. You should find yourself someone else and annul the marriage."

"Elizabeth, look at me," he cupped her face, making sure their eyes met. "There is nothing wrong with you. I do not know how many times I have told you that you are the only one for me! Simply, you are not ready. You have been through so much lately, and it is perfectly understandable that your body responds to it in its own way."

"You are very gracious to say that," she whispered brokenly, allowing him to cradle her to his chest.

"Shush. All is well. No need to fret about this." He spread kisses all over her face. "Everything will be well."

Despite his assurances and the comfort of his arms around her, she fell asleep with heavy heart. She could not understand what was happening to her.

Chapter Twenty-Four

"Are you certain that you do not wish me to accompany you to see your mother and sister?" Darcy asked from the doorway.

"No, thank you," she answered in a tight voice, putting her bonnet on. "It will be much better if I go alone."

She tied the bow under her chin, thinking that Darcy and her mother in one room was not the best idea. She knew that her husband thought little of Mrs. Bennet, and to be truthful, she could not blame him, no matter how painful it was to admit that to herself.

He made his way to her, standing close. "If I am there with you, she will not dare to say anything spiteful to hurt you."

"Fitzwilliam, she is my mother. I cannot escape from her," she said with resignation.

"You know that you do not have to go to see her." He placed his hands on her arms. "I can see how much it costs you to do that."

"I have to go." She looked up in his eyes, begging him to understand. "I deprived her of participation in my wedding, even though I knew all too well how important it was for her. Marrying her daughters off is the aim of her life. She must have been extremely disappointed not to be included. I should at least try to apologize for my behaviour."

"You had your reasons not to include her," he tried to convince her. "It is good for one's peace of mind to be selfish from time to time. You always put the needs of others above your own, and that is not healthy."

"She is my mother," she repeated. "I have to go to see her."

"You do not have to if you do not wish to," he repeated with force. "You have your own family now, one that loves and accepts you." She was about to respond to his words, opening her mouth, but he placed a gentle finger on her lips, silencing her. "I do not ask you to break bonds with your sisters. They are welcome to visit us, I assure you. Georgiana would certainly like the company of the girls her own age. But your mother... she is spiteful, cruel even. I cannot calmly abide witnessing as she intentionally hurts you time and again with her heartless remarks."

"She does not do it on purpose," Elizabeth protested. "We are so very different, that is why it is difficult for us to find common ground."

"Nonsense, she does not care for anyone but herself. I have had enough proof of that. Let me accompany you."

She lowered her head down, staring at her pointy, soft skinned shoes. "I prefer to go alone," she murmured.

"As you wish," he agreed with a heavy sigh. Taking her hand, he led her towards the window. "I observed you many times from this window."

She looked up at him, confused, her mind still engrossed in the previous topic of their conversation to catch his meaning. "When? Since we came here yesterday evening, we have not left the house."

He shook his head with smile. "It was my room when I visited here last year. When you stayed at Netherfield for those few days when you nursed your sister..." He paused to touch her cheek. "I could watch you safely from here as you strolled down the lane or played with dogs."

She frowned. "You spied on me... why?"

"You cannot guess?" His hand moved from her cheek to the back of her waist, bringing her closer.

"I would have never believed it if someone had told me at that time that you had been interested in me."

"You had no suspicions, truly?" He viewed her with a degree of shrewdness. "I have always thought that women could feel a man's interest? All the times you caught me staring at you... I do know that you noticed my eyes on you too many times to ignore it. You must have explained my behaviour to yourself in some way."

"I noticed your staring," she agreed. "However, you rarely said anything to me... Moreover, you seemed so very cold, distant and disapproving... I thought that you looked at me for amusement just to find a fault with me."

He gave a short laugh, pulling her to his chest. "Only a complete innocent may think something like that. Perhaps my jealously over other men is truly unfounded... How could you be so naïve, love? I had to bite my knuckles not to throw myself at you, and you noticed nothing of that?"

"This is the most shocking intelligence, Mr. Darcy." She raised up on her toes, a small smile curling her lips as she placed her arms around his neck.

Their lips met for a slow kiss, which was soon interrupted with a muffled cough, coming from the direction of the door.

"Bingley, come in, please," Darcy cried jovially in a rich voice, keeping Elizabeth firmly to his side, his arm around her waist.

Elizabeth smiled brightly at their host as he walked in, his expression obviously embarrassed at what he had just witnessed.

"I hope you rested well," he said, standing in front of them, his hands clasped behind his back.

"Very well," Elizabeth assured quickly. "We apologize that we were not such amiable company last night."

"Oh, that is perfectly understandable," Bingley spoke smoothly. "You arrived so late, you must have been tired."

Elizabeth nodded. "Yes, indeed. Travelling in such heat is tiresome, even in the most comfortable carriage. Let us hope that the rain will come today; it is so sultry, nothing to breathe with."

Bingley shifted from one foot to the other, before his eyes locked directly at Elizabeth. "Mrs. Darcy, if I may be so bold to ask..." he cleared his throat. "Your elder sister... Has she any immediate plans of returning home? Or does she plan to prolong her stay with your aunt and uncle in London?"

Elizabeth fought hard not to show an overwhelming joy on her face, caused by Mr. Bingley's enquiries.

"I had no opportunity to ask her, but I believe that she may stay in London for the next several weeks, at least," she answered animatedly.

"Mr. and Mrs. Gardiner are expected at Pemberley this summer, together with their children, and I dare say Mrs. Darcy would like Miss Bennet to join them," Darcy explained, looking down at Elizabeth for confirmation of his words. "In that case, Miss Bennet may very well not return to Hertfordshire sooner than September."

"We have not yet discussed the summer plans in detail with my sister, but I would dearly wish for her visit in Derbyshire," Elizabeth added.

Bingley nodded his head slowly. "A trip to London is in order for me then. Would she mind if I called on her there?" he asked unsurely, looking from one Darcy to the other.

Elizabeth openly beamed at him. "I think she would be very pleased, the same as our aunt and uncle. You will be most welcomed there. I shall write down their address for you."

Bingley thanked her profusely, before excusing himself from their company.

"Is it wise to encourage him like that?"Darcy asked, as they were left alone.

"He seems very much decided to make her an offer," Elizabeth spoke excitedly. "Why should I not encourage him? He is a decent young man of sufficient means, and he is very much taken with her. He is your friend too."

"What about Richard?" Darcy asked uneasily, frowning.

"Jane barely knows your cousin, and I know that he is a good man, and I understand your point, I truly do," she answered patiently. "You wish him happiness with someone as kind and beautiful as my sister. However, there is no guarantee that Colonel Fitzwilliam would ever be in position to afford to marry Jane."

Darcy said nothing to that. She was right, after all. Still, he thought that Richard and Jane would make an excellent match.

Elizabeth stepped away from him, walking to the side table to gather the presents she had put aside for her mother and younger sisters.

***

"Oh, Lizzy, it is so beautiful!" Lydia exclaimed as she turned in her hands a wide rimmed, straw bonnet adorned with bright blue ribbons.

Elizabeth smiled at her youngest sister. "I am pleased you like it, Liddy. I picked it for you thinking that it would match the colour of your eyes quite well."

"Tis perfect! Thank you!" Lydia rushed from her chair to give her a hug.

She joined her sister who stood in front of the mirror hanging over the mantle. Kitty was modeling her own new hat, similar to her sister's but with yellow ribbons.

"I knew you would not forget about us, Lizzy," Kitty said, admiring her reflection. "Mama said you cared nothing for us since you were such a grand lady now, but I always hoped that it was not the case."

"I could never forget about you," Elizabeth assured, glancing at her mother, who was sitting stiffly on the sofa next to her. "Mama, will you not open your present?" she asked timidly, pushing the elegant parcel in the direction of the older woman. "It is a lace shawl like the one you have always wished for."

Mrs. Bennet took the package in her hands, only to put it aside without opening it.

Elizabeth reached for her mother's hand, but Mrs. Bennet pulled away.

"Mama, please," Elizabeth whispered, the instant tears standing in her eyes.

Mrs. Bennet's round eyes narrowed as she examined her second daughter. "You think that some scrap of cloth is enough for me to forget about what you have done!?" she screeched. "I prepared everything for your wedding, every detail, and you did not show up! You made a fool of me! I can barely face my friends after what you have done. How can I explain this to them? My own daughter refused her mother to participate in her wedding. You invited Jane, but left all of us behind."

"Mama, I did not do it on purpose," Elizabeth spoke slowly, her voice trembling. "I was not feeling very well at that time, and I had no will to travel to Hertfordshire. I know you must be disappointed, but please try to understand my feelings. I did not do it to spite you. I wanted a quiet wedding. I am not certain whether I would be able to say yes with the church full of strangers. I—"

"These are all your usual excuses, Elizabeth!" Mrs. Bennet interrupted harshly. "You made me the laughing stock of the entire neighborhood because you could not say your vows in a church full of strangers? These people are not strangers! They are our friends and neighbors. You are a selfish and ungrateful girl who thinks only about herself!"

With those words, Mrs. Bennet stood up, and not giving a second glance to anyone, stormed out of the room.

Elizabeth sat frozen in her place, trying hard to fight the tears coming to her eyes.

"Do not fret, Lizzy," Mary walked to her, placing a gentle hand on her shoulder. "Mama will forgive you; only some time must pass."

Elizabeth nodded, but did not dare to lift her head up.

"Thank you for the books and music sheets, sister," Mary added.

"You are welcome," Elizabeth's voice cracked. She rose to her feet. "I will go."

"Stay, Lizzy, stay with us a little longer." Mary took her hand to stop her. "You must tell us about your trip to Brighton."

"Oh, how I would wish to go to Brighton and try sea bathing!" Lydia cried, turning in their direction. "You are so fortunate, Lizzy, that Mr. Darcy took you there!"

Elizabeth managed a pale smile. "I should go; Mr. Darcy awaits me."

The carriage was waiting for her in front of the house. As soon she emerged on the graveled path, Mr. Black, the driver, began to climb to his high place, the other servant opening the door for her.

She stopped them in their tracks with her words.

"I will not need you today," she said, trying to give her voice a decided note. "Please return to Netherfield without me. I will return on foot later on."

"Mistress," Black climbed down, standing in front of her. "Master gave us the direct instructions to bring you to Netherfield."

"I want some fresh air," she insisted. "Tell Mr. Darcy that I wish to visit my father's grave."

She marched past the carriage, hurrying across the small park surrounding Purvis Lodge towards the fields she knew so well.

***

Darcy had a bad feeling about Elizabeth visiting her mother alone. He was decidedly against it. God knew what that horrible woman would tell his wife this time. Sometimes he wished he had wrung Mrs. Bennet's neck for being so insensitive and unloving towards her second daughter.

Elizabeth seemed in good spirits these days, despite her obvious upset about her 'inadequacy in the bedroom,' as she phrased it. She was so worried about their failed second attempt at lovemaking, blaming herself. She gave the impression that she was scared to death that he would run to the nearest brothel because she was not giving him what he needed. He could see why the situation was upsetting for her, but he was not overly concerned about the slow progress of their marital relations.

He had no doubt that when the right time came, they would do brilliantly loving one another. Her passion was there, but buried under the fear and apprehension. He liked to think that her body refused to cooperate because she had not yet admitted to being in love with him. One day in the future, she would open herself to him, both figuratively and literally. Then he would have the proof of her love for him. She was not one to share her body without true and honest love for her husband. He could only admire her for that and be proud that he had chosen such a woman for himself.

He was in awe with himself over the fact that he did not mind terribly that physical closeness was postponed between them for the time being. He desired her, there was no question of that, however some newfound patience developed in him. It was astounding that it was almost enough for him to simply hold her chastely in his arms while she slept.

Nevertheless, the unpleasant encounter with Mrs. Bennet could only set Elizabeth back to her previous bleak frame of mind. It was the last thing he wished for her, for both of them. Over the last months, he had learned that the outspoken and confident Elizabeth, with her witty ways and sunny personality, the one he had fallen in love with, was in truth, a very sensitive and fragile being. She felt deeply for her loved ones, and had a rather complex perception of the world and the people around her. There were moments when, in his opinion, her sensitivity stretched too far, making her worry about mostly irrelevant matters, or even create new dilemmas for her to fret about with no rational background to them.

At last he spied through the window that his carriage had returned. He ran out of the room, and soon was in front of the house.

"Mrs. Darcy said that she wanted some fresh air and time alone," Black spoke without preamble. "She ordered us to return here without her."

Darcy opened his mouth to scold his man, but then he realized that there was very little they could do, apart from putting her in the carriage by force, when Elizabeth set herself on something. They must have tried to stop her from returning to Netherfield on foot, but she probably did not listen.

"Did she say anything more?"

Black nodded, his expression compassionate. "She was sad, crying almost, and she said that she wished to visit her father's grave."

"Ask to prepare one of the horses for me. I will look for her. It may start to rain at any moment." He frowned in concern, looking up at the grey skies.

Black nodded eagerly. "Right away, Master."

***

The first drops of rain fell over his hat as he rode along the wall of the graveyard where Mr. Bennet had been buried. To his relief, even from a distance, he could see a small, all too familiar figure, kneeling on the ground in front of one of the graves.

He tied the horse beside a spot grown with tall, juicy grass. The animal started to graze instantly, entirely oblivious to its surroundings.

He expected her to hear him coming and acknowledge him as he approached her. She did not make a move though, or give any indication that she was aware of someone's company.

"It is time to return home, love," he said, putting a hand over her shoulder, hoping not to startle her. "The downpour will come any minute," he added worriedly.

Slowly, she stood up, hiding her face behind the wide rim of her bonnet. He leaned down to see how much damage his mother-in-law had done.

At the sight of her tear-streaked face, his heart clenched in rightful anger. "What did she say this time?" he asked, pulling her to him.

"Nothing which I did not expect her to say," she answered hoarsely, her voice cracking.

He wished to say something to make her feel better, but he lacked the right words. Having this kind of relationship with a parent was a completely new experience for him. His father and he had had their disagreements, but the man was grief stricken over the death of his wife. When his mother had been still living, he had been the best father a boy could wish for.

He cleaned her face with his handkerchief the best he could before placing a chaste kiss on her salty lips.

"I am well," she assured, attempting a weak smile.

"Come." He gathered her to his side, directing them to his horse. The rain was getting heavier with every moment. Without second thought, he removed his great coat, placing it over her head and around her.

He untied the animal and led him closer. He lifted her up, sitting her sideways on the saddle, before mounting himself behind her in one practiced, fluid movement.

"Let us go home," he murmured, his arms wrapped securely around her as he kicked the horse into a faster pace.

Chapter Twenty-Five

Mrs. Reynolds stood by one of the windows in the spacious foyer of Pemberley manor. Through narrowed eyes, she tried to recognize the shapes outside where a moonless night, combined with drizzling rain, created pitch darkness.

Master Fitzwilliam and his bride should have arrived hours ago. It was nearly ten in the evening. Mrs. Reynolds began to believe that their plans must have changed and that they had decided to delay their arrival for a day or two. She was not allowing herself to think that something dangerous might have happened to them on the road. Mr. Black was the best coachman they had ever had, and he had driven the family safely to various destinations in much worse conditions.

"No sign of them?" A sweet voice called from behind.

The housekeeper turned to look at the young girl. Georgiana was like a daughter to her, the one she had never had. She had raised her from a toddler after Lady Anne's premature death. Her two sons had lived their own lives for many years now away from her. She could not be more pleased for them, or more proud. Both of them had gained respectable professions, one being a solicitor in Bath and the other, with the help of Colonel Fitzwilliam, doing a fast career in the army. However, she had seen them only a few times in recent years; and even though her older son had invited her to live with him many times, she had always refused. The Darcys were her second family, equally dear to her heart, and she felt that the siblings still needed her more than her own children.

Mrs. Reynolds could not wait to watch the new generation growing up, small children running the wide halls of Pemberley again. She could only pray that the boy had picked for himself a woman of a good heart, someone who would love and appreciate him the way he deserved.

Master Fitzwilliam had been very vague so far in divulging information about his bride, which was not in the least surprising. He was a man of a few words, and very private about his personal life. All Mrs. Reynolds knew was that her name was Elizabeth, she was a daughter of a gentleman from

Hertfordshire, and they had met last autumn when the boy had visited Mr. Bingley's new estate. Other information was that she had lost her father a few months ago, which was the reason for a very quiet wedding.

Fortunately, Georgiana, contrary to her brother, was quite eager to speak about her new sister. She was all but enchanted by 'Lizzy' as she referred to her. She had never been so enthusiastic about anyone else, including Mr. Bingley's sister. It gave hope that the new Mrs. Darcy was nothing like Caroline Bingley. Mrs. Reynolds had disliked her from the first sight when she had come to Pemberley with her brother. Even though it had been obvious to everyone that the boy would never touch her with as much as a very long stick, not to mention considered asking for her hand in marriage, she had already behaved as if she owned the place and had been his Mistress. Her calculating eyes had looked with greed at every piece of furniture, every painting on the wall, and every piece of silverware on the table, as if adding in her head their combined value.

"It must be them!" Georgiana exclaimed, bringing Mrs. Reynolds instantly from her thoughts to the present moment.

Indeed there were noises of tired horses heard, followed by the not so subtle banging on the door.

The servants were running with umbrellas, and soon the doors were wide open, and the Master stepped in, carrying a small figure.

"Brother, what happened?" Georgiana asked first. "We were so concerned."

"Shush," he spoke in quiet voice, looking down at the sleeping person nestled in his arms.

Mrs. Reynolds followed his eyes. It was not a woman but a girl! She was not sure what she expected, but definitely someone older, and bigger. She could not see the girl's face well, as it was hidden against her husband's chest, but she appeared to look younger than Georgiana. She hoped that her Master had not decided to rob the cradle, marrying a fifteen-year-old. It would be so unlike him. What would they do with a child as a Mistress of such a grand estate?

"She fell asleep in the carriage," he spoke with obvious tenderness, his eyes glued to the unmoving figure of his wife.

With that one look, Mrs. Reynolds knew that he was head over heels for that girl. There was nothing rational in the way he stared at her, nothing sane. He would do anything for her should she ask him. The housekeeper sent a quick prayer to the heavens, hoping that the new Mrs. Darcy was not a spoilt brat.

"Is she well?" Georgiana whispered worriedly.

"Yes, only tired," he responded, whispering as well. "One of the horses lost its shoe, and it took us three hours to restart our journey. Black deserves a large pint of the very best ale for delivering us safely in such weather.

"We will talk tomorrow," he added, leaning to place a kiss on the top of his sister's head.

"Mrs. Reynolds, it is good to see you," he acknowledged her with a smile, before directing himself towards the staircase.

The housekeeper followed his retreat with her eyes, the same as all the others gathered around her. Their livelihood depended on that small lady cradled in Darcy's arms. Should she turn moody and selfish, there would be no peace and happiness in the house. She could only hope that the girl would prove to be worthy of the Darcy name and make the boy happy.

***

Mrs. Reynolds woke up early the next morning, as was her custom, eager to learn more about the new Mistress. The little lady whom the boy had brought home last night had very large shoes to fill after Lady Anne.

For breakfast, she made sure that the cook prepared a large variety of dishes, not being sure what Mrs. Darcy's tastes were. However, when she peeked into the breakfast room, to her disappointment she only saw only the Master and Miss Georgiana, talking animatedly.

Darcy explained that his wife was still sleeping, tired after the long journey. He excused himself quickly, and went upstairs. A bath was to be prepared for the Mistress, and a tray with breakfast delivered to her room.

Mrs. Reynolds was not certain what to think about it. She did not wish to judge the girl too harshly nor unfairly, but Lady Anne had never slept so late. She had started her days early, dealing with many household affairs from seven in the morning, and sometimes even earlier. On the other hand, the girl had indeed looked exhausted last night. She looked so small and frail, perhaps she tired easily? What if she was a weakling, sickly and cross?

Would she be able to bear an heir to Pemberley with such a weak constitution? Perhaps she was already with child, which could explain her exhaustion.

It was nearly one o'clock when Mrs. Reynolds caught the first sight of the new Mrs. Darcy. The boy was touring his wife around, showing her the house.

"Mrs. Reynolds," he cried jovially, gesturing for her to come closer.

As he made the introduction, the housekeeper's eyes rested greedily on the girl's face. What first struck her was that she was so plain... not pretty enough for her handsome boy. At least she was not a child, she looked around twenty years of age, and there was a certain maturity in her face. Unfortunately, she was not only short, but thin, all skin and bones. She was tanned as well, which could be explained by their recent stay at the seaside. Mrs. Reynolds instantly made a firm resolution to do everything in her power to fatten the girl up.

She had a beautiful voice though, sweet and uplifting with singing quality to it. She was probably a good singer. Georgiana mentioned that her brother had said that Elizabeth could play the pianoforte and sing very well, and with great feeling. Mrs. Reynolds was little impressed with that intelligence, finding it not surprising and most expected. It was natural that the boy had picked someone accomplished like his sister and bookish like him. Mrs. Reynolds had managed to look discreetly through Mrs. Darcy's trunks sent to Pemberley in the last weeks. The main reason for which they were so heavy was that most of them contained many books, journals and music sheets. The fact that she liked books, gave hope that she was a rational creature, not empty headed like many of the young females nowadays.

The young Mrs. Darcy did not seem shy, but neither was she overly confident or conceited. She was polite, but outspoken at the same time, and not in the least intimidated. The longer Mrs. Reynolds talked with her, the more she was convinced that her first impression had been wrong. While not a classical beauty, Mrs. Darcy possessed a lot of charm, especially when she smiled. Her big, dark brown, cat-like eyes showed many emotions. It was difficult to take one's gaze from her animated face.

The housekeeper talked with her for about five minutes, mostly exchanging pleasantries, before the boy cut the conversation short. He excused them, saying that he had much yet to show to his wife. He sounded very proud when he said the word *wife*.

The way he looked at her... It made Mrs. Reynolds's heart beat a little faster. She remembered the times when she had been young and her late husband had courted her over thirty years ago.

The boy's eyes devotedly followed his wife's every move, her every expression. He smiled when she smiled, became serious when she listened intently. His arm was casually draped around her back with his fingers gently grasping her shoulder. It was so very unlike him to be so open with his affections in public. It all confirmed what Mrs. Reynolds had already guessed when they had arrived the day before. He was completely and utterly besotted with her. Still, the housekeeper was unsure whether the girl reciprocated his feelings with equal ardour.

She gave the impression of being at ease in his company, leaning into his side trustingly, that much Mrs. Reynolds could judge from the first encounter.

***

Mrs. Reynolds saw little of her new Mistress that first day, the same as the second and the third. Master commanded her entire time, showing her the house and the vast grounds of Pemberley. In the evenings, they were closed together in the library, or they listened to Georgiana's singing and playing.

Even though the housekeeper had little contact with Mrs. Darcy during those first few days, she gained much coveted valuable information about her from the servants who interacted directly with her. The maids claimed that she was kind, smiled at them and was very undemanding, doing many of the tasks by herself. She rarely summoned for their help.

Moreover, Mrs. Reynolds learned a little from their coachman, Mr. Black. He did not divulge any details, even though his face told her that he could tell a lot about the girl and her family, if he only wanted. It was clear that he approved strongly of the new Mrs. Darcy, and would not say one bad word about her. All he said was that the girl had had a hard life so far, but was good to the core and very kind. According to him, she had inner strength and was not afraid to stand up to Mr. Darcy, telling him what she did not like.

Mrs. Reynolds had an opportunity to develop her own opinion about the new Mrs. Darcy when on the fourth day since her arrival, the girl sought her out early in the morning. She asked to be introduced to the staff and become acquainted with household matters.

While the housekeeper presented the numerous servants to her, she had a smile and a kind word for each one, from the scullery maids to her husband's steward. She already knew some of them, and instantly learned the names of the others. She seemed to have a good knowledge of the housekeeping business. She asked about the prices of food and their source, telling her how much this or that cost when her mother ordered it at Longbourn, which had been her family's estate. It was obvious that Mr. Darcy's mother-in-law had prepared her daughter very well to the life of a country squire's wife. The girl was intelligent, sensible, and down to earth.

By the end of the first week, it was not a secret to anyone at Pemberley that the Master spent every night in his wife's bed, and was most attentive to her. The maids were apprehensive about going into the Mistress's chambers early in morning, fearing to encounter the Master there. Mrs. Reynolds had witnessed herself a few times as he kissed and embraced her within open view. Those were chaste exchanges, but still spoke volumes about his feelings for her.

The boy seemed to be even more protective of his wife than he was of his sister, which was difficult to imagine. One day he asked for a private conversation with her. He wanted one of the footmen to be appointed for the task of accompanying his wife on her daily walks, but in such a way that she did not notice anything. Mrs. Darcy walked daily, usually for an hour or two in the early afternoon after she had finished with the household duties.

Seeing that the boy could not be reasoned with about it, Mrs. Reynolds did as she was told. After a mere week of this duty, however, the servant whom she had chosen asked kindly to be released from the task, as it was hard for him to keep pace with the Mistress. Not to mention that she had lost him more than once. The problem was solved on it own when one day Mrs. Darcy approached her personally on the matter. She said that she had talked to Mr. Darcy, and he agreed with her that she was familiar enough with the grounds by now, and she had no need for company on her walks.

It seemed unlikely to Mrs. Reynolds that the boy had surrendered on the matter so easily, and she was right. The next day he returned home with a small ball of yellow fur tucked inside his great coat. Both his sister and wife were delighted with the playfully energetic Labrador pup, who became Mrs. Darcy's most faithful companion. She named him Brutus.

By the end of the first month since new Mrs. Darcy had come to live at Pemberley, Mrs. Reynolds was able to breathe with some relief. She was not one to judge others easily, but nor was it easy to gain her trust either. So far, Elizabeth Darcy had done nothing which could be held against her. She had made no mistakes. She was a true lady, carried herself with dignity, was kind to others, and she was always mindful of her new position and her duties as a Mistress.

There was only one matter which worried the housekeeper – Mrs. Darcy seemed to be less invested with her feelings than her husband. She genuinely liked him, that was obvious, the older woman could clearly see that. She respected him, and she was grateful to him. Over time, Mrs. Reynolds managed to draw some more information from Mr. Black. He did not say much, of course, but she could read between the lines, and it seemed that Darcy had rescued her mother and sisters from certain destitution after her father's death.

However, whether she had sincere love for him was less certain. Mrs. Reynolds could only hope that the boy did not notice the lack of his wife's deeper feelings for him. She did not wish to see him hurt; he deserved happiness in his life, not another heartache.

Chapter Twenty-Six

Darcy again turned the letter which he had been holding in his hand for the last ten minutes, inspecting it from every angle. It was unusually thick for a private correspondence, and his wife's name was written on the top in an all too familiar hand. His cousin, Colonel Fitzwilliam, had decided to keep a private correspondence with his wife. Why?

His reasonable side was telling him that his cousin Richard, who was as close as a brother to him, would never have betrayed him in such a way, but the insecure, possessive, and jealous part of him nagged, persistently, asking why his cousin would feel the need to write personal letters to his wife.

Perhaps Richard wanted to ask for advice concerning his courtship of Jane? That was the only reasonable explanation which came to Darcy's mind. He knew what he should do in this situation – he should give the letter to Elizabeth, later asking her casually on what matter his cousin had addressed her personally.

A soft knock on the door brought his attention to the present moment. Knowing that it was Elizabeth, he dropped the letter hastily into the open drawer of his desk, shutting it with quiet click.

"Enter," he called, surprising himself with the sudden coldness of his voice.

"I heard that the post came," she spoke with smile, walking closer. Brutus, the pup he had given her a few weeks ago, followed her closely.

"Yes, these are for you," he pointed to a neat pile he had separated earlier from the estate correspondence.

She nodded, still smiling, as she stood close to him by the edge of the desk. Her long, delicate fingers began to sort through the mail, checking who had sent her each letter.

He watched her face, and his heart clenched painfully in his chest, as he observed a visible shadow of disappointment crossing her expressive features. She lowered her head, the smile gone from her pretty lips. Was she looking for the letter from his cousin? Was she expecting it?

"I will go to the park to read my letters." She gave him a faint smile, which did not reach her eyes.

Before she could step away from the desk, he rose fluidly from his chair, grasping her elbow.

She looked up at him, her eyes questioning. "Stay here," he spoke. "You can read your letters here."

"I do not wish to disturb you. You said earlier today that you have numerous correspondences to attend to."

"Your presence is always welcome," he assured, pinning her with his steady stare. "I like having you close."

"Very well then." She smiled again, lifting to her toes to place a small kiss on the side of his jaw.

He could read the surprise in her eyes when he did not react to her gesture, as he usually did, by pulling her into his arms to kiss her more deeply.

Through narrowed and calculating eyes, he observed as she walked to the sofa, the one placed nearest the windows. She settled herself comfortably, tucking her feet underneath her skirt, her shoes abandoned on the carpet. Brutus climbed after her, stretching against her. Elizabeth reached to stroke his back and scratch behind his large ears. The animal purred like a cat, straining against her hand.

Darcy began to think that the dog was turning out to be useless and disappointing. He had selected the pup himself, and with great care, when he had heard that one of his neighbors' Labrador bitch had just had a new litter.

He had received a Labrador from his parents as a little boy, before he even had been able to walk properly, and had wept when the dog died many years later.

Darcy knew well how gentle, intelligent, and eager to run and swim this breed of dogs was. They were perfect companions for someone who, like his wife, enjoyed the outdoors. He felt calm about her safety when Elizabeth was not alone on her long walks, but having a dog accompanying her. He also knew that she would feel attracted to the pup's rare, yellow fur. Most Labradors he had seen in this part of the country were pitch black.

Elizabeth, however, spoiled the animal with her attention, having no measure whatsoever. She refused to allow her pup to sleep with other dogs in the stables, saying he would feel lonely and cold. She insisted on placing a rug for him in the corner of their private sitting room, where Brutus snored soundly through the nights.

She cuddled the pup at every opportunity, cooed to him, as if he was a newborn child, while carrying him around. Thankfully the dog was growing fast, becoming heavier every day, and soon he would be too heavy for her to do so.

Brutus visibly adored Elizabeth, thrived with her attention, at the same time consequently ignoring Darcy and the other dogs around the house. He did not listen to Darcy's commands, and he even dared to growl, baring his teeth at him on one occasion. Enough had been enough, when the pup had attempted to take Darcy's place in their bed. Darcy kicked him out of their bedroom, shutting the door right in front of his face. Understandably, he made sure that Elizabeth was busy changing in her dressing room and could not see him doing so.

Since that incident, Darcy and Brutus had forged a truce of sorts. They tolerated each other, united with the task of bringing a smile to Elizabeth's face, but there was no love between them.

He watched as Elizabeth lifted her eyes at him once before opening the first letter, her gaze confused. She smiled again, but as he did not return her merriment, her attention focused on the task at hand, and she did not look at him again.

***

Elizabeth sorted her letters in the order she wanted to read them - the first from Aunt Gardiner, next from Jane, then from Mary and Charlotte. She was disappointed that her mother had not replied to any of her letters, but not truly surprised with such a turn of events.

She marvelled about the sudden odd behaviour of her husband. He had acted his usual affectionate self only this morning. She wondered what could have put him into such a sour mood. He resembled the Mr. Darcy she had met last autumn in Hertfordshire, reminding her how cold and sober in his attitude he could be if he wished to. She had forgotten this side of him almost completely during the last few months.

As she tore open the letter from her Aunt Gardiner, she decided not to ponder on her husband's behaviour. After all, he had asked her to stay with him, which allowed her to believe that she was not the reason for his blackened mood. Perhaps he had some business or estate related problems. She would try to approach the topic later. She wished him to share his worries with her.

Greedily she began to read.

My dearest niece,

In the first words of this letter, let me apologize to you for being so lenient with my response to your letter. My only justification is that I have my hands full these days. Your uncle was forced to let go one of his thus far most trusted clerks, who proved to be unreliable. In consequence, I am helping him with the correspondence and all the other current paperwork till he can find someone new for the position. Even now, I am sitting in the office, summing up the account books. Thankfully your sister Jane is still with us, supervising the children, because truly I would not know how to manage everything without her help.

We thank you again for your invitation to spend summer at Pemberley. The children are especially beside themselves with anticipation. They rarely have the opportunity to spend time in the country, and they are always so curious of animals. Every day they ask me when we will go to Pemberley. You can expect us two weeks from now, in the last days of July. I am afraid that your uncle will not be able to come with us. He may, however, come later, for which I sincerely hope. He needs his rest and some quiet fishing time more than anyone.

Returning to the most important matter - I read your last post several times, and have given much thought to it, let me assure you.

Oh, Lizzy, my heart goes out to you when I read your letter. First and foremost, I wish to you assure you that you are a perfectly normal, healthy, young woman, and there is absolutely nothing wrong with you. Simply, some physical activities take longer to master, let us look at little Fred. He did not learn to run like he does now in just one day. The same is true with physical intimacy. Some people require more time to acquire fluency in it.

The discomfort you mentioned is nothing unusual, I assure you. Your husband is much bigger than you, so it may take some time and practice before you fit together just right. I remember feeling some discomfort as well for the first few weeks after our wedding.

You mentioned the pain to be unbearable each time you attempted to couple with him. That was my experience as well at one time. You may not remember this, but the birth of twins was especially difficult for me. Even though I healed completely within two months, I could not bear the thought of being intimate again with my husband for another year or so. Each

attempt ended in such a pain for me that I kept asking him to stop. Moreover, at that time, your uncle started a rather risky (in my opinion) business with a man I considered unreliable. This only added to my low spirits.

I know that the circumstances are different for you. However, I wish to tell you that what you are experiencing is not uncommon. You are not the first nor are you the only woman suffering from such a predicament. In time, when you feel less depressed and more secure in your new life, I am certain that your problem will resolve itself on its own.

You also voiced concern as to whether your husband may look for someone else when you are not able to give him what he needs. I would not worry about that. He loves you; a blind man could see it. You are writing that he spends every night in your bed, that he does not avoid physical contact, even though he stays respectful to your boundaries, and never demands more. Consider this, my niece; when would he would find time to entertain a lover if he spends the nights with you, holding you chastely, while his days are divided between you, his sister, and his numerous duties?

You seem to dread trying again in anticipation of another failure. I suspect that this fear raises your anxiety all the more. My dear, this should not be and nor does it have to be.

My advice to you is to relax about this matter and stop torturing yourself with thoughts and suspicions like I found in your last letter. When the right time comes, you will feel you cannot bear waiting any longer to have him inside you, to put it bluntly.

I cannot tell you when this moment will happen, but be certain that it will come, and sooner rather than later.

If you are impatient, you may try to let him closer, without allowing things to go too far, if you understand my meaning.

I am certain that he would be more than happy with kissing and intimate touching in the privacy of your bedroom. A little practice cannot harm anyone. On the contrary, it may only add to your confidence which you seem to need so much. A small glass of good wine before sleep will help you to relax (not too much though, and not on an empty stomach, because the result may be quite the opposite).

When you are in his arms, do not think that something must happen, that you must conceive a child, that you must fulfil your duty to him, his family and his estate. Allow yourself to have a pleasant time with your husband.

May I remind you that, your uncommonly handsome, affectionate, and very much enamoured of you husband who is completely in love with you. Never forget that, my dear, and all will be well.

"I love you," she heard his deep voice close to her ear.

She jerked, closing the letter abruptly. Fitzwilliam was seated beside her, staring into her face intensely.

"You scared me," she said, blinking her eyes at him. "I had not heard you coming."

She saw that poor Brutus must have been unceremoniously pushed down to the floor, his expression sad as he stared at them with hurt in his eyes.

Darcy pushed his head onto her lap, causing some of the letters to fall to the floor. His long body stretched on the sofa with his booted feet extended on the other side.

"What is the matter?" She tugged at his hair affectionately.

In response, he took her other hand placed it on his chest, his eyes closed. He seemed to need physical contact, so she held him closely, stroking his hair leisurely to give him comfort.

"Aunt Gardiner is writing that we should expect them in the last days of this month," she said after a moment.

"That is good," he murmured.

"Uncle may not come; he is very busy with his business. Aunt will arrive alone with Jane and the children."

"I see," he said with a sigh, opening his eyes.

Her heart tugged in worry. "Are you not pleased with their visit? I know that you are not accustomed to small children, but we will take them out of your way, I promise."

He shook his head. "I like the Gardiners very much, and I do not mind children. I should be getting used to them, after all."

"Then why are you in such a strange mood?" she questioned, frowning.

He sighed again, before lifting up from her lap and sitting properly next to her. "You shall be angry with me," he announced.

"What did you do?" she asked, amused.

"You will not be angry?" he questioned childishly, resembling a five-year-old guilty of eating too many cookies before dinner time who was afraid to confess his misdeed to his mother.

"I cannot promise that I will not be angry; however I will try to understand why you did it—whatever it is that you have done."

She felt something being pushed into her hand. Looking down she noticed that it was a letter addressed to her, but written with an unfamiliar hand. She read the name of the sender, her eyes widening in surprise.

"Why would Colonel Fitzwilliam write to me?" she mused, turning the letter in her hand, before she saw that the seal was torn.

"You opened it?" she gasped.

He wrapped his fingers around her wrists. "I will never do it again." He swallowed visibly. "Forgive me."

She ignored his words, opening the post. "What is he writing?" she asked curiously.

Strangely, the inside was blank, but there was another letter inside, addressed to Miss Jane Bennet.

"What is the meaning of this?" She frowned. "He wants me to send this to Jane?"

Darcy nodded. "It would seem so."

Elizabeth reached for Jane's letter, picking it from the floor. She tore at it impatiently. The inside was filled with her sister's tight handwriting, but there was another letter enclosed inside.

"Can you believe that?" she asked, showing to Darcy a letter addressed to *Colonel Richard Fitzwilliam.*

"They want you to help them correspond with one another," Darcy stated the obvious. "Richard cannot send letters directly to Jane, as he is not her family and they are not engaged. You, as Richard's relative and Jane's sister, can send the letters to both of them."

"This is most shocking!" Elizabeth remarked, shaking her head. "What about poor Mr. Bingley?"

Darcy shrugged. "Bingley seems to be out of the cards here."

He did not say it, but he thought that it was his friend's own fault that the matters had taken such a turn. Bingley was still undecided where Miss Bennet was concerned while Richard seemed to have a clear strategy and played accordingly with some apparent success.

"I cannot believe that Jane would do something like this. It is very unlike her. All this secrecy," Elizabeth marvelled.

"Perhaps Jane wants to simply get to know my cousin better," he suggested, hoping to ease her mind. "How can she achieve that when she is in London while he must remain at Kent for the time being?" he questioned reasonably. "This is a very safe solution and very wise. She does not risk her reputation, and it does not ruin her relationship with Bingley. They picked the right person to help them as well. They both know that they can trust you implicitly."

Elizabeth folded Jane's letter neatly, before setting her eyes at him. "You opened the letter from your cousin because you thought that I was writing to him behind your back," she stated. "Why do you distrust me so much? Have I ever given you reason for that?" she asked, not being able to remove the hurt from her voice.

He leaned forward and buried his face in her neck. "I thought that it would be easier for me once we were married, once you were mine, but I cannot help feeling insecure," he confessed.

She cupped his cheek, making sure their eyes met. "The only times I think about your cousin is when you bring his name into our conversation. It is my husband who occupies my thoughts and heart to such an extent that there is no place for another man," she whispered the last words.

Remembering her aunt's advice, she wrapped one hand around his neck, and with all her strength, she pushed him backwards, looming over him.

"Touch me," she whispered, before meeting his lips in a kiss.

He seemed surprised, but it lasted only a moment. His hands took firm possession of her waist, as he was responding to her kiss with enthusiasm.

Taking one of his hands, she moved it up her chest. His eyes opened for a moment, focusing on her face as he gave her breast a gentle squeeze.

"Touch me, touch me," she chanted, straining against his searching over her bosom hand. "Love me if you will, Fitzwilliam."

"Let us go upstairs," he murmured into her neck, his hand running down her body, stopping on her backside.

"I thought that you had numerous correspondence to attend to," she whispered breathlessly, perfectly aware that she was teasing him.

"To hell with correspondence," he spoke before pulling both of them to their feet.

She giggled. "What will the servants say when we disappear upstairs in the middle of the day?"

"I do not care. Servants be damned!" He spoke hoarsely.

She sobered instantly. "I care."

"It is my home, and I will not answer to anyone if I want to spend time alone with my wife in the middle of the day," he announced arrogantly, taking her hand.

They exited the library, hurrying through the long corridor towards the staircase. She and Brutus were forced to run in order to keep his pace.

"Nephew, nephew, where are you going?" a high pitched, distinctively female voice called, rooting them in place.

Slowly they turned towards the fast approaching woman.

"I can see you, Fitzwilliam! What is the meaning of this, and why are you hiding from me?" the elegant lady, looking to be in her early fifties questioned. "We have been expecting you for weeks now, you and your new wife." Her gaze rested on Elizabeth.

Darcy regained his composure for a moment. "Aunt, allow me," he motioned with his hand. "This is my wife, Elizabeth. My dear, this is my aunt, Lady Eleanor, Colonel Fitzwilliam's mother."

Elizabeth dropped a curtsey, looking into the older woman's face. She saw blonde hair and laughing blue eyes, as if exactly copied from Colonel Fitzwilliam's face.

"Well, my dear," Lady Eleanor gave her an assessing look. "I've heard so much of you from my son that I expected someone bigger. You seem a nice girl though," she acknowledged with a warm smile.

Darcy and Elizabeth stood, still holding hands, as if frozen in their astonishment at the unexpected guest.

"Well, will you not invite me in?" Lady Eleanor questioned, her voice turning impatient. "Am I to stand here all afternoon, not being offered even a cup of tea?"

Elizabeth blinked, recollecting herself at last. She started to speak, greeting her husband's aunt in a most polite way.

Chapter Twenty-Seven

"I thought she would never decide to retire," Darcy whined as they entered their bedroom late in the evening.

Elizabeth walked past him into her dressing room. "I believe that Lady Eleanor missed both you and Georgiana, having not seen you for so long, and she wished to hear all the news. Moreover, she must have been curious about me," she responded to his comment as she moved to retrieve a pair of soft, well cushioned slippers she always used when in the privacy of their rooms.

Darcy's dark head peeked inside while he supported his arm against the door frame and stared down at her with serious eyes, as she was removing her shoes and stockings.

"Your aunt was most kind to me," Elizabeth said happily as she turned her back to him, indicating that she wished for him to open the row of tiny buttons at the back of her dress. "I had a feeling that she truly wanted to know me better for who I was," she mused as his fingers glided along the length of her back, working patiently on the buttons. "There was neither judgment nor any previously held misconceptions concerning my person in her tone or expression as we conversed," she continued. "I can see now from where Colonel Fitzwilliam derives his kindness and pleasant disposition."

The dress began loosening around her shoulders, and she had to hold it at her bosom to keep it from falling down completely. Darcy wrapped his arm around her waist, and she felt his lips on her neck.

She sighed, biting her lip worriedly. "I hope that Lady Eleanor was not disappointed with me. I would wish at least one member of your family to approve of me, apart from Colonel Fitzwilliam, of course."

She did not mention Lady Catherine's name, but she was certain that they both knew to whom she referred. Their last meeting with Lady Catherine was deeply buried in her mind, and she doubted whether she would ever forget about it.

Her husband's arm dropped from her waist and she heard his retreating steps on the hardwood floor.

"I will leave you to finish your toilette," he spoke in an odd voice, and a moment later, she was alone in the dressing room.

She cleansed herself quickly, her mind still occupied with Lady Eleanor's unexpected visit. Dressed in a nightdress and a dressing robe, she returned to the bedroom.

The room was empty, and she assumed that her husband had departed to prepare himself to sleep. She sat at her vanity, looking distractedly at her reflection in the large oval mirror. Her fingers were busy removing her elegant but simple earrings, which were a present from Darcy for her twenty-first birthday. They were beautiful, and even though she cringed at the thought of how expensive they must have been, she wore them every single day.

"She could have announced her visit." Darcy's words signaled his return.

Elizabeth's searching eyes locked on her husband. He was already dressed in his nightclothes, his hair slightly wet and combed neatly away from his handsome face. His entire posture informed her of his ill temper.

"Why are you so irritated?" she enquired gently, placing the earrings neatly in the small case. "You barely spoke a word to our guest. Lady Eleanor cares a great deal about you and Georgiana; that much was obvious. Your aunt is very fond of you. She invited all of us to Matlock, and I think that it was very thoughtful of her. "

Darcy dropped on the chair next to her. "Do we have to go there?" he fumed. "Why did you accept the invitation so readily in the first place? You could have refused, saying that we are expecting your relatives."

She turned with her whole body to him, more and more astonished with his angry attitude. "We will be in Matlock for a few days only," she spoke calmly. "We will return in time to welcome the Gardiners. Mrs. Reynolds can see to the preparations concerning their visit."

"I would prefer to stay home," he grunted, not looking at her. "You should have asked me before accepting the invitation," he insisted.

There was a long silence after his last words. Elizabeth turned back to her vanity, pretending to be busy with her combs, jewelry cases and bottles of perfumes sitting on the smooth white surface. She refused to look at her reflection, afraid to detect tears in her eyes. She began to remove the pins from her hair, trying to stop her trembling fingers from shaking so violently while she worked.

Why was he speaking to her in such a harsh manner? She re-evaluated today's afternoon and evening, finding no lapses in her behaviour towards Lady Eleanor. She thought that her husband would be pleased that his aunt was welcoming and accepting towards her, but she might have been wrong.

"Are you ashamed to show me in Matlock?" she asked quietly.

"Do not be ridiculous," he murmured only.

She froze at his words; a part of her wanted to call him on his harsh words, on the fact that he had just called her ridiculous, but she found that she had no strength for that. She was exhausted after a long, emotional day, and she needed her rest. Perhaps tomorrow her husband would be in a better frame of mind, and she would find the true reason for his dark mood.

Avoiding eye contact with him, she finished her nightly routine. She was still not accustomed at having a personal maid at her beck and call, and preferred to do many things on her own.

Brushing her long hair, she walked towards the bed. It was high time to cut some of its length. It reached well past her waist, and it was getting difficult to pin the heavy mass up in an orderly fashion.

Darcy was already seated on his side of the bed, with his back supported against a large pillow. She put the brush on the bedside table as she sat on the edge of the bed. She divided her tresses into three sections, intending to plait them for the night.

"You know that I like your hair let free," his disgruntled voice came to her.

She rolled her eyes, but did not turn to look at him. "You do not have to comb the tangles out of it in the morning though."

"You do not need to do it either. You have a maid at your disposal to do that, I believe."

She stopped her task and turned with her entire body to him. "What is the matter with you tonight?" she asked.

The only answer she received was a shrug of his broad arms. With a sigh, she flipped the half-made braid to her back and crawled across the bed to him.

"Talk to me," she pleaded, kneeling beside him. "What put you in such a bad mood?"

"You cannot guess?" he asked, his voice gentler, his expression suddenly vulnerable.

Slowly, the realization began to dawn on her. "You wished to spend the afternoon with me?"

He refused to look at her, and he did not confirm her suspicion with words, but she could feel that she had guessed correctly.

"You seemed to forget about our plans completely," he murmured, his voice thick with hurt.

She put a hand on his shoulder, stroking it. "Forgive me; it was not my intention to forget about you. However, what else could I do when she showed up on the doorstep? Should I have ignored her, or perhaps left it to Georgiana to entertain her? I wanted to make the best impression on your aunt. It was my first time to perform my role as Mistress of Pemberley in front of a stranger. Can you not see that?"

He turned away slightly before answering, "I am nothing more than a duty to you, coming at the far end after more important tasks…keeping my sister and relatives company, attending to household matters, and let us not forget your dog." The words fell from his mouth quickly with open bitterness.

She stared at him in astonishment, blinking her eyes. She had no suspicion that he could feel that way.

"You are most unfair," she protested. "I have tried very hard to find my place here, to prove myself. I want to be a good wife to you, so you will not regret your choice. I wish to be useful."

As soon as she finished her small speech, she knew from his expression that it was not what he had hoped or expected to hear.

"You are right, I am in a foul mood tonight," he agreed, his voice cold, his face blank. "Will you put the candles out?" he asked, as he laid down, showing her his back.

She sat on the bed next to him for a longer moment, undecided in what to do. Finally, she slipped from the bed and took a turn around the room, putting out the candles as he had asked. She wanted to weep.

As the room darkened, with only the faint light from the fireplace illuminating it, she returned to their bed and slipped under the covers.

She lay on her back, staring at the canopy of their large, four poster bed. She guessed from his breathing that he was only pretending to sleep—he was too quiet for real sleep. Usually when in deep slumber, he produced low wheezing sounds while taking every breath. She also realized that it had been the first time since their marriage that he was so physically distant from her, not touching her in any way.

Without farther consideration, she rolled closer to him, plastering her front to his back.

"I cannot fall asleep without your arms around me," she confessed in a clear voice, despite her uneasiness at admitting her true feelings to him.

Slowly, he shifted onto his back and raised his arm over her head, allowing her to snuggle closer.

"Sleep," he whispered roughly, without his usual tenderness. But he kissed the top of her head, which uplifted her spirits vastly, and she felt as if a heavy weight had been lifted from her heart. She moved yet closer, lifting her leg over his body.

They both stilled when her thigh brushed against his middle and felt his hardness.

The silence between them was complete. He did not remove his arm from around her and seemed to stop breathing. She realized that lately she had not felt him like that against her. He had always handled her very gently, and when embracing her, he had never pressed her with too much force. Her heart melted as the thought crossed her mind that in all probability, he had kept himself in check so she would not feel pressured into intimacy that she was not ready for.

She, Elizabeth Darcy, was a fool indeed, as she had not guessed the true reason for her husband's foul mood.

"Fitzwilliam," she whispered, moving onto her back, pulling him firmly with her, her fingers twisted into the front of his nightshirt.

He laid down on her, not sparing her his full weight, his face buried in her neck.

She shifted under him with some effort, at last freeing her legs, so she could bend and wrap them around his lean body. Her hands slid down his back, till she grabbed his nightshirt, attempting to pull it up.

His weight lifted from her then, and his eyes bored into hers as he stared down at her, supported on his outstretched arms. She pulled up his nightshirt farther, uncovering the hairy planes of his chest till she succeeded in removing the garment completely.

As she disposed of his nightshirt, she captured his lips with hers, her hands stroking their way down his chest, stomach and lower. Hesitating only for a short moment, she took a hold of his still erect manhood.

"You are certain?" he breathed above her, his voice resembling a tortured moan.

In response, she grabbed the hem of her own nightgown, removing it hastily, throwing it blindly aside.

"Oh, Lizzy!" She heard a throaty exclamation, before he dropped back on her, she felt the presence of his hands and lips suddenly all over her body.

She gasped in the first moment of his ferocious attack on her body, but then she reminded herself that he was the last person in the world whom she should fear physically. He had always been nothing but gentle with her. Even when they strolled together, and she, lost deep in her thoughts, walked off the beaten path, his fingers wrapped so very carefully around her shoulder as if a butterfly touch to steer her in the right direction. He had never left as much as a slight bruise on her skin. With his strength, it would be enough for him to press or squeeze a bit harder, and he would mark her easily, probably without even realizing it.

He had hurt her that first night, true, but she could see now that the disastrous outcome was as much her fault as his. She had stubbornly insisted that he continue, even though she was anything but ready to accept him at that time.

Remembering her aunt's letter, she lifted her hands to his head, burying her fingers in his hair, as he suckled at the tip of her breast. With her eyes closed, she enjoyed his ministrations, trying not to think about anything but the pleasurable sensations that his touch brought to life in her body. She lifted her hips when his hand found its way between her thighs, silently encouraging him to continue.

Clasping him to her with all the might of her right arm, the fingers of her left hand gripped the sheet beneath her. She concentrated on the pleasure coming from his caresses inflicted on her sensitive folds. Every few moments, his thumb seemed to brush one special spot, bringing such a thrill every time he stroked her, her fingernails dug in the supple skin of his back, surely causing him pain.

At last the sensations became too intense, and a wave of shattering pleasure enveloped her entire body. It could be compared only to what she had felt when he had taken her to his bedroom before their wedding and touched her intimately for the first time. Nevertheless, it was stronger now, and she clung to him, never wanting to let go, her heart pounding erratically in her chest, her legs trembling, choked sounds coming from her open mouth.

She lay lifelessly for what seemed to be a long moment after that, her limbs weak and thrown awkwardly around his body. From time to time, a pleasant current ran through her, and she did not possess the strength nor the will to lift her head or even open her eyes.

"Is it painful?" His question brought her attention back to the present moment, and she looked up into his concerned face.

"Is what painful?" she murmured, following his gaze down. The light from the fireplace had died down completely, and she could see little; only that his right hand was firmly wedged between her legs.

"This," he said, and something moved inside of her. She sat up abruptly, now clearly seeing that one of his fingers was pushed inside of her.

"It does not hurt?" she questioned unbelievably.

He laughed in response. "It is I who should be asking." He wrapped his free arm around her arms, kissing her forehead.

She joined him in his laughter, immense relief washing over her as they fell back together on the pillows.

Soon, his finger was replaced with his manhood, and she felt him poking hesitatingly at her.

"Do it," she ordered impatiently, eager to see whether the feeling of his manhood inside of her would be as painless as his finger.

At last he pushed, and there was pain, but small, and of entirely different intensity. There was no burning or tearing, and she did not feel as if she was split in half. The stretching was uncomfortable - it was a dull pain, or rather discomfort, resembling nothing she had experienced before, but still perfectly bearable.

"You are well?" She heard his frantic voice asking.

"Yes," she answered slowly.

"You are not pretending like before?" he demanded, hovering over her, his eyes staring into hers with intensity.

She shook her head. "I feel stretched, rather uncomfortable, but there is no tearing sensation like before. You can try to move, I think."

Unlike the other two times, she did not avoid looking at him while he moved inside her. The difference in their heights was reflected even now when they were together like this, joined intimately. He was supported on his outstretched arms, his head well above hers, so when she looked directly up, all she could see was his upper chest and chiselled collarbones. She doubted that it was comfortable for him to loom over her like that.

The sensation of discomfort between her legs was still present, but less so. His pushes were gentle, but a few times, he seemed to go a bit farther or perhaps at a different angle, and then she felt a pleasant sensation, as if he managed to hit the right spot inside of her. She began to wonder how to communicate to him what made her feel good, but then his breathing and movements changed, turning fast and shallow. Once again, she felt a surge of unexpected pleasure as he drove with more force inside of her the last time, before producing a grunting sound, and trembling above her.

Her heart swelled with joy and immense pride, and she hugged his heavy, sweaty, now relaxed body, to her, using both her legs and arms, grinning wildly above his shoulder. She had managed to successfully bed her husband, or rather he bedded her. Everything went smoothly, without the searing pain, humiliation, and without asking him to stop before he even started. She indeed deserved to be called an accomplished woman tonight.

Chapter Twenty-Eight

"Out," Darcy ordered, as he saw Elizabeth's dog peeking through the crack in the door leading from the private parlour of their chamber to their bedroom.

Darcy, who had awakened to an empty and cold bed, was naturally displeased at his wife's absence. He wondered where she could have gone so early in the morning. He had knocked at the door of her dressing room, but she was not there. Now, that he saw her dog, he knew that she must be somewhere close by.

"I do not comprehend why you always have to be so short with Brutus. He is such a darling." He turned to the sound of his wife's clear, singing voice as she walked into their bedroom.

She was dressed in a nightdress and robe, her hair pulled back into a low ponytail, tied with a plain white ribbon. Leaning down she patted Brutus' head, causing him to let out a short, happy bark.

Darcy, however, was the one who had set the rule that the dog was not allowed inside their bedroom, and he had every intention of sticking to it.

"Out," he repeated, staring down at Brutus. The pup moved behind Elizabeth's skirts, turning his back to Darcy.

"That is enough," Darcy grunted as he picked up the dog by its yellow fur and carried it outside into the sitting room, closing the door right before its black, wet nose could wedge back inside.

"Where have you been so early in the morning?" he asked, focusing his attention back on his wife.

"When I awoke, I remembered that yesterday I had left my letters in the library." Only after she had spoken the words did he notice the few letters she held in her hand. "I thought I should go and collect them."

As she offered her explanation, her eyes carefully avoided him; not once did she look at him. Instantly worried that she might feel disappointed after the events of the night, he pulled her closer and cupped her cheek.

"Will you not look at me, my love?" he asked softly, turning her face to his.

She blushed, her gaze escaping to the ceiling. "You are naked," she murmured.

He looked down at his body in confusion. She was indeed right; until now he had failed to notice the state of his undress.

"You are shy of me?" he cried unbelievably. "After last night?" A rich laughter echoed in the room.

She crossed her arms over her chest. "There! Tease me about it, will you?" she huffed. "I cannot help but feel some embarrassment as you parade around naked in broad daylight." She swatted his arm in a playful gesture.

"You never cease to amaze me, love," he murmured, wrapping his arms tightly around her so that she was not able to move away from him, even if she wished. "Let us return to bed." His hands moved from her back and waist down to her hips, clearly stating his intentions.

She pushed at him, shaking her head, her hands splayed flat on his chest. "It is almost seven; I should prepare myself for the day. We have a guest, and I should see to breakfast…"

"My aunt will not awaken before ten o'clock, I assure you," he interrupted. "And when she does, she will take breakfast in her room, as she always has. We should not expect her below stairs before noon. I know her routine well."

Their eyes met, and she held his gaze steadily for a moment before she looked away. "Still, I would wish to read my letters. I may not have time later, as we are to depart for Matlock tomorrow. Besides, I must speak with Mrs. Reynolds so that she knows exactly what to prepare for the Gardiners arrival."

"Just a few minutes then," he said, trying to fight back the sharp feeling of rejection aching painfully in his chest. "Please."

As they lay down on the bed, he drew the covers over them. She quickly snuggled close to him, placing her head on his chest.

"Do you regret what happened last night, love?" he dared to ask, after a long moment of silence.

"No, of course not!" she cried instantly with feeling, looking up at him. "No," she shook her head, "I am most pleased that we at last…" She blushed, hiding her face from him as she rubbed her cheek against his chest. "You know my meaning," she murmured.

His hand ran down the length of her hair. "Are you sore then?"

She shook her head again. "No, not at all."

"Do not hesitate to tell me if that is the case," he insisted. "It was three times, after all," he reminded her proudly.

She shook her head once more, quite vehemently, her fingers tugging at his chest hair.

Darcy was amiss at what could possibly be the cause of her current mood. What wrong had he done? She had been so wonderful last evening, so open and uninhibited, while this morning she seemed to be an entirely different person. This marriage business was certainly a complicated one. His previous contact with women had always been so simple in its nature, shallow to be sure, but always straightforward.

He had imagined the morning after he loved his wife fully and completely for the first time in an entirely different way than his previous bumbling, that everything would be different—that she would be more willing to be his lover. He did not expect to wake up alone without her in his arms. At the least, he expected her to be resting close to him so he could reach for her at his leisure and love her as he pleased.

Darcy took a deep breath. To be sure, last night could be counted as the best night of his life thus far. He was elated with the awareness that the last barrier between them had been lifted—the last obstacle to their truly being together.

"I feel different," she said quietly.

Surprised to hear her voice interrupting his troubled thoughts, he frowned. "Can you elaborate?"

Still playing with his chest hair, she replied. "I am not certain. I just feel as though I am not the same person I was yesterday."

Kissing the top of her head, he had no clue as to how he should answer her; nor did he know to what she was referring. He felt exactly the same as he had yesterday, only much happier in both body and soul—especially in body. The last months, when he had had no release other than his own hand, had been trying for him.

Was she happier with things as they had been? Was that her meaning? She had said that she had not regretted their passionate night and that she was pleased with what had transpired between them. So what was her meaning?

"Are we going to do it every night now?" she asked, a slight smile gracing her lips.

"Yes, we are," he answered without hesitation.

In his view, there was no reason why they should not. There was no physical obstacle to inhibit them. She no longer felt pain like before. Moreover, he could tell from the way her body responded to his that she derived more pleasure with each time they made love. When he touched her, there was no doubt that he had her in the palm of his hand. She was his for the taking—and take her he had. Her next words amazed him.

"I cannot wait for the night."

Turning his head, he gazed at her in confusion. She could not wait for the night? Her last words played over in his mind several times as he tried to make sure that he understood her correctly. If she was eager for him to bed her again, then why had she just given him the speech about feeling different than before and not being the same person?! She made no sense!

"Elizabeth," he said. "You know very well that we do not have to wait for the dark of night," he changed their positions, shifting so that she was beneath him.

Her legs lifted and parted eagerly, wrapping around his hips. He tugged at her gown in order to see her pretty, high, perky breasts. They were perfect, so delicate, with soft, pink peaks. He knew that he could stare at them for hours, and the view would never bore him. He even toyed with the idea of asking her to keep the bodice of her dress lowered whenever they were in the privacy of their rooms—similar to the women in some of the ancient civilizations he had studied while at university.

As he pushed her skirts up to gaze between her thighs, he felt her stiffen. She no longer protested against his looking at this part of her as she had before, but he could feel the tension in her body as he examined her.

"I am not clean," she murmured. "I should bathe." She attempted to sit up, but he put her down with a hand firmly pressed against her shoulder.

Clearly visible were white, dried smudges on the creamy skin of her inner thighs, which he presumed were the remains of his seed. What he had said when he had seen her that first time in his bedroom in London before their wedding was true. She had an uncommonly pretty and delicate slit, completely symmetrical and even. Her skin was visibly reddened now though. However, as he touched her, she did not cringe in discomfort, so he had to believe her assertion that she was not sore. He truly wished to kiss her tender flesh, but was not certain whether she would welcome it. He had never done such a thing before, but naturally he had heard of it. Nor had he ever wanted to perform such an intimate act on any of the women he had known in his past, but with Elizabeth it was entirely different.

"Have you finished?" Her cranky voice reached his ears. "I cannot imagine what you find so interesting that you would be this occupied with my personal parts for any length of time. I will fall asleep if you do not end your staring soon."

He grinned, moving up her body. A few minutes later, when he found her wet enough to accept him, he pushed inside. Focusing on controlling his pace and trying to be gentle, he took into account the great disproportion in their height and weight.

A frown appeared between her dark eyebrows. She began wriggling beneath him, shifting her hips in small sharp movements which made it very difficult for him to go slow.

At last her hands found a place on his buttocks, and she lifted herself up to meet him. "Harder," she ordered.

Stopped in a half thrust, frozen above her, he was not sure whether he heard her correctly.

"I will not break; push harder," she repeated, locking her eyes with his, filled with determination and burning with passion.

Shocked with her taking the initiative in such a way, he began surging into her depths as deep and quickly as he could go. And lifting to meet his each and every stroke, it was not long before she tightened rhythmically around him, gripping him in a passion such as he had never known before.

Finally, they both collapsed, utterly spent.

As he cradled her in his arms, both of them trying to catch their breath while their hearts raced, he wondered whether he would ever be able to completely understand her. She was a mystery, however he prayed that little by little her secrets would be completely revealed to him.

With a contented heart, his body finally sated, he closed his eyes in restful sleep once more. This was the best sex he had ever experienced, and he had the rest of his life to look forward to more of it.

***

It was quite late in the evening when Elizabeth found the quiet time to read her letters. Lady Eleanor had proved to be a rather demanding guest who liked to be entertained. Whether it was a simple tea or an open carriage ride around the grounds, she certainly liked to have company around her at all times.

Elizabeth released a sigh as she lifted Jane's letter from the pile in her lap and began to read, hoping to find some explanation for her sister's relationship with Colonel Fitzwilliam. Unfortunately, Jane was very laconic, only revealing that she and the man in question had shared a few pleasant conversations. However Jane wished to continue their friendship, asking Elizabeth to help her correspond with Darcy's cousin.

Elizabeth could not wait to have an eye to eye conversation with her elder sister. What amazed her most about the current situation was that Jane did not appear to have completely lost her interest in Mr. Bingley, having seen him in London several times over the last few weeks. Jane wrote quite plainly that Mr. Bingley had every intention of visiting Pemberley this summer. Having a standing invitation from Darcy to come whenever he wanted, and knowing that Jane would be there together with the Gardiners, it appeared to please him to come when they would be present.

In her limited experience Elizabeth could hardly imagine how a woman could be courted by two men at the same time. Understandably, Jane was too beautiful and good to go unnoticed, and it was expected that many men would be taken with her charms. But the astonishing part of this situation was that Jane seemed to be seriously interested in both suitors equally, as if she could not decide between them.

Closing Jane's letter, Elizabeth gazed down at her husband, who was sleeping soundly with his head nestled in her lap. The rest of his was body stretched comfortably along the oversized sofa, which suited his height perfectly. Perhaps she should consider asking him about his opinion on Jane's relationship with Mr. Bingley and Colonel Fitzwilliam? Darcy knew both men very well, after all. It was clear, however, that he would be more welcoming towards his cousin's suit rather than Mr. Bingley's. On the other hand, she concluded, it was a private matter between only three adults—her sister and the two gentlemen in question. Neither she nor Darcy had the right to interfere, though Jane had asked her to pass along her letters to Colonel Fitzwilliam. Elizabeth did not see any valid reason why she should refuse such a small favour. Above all else she wanted her sister's happiness, and she prayed that Jane knew what she was about.

The next letter she opened was from Charlotte. She and Mr. Collins were well settled into Longbourn now, but her friend tactfully wrote very little about it—one sentence stating that they were comfortable in their new home. The rest of the letter was quite entertaining, containing all the gossip from the neighbourhood. In the last few lines Charlotte revealed that she was with child, expecting to deliver around Christmas or early in the New Year. Elizabeth was very happy for her friend. She hoped that soon she would have good news of the same nature to share with Charlotte.

In her letter, Charlotte said nothing about Mrs. Bennet, so Elizabeth was more than usually curious about the content of Mary's letter. Nevertheless, she did not expect to gain much information from her sister concerning her mother or the younger girls. Elizabeth released a contented sigh as she unfolded the missive and began to read. Mary wrote to her regularly, every two weeks or so, contrary to the younger girls, who seemed not to know what a pen and paper were for. Nevertheless, Mary always concentrated on the same topics, mainly what books she was reading and what compositions she was currently learning to play, eager to know whether Elizabeth knew those books or played that particular music.

"Oh, no!" Elizabeth exclaimed, jerking as she sat up straight. She reread the second paragraph of Mary's letter again, eager to be certain that she understood the meaning correctly. "That cannot be! What is Mama thinking to allow such a thing?"

Roused by her sudden movement, Darcy lifted his head from her lap. "What?! What happened?"

"Mama has agreed for Lydia to go to Brighton for the summer," she explained, frowning at the letter in her hand.

"During her mourning?" Darcy questioned incomprehensibly, still not quite awake from his recent nap.

"It is tragic, simply tragic," Elizabeth moaned, clenching the letter as she stood and began to pace.

Darcy reached to take the now slightly crumbled letter from his wife's trembling hand. Rubbing his eyes and stifling a small yawn with his fist, he began to read.

"It is clearly written here that Lydia accepted the invitation of Colonel Foster's wife," he said after a moment. "Surely it is not so bad if she is to stay under the care of the colonel of the regiment—and in their house at that?"

"How can you say so, Fitzwilliam?" Elizabeth cried passionately, her voice laced with desperation. "You met Harriet Foster. She the silliest, most irresponsible and empty headed woman in the country, and the worst possible company for Lydia! As long as Papa lived he was able to curb Lydia, to somehow tame her wild behaviour. He was the only person to whom she would listen. Now, without Papa here, she is most surely lost to any reason. I am certain that if she should go to Brighten, she will soon be lost to us forever."

Darcy stood up, pulling her gently into his arms. "Love, you worry too much about something of which you have little to no control," he murmured thickly.

She locked her eyes with his. "Jane knows nothing about it, because if she did she would have surely mentioned this matter in her letter. I can only imagine how badly Lydia will behave while unsupervised in Brighton with all those officers about! If she returns home with her virtue intact, I would be very much surprised."

"Are you not exaggerating? Surely she would not allow... she is so young."Darcy stuttered.

"She would, believe me," Elizabeth said passionately, shuddering in his arms. "Last summer Jane and I caught her with the stable boy near the hedgerows. She had the upper part of her dress completely removed and his hand was under her skirts. She did not seem displeased with his actions and she had just turned fifteen. She is now a year older."

"What happened after that? What was your father's reaction?"

Elizabeth sighed. "Papa did not beat her—he never used force with any of us— but she was not allowed to leave the house for weeks. Later, however, all was forgotten as if it had never happened. Mama just seemed pleased that nothing more serious had transpired, if you know my meaning."

Darcy frowned, pausing for a moment. "I think that only your uncle, Mr. Gardiner, might influence your mother to change her mind and refuse to let Lydia go."

"You are right, of course! You are perfectly right!" she exclaimed, new hope rising in her voice. "Uncle Gardiner is the only person who can convince Mama that allowing Lydia to go to Brighton, without even one reasonable person to watch over her, is a disaster in the making. The Gardiners, however, know nothing about what happened last summer. I must write to them today, informing them of the situation and asking for their help."

"It is late and you are tired." Darcy interjected. "Wait until tomorrow."

"We go to Matlock early in the morning," she protested. "There will be no time for letter writing tomorrow. I must send it as soon as can be as there is no time to tarry."

He hugged her close to him, kissing her forehead. "Try not to stay up too long, my love. I know they are your family, but I hate to see you so worried."

With those words, he stepped away and entered the bedroom, leaving her alone in their private sitting room to attend to her most urgent business.

He hoped that she was exaggerating her expectations concerning her younger sister, for if she was not, trouble would follow. And that kind of trouble he would rather not have to deal with.

With a heavy sigh, Darcy pulled back the counterpane and slid under the covers to await his wife and another night of passionate love making.

Chapter Twenty-Nine

"And here is the coin that I acquired lately from a university professor in Edinburgh. It is the newest of my collection and was issued during the reign of James VI of Scotland, late sixteenth century just prior to him becoming James I of England," Lord Matlock declared, handing the coin to Darcy.

Darcy took the gold piece between his fingers, examining it with great interest. The Earl of Matlock's passion for acquiring antique coins was well known in the family, and Darcy himself had added a few items to his collection in the past.

"It cannot, of course, compare with the coins I received from your father—the ones dating back to the Roman rule in Britain. Not many people in the country have those. They are a true treasure—one I shall always keep."

Darcy nodded, remembering the story he had heard many times from his parents as a child. During the time when his father had been courting his mother, there had been an occurrence at Pemberley. It seemed that while building the new addition to the stables a small pot had been found containing several old coins. His father had recognised that they were quite old, but having little interest in such matters, and at the same time being aware of the Earl of Matlock's passion for all things historical, brought them to Matlock upon his next visit. Lady Anne, Darcy's mother, had claimed that this one event had convinced her brother to give his approval to their union.

"Unfortunately, neither Richard nor Henry seem to show any interest in my collection," the Earl of Matlock continued, the sadness in his voice obvious. "When I am gone, no one will care enough to add to it."

Darcy clasped the older man's arm. "You are in good health Uncle, and many years are yet before you." His words did not seem to lift the man's spirit, so he added, "Perhaps one of your grandchildren will be interested in your collection."

"I would prefer to leave it to the museum than to one of those little devils!" the Earl whispered loudly, looking with accusation across the room where his daughter-in-law, the mother of said grandchildren, was sitting by the fireplace with Elizabeth, Georgiana, and Lady Eleanor. "Little rascals... cruel brats they are! Can you imagine what the older one did this last week? Why the little imp tortured your aunt's cat, Miss Pat. Poor animal has not dared to leave our private rooms till this day." Shifting closer, he beckoned with his hand for Darcy to lean down. "I asked Henry to take his family to London, or to the house in Bath, so we may have some peace in our own home, but he will not! He says he prefers for them to stay in the country. It seems she fell into terrible debt during their last season in London. So now he leaves her here with us and goes his own way, not giving a second thought as to what we must suffer!"

Darcy watched as his uncle's face turned red and drops of sweat appeared on his temples. "May I fetch you a glass of water?" he asked with concern.

Shaking his head no, the Earl of Matlock began closing the large, leather bound case that held his treasures. Speaking in hushed tones, he continued, "I doubt whether your aunt and I can stand this much longer. We may be forced to live in Bath."

"You always claimed to hate Bath, Uncle," Darcy reminded him quietly.

"What else are we to do?" The earl looked at him, his eyes blank and glossy. "We only want peace and quiet in our old age."

Darcy fell silent, trying in vain to find the right words to say in order to console him. Henry's wife, born to the house of the Duke of Richmond, was spoiled and cruel, and everyone in the family felt the sting of her vindictiveness rather painfully. She had always been quite polite to Darcy, though and he suspected he knew why. The fact that she had two unmarried younger sisters vying for his attention would have been reason enough.

"Uncle, I want you to know that you and Aunt are always welcome at Pemberley if the situation here becomes unbearable for you," he assured sincerely.

"Thank you." The older man nodded, his voice trembling with emotion. "You are a good boy Darcy. You always have been a good friend to our Richard and your wife seems to be a sound choice despite her lack of connections and a proper dowry. Your aunt and Richard think very highly of her."

Darcy's eyes went to the other end of the room where the women were seated. Elizabeth's face was calm and polite, as she listened intently to what Lady Eleanor was saying. Neither her posture nor expression suggested that she might be upset. The awareness that Elizabeth was perfectly capable of protecting herself against malicious remarks—which she had proved many times—not only standing up to Caroline Bingley, but to Lady Catherine, and at times to him, did not ease his concern. Her spirits had not yet recovered after Mr. Bennet's death, and she was much more vulnerable than when he had met her last autumn. He excused his uncle's company and walked across the room towards the women.

"Darcy," the Viscountess of Rockford exclaimed as she noticed him approach them. "We have just been talking about you." She raised her chin in smug confidence.

Darcy said nothing to this as his eyes rested upon his wife. Moving to stand behind her chair, he put a hand on her small shoulder causing her to turn and look up at him with a reassuring smile. He returned it. It never failed to warm his heart when her dark eyes sparkled with amusement as they did now.

"I was telling Mrs. Darcy how many hearts were broken when the news of your upcoming nuptials reached Town." Lady Rockford looked directly at him." My own sisters were desolate with grief, I assure you. The most desirable bachelor caught by a country girl from Hertfordshire who was unknown to anyone." She laughed loudly, her gaze shitting from Darcy to Elizabeth. "Tell me, Mrs. Darcy, how you can possibly sleep peacefully at night knowing that your husband was so sought after and desired by the most beautiful, fashionable and accomplished women of the ton. You cannot imagine how fortunate a woman with your background is to have accomplished what so many others could not."

Darcy felt his hand clench on Elizabeth's shoulder with more force than he ever intended to use when touching her. He lessened the pressure only when he felt her small, cool hand cover his.

Elizabeth smiled brightly at Lady Rockford, her eyes dancing with merriment. "You guessed correctly. My nights are far from peaceful; however, the reason for it is quite the opposite of what you might imagine. My thoughts and attention during the night are completely taken by my husband—and I assure you, Lady Rockford, it is not his bachelor past which occupies us."

Darcy bit his lower lip hard, fighting the urge to laugh out loud as he observed the expression on Lady Rockford's face once she realised what Elizabeth had said. He doubted whether the woman would ever again try to embarrass his wife with cruel remarks. Then, to his great consternation, he remembered his baby sister was among the company and his eyes darted to

Georgiana. Her gaze was lowered as she sipped her tea, but he could swear that there was a satisfied smirk upon her lips.

Relieved that his sister did not seem particularly disturbed with the direction of the conversation, he put his hands on both sides of Elizabeth's arms and leaned forward. "If you will excuse us Aunt, I wish to show Mrs. Darcy around the grounds. She is very fond of the outdoors, and I do not believe she has had the opportunity to see the entire park yet."

"Of course, off you go! We understand," Lady Eleanor offered hastily, obviously relieved at the change of subject.

Darcy offered his arm, which Elizabeth accepted with a beautiful smile as her eyes locked with his. A smile graced his lips as well. Each time she gazed at him in such a manner his chest tightened pleasurably.

They walked for quite a while before Elizabeth spoke, getting right to the point. "Why did your cousin marry such a woman? Was it a love match?"

Darcy laughed mirthlessly. "Hardly. It was time for him to marry, I suppose. My uncle was eager for an heir to assure the line, and so he strongly advised my cousin to seek a wife. The daughter of the Duke of Richmond, in theory, was a good match for him. She is from an honourable family and had a large dowry."

"Could he not have found someone kinder, less vicious?"

"I do not know the exact circumstances of their courtship; I was just beginning university when they were courting. Later when I had opportunity, I was never curious enough to ask about it. Henry and I were never particularly close, you see. However, I will say that for the son of an earl to marry the daughter of a duke is considered a splendid match. Personalities, as well as likes and dislikes, are normally not taken into consideration in matters of marriage. Rarely does one from our rank marry for love as it is a luxury we cannot afford."

While her husband spoke so casually, Elizabeth pondered his words carefully. *Rarely does one from our rank marry for love.* And yet her husband claimed to love her and had fought very hard for them to be together.

"Lady Rockford reminds me of Caroline Bingley," Elizabeth declared at last.

"I think that Caroline Bingley might quite easily grow into Lady Rockford if she had the right connections and was titled."

They strolled along in silence until Elizabeth eyed a stone bench under a large oak tree. She released his arm, taking a seat. Stretching out her hand, she patted the place next to her, indicating that she wanted Darcy to join her.

"Is it allowed here?" she questioned, shifting with her back to his chest.

"This?" he murmured, kissing her neck as his arm wound around her waist bringing her closer.

She nodded, closing her eyes as she rested her head against his shoulder. "Everyone can see us. Such public acts of affection may be frowned upon."

"Do you think that I care?"

"You have changed." She covered his arm with her hand.

"I must disagree. When we met for the first time, you perceived that I was very private person, but you did not see this part of me. Still waters run deep and things are not always as they appear."

She said nothing for a moment, but only stared into the gardens beyond. "I like the landscaping at Pemberley much better. French gardens like these are beautiful, to be certain, but are much too controlled for my taste."

He squeezed her tightly. "Nothing can compare to Pemberley, my love."

Turning in his arms, she studied his face. "Please say we will return home tomorrow."

His eyebrows raised in surprise. "Two days earlier than was planned? I thought that you were enjoying the visit."

"I am enjoying it."

He frowned. "Is it Lady Rockford? Did she say something hurtful to you?"

She shook her head. "She does not bother me, nor will her attempts at unsettling me succeed. Nevertheless, she made me realize how much I appreciate what we have at Pemberley. It is not common for some families to genuinely love and respect one another. After a long day, most would expect to spend time with their loved ones in peaceful harmony—deriving joy from each other's company without quarrels, misunderstandings and pettiness. It is something we have at Pemberley, have we not?"

"We certainly have," Darcy confirmed with no little emotion. He was not certain whether she had even noticed that she had used the word love.

"We certainly lacked it at Longbourn, although I often witnessed such a home when visiting the Gardiners," Elizabeth stated earnestly. "It is rare enough that we should not forget our good fortune."

"My wise, Lizzy," Darcy murmured, capturing her lips with his in a chaste but tender kiss.

"What about Georgiana? Do you suppose she may be displeased with our early return?"

"I doubt it. She is very eager to see the Gardiners again. I dare say your aunt and the children especially."

"Aunt Madeline is certainly a person whom every woman would like to have for a friend."

"It is settled then," Darcy said, lifting fluidly to his feet and extending his hand as he helped Elizabeth to stand as well. "I know that you would wish to stay in the gardens longer, but I do not like those clouds. Rain threatens and I do not want you to get wet."

Nodding her head, Elizabeth accepted his arm and they strolled slowly back to the manor.

***

The Matlocks expressed their displeasure at the news that the Darcys wished to abandon their company earlier than initially planned. Lady Eleanor attempted to change Elizabeth and Georgiana's mind, promising a picnic and a shopping trip in the village. Darcy gave Georgiana the choice of staying longer, but she refused without any visible regret.

The return home proved to be joyful for everyone. Reaching Pemberley, Georgiana ran to grab her music sheets and then to her pianoforte, while Darcy hurried to greet his horses. Elizabeth was happy to take a long walk around the park, amazed that she had managed to grow so attached to Pemberley in such a short time. She had begun to consider it a magical place with wild, untamed beauty, isolated from the outer world by hills and forests. And she understood why her husband was so proud of his ancestral home and could not hold his pride in all that he held dear against him. She was beginning to realize that she was now a part of all that he cherished. He had defied convention, marrying for love and she felt humbled by this knowledge, though she failed to understand what she had done to deserve such good fortune. Of all she surveyed, she was mistress.

***

The day of the Gardiners' arrival, Elizabeth spent her morning checking to see if everything was prepared for their visit. It was to be the first time since Georgiana was a child that small children would inhabit the house, and Elizabeth devoted much attention to readying the nursery. She had not discussed the details with her aunt, but she had one room prepared for the

twins and little Fred, for whom a small bed was secured from the attic. There was a separate bed for Anne, who was to stay in one of the regular guest bedrooms. Elizabeth and Georgiana thought that the older girl would appreciate being treated like a young lady. Naturally, the arrangements could easily be changed if Aunt Madeline had different ideas.

The guests were expected in the late afternoon to early evening, but Elizabeth began to look for them at midday. Eventually, restless and unable to focus on any task, she decided to go for a walk, hoping to find her husband who had left the house in haste shortly after breakfast. Heading in the direction of the stables, she indeed found Darcy in the paddock standing next to a small horse.

"I have not seen him before," she proclaimed, walking closer.

Darcy straightened up from inspecting the animal's legs. His whole face brightened at the sight of her, which warmed her heart. Extending his hand, her feet carried her to him without conscious thought.

"Our newest addition," he offered, wrapping her in his arms and bringing her close. "It came today."

"You bought a pony?" she asked, confused.

"Georgiana's old pony died a few years ago. I figured that since we were to have children among our guests, they would enjoy it. Perhaps the twins would like to learn how to ride and it is safer to start with a pony. He is young but already quite well trained, though he does not have a name as yet."

"How thoughtful of you!" she exclaimed, throwing her arms around his neck.

"Easy," he crooned, holding her to him with one arm, while the other hand held on to the pony's bridle.

"You are too generous," she stepped back to look into his face. "I know that the children will be delighted with your gesture."

"I thought that in a few years our own child may use him as well," he mentioned casually.

She stilled, her eyes searching his expression as she held her breath. "You are not opposed to the idea then?"

He held her gaze steadily. "I never was."

"Oh, Fitzwilliam," she whispered, stepping close to place her head against his chest.

His tightened his grip, whispering in her hair, "A man needs an heir—a son to whom he may pass his legacy . At first, I wanted to wait and have his mother to myself for a little while, but then I realized that a child born of love can only strengthen a marriage. And Lizzy, I—"

The sound of someone behind them loudly clearing his throat made Darcy stop and turn. One of the footmen stood with his face to the ground, looking very awkward. Elizabeth stiffened, attempting to step away from Darcy so as to keep the proper distance between them, but he would have none of it, holding her firm.

"Excuse me, sir, but Mrs. Reynolds asked me to find Mrs. Darcy and tell her that her relatives have just arrived," the servant said, appearing embarrassed at what he had observed.

"They have arrived and I was not there!" Elizabeth cried.

"Calm down, my dear; they are earlier than expected. Surely they did not expect to find you waiting on the portico."

"We must go to the house at once," she cried, her eyes beseeching him.

"Of course." He called for the stable boy to take the pony back inside and care for him.

Going on ahead, Elizabeth traversed the distance between the stables and the manor house as quickly as possible. Only the fact that she was Mrs. Darcy now and not Lizzy Bennet stopped her from breaking into a full run. Slightly out of breath, she stepped into the main foyer, only to find it empty.

"They are already in the sitting room, Mrs. Darcy," Mrs. Reynolds said from close by. "Miss Georgiana is with them."

Smiling, Elizabeth breathed her thanks to the housekeeper just as Darcy entered the house. Extending his arm to her, he asked, "Shall we?"

As they approached the sitting room, she could hear the children's voices.

"Lizzy!" Jane saw her first.

The next few minutes were filled with laughter and warm greetings even though the children seemed to be unusually subdued, hiding timidly behind their mother's skirts, or in little Fred's case, on Jane's shoulder.

"Robbie." Mrs. Gardiner whispered something into her oldest son's ear and pushed him forward. The little boy's face flushed as he reached inside his navy blue coat to retrieve two small bouquets of pink daisies. Shyly he handed one to Georgiana and the other to Elizabeth

Much to his embarrassment, he was thoroughly kissed and hugged in return by both ladies.

"How was your journey?" Darcy asked in a pleasant, rich voice when the women grew quiet enough for him to speak.

"It was well; thank you for asking," Mrs. Gardiner answered, smiling kindly. "Even though the twins were poisoned by something they ate on the road yesterday."

Elizabeth's eyes sought Emily and Robbie, who indeed looked paler than usual. "Oh, no!"

"I threw up three times," Emily announced proudly, deciding that it was time for her to take part in the conversation. "And my tummy hurt, but Robbie threw up more than I did."

"Oh, you poor dear," Elizabeth said, pulling the girl onto her lap.

"We were afraid to feed them again today, which is the reason why we came so much earlier," Jane explained.

Mrs. Gardiner nodded. "I do not trust the food at the inns anymore."

"You must be famished!" Elizabeth cried. "I will have Mrs. Reynolds see to some refreshments this instant."

"Something light, Lizzy, if it is possible. A plain sandwich would be best," her aunt added.

As the maid showed the guests the way to their bedrooms, Mrs. Gardiner pulled Elizabeth aside, allowing Jane and Georgiana to assist the children up the stairs.

"I dare say, Lizzy, that your problems in the bedroom must have been solved," she whispered, eyeing the younger woman with amusement.

Elizabeth blushed, giving a slight nod of her head. "Yes, indeed. How could you have guessed? Is it written on my face?"

Mrs. Gardiner shook her head in amusement. "You look lovely, my dear, and no, it is not written on your expression. Mr. Darcy, however, looks much too relaxed and pleased with himself to suffer from conjugal difficulties. Remember, I have been married for ten years, and I do recognise that look."

A small smile graced Elizabeth's lips, "Indeed, Aunt Madeline. The advice in your last letter was sound and most appreciated, and I dare say that he has no reason to repine."

The older woman threaded her arm through Elizabeth's, giving it a light squeeze. "I am truly glad for you, my dear."

Their conversation was interrupted as Anne ran up to them, excited to show her mother her very own guest bedroom.

As Elizabeth watched mother and daughter take the stairs, she realised that she could not wait until that evening. Maybe then she would have more time to talk privately with both Jane and her Aunt Madeline.

Chapter Thirty

"Do you think badly of me, Lizzy?" Jane asked with visible worry etched in her tone and expression.

Elizabeth and Jane, in their nightclothes, were huddled together on the bed in the same guest bedroom which Jane had occupied during her stay at Pemberley. Three days had passed since Jane and the Gardiners' arrival, but only now had the sisters found time for their much awaited private talk. It was a few minutes past eleven in the evening and Elizabeth felt like a maiden again, whispering with her beloved sister late into the night, sharing secrets and wishes for the future.

Brutus was sprawled at the foot of the bed, pleased with having his floppy ears rubbed from time to time.

"No, Jane, certainly not," Elizabeth assured quickly. "I am simply concerned for your happiness. I care for you, sister. I want you to find happiness with a man whom you can love. I always thought that Mr. Bingley was that man. And now…well…I cannot make you out."

Jane let out a long sigh, and fell back on the pile of pillows heaped against the headboard. "I thought that too, Lizzy, but," she stopped, staring at the canopy above her.

"But…" Elizabeth prompted gently, eager to hear more.

Jane was about to speak, when there was a quiet knock on the door.

"Who can that be?" Elizabeth wondered aloud.

"Perhaps Mr. Darcy is looking for you," Jane ventured.

Elizabeth shook her head. "No, he needs to answer several important letters in order to send them out in tomorrow's post. He is locked in his study."

The knocking was repeated with more force, and the sound of a muted male voice was heard. "Excuse me the late hour, however, I am looking for Mrs. Darcy."

Jane giggled, while Elizabeth rolled her eyes.

"Told you," Jane murmured, still grinning as Elizabeth climbed down from the tall bed and ran across the room to open the door.

"I thought I heard your voice," Darcy said as she stepped out into the darkened hall, leaving the door ajar behind her.

He held a single, thick candlestick in his hand, which illuminated his face in a ghostlike fashion.

"Have you finished your letters?" she enquired.

He shrugged noncommittally. "I wrote only one. I decided to deal with the rest early in the morning. Are you coming to bed?"

She shook her head vigorously. "There are matters which I wish to discuss with Jane."

He scowled. "It is late. Can you not do it tomorrow?"

"No, I cannot," she replied impatiently. "Go to bed."

His frown deepened, and his bottom lip protruded in a pout more appropriate for five year old Robbie than for a man of eight and twenty.

"Lizzy," he whined.

She rolled her eyes. "I will return as soon as Jane and I finish our conversation. Do not wait up for me. You must be exhausted."

He gave her a sad look, which made her even more exasperated with him. "Fitzwilliam, you are acting like a child," she said sternly. "Now, go!" She motioned with her head towards the other end of the hall where their private rooms were located. Closing the door behind her, she leaned against it and puffed out her cheeks.

"Lizzy, you were so mean to poor Mr. Darcy," Jane said earnestly, a smile twitching the corners of her mouth.

Elizabeth produced a low, growling sound. "He is so infuriating at times. It is as if he cannot stay away from me for a minute."

"Would you prefer your husband to be cold and distant, ignoring you like so many others we have known?" Jane asked, completely serious now. She was referring to their parents, but would not say it.

"Of course not! Do not concern yourself with him, Jane. He is overly anxious as it has been three days since we..." she cleared her throat. "I have been tired these last days. Occupied with making preparations for your visit, and then trying to make you feel welcome and comfortable. We have not...well, I am sure you know my meaning."

Jane's laughing eyes met hers. "Yes, I believe I do."

Elizabeth reached for one of the soft, woollen blankets, before climbing back onto bed. "We were talking about Mr. Bingley though," she reminded her sister as she wrapped the soft material around herself and sat crossed legged.

"I still like him," Jane confessed. "I truly do. However, Colonel Fitzwilliam...oh, Lizzy."

Elizabeth's eyes widened as she took in her sister's dreamy expression. She had never seen her in such a state.

"Jane, you barely know the man."

"That is why I asked him to keep a correspondence."

"It was you who suggested that?" Elizabeth exclaimed, greatly surprised.

"Was there another way for me to learn more about him?" Jane questioned rationally. "Especially since he is in Kent and will remain there at least till the end of the year, as I understand it."

"Jane, you do realise that you are raising his expectations and giving him hope that he cannot afford. If Lady Catherine hears a word about it, she will leave Rosings Park to the Church of England rather than to him. She hates me and will hate you because you are my sister. Colonel Fitzwilliam can ill afford to marry you." She spoke the last words slowly and evenly, looking her sister in the eye.

Jane lowered her gaze, her long eyelashes sweeping across her creamy cheeks. "Not now, but in the future..." her voice trailed off. "He is not that poor, Lizzy. He told me that he is well compensated while in the army."

"Did he promise you something? Are you engaged?" she pressed.

"No. He said that he was not in a position to ask me—not now, not yet."

Elizabeth reached for her sister's hand. "Jane, it may take years before he inherits his aunt's estate and even then... Are you willing to wait? You know him so little."

Jane's earnest gaze met hers. "You always spoke very highly of Colonel Fitzwilliam," she reminded. "I still have the letters you wrote to me from Hunsford, praising his goodness, kindness, and easy manners. I even once thought him a favourite of yours. Now you speak as if he purposely wants to hurt me."

Elizabeth let go of Jane's hand slowly, flushing furiously. "My opinion of Colonel Fitzwilliam has not changed in the least. All I want is for you to be careful. I do not wish anyone to toy with your feelings. And Colonel Fitzwilliam was never a favourite—only a friend."

"That is well and good, Lizzy, but it was Mr. Bingley who toyed with me, not Colonel Fitzwilliam."

"Jane..." Elizabeth began, only to pause. "Sister," she said at last, touching

Jane's arm. "Have you fallen in love Colonel Fitzwilliam? Is he more than a friend to you?"

Now it was Jane's turn to blush. "Oh, Lizzy..."she sighed, pressing her hands to her chest. "He is so different from any of the men I have ever known. He has travelled to France, Spain, the West Indies and even America. He had so many adventures and he is blessed with the ability talk about it in such a captivating manner, as though I was there with him. I think that he should write his memoirs, cataloguing all his adventures, and have them published."

Elizabeth frowned, wondering whether they spoke of the same man. She had had a few lengthily conversations with the colonel while in Kent, but he had never said a word about his professional life or of his travels.

"I did not know that he was stationed in France," Lizzy murmured. Even Darcy never mentioned the fact.

"Many times, but he was not in a battle," Jane explained. "He dealt with different matters. I cannot tell you exactly what it entailed, as I swore to keep the secret. Do you know that he speaks fluent French? Frenchmen would never guess him to be English."

"Are you telling me that he was a spy?"

"Shush." Jane whispered nervously, putting a finger to her lips. "I have said too much already."

Elizabeth stared blankly at her sister for a long minute. "And you believe him?"

"He would not lie to me," Jane proclaimed, her jaw line tensing.

"I do not know what to think about it. I will worry even more about you," Elizabeth said after another moment of silence.

"Sister, please do not," Jane pleaded, her expression softening. "I know what I am about. We are only exchanging letters. There is nothing more."

Elizabeth crossed her arms against her chest. "What about Mr. Bingley? Fitzwilliam received a letter from him today. We are expecting him at any time and he is coming to see you, Jane."

Jane looked to the side but offered no answer.

"He loves you," Elizabeth continued. "Yes, he made a mistake in abandoning you after the Netherfield ball but it was not entirely his fault. It was his sisters and my dear husband who talked him into believing you were indifferent. I assure you Fitzwilliam has atoned for his ill advice to his friend tenfold and Mr. Bingley is contrite over the past events. I am certain that he wishes to make amends for his mistakes, if only you will let him."

"You want me feel guilty," Jane complained. "I like Mr. Bingley and I like his company, but he does not..."

Elizabeth leaned closer. "Does not what?"

An intense blush covered Jane's creamy complexion. "I do not have naughty thoughts about him."

"Jane, what has happened to you?!" Elizabeth exclaimed, finding it almost impossible to believe this was her beloved sister. "You have never spoken in such a way!"

"Mr. Bingley has never once tried to kiss me," Jane offered. "He had numerous opportunities while he visited me at uncle's house in London and yet did nothing."

"Still, you must allow him some consideration. Mr. Bingley is a perfect gentleman. He is coming to see you and has followed you around England just to be in your company."

Jane shrugged her pretty, rounded shoulders, now uncovered by her light, summer nightgown. "He never once tried to take my hand or speak words of affection as men in love are prone to do."

"He respects you," Elizabeth continued in defence of Bingley. "He may be shy with women but let me advise you that such an attitude has its advantages. You will most likely never have to deal with legions of past lovers. While with Colonel Fitzwilliam... well...while I have no proof, I know that he and my husband were thick as thieves in more ways than one."

"Perhaps," Jane agreed quietly as her slim fingers began twisting the ribbon at the end of her long braid.

"He kissed you, did he not?" Elizabeth asked on a sigh, her voice resigned. "Colonel Fitzwilliam kissed you. Yes, he did!"

A blissful smile graced Jane's face, a new blush blooming on her cheeks. "I forgot about the whole world for that short moment in his arms. You cannot imagine..."

"Oh, I can imagine, Jane." Elizabeth interrupted dryly. "I truly can. It seems that some skills run in this family. I only wonder at him finding the opportunity to do such a thing."

The pink returned to Jane's face with double intensity. "Do you remember the night of the dinner—the one before your wedding?"

Elizabeth nodded slowly. "I did not notice the two of you disappearing."

"You had other matters on your mind back then. It is only natural that you did not notice."

Elizabeth kept shaking her head. "Jane, was that not just the third time you had seen him?"

"I believe so," she confirmed, not lifting her head.

"Still, you allowed him to kiss you?"

"Why are you being so harsh with me?" Jane's voice was laced with hurt.

"Because the way you speak is so unlike you," Elizabeth explained gently. "You wish to disregard a good man, because he has not kissed you yet?" Elizabeth shook her head. "Forgive me for saying this, Jane, but it is as if I am speaking with Kitty or Lydia."

Jane's blue eyes watered. "I am so confused."

"Oh, sister."

Elizabeth pulled her into her arms and they spoke no more. Glancing at the mantel clock, she noted that it was very late—an hour past midnight. So Elizabeth said goodnight and ran to her bedchamber. As quietly as possible, she crept through the sitting room and into the room she shared with her husband. Being careful not to wake him, she slipped under the covers and closed her eyes with a quiet sigh. She hoped that the sleep would come despite the disturbing conversation she had just had with Jane.

"At last," a rich voice whispered as a strong hand pulled her into the folds of a large, warm body. "What took you so long? You spent all day with Jane. What had you to discuss so long tonight?"

"I shall have a long talk with your cousin once he comes to visit," she announced sternly.

"Richard? What did he do?" Darcy murmured, his tone suggesting that he was not in the least interested in the answer.

"Well, he has filled Jane's head with such nonsense, swept her off her feet! Now, she questions her feelings for Mr. Bingley."

Not minding the darkness in the room, she peered closely at Darcy. She could have sworn that she had heard a small chuckle. "Why are you laughing?" she swatted him. "There is nothing amusing in this."

"Nothing?" he asked, completely serious. "My only question is why you are keeping Bingley's side so strongly?"

"He is a safe choice for her."

"Collins was a safe choice for you, but you refused him."

"How can you even compare the two situations or these two men?" she cried as she sat up, now quite agitated. "Mr. Collins is nothing like Mr. Bingley. My cousin is repulsive—not only as a man but as a human being, beginning with his total neglect of personal hygiene and ending with his utter stupidity."

Darcy sat up as well, placing his chin on her shoulder as she had turned her back to him. "When I brought up Collins, I did not mean to offend you. I did it to remind you that you followed your heart, even if your mother thought your cousin was a good match for you. Did Jane criticise you? Did she try to change your mind?"

"No, she supported me, but..."

He turned her face to him, covering her lips with his finger to silence her. "You sister's concerns in matters of the heart seem very similar to yours, I dare say. Moreover, they are adults—Jane, Bingley, and Richard. We should not intervene."

"I cannot help but worry. I do not want Jane hurt again."

"Your sister is a smart woman. She knows what she is doing. You worry too much."

"I only want what is best for her."

"I know you do, love. You have a good heart. Nevertheless, some things should be left to the people involved. I think that she would be grateful for your support no matter what her decision."

Silently, she pushed at his chest. He obediently lay back.

Pulling up her nightgown, she crawled atop him.

"I think this is your favourite way," he mentioned casually, as he helped her to settle herself.

"You do not enjoy it?" she asked shyly.

Securing his arms around her, he pulled her down, so their chests pressed together. "Always, but later I would wish to try something different."

"Hmm." she murmured, as his hands ran down her back, then back up to remove her gown entirely. Not needing to be reminded, she untied the ribbon at the end of her braid, freeing her hair and letting it fall down her shoulders.

"Easy," he crooned as she took his manhood into her hand, rubbing it against her tender flesh which was already wet from the earlier touch of his fingers.

Slowly, she fit him inside of her. Each time she did this, she needed a short moment to adjust to the sensation. Catching her lower lip with her teeth, she rotated her hips slowly. This was a sign for her husband to push up as he held

her firmly, his hands splayed on the top of her thighs. He was correct. This particular way of loving was a favourite of hers as it was the easiest and fastest way for her to reach her pleasure. And as he hit the perfect place inside in well measured thrusts, his thumb rubbing insistently at her special spot, she started to moan loudly and clench around him in what seemed only a minute.

Her heart racing, the pleasant currents running through her body, she slumped on his chest, even though she felt him still rigid inside of her.

"Here we go," he groaned, lifting her off him and placing her face down on the bed.

"What are you doing?" she murmured as he lifted her bottom up and positioned himself behind her.

It was too late to object, as he was already slowly pushing inside of her. "I am not your horse" was at the tip of her tongue until he surged forward, making her moan instead.

Later, as they rested together on the pillows, her back to his, he enquired, "How did you like it?" He was very direct while in their bedroom and always questioned whether she enjoyed what they had done. For her it was still difficult to talk so openly about their lovemaking.

"It was different, but very pleasurable," she assured, pulling the sheet over herself as a slight shiver shook her body.

"Cold?" he asked.

"A bit. If you could, would you please build a fire? I am aware it is the middle of the summer but... "

"Shush." Then he silenced her with a kiss.

When she had lived at Longbourn, Mrs. Bennet had never allowed them to start a fire in the bedrooms in the period from April to October no matter how cold it was at night. At Pemberley Elizabeth could have a fire whenever she desired.

"What time is it?" she asked sleepily a few minutes later as the bright flames of the fire danced in her eyes.

"Almost three."

"So late." She snuggled into his chest when he returned to bed. "How will I ever get up in the morning?"

"I will tell your maid not to awaken you," he said, tucking the coverlet about her.

"We have guests," she murmured, her eyes closing. "I must see to them."

"You need your rest. They will understand."

The awareness of her husband's strong arms wrapped around her, enveloping her in a cocoon of love and security, was the only comfort Elizabeth required in order to fall into a sound slumber.

Chapter Thirty- One

Anne Gardiner's dark blue eyes focused intently on the sheet of music in front of her. A small frown formed between her eyebrows as she played her way through the complicated sonata.

Georgiana sat on the piano bench beside her, her eyes glancing between the notes and the child's fingers which moved with a slight degree of awkwardness over the black and white keys.

The rest of the family was seated comfortably in the main area of the spacious drawing room. Elizabeth and Darcy sat close together with little Fred upon Elizabeth's lap. On the opposite sofa was Mrs. Gardiner, listening intently to her daughter's playing, with Robbie and Emily on both sides of her. Mr. Bingley and Jane occupied the smaller settee.

As soon as the last chord was played, loud, sincere applause echoed in the spacious room. Mrs. Gardiner rushed to the pianoforte and hugged and kissed her daughter.

"That was very good Anne. This is very difficult composition," Georgiana offered enthusiastically, patting the child's back.

Blushing furiously at all the attention, the girl whispered shyly, "I made mistakes."

"Your fingers are simply too short yet to reach some of the chords," Georgiana soothed her concern. "I was twelve before I was able to play Handel well and you, my dear, are not even ten."

Anne's blush intensified as she ducked her head, mouthing a soft thank you.

Georgiana addressed Mrs. Gardiner. "I cannot believe that Anne has never had a proper master."

Mrs. Gardiner hugged the girl to her again, stroking her long blond hair, while motherly pride oozed from her expression. "Only what Elizabeth and Mary taught her while we visited at Longbourn. We bought a pianoforte this March for her use only as neither I nor my husband ever learned music."

"Yes, I noticed it during my visit. You chose a very good instrument. We have an identical one in the music room. "

"She has spent every free moment practising since the day the pianoforte appeared in our home," Mrs. Gardiner boasted.

"She has a tendency to place her fingers in wrong order while playing more difficult passages, and her wrists are not relaxed enough," Georgiana assessed professionally. "Nevertheless, these are small things and there is still plenty of time to correct those flaws before they become a bad habit and possibly make it difficult to advance in technique. However, she needs regular lessons from a good master."

"We thought to start the lessons once we return home. We do not know any music masters though. I would be afraid we might place her in hands of someone unreliable."

"My music master, Mr. Keiser, has not accepted a new student for many years but I could ask him to take on Anne. He enjoys the challenge of a talented student but absolutely refuses the mediocre ones. He is considered to be an eccentric, and from my own experience I can say that he is very demanding, but I could recommend no better. Be advised that at your first meeting his English may seem a bit difficult to understand, even though he came from Hamburg to London some twenty years ago and his wife is English."

"What do you say, Anne?" Mrs. Gardiner peered at her daughter who nodded with enthusiasm.

Gaining Anne's attention, Georgiana added, "You will have to practise several hours a day."

Anne nodded. "I will practise, I promise."

Georgiana's expression clouded and she hesitated. Then she lowered her voice so that the others in the room could not hear her. "He is very expensive though as he usually writes music for operas and allows only a few students."

"We will spare no expense," Mrs. Gardiner spoke firmly in a proud voice. "If Anne has a talent, she deserves the best teacher."

"Excellent," Georgiana clapped her hands together. "I will write a letter to him and give you his address and a letter of recommendation as well. I think that it would be best for Mr. Gardiner to pay him the initial visit. He usually has more patience with fathers than mothers. If it becomes necessary to convince him, I will meet with him in person."

Anne thanked both her mother and Georgiana, as a wide smile graced her pretty face.

"Papa!" A high pitched child's cry brought everyone's attention to Emily as she ran to the man who stood in the open door.

"Papa, Papa!" All the little Gardiners jumped from their seats. Even little Fred managed to struggle down from Elizabeth's lap.

"I think that we should give them some private time," Darcy suggested, his head tilting to the Gardiner family who were gathered in the middle of the room, hugging, kissing, and talking all at once.

Standing, he offered his hand to Elizabeth which she accepted with smile, her fingers wrapping around his palm.

Nodding in agreement with his friend's words, Bingley stood as well, offering one arm to Georgiana and the other to Jane.

Elizabeth's eyes narrowed as she observed an intense blush spreading over Georgiana's cheeks when she accepted Bingley's arm. She looked up at Darcy to see whether he noticed, but her husband was oblivious to everything except the Gardiners. A smile tugged at his lips as he watched little Fred trying to climb higher in his father's arms.

"We shall take a walk in the park," Darcy announced, bowing his head as they passed by the merry family. "We will meet for afternoon tea."

Mr. Gardiner made a move as if to greet the Darcys, but his wife and children, now firmly attached to his arms and legs, made it impossible.

The entire company decided to take a stroll around the lake as it was a pleasant walk and it was not so long a distance as to cause fatigue. However, the path was narrow, allowing only two people to walk the pathway side by side. There were five of them, so naturally one person was left to walk alone.

Elizabeth glanced with concern at Georgiana. Her face was turning red again, this time obviously in embarrassment. She had let go of Bingley's arm and was taking slow steps backwards. Elizabeth knew that she was likely going to excuse herself, stammering that she needed to return to the music room in order to practise.

Shifting her gaze to her sister, Elizabeth gave Jane a beseeching look then nodded in Georgiana's direction.

Jane had no trouble understanding what Elizabeth wanted from her, so she dropped Bingley's arm and stepped around him to take Georgiana's.

"My dear, let us walk out first. Our brother and sister always crave their privacy, and, as a dog lover, Mr. Bingley would like to inspect Brutus's swimming abilities I am sure."

Georgiana nodded with a shy smile, answering that Labradors are indeed known for their excellent swimming.

Bingley, not at all disappointed with the development, called for Brutus, then went into the nearest brush to look for the right stick. The pup seemed to guess what was coming, as he quickly abandoned his place by Elizabeth's skirt and began running circles around Bingley, waggling his tail excitedly.

Making a wide gesture with his arm, Bingley threw the stick far out into the lake. Brutus shot like an arrow into the water and soon was back with a dripping wet stick in his mouth.

"See," Darcy said to his wife as he pointed to the animal. "That is what he is supposed to do rather than cuddle with you in front of the fireplace."

Brutus dropped the stick at Bingley's boots and looked up at him with his tongue hanging out, clearly eager to repeat the experience.

"He likes both," Elizabeth insisted.

"He should run and swim every day, Mrs. Darcy," Bingley agreed as he again threw the stick into the water. "I have a good Labrador bitch, but she is brown, not yellow. I am curious what colour their litter would be."

"We may try to cross them," Darcy declared. "We can bring Brutus with us to Netherfield next spring when we travel for your wedding to Jane."

Bingley stilled, staring blankly at his friend.

"Fitzwilliam," Elizabeth hissed, tugging sharply at her husband's arm. "Jane told me about her engagement to Mr. Bingley in confidence. It was supposed to be a secret." She glanced worriedly into the direction of her sister, afraid that she might have heard. Thankfully Georgiana and Elizabeth were a good hundred feet ahead of them and talking animatedly.

Darcy gave a dismissive shrug. "I understand that your sister wants to keep the news about the engagement private, not announcing it to the public, still this is my future brother," he motioned to the Bingley. "Why should I not speak of it to him? He knows that he proposed and was accepted. When it was, Bingley? Two days ago?"

Bingley's handsome face split in an ear to ear grin. "Yes, indeed two days ago I was blessed with the acceptance of my lady."

"Congratulations," Darcy gave Bingley a hug. "I hope that you will be as pleased with the marital state as I am."

"I dearly hope so," Bingley clasped Darcy's back. "I would marry tomorrow, but Jane wishes to wait until the end of the mourning period which is only proper."

"My sincere congratulations, Mr. Bingley. I cannot think of the better man for my beloved sister," Elizabeth said warmly. Then her eyes shifted to Darcy and the smile disappeared from her face. "You must forgive my husband who it seems does not understand the concept of keeping a secret."

Darcy chuckled, tucking Elizabeth to his side. "Come here you little imp." He leaned down to kiss her lips. The kiss was chaste and innocent compared to the kisses bestowed behind closed doors. Nevertheless, she hid her face into her husband's chest when it ended, embarrassed at such a public display of affection.

"We are alone," Darcy whispered above her ear.

Looking up, she saw Mr. Bingley walking away from them, Brutus following at his feet.

"You must be pleased," Darcy noted, threading his arms around her waist. "Jane chose the one you wanted her to choose."

Placing her hands on his arms she shook her head. "I am not certain of that."

He frowned in confusion. "He proposed, she accepted, it is decided."

She sighed. "Not exactly. Jane asked me to send a new letter to Colonel Fitzwilliam."

"There is a simple explanation for that, I dare say. She may want to finish the matters with my cousin and inform him about her engagement to Bingley."

"I think not," Elizabeth said, turning to stare at the lake.

"Why?"

"My suspicion is that she wants a long engagement not to respect the mourning period as she told Mr. Bingley, but to secure herself some time. Colonel Fitzwilliam needs time to settle his affairs in Kent, does he not? An engagement is not a marriage. It can be broken."

Darcy cocked his head. "Do you approve of such scheming? It seems cruel."

"I..." she hesitated. "I have given some thought to it. Jane will always have my support. It is her life and her decision and it is not easy being a woman. I cannot reproach her conduct as my own life is far from exemplary."

"What do you mean?"

Her expression was exceedingly sad as she faced him. "I married a man only for his fortune and the protection he could afford me and my family. He loved me, and yet I could not...I did not want to reciprocate. Was I not being equally as cruel towards him?" she whispered softly, her eyelashes sweeping over her pale cheeks as she avoided his gaze.

He cupped her cheek and tiled her face so that she looked him in the eye. "He did not mind."

She took a deep breath and released it slowly. "I fell in love with him," she confessed, her voice trembling. "So much so that it sometimes frightens my heart." She took his hand from her waist to put it against her bosom. "Can you feel how rapidly it is beating?"

His only response was to lean down, burying his face in her neck. Soon she felt wetness on her skin.

"Come," he murmured thickly, pushing away from her and brushing the tears from his eyes with the back of his hand.

"Where?" she giggled as she tried to keep up with his fast footsteps across the lawn. They moved away from the lake.

"You shall see."

As they approached the stables, Darcy barked orders to have his horse prepared.

"Where are we going?" Elizabeth questioned as finally he lifted her up on the saddle and mounted behind her.

"For a ride," he answered, kicking the horse into a fast trot. "I have wished to show you a certain place for some time, but for whatever reason I have not. I suppose I did not feel the time was right, but now it is."

They rode fast for at least half an hour through a mostly unbeaten path to a hillside before they stopped, leaving the horse at the foot of the hill.

"What is up there?" Elizabeth asked, staring at the tall trees growing above them.

Darcy tied the horse to a low branch of a nearby tree, so he could graze. "It is a surprise, but I assure you that you will not regret coming here."

He went first, helping her to climb behind him. The ground was rocky in places and her slippers were hardly appropriate for such activities, but his strong hold kept her safe from falling.

She was visibly out of breath once they reached the top. Pulling her hand, Darcy insisted she continue, his face animated with excitement. "Come, it is only a few yards from here."

Suddenly the trees and bushes gave way to a clearing where she could see a breath taking view of Pemberley. It was nestled in the wide valley below them, surrounded by dark forests, hills and the lake.

"How beautiful," she breathed, her eyes devouring the scene.

"This, my dear wife, is the most spectacular view of Pemberley according to the Darcys. As far I know, only the family is aware of it."

"I lack the words," Elizabeth marvelled. "Someone should paint it."

"Perhaps one day. It would take a true master with exceptional talent to give this view justice."

"I cannot argue that," she responded, tearing her eyes from the view, to look at Darcy. "Thank you for bringing me here."

He accepted her thanks in silence as his gaze focused on her lips. She took a step forward and stood on tiptoes. Staring into his intense eyes, she leaned in to kiss him.

One by one pieces of clothing fell to the ground and Darcy took his greatcoat and spread it on the grass. Elizabeth lay down and opened her body to him. This time was not slow and careful like their usual lovemaking, but fast and impatient. As they lay spent, he adjusted her head on his arm and shoulder so she would be more comfortable. And after a moment, he noticed tears brimming in her dark eyes.

"Are you well?" he whispered, his concern evident as he stroked a wisp of hair away from her face.

She nodded as the tears ran down her cheeks one by one. "So beautiful," she whispered. "I love you." She pulled herself higher, hiding her face in his neck.

His rich laugh echoed among the trees. "And I love you, but I believe that it is not a reason for tears." His hand moved up and down her back in a soothing gesture.

"I know." She sat up, unashamed of her nudity, and reached into the pocket of her dress for a handkerchief to dry her face. "I am sorry, I am being silly."

"Shush," he tucked her back to him. "Sensitivity is not silly."

She must have fallen asleep in his arms, because the next thing she felt was a nudge to her shoulder followed by the sound of a sharp voice. "Elizabeth, Elizabeth wake up, we must go."

Blinking several times, she brought her fists to her eyes, trying to rub the sleep from them. Why was it so dark? Darcy had rolled her off his shoulder and stood gathering his clothes.

Elizabeth rose up on her elbows as shattering thunder rumbled, shaking the ground and making her shriek.

Darcy was already dressed. Taking her arm, he pulled her to her feet.

"What time is it?" she asked worriedly, noting the black sky.

"Seven; we overslept," he exclaimed before a string of curses left his mouth. Elizabeth stared in shock, wide-eyed. She would have never suspected that her husband possessed such a vivid and colourful vocabulary.

"Get dressed," he ordered, his tone the harshest he had ever used with her.

With shaking hands she began gathering her scattered undergarments, putting them on. As soon as her stays were secured, he helped her step into her dress, buttoning it at the back with quick fingers. The cold wind whipped through her thin dress, making her shiver. Seeing this, Darcy put his great coat over her shoulders.

"You will be cold," she protested as he hurriedly buttoned it around her.

Ignoring her objection, he took her hand firmly in his. "Come, we must get down the hill before the rain catches us."

The wind grew stronger every minute, blowing her long skirt like a parachute sail making it difficult for her to move. Big raindrops began to fall, hitting them like angry fists as they descended. Elizabeth had always prided herself in having no fear of storms and loud thunder. Ever since she was small, she had liked to sit by the windows and watch magnificent bolts of lightning illuminate the sky. She realised now how ignorant she had been of the danger. Observing a thunderstorm from the safety of a warm home and being caught in the midst of one was vastly different.

Reaching the bottom of the hill, Elizabeth was very relieved to be standing on flat ground once again. Clinging to Darcy's arm, she could not see very far ahead as a wall of rain in front of them plunged the area into darkness.

Suddenly another string of vulgar words escaped her husband's mouth causing her to look about. Their horse was gone.

Chapter Thirty-Two

"Where have you lost my sister and your friend, Mr. Bingley?" Jane asked archly as she and Georgiana rounded the lake.

"I thought it would be better for my chaste soul to leave their company," Bingley replied, eliciting a soft giggle from Georgiana with his comment. Seeing the girl's reaction, he leaned towards her. "I dare say Miss Darcy here can tell us more on the subject."

Georgiana blushed, her eyes downcast, shaking her head no as a small smile played on her lips.

"Do not tease Miss Darcy, sir," Jane declared. "You cannot expect Georgiana to gossip about her own brother and sister."

"I am pleased with how happy my brother is," Georgiana spoke up with sincerity. "I have never seen him so content. I can remember all the years he was often sad. He seemed burdened and lonely."

"They are a good match," Bingley offered.

"Oh, yes, the very best," Georgiana agreed with feeling. "Elizabeth is such a good influence on Brother, on all of us really. I feel as if she has always been with us."

The three of them stood for a moment, silence prevailing as each was lost in their own thoughts.

Bingley spoke first. "Shall we join Mr. and Mrs. Gardiner for tea?"

Jane nodded. "Yes, indeed; it is becoming increasingly hot."

In a slow stroll they returned to the manor.

***

"Uncle, let us speak now before Lizzy joins our company," Jane said quietly as she sat down beside Mr. And Mrs. Gardiner with a cup of tea in her hands. "Can you tell me whether you had an opportunity to talk with Mama about Lydia?"

Mr. Gardiner nodded, a heavy frown marring his forehead. "I stopped by Meryton on my way here. Initially I planned to spend a night at Purvis Lodge, but I must say that after only one hour in my sister's company I changed my mind. I am not certain whether it is the grief after your father's death being displayed in an unusual way, but she was insufferable. It was impossible to have a rational conversation with her."

"I suspected as much," Jane whispered. Her hands beginning to shake so much that she set the cup on a nearby table.

"I do not even wish to remember the things she said to me," Mr. Gardiner said with lowered voice, before leaning towards his wife and niece to be sure no one could overhear them.

A quick glance about determined that the children were playing by themselves on the terrace while Georgiana was occupied with her music sheets and Bingley stood beside her.

"The very comfortable home she now occupies she referred to as a rat's nest," he continued. "She spoke badly of Lizzy, claiming that she has abandoned her and your sisters to poverty while living in luxury herself."

Jane grasped the material of her skirt, her lips pressed in a thin line. "Poor Lizzy sacrificed herself for Mama, for all our sisters, and this is how she repays her. Thank God that Mr. Darcy loves her, but what if he was a different kind of man? I cannot understand Mama, I cannot. I know that she was very harsh with Lizzy the last time they spoke."

"Forgive me, Jane, but I was not able to speak with her about Lydia the way you and Lizzy wanted." Mr. Gardiner's expression was apologetic. "I left before I said too much, afraid of stressing our relationship even more, possibly severing it forever."

"What about Kitty and Mary?" Jane enquired.

"Mary was closed up in the music room with her pianoforte while Kitty was visiting your aunt Philips. It seems that poor girl spends the whole of her days at my sister's house."

"I understand, Uncle," Jane sighed, smiling sadly. "Thank you for trying. I only hope that Lydia will not involve herself in anything scandalous while in Brighton, ruining her reputation forever."

"I think our only hope is that she is too poor to entice anyone, even with Mr. Darcy's settlement," Mrs. Gardiner remarked. "As for my sister, I am pained to say, if she continues with this behaviour she will alienate everyone. She will be left alone in the world, never to see her daughters or grandchildren."

Their conversation ended when Georgiana walked over to them.

"I am beginning to worry," the girl said, glancing in the direction of the tall

windows. "Lizzy and Brother have not returned and the clouds are gathering. It is so hot and suffocating today that I am certain there will be a thunderstorm."

Bingley came to stand behind her. "Do not fret, Miss Darcy. I am certain they will return any moment," he offered brightly. "Even if the rain surprises them, Darcy is perfectly capable of finding shelter. He would never allow anything to happen to Mrs. Darcy."

***

Elizabeth slowly awakened to the sensation of a gentle finger stroking her cheek. She snuggled closer, inhaling the familiar scent of her husband. Yesterday had been a very eventful day, to say the least. For a short while she had been truly frightened when they had discovered their horse had bolted and run off.

Thankfully, her husband had not lost his composure even if he had said a few choice words about the horse. Stating that there was a farmhouse half a mile away, he led the way confidently despite the fact that their visibility was obstructed by a thick curtain of rain. Elizabeth had succeeded in visiting all the tenant families, but still had little idea which household they had approached. Only after Darcy's persistent banging, when the door had swung open and they were ushered inside the warm house, did she recognise the Finney family. They had four sons and one baby girl, recently born. Mrs. Finney was a very lively, talkative woman while her husband and sons were mostly silent, speaking mainly when they must.

Darcy and Elizabeth had been given dry clothes, a seat by the open hearth and fed a hearty dinner. Her husband had agreed with Mr. Finney that the storm might very well last the entire night, and thus it was too risky to attempt to return to the manor before morning.

Mrs. Finney had proudly shown them to the back of the house, to what she called a guest room. It was a small chamber, rather narrow with one window. A small dresser and a moderately sized bed was all it held. Nevertheless, it was very clean. The floor was painted white and the flowery design of the wallpaper matched the window curtains. The tenants were accustom to retiring much earlier than the inhabitants of the manor, so therefore the entire family was in their beds quite early, with all the lights out.

A kiss on her forehead had made Elizabeth open her eyes. "Good morning," she whispered, her voice hoarse.

Darcy raised on his elbow, studying her closely. "Are you well?" he questioned, his voice full of concern.

"Very well," she answered. "I had a good night's rest."

He frowned. "Does your head or your throat hurt? Your voice is hoarse."

"I always sound like that in the morning. I feel quite well, I assure you."

"I do not wish you to catch a cold due to my negligence."

She yawned into her open palm, and began rubbing sleep from her eyes with her other hand. "First, I am never sick, and you certainly were not negligent last evening. You knew what to do, never once losing your head; you brought us safely here."

"I put us in the dangerous situation to begin with."

"Hardly," she dismissed his assertion. "We both fell asleep."

"I should have known better." Despite her reassurances Darcy kept chastising himself. "I should have perceived that a storm was coming."

She leaned over his chest. "Nonsense! You saved us."

"It is very gracious of you to say that," he said, a small smile beginning to play at the corners of his mouth.

Feeling the tension in his body, she ran her hand over his chest. "You are so tense, relax." She kissed the dimple between his collarbone. As her hand moved lower, she teased. "So hard."

"Do not tease." His expression was raw, his eyes vulnerable.

"Me?" She pointed to herself before tugging at the opening of his nightshirt so she could place kisses on the exposed parts of his chest. They had been given clean nightclothes, long and practical, made of thick, white cloth—the sort of clothes this family wore.

Gathering a handful of the crisp material in her hand, she pulled the nightshirt up, exposing her husband's body from the waist down. Slowly she shifted, lowering her head to kiss the dark line of hair leading from his stomach downward. Then confidently she took his manhood in her hand, touching him softly and eliciting a low groan.

"Shush." She looked up at him. "You must be quiet or I will stop."

Giving a quick nod, he put a fist in his mouth, while burying his other hand in her hair.

She kept stroking, all the while placing small kisses on his stomach.

"Could you...?" he whispered, as his voice hitched.

"What?"

"You know..." He gazed down at her hand. "...with your mouth." When she hesitated, he shook his head. "Does not matter; just keep to what you were doing." His head fell back on the pillow.

Slowly, Elizabeth resumed her stroking. She was not certain what he wanted from her and she hated to think that he had received this type of thing from the women of his past—from Annette. Quickly, she pushed those thoughts aside. She was his wife. She, Elizabeth, and those women were of no importance now. She prayed that he had no cause to repine when it came to their intimate relations, though some things he liked were very strange to her. Still, she saw no reason why she should refuse him. Bending forward, she placed a small kiss on the pinkish end of his manhood.

"Oh, yes, Lizzy," was his immediate reaction, while his strong hand cupped the nape of her neck, guiding her gently down.

While indeed it was a most strange thing to do in her opinion, she was neither repulsed by it nor did it make her feel humiliated.

"Just like that," he murmured. As she observed him, not interrupting her work, she noted that his expression was one of pure bliss, even more so than when he was inside of her.

Soon enough she sensed that he was nearing his completion, so she sucked hard one last time, replacing her mouth with both of her hands. She made certain that he emptied himself into her hands until not a drop was left as she did not wish to soil the sheets, or the borrowed nightclothes. They were guests here, and Mrs. Finney had most likely given them her very best linens. It would be very rude to dirty them in such a manner.

She padded to the dresser, where she cleansed her hands in a bowl of cold water, before opening the window and pouring it out on the ground.

"Are you pleased?" she enquired, returning to bed and snuggling against him.

His arm draped lazily around her, a small smile playing on his lips. "You are the best, Lizzy, the very best."

A warm sensation filled her chest at his words. Some might think that she would feel offended with his words, but she was not in the least. No, she was proud of herself.

A knock on the door got their attention. "Master Darcy, your clothes are dry. I will leave them by the door," Mrs. Finney proclaimed. "Breakfast is ready. Our eldest boy rode to Pemberley at first light to tell them that you are with us."

"Thank you kindly, Mrs. Finney," Elizabeth replied. "We will join you shortly. However, may we ask for more water as we used most of the bowl?"

"Right away, Mistress!" she exclaimed cheerily.

Elizabeth crept to the door, and after a moment of listening to determine that there was no one outside, she opened it and reached for their clothes with a quick hand.

A few minutes later there was another knock. "Water for you," this time a high pitched boy voice spoke, and Elizabeth guessed that it must have been one of the sons. Upon opening the door no one was about, but a small water pail sat in the hall. She brought it into the room and as she poured the water into the bowl, she became aware that their clothes were not only dried but ironed as well.

"Can you believe that?" She pointed to her dress. "Only Heaven knows how early Mrs. Finney had to wake to press our clothes."

Darcy nodded with a yawn, deciding at last to rise from the bed. "I will send them a milk cow in return for their hospitality."

A quarter of an hour later they were both dressed, but as Elizabeth had lost most of her hair pins in the rain, she left her hair free. It hung in a heavy mass of curls down the middle of her back. Unfortunately, her elegant, yellow leather slippers had been completely ruined. Once they reached home, she knew that her maid would simply throw them away.

"Good morning," Elizabeth said with a wide smile as they entered the main area of the house, which consisted of a large kitchen combined with a dining room.

"Good morning, good morning," Mrs. Finney replied with a smile of her own.

Looking about, Elizabeth noticed that Mr. Finney and the boys were absent. She guessed they had eaten and were already seeing to their animals' needs.

"Sit down please." Mrs. Finney fluttered around the table, pulling out the chairs.

"We thank you, but we should return to the manor," Darcy said. "They must be quite worried about us."

"Joe, our oldest, returned from Pemberley a few minutes ago. They said they would send a carriage for you, but it has not arrived yet."

Elizabeth gave Darcy a hard look. She gestured for him to take a seat, discreetly pushing him forward. She could see how much work Mrs. Finney had put into preparing their breakfast. There was a white and red checkerboard tablecloth and even a vase of fresh flowers on the table.

They ate for a bit in silence, but soon Darcy stood up, excusing himself. "Thank you for the breakfast and your hospitality, Mrs. Finney. I will await the carriage outside."

As soon as he left, a small cry came from the crib placed near the window. Elizabeth stepped over to look at the bundle now waving its fists and legs wildly. The baby girl had blue and yellow flowers embroidered on the front of a white frock and pink knitted socks on her tiny feet. She was mostly bald, with only a small tuft of blonde hair above her wide forehead.

"May I?" Elizabeth gestured towards the child.

Mrs. Finney grinned, exposing surprisingly good teeth. "Aye, Mistress."

With utmost care, but at the same time sure of herself, Elizabeth picked the girl up from the crib. As she began cooing to the baby, the child's wide blue-green eyes stared at her in fascination.

"You are a natural, Mistress," the other woman commented from her place at the stove.

"I have three younger sisters and little cousins, one of them is my godson, not much older than this little one," Elizabeth explained.

"Watch my word, Mistress. This time next year you will have your hands full with your own little one."

Elizabeth caught the tiny hand with her fingers, admiring the alabaster skin and perfect pink nails. "I hope so." She bounced the child in her arms, eliciting a smile. "She is smiling at me!"

Mrs. Finney dried her hands on her apron and stepped closer. "This one is spoiled, she is. Even fed and dry she will not be quiet in her crib, always wanting to be carried about. Tis her father's fault, you know. He picks her up every time he is home from the fields, even when she is sleeping. He never did that when the boys were little."

"Your husband must be very proud of her."

The woman nodded. "Aye. Men always say they want sons, but we have four and Mr. Finney wanted a girl. Not that he would ever admit it, mind you, for talkative he is not. I thought that I could have no more children as it had been six years since our youngest and then this little lass surprised us."

"That must have been quite a shock for you," Elizabeth said kindly.

"I thought for sure while I was carrying her that this one would be another boy."

"She is beautiful." Elizabeth stared adoringly at the child. "What is her name?"

"Mary."

"Little Mary, you are beautiful, are you not? Yes, you are, yes-yes, you are." Elizabeth cooed at the girl, before looking to her mother. "I have a sister with the same name."

"Mrs. Darcy, our carriage has come," Darcy announced, poking his head through the window.

Elizabeth nodded at him and regretfully placed the babe back in her crib.

"We thank you for your hospitality, Mrs. Finney," she said, bowing her head slightly. "I do not know what would have happened to us, had you and your husband not taken us in last evening."

"Twas an honour, Mistress," the woman dropped an awkward curtsey before adding with enthusiasm, eyes sparkling, "I cannot wait 'til the other women in the village hear that Mrs. Darcy herself spent the night in my guest room."

Elizabeth laughed at her words and with one last look at little Mary, quitted the house. As soon as she stepped outside, her skirts were attacked by Brutus, while Georgiana and Jane nearly made her trip with a fierce embrace.

"Lizzy, we were so worried!" Jane exclaimed, her voice unusually agitated.

"The storm lasted until nearly dawn and we could not start searching for you," Georgiana explained. "Poor Brutus howled by the door for hours. When your horse returned to the stables alone, we feared the worst. Only when the Finney boy came...," his sister's voice broke as her eyes watered.

"We are well and there was no danger," Elizabeth replied calmly, patting Georgiana's back in a soothing gesture. "Fitzwilliam knew where to find shelter once we realized it was too late for us to return home."

She looked to see one of the open carriages from Pemberley waiting, Mr. Bingley acting as a driver.

"Good morning, sir," she greeted her husband's friend as they neared the carriage.

"Delighted to see you unharmed, Mrs. Darcy," Charles proclaimed as he looked down at her. "Pray, do not disappear anymore in the near future and leave me with the task of consoling those two fair ladies."

"Let us proceed," Darcy stated brusquely, as he handed his wife and sisters into the carriage, visibly impatient to be off. "I must see whatever damages the storm may have caused. Finney told me that several trees nearby have been broken or uprooted so I expect to find some in other areas. I hope that no buildings were damaged or destroyed."

On their way to the manor, at Jane and Georgiana's demand, Elizabeth told them in detail about the events of the previous evening. Understandably, she edited some of the details which were much too private for their ears.

Chapter Thirty-Three

Four days after the great thunderstorm, which had succeeded in uprooting a few old trees in the park and ripping the roofs off several barns, Mrs. Gardiner and Elizabeth sat beside a window in Pemberley's drawing room. They talked while observing the children playing outside on the lawn, riding the pony Mr. Darcy had recently bought for the Gardiner children.

"I agree completely, Aunt. It is only fitting that you and Uncle should go. You deserve time alone, away from the children," Elizabeth said with great conviction. "I hear the Lake District is particularly beautiful this time of the year."

Mrs. Gardiner gave her niece an indecisive, guilty look. "I do not wish to burden you and Mr. Darcy, Lizzy. He was kind enough to host us here, but leaving you alone with four children is an entirely different matter. Fred is so small; he wakes in the middle of the night quite often, and Robbie sometimes wets the bed."

Elizabeth placed her hand over her aunt's. "It is not a burden, Aunt. In fact, it is far from it. I think of all the times Jane and I have stayed with you in London." She paused. "We owe you and Uncle much more than you will ever know," she added fervently. "I will never forget everything you have done for us, and if I can repay you in such a small way, please allow me to do so. Look about you. This house is so big with an abundance of room for everyone. And as for Mr. Darcy, he will have nothing against it, believe me. This time of the year he spends most of his days out of doors attending to matters of business on the estate. He will not even see the children that often." Elizabeth smiled and shook her heard at her aunt's quizzical expression. "I know what you may think, but it is not how he really is. My husband might give the impression of being reserved, sometimes displeased even, but he always means well. His flaw is that he cannot express himself as well as others do and lacks the social skills. However, in his defence, I must say that he is very thoughtful. For instance, it was solely his idea to buy the pony you see before you. He thought it fitting that the children might have a pleasant time during your visit. As you see, Aunt, he truly welcomes you here."

The older woman watched her niece with warm eyes. "I can see that you have finally learned to understand him."

Elizabeth nodded, her expression thoughtful. "There is much depth behind those dark brooding eyes. He is always thinking even when he is silent or speaks little. People often mistake his meaning in the way he expresses himself, as did I in the beginning of our acquaintance. He is a very private person and keeps many at an arm's length. But he is as good and caring as any man ever was—a loyal friend to those whom he loves and a good brother. My husband is an honourable man even if it is a well-kept secret from the masses," Elizabeth said with a chuckle as she gazed at the children playing on the lawn.

"You sound as though you have fallen in love with him."

"I have," Elizabeth affirmed, a soft smile curling her lips as she faced her aunt. "But do not think that I am blind to his faults, for I am not. They are part of him," she paused, before adding with a voice slow and even, "and I am happy with him."

"I am so relieved to hear this confession from you, Elizabeth," Mrs. Gardiner said. "The days following your wedding, your uncle and I discussed you and Mr. Darcy often, wondering whether we were right in convincing you to marry him. We had a good feeling about him from the start, but in truth, we knew so little of him. It also concerned us that you seemed sad on your wedding day, terrified even. You trusted our judgment, and I feared we might have failed you."

"No, Aunt," Elizabeth shook her head. "You and my uncle are true friends to me and to Jane as well. Your house was always open to us. By your example I learned what a happy family should be, how spouses should treat one another, how to love and bring up children wisely. As for my wedding day, I am afraid my spirits were down. I was so stubborn, putting too much pressure on myself." She let out a heavy sigh. "Poor Fitzwilliam, he did not know how to approach me, how to talk to me. I hardly knew myself."

The two women sat in quiet reflection for a moment before Mrs. Gardiner returned to the subject of their trip.

"Will ten days be too long?"

"No, of course not; there is no point in travelling to the lakes for a shorter stay, and therefore, it is settled." Elizabeth clapped her hands, smiling. "The children will be safe here with us."

"I have no doubt they will be under the best of care," Mrs. Gardiner assured. "Thank you, Lizzy. We do appreciate your generosity."

Elizabeth excused herself from her aunt's company to seek out her husband and explain her plans for the next two weeks. He was supposed to be in his study where he had sequestered himself in order to catch up on estate matters that had been neglected over the last few days. Elizabeth smiled as she walked, well pleased to be of assistance to the Gardiners. After all, it was only right that she repay their kindness with this small gesture, and she was sure her husband would agree.

Standing before the tall, dark and imposing door, she knocked, but received no answer.

"Fitzwilliam?" she called, knocking again. "Are you there?"

With a frown, she pushed open the door. Elizabeth's eyes swept over the room before coming to rest on her sleeping husband, his large form curled awkwardly on the sofa.

Kneeling beside him, she placed a hand and then her face against his forehead. It was warm. The fever was not high, but there was one nonetheless.

"Fitzwilliam," she whispered, stroking strands of damp hair away from his face. "Wake up, my love... please. You must go upstairs and rest."

Getting no reaction from him, she tried to pull him up by his arms, but he was too heavy. She touched his face again, worry tugging at her heart. Looking around she saw his coat hanging on the back of one of the chairs. Reaching for it, she placed it over him, pulling it to his chin.

Stepping into the hall outside the study, she looked around for a familiar face.

Out of the corner of her eye she noticed Mr. Bingley descending the stairs dressed for riding. Elizabeth cried out, her voice carrying through the hall and instantly gaining his attention. "Sir? Mr. Bingley, can you assist me?"

"Anything for you, Mrs. Darcy." Smiling eagerly he approached with quick steps.

Leading him inside the study, she gestured to Darcy. "He fell asleep here as you see. I fear that he has developed a cold as he has a fever. I tried to wake him, but he does not respond. My attempts at lifting him were futile. As you might suppose, he is much too heavy for me."

Thankfully, Mr. Bingley did not need to have the situation explained twice. "Do not fret, Mrs. Darcy." He walked to the sofa, grasping his friend by the

shoulders and pulling him up into a sitting position. "We will have him upstairs and into bed before you can turn around."

Bingley hoisted Darcy to his feet, supporting him against his side. Both men were of similar height with Bingley having only a slightly slimmer body build. Nevertheless, he had little trouble with bearing Darcy's weight, something entirely impossible for Elizabeth.

"Bingley, what are you doing?" Darcy awakened at last, blinking his eyes.

"You have your lovely wife quite worried, my friend," Bingley replied, taking a step forward and pulling Darcy with him.

"Bingley! Stand aside!" Darcy pushed the other man away, standing straight and proud. "I am perfectly capable of walking on my own."

Not in the least bit offended with his friend's response, Bingley looked in Elizabeth's direction, saying in a bright voice. "I think he is not as sick as you may think, Mrs. Darcy. He is not so much different from his usual cranky self, I dare say."

"Thank you, Mr. Bingley." She smiled at the fair haired man before eyeing her husband, her expression sober. "Let us get you upstairs, Mr. Darcy. You must lie down. I will send for a nourishing broth. And you, good sir, will eat it. It is essential that you do as I say so that your body can fight this fever you have acquired. I will ask the cook to kill our fattest chicken. It is the best thing for a cold."

Darcy scowled down at her, trying to intimidate her with his sternest look. "I am not sick, madam. I do not understand why you brought Bingley here, asking him to help me to the bed as though I was a child unable to care for my own needs. I assure you I am no child, Mrs. Darcy."

Elizabeth's dark eyes narrowed and she placed her hand on her hips. "You certainly act like one! I tried to wake you up for several minutes, but you would not move. Do not tell me that it is normal."

"I am not sick. I am simply fatigued," he protested.

"You are sick, and you will go upstairs to our rooms this very instant and rest for the remainder of the day."

They stared at one another, both unyielding, while Bingley followed their exchange quite fascinated.

Darcy murmured gruffly at last, avoiding meeting her eyes, "Very well, if you insist, Mrs. Darcy. I will do as you ask, even though I am perfectly well…a bit tired perhaps. Overseeing the repair work after the storm took much of my energy these last few days. That is all."

Instantly Elizabeth's demeanour changed, and she stepped to Darcy with a smile on her face. "Thank you." She took his hand, lifted it to her face and placed a kiss on the inside of his palm. I shall find Mrs. Reynolds."

She moved to leave, but stopped at that door. Turning, she raised an eyebrow, her voice firm. "I expect you to be in our rooms. I will meet you there in five minutes."

Darcy glanced at Bingley who laughed into the fisted hand now against his mouth.

"Do not dare say anything, Bingley. Not one word..." Darcy warned. "I simply do not wish for her to become overly concerned with my wellbeing. She is a bit sensitive."

"I comprehend perfectly." Bingley clapped his back. "Now, you had better go upstairs. You do not wish to worry her, after all."

***

Elizabeth found Mrs. Reynolds in the servants' wing giving instructions to the chambermaids. The housekeeper stopped instantly upon the mistress's entrance and listened while Mrs. Darcy explained the situation to her. Elizabeth asked that she talk with the cook about preparing a rich broth made with herbs and plenty of black pepper.

The housekeeper was amazed to learn that Darcy had agreed to put himself to bed in the middle of the day. The woman looked at Mrs. Darcy with a newfound respect, openly stating that it must be Elizabeth's good influence, for in all the years since Mr. Darcy had become Master of Pemberley, it had been impossible for anyone to achieve such a feat.

***

When Elizabeth entered their private rooms later, she found her husband slouching on a chair in front of the fireplace.

She came to stand by his side, touching his face. He leaned into her hand, his eyes drooping.

"You must tell me truthfully," she pleaded. "How are you? Sore throat? Headache?"

"Both," he acknowledged quietly.

"My poor dear." She kissed his forehead. "Why did you not say something sooner?"

He shrugged. "I thought that it would go away of its own accord."

Shaking her head she asked, "What am I going to do with you?"

"Keep me?"

She laughed, ruffling his hair. "Come; let us move from this chair before you doze off again. If you are unable to move, I will need to call someone to carry you."

He shot her a guarded look. "You want to put me to bed?"

She raised an eyebrow.

"I can walk on my own, thank you very much!"

"Very well," she said. "Then move."

Taking his hand in hers, she led him through the open door of the sitting room into their bedroom. Lightly, she pushed at his chest, so that he sat down on the edge of the bed.

"Will you stay in bed for the rest of the day?" she pleaded, "Please, for my peace of mind do as I ask."

He regarded her for a moment. "Will you remain with me and not go downstairs to attend our guests?"

"Of course," she agreed instantly.

He seemed content with her response and allowed her to unbutton his waistcoat and remove his neck cloth, along with the rest of his clothing. A quarter of an hour later, Darcy was in bed, dressed in his nightshirt, supported against a mound of soft pillows as Elizabeth drew the covers to his chin.

Reaching for her hand, he murmured, "Stay. You said you would."

"Shush." She leaned forward, kissing his forehead repeatedly. "Try to rest."

His eyes dropped, his hand wrapped tightly around her much smaller palm, resting on his chest. They sat this way for the next half hour until his grasp around her fingers weakened. Removing her hand from his, she tiptoed into the dressing room and brought out another warm blanket and spread it over his body.

There was a gentle knock on the bedroom and as she whispered for them to enter, Georgiana peeked inside.

Silently, Elizabeth waved her closer. The girl gazed at her brother with concern written across her face.

"Mr. Bingley told me what happened in the study," she explained quietly. "How is he?"

"He claims to be only fatigued, but I fear that he is unwell. He is far too complacent. He did not resist much when I asked him to lie down."

Georgiana glanced at her, her expression changing to panic. "He will recover though, will he not?"

Elizabeth rubbed her arm. "Of course he will. It is only a cold. He will stay in bed for a few days and will be himself soon enough."

Georgiana's fears calmed with Elizabeth's assertion.

"I must ask you to take care of our guests for the remainder of the day," Elizabeth said. "I promised him I would stay by his side."

The girl bit her lower lip, her eyes fearful. "I am not certain whether I am capable."

"You are certainly capable and will do an excellent job," Elizabeth told her. "I truly need your help today."

Georgiana nodded. "Of course, Lizzy. I will do my best."

Elizabeth leaned over to kiss her cheek. "Thank you, my dear sister."

As Georgiana left, Elizabeth rang for the servants to build a fire in the room. It was a warm day, but she thought that it would be best if he sweat out the illness.

When at last the freshly made broth was brought, she thanked the servant and asked to be left alone.

"Fitzwilliam, Fitzwilliam…wake up, dearest. You must eat," she urged, shaking his shoulder until he opened his eyes.

"Come, you need to sit up." As he listened to her, she rearranged his pillows supporting his back so he could sit more comfortably.

Placing the wooden tray on his lap, she stirred the fragrant soup. "Open your mouth," she prompted, placing a spoonful in front of his lips. He listened obediently, opening his mouth and swallowing the warm liquid. She thought that he might take the spoon from her, saying that he was not a child, but instead he allowed her to feed him until the bowl was empty.

Putting the tray away, she sat down beside him again. "Is that not better?"

He curled on his side, again capturing her hand in his, bringing it to his chest. "My throat feels better," he admitted.

"Sleep," she whispered, leaning over him. "You need your sleep to recover. I love you," she added, kissing his temple.

She saw him smile as he pulled her hand closer to his chest. Darcy slept without interruption until the evening. Georgiana returned twice, asking for him. Mrs. Gardiner and Jane, hearing of his state, came as well.

Mrs. Gardiner enquired whether or not they should postpone or even cancel their trip to the lakes. Elizabeth assured her that the illness was merely a trifling cold and there was no reason for them to change their plans. Jane supported her instantly, stating that she was perfectly capable of caring for the children on her own.

Elizabeth spent the night on the sofa next to their bed, waking up quite often as Fitzwilliam tossed and turned, mumbling in his sleep and kicking the covers to the foot of the bed. The result was that he uncovered himself often throughout the night. But it was not her husband's restlessness that worried her most. Whenever she touched his forehead she found that he was warmer as the night wore on. Greatly concerned, she wiped his brow with a soft cloth dipped in cool water from a bowl on the bedside cabinet. This she continued all through the night and into the early hours of the morning and by dawn he had begun to cough.

Finally, by the time the cock crowed twice, she had another bowl of broth brought up which he ate eagerly before falling back asleep. Reassured at last that he was resting comfortably, Elizabeth asked Georgiana to sit with him while she bathed and broke her fast.

She made an effort to dress in one of her more elegant morning dresses before descending downstairs to eat breakfast with the rest of family. Although becoming more worried, Elizabeth was determined to display a cheerful mien. She wanted very much for her aunt and uncle to have their holiday, and if they knew the truth about her husband, she feared they would not depart for their much needed time alone in the Lake District.

After their morning meal together, which included Jane, Bingley and the children, they waved their goodbyes to Mr. and Mrs. Gardiner. Jane had plans to make use of the pleasant weather, planning to take the children for a ride in an open carriage around the park and later a picnic in the meadow. Bingley was to assist her in entertaining her cousins.

On returning upstairs to their private rooms, Elizabeth hoped to see her husband sleeping or talking with his sister, perhaps even complaining that he had to stay in bed yet another day. She certainly did not expect to find him bent in half, coughing heavily in his hand as though he might spit out his lungs.

"Oh Lizzy, my brother is not better. In fact, he is far worse than he was before you left," Georgiana whispered, as they settled him back against the pillows.

Darcy's eyes were closed as he rested after his round of violent coughing.

"Find Mrs. Reynolds," Elizabeth cried, her eyes wide, the fear in them mirroring Georgiana's. "Tell her to send to Lambton for the doctor. Tell her to make haste."

Georgiana fled from the room in a hurry, knocking over a small table in her haste.

Elizabeth sat on the edge of the bed, careful not to disturb her husband. Placing a hand on his forehead, she shuddered, alarmed by how hot his skin had become. He was on fire!

"Lizzy," he whispered.

"Yes, my love. I am here," she said as calmly as possible while choking back her tears.

"Come lie beside me," he murmured, his breathing laboured and eyes glazed with fever.

Crawling onto the bed, she lay down beside him and reached to stroke his cheek gently.

"All will be well, my love. All will be well," she whispered more in assurance to herself than to him. After a moment, she added, "You only need to rest."

Chapter Thirty-Four

Doctor Sharp leaned over Darcy with a frown, listening to his chest. His expression was grave as he pulled away from his patient. Elizabeth retied her husband's nightshirt and pulled the covers over him, then turned to the doctor.

"Doctor?" she asked, her voice trembling.

The man's frown deepened as he looked down at her husband. "Let us step outside," he said.

Elizabeth placed a kiss on her husband's burning forehead, whispering that she would return soon. Stepping into the sitting room, she noticed how pale Georgiana's complexion had become as she stood watching at the door.

"Is he very sick, doctor?" the girl asked, her eyes wide with fear.

Doctor Sharp, who had been practising medicine in Lambton for the last thirty years, glanced at the faces of those assembled who awaited his answer. Miss Darcy, young Mrs. Darcy and Mrs. Reynolds were all waiting anxiously for his prognosis. By now he should have been accustomed to relaying bad news to the families in his bailiwick, having been a doctor for so many years. But still it was difficult, especially when it came to the Darcys who had faced so many deaths over the years.

"This night will show," he said at last. "This is a case of a very severe and malicious fever. What is more, his lungs are congested. He has the beginnings of pneumonia which," the doctor cast a worried glance at the entrance to the bedroom, "is developing fast. This, combined with high fever, makes his chances for survival quite slim. We should prepare ourselves for the worst."

Quiet sobbing came from Miss Darcy as she stepped into Mrs. Reynolds arms, who was weeping as well.

With compassion he glanced at the young woman in front of him, the new Mrs. Darcy. Poor girl, so young, married barely a few months and already facing such a tragedy.

"How can this be?" Elizabeth questioned. "My husband is young...strong and fit."

"It was a similar situation with his mother. The illness that took her life also started with a cold and she was gone in the course of a few days," he kindly reminded her.

"No! He will recover!" she stated vehemently.

"Mrs. Darcy," he said gently. "I have seen such cases as these many times in my life, and I must tell you that only one in ten survives, if that. He has a chance, yes, indeed he does, but you must prepare yourself for the worst."

Her large, now almost black eyes bore into him and she spoke purposely. "He *will* recover. He has people to live for—people who love him very much."

It would have been easy to say that the late Mrs. Darcy had had people to live for as well—a young son, husband and a baby girl not even two years of age but it had not helped her. Nevertheless, in the end he bit his tongue as that was not the words she wished to hear.

Mrs. Darcy turned on her heel and without another word, stomped back into the bedroom. Through the door he could see her sitting beside her husband, his hand in hers, whispering softly to him.

***

"I will not listen to him, my love," Elizabeth said, clasping his hot hand in both of hers. "You will be well; you will fight this and you will win! I know that. What kind of a doctor he is?" she huffed. "When our first child is born I do not want him anywhere near me; do you hear? You must promise me that, Fitzwilliam. You will secure me another doctor, a more understanding one."

There was no response. His eyes were closed and his breath came in short pants. Leaning forward, she lightly kissed a path from his forehead and temple to his cheek and then his ear. "I love you; do you hear me? You must fight! I know that you will not leave me. You must fight and we will help you."

Tears blurred her eyes, but she quickly dried them with the backs of her hands.

"Mrs. Reynolds," she called in a slightly raised voice and the grief stricken housekeeper entered the room to stare sadly at Darcy. "Mrs. Reynolds," she said more sharply, commanding the woman's attention. "Tell the cook to kill more fat chickens so there will be fresh broth always ready. Then we will need more cold water and soft rags, hot tea with fresh raspberries added, and tea with a drop of honey instead of the raspberries, two pints of curd, as well as lemon juice mixed with honey and whiskey for his throat. Please bring all of these to me as soon as possible."

Mrs. Reynolds stared at her, unmoving.

"Should I repeat myself?" she asked, growing impatient. The woman shook her head no.

"Good; make haste then!" Remembering the little Gardiners she added, "One more matter, Mrs. Reynolds. When my sister returns from the picnic with my cousins, tell her that they cannot enter the house because of the illness. Pack their things and put them in a carriage, and ask Mr. Bingley to drive them into Lambton. He is to rent rooms in the best inn where they will stay until their parents return."

Mrs. Reynolds blinked several times before dropping a quick curtsey and dashing out of the room. Alone, Elizabeth looked back at her husband and placed her hand against his cheek. He calmed whenever she did that, and it gave her hope to know that he was aware of her presence. She knew that in his own way, even with the fever, he was doing his best to fight the illness.

"Lizzy?" the quietest of voices caught her attention as Georgiana walked around the bed and sat on the other side. "What are we going to do without him?" Big tears began to stream down her pale cheeks.

"Why do you say that?" Elizabeth replied sharply.

"You...you...heard the doctor," her sister stuttered.

"Do not listen to him, Georgiana. You will not have to worry about that for the next forty years or more."

She looked hopeful. "Oh, Lizzy, are you certain?"

"Yes, he will not die, not now," she declared with all the force she could muster. "Now, will you help me or are you just going to cry?"

Properly chastised, Georgiana nodded furiously. "I will help."

Elizabeth gave her an encouraging smile. "Good; one of us should always be with him." Her expression softened as she searched his darling face. "He does not like to be alone."

The girl dried her eyes with a handkerchief. "Yes, Lizzy."

Soon the medicinal items she requested were brought in. So she began by wetting the soft cloth in the cold water and had Georgiana put it on his forehead. Then she opened the wardrobe and removed a large towel from the top self, which she dipped in the large jar of curd.

"What are you doing, Lizzy? Georgiana asked curiously.

"I read in a book once that curd placed on the chest pulls the illness from the lungs," she explained. She gestured to Georgiana to open his nightshirt then placed the wet material soaked in curd over the area from his collarbone to his stomach.

"Are you certain? I have never heard of such a thing..." the girl's voice trailed off as she wrinkled her nose in disgust at the scent. She cleared her throat. "It smells unpleasant. What kind of book was that?"

"It may smell bad, but it will not hurt him, I assure you," Elizabeth reasoned. "The book was about the customs and traditions of Russian peasants living in the outer limits of civilization. We must do everything we can to help him."

An hour later she and Georgiana removed the curd plaster from Darcy's chest and cleaned his skin with cool water. "Let us change his nightshirt," Elizabeth said wearily.

"I will bring the clean shirts," Georgiana offered, moving to the door.

"Thank you," Elizabeth whispered, not taking her gaze from her husband. His eyes were closed, but he did not sleep peacefully. And when she spoke to him, he did not respond. Every few moments his head moved from side to side, as though he was having a bad dream. Sometimes his hands shifted under the covering, but the movement was unnatural, a jerking motion.

Georgiana returned with the nightshirts in her hand, Mr. Bingley following behind her. Elizabeth rose to talk to him while Georgiana took her place beside Darcy.

"I rented the entire floor at The King's Clock in Lambton for Jane and the children. They should be comfortable there."

"Thank you, Mr. Bingley. I appreciate all your help in this matter. I would be very uneasy knowing the children could be in danger should they remain here."

"What more can I do?" he asked, gesturing towards the bed.

Seeing the deep concern in his eyes, Elizabeth responded, "We will need someone strong to lift him while we change the bedding and his shirt. Georgiana, dear, can you pass me one of the clean shirts?"

Elizabeth pulled the covers down, while Bingley lifted his friend. Quickly they stripped off the sweat dampened nightshirt and pulled on a clean one while Georgiana turned her back.

The rest of the day passed in the same manner. They fed him broth and hot tea with honey interchangeably with a whiskey, honey and lemon mixture, changed the compresses, and every so often placed a curd plaster on his chest.

In the evening they heard a bell tolling and Mrs. Reynolds came in to explain that people from the village were now gathering in the church to pray for their Master's health. As the evening wore on they tried to feed him the warm broth and raspberry tea but with little success. He seemed to gag on everything Elizabeth put in his mouth, gasping for air.

Sometime around midnight Darcy calmed down, falling asleep and allowing those who took care of him to sleep a little too. Georgiana was curled on the sofa while Elizabeth lay on top of the covers by his side. Bingley slouched uncomfortably in the armchair. Suddenly, Elizabeth was awakened from her light sleep.

"Miss Bennet, Miss Bennet, pray tell me what are you doing here?"

Blinking, she tried to focus on Darcy. He was sitting up in bed, seemingly alert and conscious.

"Are you feeling better?" she murmured, her heart filling with hope. Reaching out to touch his cheek, she found it burning hot. He was looking right at her, but his eyes were unseeing and glazed with fever.

"What are you doing in my bed, madam?" he answered haughtily. "I believe that you should be in your room or nursing your sister."

Mr. Bingley rose from the armchair and stepped to bed. "I believe he thinks that he is at Netherfield—as we were last October."

Elizabeth was certain that if she had been standing at the moment, her knees would have given way. Her husband was hallucinating and not only did not know where he was, he did not remember that they were married.

"Darcy, my friend," Bingley moved closer to the bed putting his hand on his friend's shoulder. "We are at Pemberley."

Darcy lay back down, focusing now on Bingley. "What is she doing here with us?"

"She is your wife. You were married this past spring."

Darcy's turned to look at Elizabeth. He stared at her for a long moment before asking shyly. "Kiss me?"

Blinking away her tears, Elizabeth scooted closer and placing one hand over his chest, she leaned in to touch her lips gently to his. "I love you," she whispered. "Stay with me."

Gazing into his eyes, she prayed that he had understood. Slowly his hand lifted to cup her face. "Such beautiful eyes...uncommonly intelligent," he whispered. Then his hand dropped and his eyes closed.

"Fitzwilliam! Fitzwilliam!" she shrieked, shaking him and waking Georgiana in her panic.

Bingley, who was checking Darcy's pulse, placed a calming hand on her back. "Do not worry. He has only fallen asleep."

Georgiana raced to the foot of the bed. "Was he talking?"

Elizabeth wiped her tears with the backs of her hands. "He was hallucinating. He did not even remember that we were married."

Georgiana moved to sit beside her, pulling her into an embrace. "It does not mean that he loves you any less."

For the rest of the night he woke several times, sometimes recognising people around him, and other times not. Once he opened his eyes, staring into the space, and talked to someone only he could see. It took only a moment for them to realise that he was having a conversation with Lady Anne. Listening to him talk to his dead mother sent icy shivers down Elizabeth's back.

Often he called for Colonel Fitzwilliam and only calmed when Bingley promised to write to his cousin requesting he come to Pemberley. By early morning Doctor Sharp had returned. Though distrustful of him, Elizabeth allowed him inside. He announced that the fever had dropped a bit, as though she could not tell, quickly adding that it did not mean that the danger was past. She was well aware of that, dreading the upcoming night.

During the day, even though the fever had decreased, coughs shook him violently and at times he had trouble breathing. The coughing eased by evening, but his temperature rose again. Elizabeth did not know which was worse, the terrible coughing or the burning fever.

That night was a repetition of the previous one with one difference—Darcy was mumbling incomprehensibly but not talking to anyone in particular as he had the night before. In the morning his fever was down again and his coughing was less strenuous, giving Elizabeth hope that the worst was behind. However, the doctor cautioned that the upcoming night would be decisive. If Darcy lived through the night, then the prognosis was very good that he would recover completely.

Elizabeth, Bingley and Georgiana took care of Darcy day and night, feeding him and making him drink hot tea and cool water. They changed his sweat soaked bed sheets and talked to him in quiet reassuring voices. But as the sky darkened and night descended, the fourth night of his fever, Elizabeth began to quake in fear. Each time she touched his forehead, it seemed hotter than before.

It was past midnight. She sat beside him, staring at his face and praying for no new traces of discomfort. Her back was stiff, her head pounded and she was tired, but she was could not sleep. Unlike Georgiana and Bingley, who had dozed off sitting together on the sofa, he with his head on her shoulder.

A sudden commotion in the sitting room caught Elizabeth's attention and she looked over her shoulder. A dark figure stepped into the room and her first thought was that it was a death banshee coming for her beloved.

"How is he?" A familiar voice questioned, coming closer. Finally the figure stepped into the light emanating from the fireplace.

A ragged sob escaped her throat as Elizabeth recognised Colonel Fitzwilliam. All her pent up emotions from the last few days came pouring out and she began to weep uncontrollably, her body shaking. Her vision blurred as she felt an arm come around her, rubbing her back.

"He is with us…he is with us," Colonel Fitzwilliam soothed. "He is fighting."

Elizabeth nodded, quieting and accepting the handkerchief he offered. Drying her eyes, she enquired, "How did you get here so promptly? Kent is no short distance."

Sitting down next to her on the bed, his eyes on Darcy, he explained. "I almost killed four horses on the way here. The message said that he wished to see me."

"He has called for you many times. But he has said nothing for some time now. The doctor said that this is the decisive night. That if the fever does not break…" She could say no more.

Colonel Fitzwilliam's brow furrowed. "I see."

Crawling onto the bed, she knelt beside Darcy's worn body. "My love, you have to wake up; do you hear me?" Her voice was sweet as she stroked his face. "Colonel Fitzwilliam came to see you just as you wanted. Wake up, love, please."

When there was no reaction, she grabbed hold of his nightshirt, trying to lift and shake him. "Wake up! Do you hear me!? Look at me!" she began to scream, her voice hoarse. "You cannot do this to me! You must fight! You cannot leave me alone! Listen to me! Fight, Fitzwilliam! Fight! You must!"

Someone was saying something, but she did not recognise who it was as she kept shaking Darcy, ordering him to open his eyes. Suddenly strong arms wrapped around her and even though she fought as hard as possible, they effortlessly removed her from the room.

As in a dream, she saw the doctor press something against her mouth while she was being held. Soon sleepiness came over her as though she was powerless. The last thing she saw before closing her eyes was the face of Colonel Fitzwilliam.

***

Eyelids heavy, her head feeling as though it was made of stone, Elizabeth opened her eyes with great effort and glanced around. The room was familiar, though dark, because the curtains had been drawn tightly to prevent the sun from peeking through.

Slowly she slid to the floor, supporting herself on the bedside table as her legs threatened to collapse. She was still wearing the same dress she had worn the day before and memories of last night came rushing back, flooding her heart with fear. Why was it so quiet? Why was she not hearing any voices?

Gathering all the courage she could muster, she walked to the door, opened it, and stepped into their private sitting room. The day was sunny, blinding light coming from tall windows. Glancing at the clock on the mantelpiece, she saw that it was four o'clock. She had slept the entire night and most of the day and no one had bothered to wake her! What was the meaning of this?

The door to their bedroom was closed and with trembling hands she reached for the handle.

As the door fell open with ease, she saw Colonel Fitzwilliam sitting in a chair, his back to her. His slightly too long, dark blonde hair rested against the collar of his coat. Hearing her enter, he stood up instantly which gave her an unobstructed view of the bed.

"Oh, God," she cried, collapsing to the floor as silent sobs shook her.

Leaning down, Colonel Fitzwilliam helped her to stand then led her to the bed.

"No need to cry, my love," she heard Darcy say clearly.

He sat there, propped against numerous pillows, his complexion pale but otherwise looking quite well for the ordeal he had been through. He was shaved and his hair was neatly combed away from his face.

He opened his arms and she climbed onto the bed and crawled over to him, hiding her face in his chest. As his arms tightened around her, she knew that she would thank God for the rest of her life for answering her prayer.

Chapter Thirty-Five

"I do not want any more," Darcy turned his head away from the spoon Elizabeth directed to his mouth, wrinkling his nose. "I dislike the broth, and there are carrots in this one," he complained, as he sat comfortably in bed, supported by numerous pillows.

Elizabeth put the spoon back into the bowl with a sigh, stirring the soup. "Carrots are healthy. A few more spoons," she pleaded. "It is good for you and will make you feel better."

"I am feeling quite well," he grumbled.

"It has only been three days since your fever broke. You are still very weak and you were coughing last night," she reminded, pushing a fresh spoonful into his mouth.

He shook his head. "I want cold ham with bread, cucumbers and some chocolate cake."

"You will have sandwiches and cake when you finish this bowl of broth."

Seeing she was adamant, he opened his mouth, swallowing obediently.

A light knock on the door caught their attention. It was Mr. Bingley, back from his morning ride.

"Good God man!" he exclaimed, grinning. "You are allowing to be fed like a child. I understand that you are still weak, but not to the degree that you cannot hold a spoon."

Darcy shrugged his shoulders, swallowing another spoonful from Elizabeth's hand. "You are simply envious of me because Jane does not spoon-feed you."

"She would if I asked it of her," Bingley boasted.

Darcy was about to give a retort when Elizabeth used the opportunity to put another spoonful of broth in his mouth. "Gentlemen, you are worse than little boys. Should I put you both in a corner?" she asked, attempting to sound strict.

Bingley hung his head, murmuring a quiet *No Ma'am*. Elizabeth laughed out loud, shaking her head in amusement as Darcy grinned.

"Now, all finished," she declared. Putting the empty bowl away, she reached over and patted Darcy's chin and mouth dry with the tail of a small cloth. "I will see to those promised sandwiches and cake now," she continued, giving her husband her brightest of smiles.

He smiled back, his eyes following her devotedly out of the room.

Bingley pulled a chair next to the bed. "You are one lucky man to have her."

Darcy straightened proudly against the pillows. "I know."

"She and Georgiana never left your side."

"So I heard. I do not remember much, but I do remember feeling their presence."

"Do not look so pleased," Bingley scolded. "You gave us all quite a fright."

Darcy sobered, his forehead creased. "I cannot believe that I became so sick from a walk in the rain."

"Most importantly you are now getting better."

"You have been riding?" Darcy guessed, glancing at Bingley's tall boots and short jacket that suggested that was the case.

"I took one of your horses—Devil is his name. I hope that you do not mind. What a beast!"

"Naturally, I do not mind. They need to be ridden, especially Devil. I bought him from Collins; he once belonged to Mr. Bennet. Elizabeth fears him though."

Bingley nodded. "Good horse, but temperamental, needs a strong hand."

Darcy gazed longingly out the window. "How I wish I could join you."

"I can tell you now that you will stay in this bed for a while longer, unless you wish to go against your wife's wishes. That I would not recommend," Bingley advised, his expression half jesting, half serious. "She ordered everyone about like a general during your illness; even the doctor seemed to fear her. She is very strong willed."

"I know how strong willed she is, believe me," Darcy agreed, amusement dancing in his eyes.

"One would never guess it," Bingley continued his observations. "She gives the impression of being so delicate and fragile. Anyway," he changed the subject. "I invited your cousin, Colonel Fitzwilliam, to join me for a ride earlier today, but he refused. He stated that he had a matter of urgent business in Lambton."

"He went to Lambton you say," Darcy's voice trailed off as he fell deep in thought. Richard's urgent business in Lambton had pale blonde hair, dark blue eyes, a pleasant figure and her name was Jane Bennet or his name was *not* Fitzwilliam Darcy.

"Yes, he is a strange fellow," Bingley said with much reflection. "I do not know him well, but I could swear that he is assessing me every time we meet. I feel he does not like me in particular. Have I offended him in some way?" Charles' expression was innocent.

"I should not think so," Darcy said hesitantly.

He was torn as he deliberated whether to tell his friend the truth behind his cousin's behaviour. He had promised himself that he would never again intervene in such matters after his last attempt had almost cost him Elizabeth. But Bingley seemed to have noticed nothing in regards to Jane and Richard, entirely oblivious to the fact that he had a serious rival just under his nose. He did not wish to offend his friend's intelligence, but he wondered how Bingley could be so unaware of what was happening around him. If someone had lusted after his Elizabeth like Richard did for Jane, wanting to steal her away, he would have known. That was irrefutable. And he would have acted accordingly.

Bingley was a good man, the best of friends, and Elizabeth and Georgiana had praised him for helping them during his illness. And knowing what heartache was, he did not wish it on anyone, Bingley especially.

"Charles, what I can tell you must stay between us." His voice was serious, which instantly commanded his friend's attention. He sincerely hoped that what he was about to say would not come back to haunt him in the future.

Bingley nodded, as his entire body tensed. "Of course."

"My cousin is interested in Jane. His intentions are honourable and very serious."

Bingley blinked. "My Jane?"

Darcy barely stopped himself from rolling his eyes. "Why are you so surprised? She is a beautiful and desirable woman. Do you think that you are the only man who admires her?"

"No, no, of course not," Bingley babbled, at a loss as to what to do with the intelligence he has just received. "I know that Jane is well admired. Is there a man who would not be drawn to her beauty and goodness? Are you certain, however, that your cousin has intentions towards her?"

"I am not in position to tell you more as I would break the confidence of people close to me, but yes, I am certain of it."

"Do you think that he has gone to Lambton this morning to see her?" Bingley asked. Before Darcy managed to answer, he stood up abruptly causing the chair to jolt. "I will go there this instant."

"Charles, keep a cool head, please—if only for my wife's sake," Darcy cried after him. "Elizabeth does not need any burdens added to those she has already borne."

"I only wish to look after what is mine," Bingley said defensively. "Do not worry though, I will control myself." Then he stormed from the room.

Darcy's head sank as he considered whether he had done the right thing in telling Bingley. In truth, he had given Bingley very little information—only a clue. He had said nothing about the letters, the kisses or Elizabeth's suspicions concerning the delayed date of their wedding.

"What has happened to Mr. Bingley?" Elizabeth asked as she and Georgiana walked in carrying trays with sandwiches, biscuits and tea, as well as slices of cake.

"He ran past as if he did not even notice us," Georgiana added. "So very odd for him not to stop and chat."

"He was in hurry to see Jane," Darcy replied, studying Elizabeth. "He is on his way to Lambton."

Elizabeth's dark brown eyes locked on his as she clumsily dropped the tray on the side table causing the china to shake and clang against one another. "Oh, my," she whispered as if speaking to herself. "Colonel Fitzwilliam has not returned from Lambton yet, has he?"

Darcy stared at her, hoping to reassure her with his gaze and ease her apprehension. The three drank tea together; Elizabeth and Darcy ate sandwiches and biscuits, but Georgiana refused anything to eat. She spoke little and soon excused herself from their company.

"What is the matter with her?"Darcy enquired.

"Have you not noticed anything?" Elizabeth's voice held slight exasperation.

He shot her a blank look. "No."

"She was upset because you said that Mr. Bingley was in hurry to see Jane. Have you not noticed the way she behaves in his presence, how she blushes every time he looks her way or speaks to her?"

"I have noticed nothing of the kind," he answered, bewildered at Elizabeth's observations. "Bingley and Georgiana? That cannot be! He is like a brother to her."

"Perhaps in the past, but I think that her feelings for him have changed, matured if you will."

Allowing a few moments to evaluate the idea, only one clear thought came to mind. "She is too young for marriage!" he exclaimed.

"Naturally," Elizabeth agreed, then added, "but in a few years..."

"I will not allow her to marry earlier than one and twenty," Darcy announced. "And as for Bingley, he is too old for her."

"No, he is not! He is but four and twenty."

"Four and twenty to her sixteen," Darcy grunted disapprovingly.

She raised an eyebrow. "The same as my one and twenty to your eight and twenty, soon to be nine and twenty."

Darcy crossed his arms over his chest, staring off into space.

After a moment, she prodded gently, "I thought you would be pleased with such a possibility."

"If I have to trust her with anyone, one day in the distant future..." he sighed. "Bingley would not hurt her, I know that. It would be easy to convince him to buy an estate close to Pemberley so I will be able to watch over her." As he started to think about it he began to like the idea of Bingley as a match for Georgiana. "But we should not forget that for now Bingley is engaged to Jane."

"We should also not forget that Colonel Fitzwilliam is quite determined to have Jane for himself. I only hope that Mr. Bingley will not meet your cousin while he is calling on Jane. I do not wish to be involved in any new drama."

Darcy gulped. "I might have hinted to Bingley that Richard is interested in Jane."

"You told me that we should not intervene." To his relief the tone of Elizabeth's voice was not angry but only surprised.

"I felt sorry for him. He had absolutely no idea. No details were revealed I assure you. I said nothing about the letters. Are you angry with me?" He wished to hear that she was not displeased.

She shook her head. "No. I am not. He is your friend and you do not wish to see him hurt."

"After what you have told me I am now more concerned for Georgiana. I do not wish her to suffer from unrequited love."

"You cannot stop her from falling in love; if not Mr. Bingley, there will be someone else."

"It was easier when she was a child. All she wanted was for me to hear the new songs she had learned, ride her pony and cuddle."

She rubbed his coverlet covered thigh. "I have an eye on her. I will talk to her whenever I feel that something is wrong."

"Thank you," he said sincerely. "It has never been easy for me to talk with her about such matters. I do not know how."

"Do you wish for more tea?" Elizabeth took the empty cup from his hand, placing it on the side table.

"No, I wish for something else," he wrapped his fingers around her wrist and pulled her on to the bed next to him.

"You should rest." She tried not to smile but ended up giggling.

"I told you that I feel much better." He buried his face in her neck. "I need this."

"Someone may walk in at any moment."

"I doubt it," he argued, kissing along her collarbone. "Most likely Georgiana has closed herself in the music room and Bingley has just left."

"The door is open and Colonel Fitzwilliam may return at any time."

"We will close the door. Richard is smart enough to guess why we have done so."

Freeing herself from his embrace, she slipped off the bed and ran to close the door, turning the key with a resounding click. Kicking off her shoes, she sat down on the edge of the bed with her back to him so he could unbutton her morning dress. This he did with quick fingers.

"Come here," he groaned, pulling her closer and pushing the fine silk down and off her shoulders.

"Wait." She sat up divesting herself of the dress before straddling him. "My stays!" With one practised movement, she sucked some air and with both hands unclasped the hooks on the front of the corset.

"Now, I have you where I want you," he murmured, pulling her down next to him and then rolling until she was underneath.

His hand moved stealthily down from her face, neck and shoulders, as he lowered the straps of her chemise. Covering one small breast with his palm, he caressed it. Looking into her eyes, he found them shimmering with moisture and one large tear running down the curve of her cheek.

His voice was full of concern. "What is the matter?"

"I thought we would never be like this again," she sniffled. "You were so sick."

"I am well now," he replied, slowly stroking the side of her face as he brushed the tear away.

She took a deep, shaky breath. "I was so scared." She trembled. "That last night, before they gave me the laudanum, I began to think that you would not survive. I felt that I could not live without you."

They settled close together, both on their sides, staring into each other's eyes.

"I am sorry that you had to go through this," he soothed.

"Those three days when you were fighting the fever and the day that I learned about Papa's death were the worst of my life."

He tightened his arm around her. "I am here. I am not going anywhere. I love you."

"I love you too," she whispered, closing her eyes and nestling against his chest.

***

When she awoke, the sun was considerably lower in the sky. They must have slept through most of the afternoon. Carefully, she slipped from his arms, not wishing to disturb him. He was still weak and needed his rest despite his assurances of recovery. He had continued to cough throughout their nap, though it was not the heavier coughs that would awaken him.

As she was dressing she heard a knock on the door. The knocking came again with more force. Then she heard Colonel Fitzwilliam's voice. "Mrs. Darcy?" Another knock. "Elizabeth, are you there?"

She opened the door and quietly slipped into her sitting room where the colonel waited. "We have been napping," she explained, smoothing her dress. "Is something the matter?"

Gently taking her elbow, he led her to the window where she beheld a carriage in the drive and people standing beside it.

"Who has come?" she asked. "Is that my aunt and uncle? No, it is not their carriage. Who are these people?" she squinted her eyes. "Is that my youngest sister? This cannot be! Lydia is in Brighton."

"Not any longer," Colonel Fitzwilliam announced gravely. "They have just arrived."

"They?"

"Let us go downstairs; we should not speak here," he whispered, glancing with apprehension at the door to the bedroom where Darcy was still sleeping."I am not certain whether he can hear us in his current state. He seems to be well enough, but he was deathly ill only a few days ago and he hates that man."

Confused and worried Elizabeth asked, "To whom are you referring?"

"Wickham," he spat out.

Her eyes widened. "Wickham is here with my sister?"

He leaned down, supporting his hand on the panelled wall, whispering quickly, "As I said, they came a few moments ago, just as I was returning from Lambton. The butler did not let them in because the last time Wickham was here, Darcy told the staff that he was not to be welcomed at the manor ever again. Mrs. Reynolds saw my arrival and not being able to reach you, asked my assistance. At first I did not believe my own eyes—that Wickham dared to show his face here after what he had attempted with Georgiana. I noted that he had a young girl with him and she introduced herself as your sister, Lydia. Wickham demanded to see Darcy. I told him that was not possible because he was ill and that is when the blackguard demanded to see you."

"What does he want? What is Lydia doing here?"

Colonel Fitzwilliam put a hand on her shoulder, his expression compassionate. "They are returning from Gretna Green."

"No," she breathed in horror. "That cannot be!"

"I am afraid that it can. Wickham showed me the marriage license."

Cradling her head with her hands, she exclaimed. "Oh Dear God, what did she do? Poor, stupid girl."

"How old is she? She looks very young."

Elizabeth's eyes watered. "She will be sixteen in a week's time."

"Bastard," Colonel Fitzwilliam muttered. "She is just a child and he is almost my age."

"I must see her," Elizabeth murmured, hurrying from the room and down the stairs, straight into a foyer. The front door was open and she could see a smiling Wickham with Lydia next to him as they had moved to the portico.

"Lizzy!" The girl's face broke into a smile, as soon as she saw her elder sister approaching.

"Are you well?" Elizabeth questioned, cupping Lydia's round face in her hands and examining her for any signs of mistreatment.

"I am well, Lizzy," Lydia confirmed, though something in her voice was amiss.

"What did you do, Lyddy?" Elizabeth asked in a whisper, her voice cracking. "What did you do?"

The girl shrugged, beginning to laugh cheerfully. "I got myself a husband in Brighton, just like Mama said I should."

Elizabeth shook her then. "Oh, sister, you have no idea what you have done."

She felt a hand on her shoulder as a sweet sugary voice whispered near her ear. "Will you not greet me Elizabeth? We are now brother and sister are we not?"

Elizabeth backed away. "How dare you!" she hissed, slapping his cheek.

At first surprised, Wickham instantly angered. Catching her wrist, his lips curled into an ugly snarl. She could feel the pain in her hand as his fingers tightened.

Coming from seemingly nowhere, Colonel Fitzwilliam grabbed her assailant from behind, twisting his arm in one fast, well-practised movement. "I will advise you to let her go Wickham, if you wish to leave Pemberley on your feet instead of in a box."

Slowly Wickham released Elizabeth's hand, noting the footmen and stable hands who had rushed forward, eager to offer their assistance.

"Look about! You do not have many friends here, do you?" Colonel Fitzwilliam taunted, still holding him captive. "How many daughters and sisters did you ruin over the years? Do you even remember? It was not very wise of you to come here. You have a very short memory it seems."

"I want to see Darcy," Wickham said.

"I told you that was not possible."

Wickham laughed menacingly. "Dying perhaps? Is he that ill?" His merriment ended and he hissed in pain as Colonel Fitzwilliam pulled his arm with greater force.

Elizabeth fought the urge to slap him again, instead turning from the vile creature to face her sister. "Lyddy, why did you agree to go with him? What were you thinking? I cannot help you now." Her voice broke as she finished. "You must go with him. You are now his wife."

Lydia exclaimed, "But he insisted we come here! He said that you would help us with his debts in Brighton. That is why we had to escape."

"You are my sister, and I will always try to help you. You will always be welcome in my home, but only without your husband. He cannot stay here. He knows why; perhaps he will tell you."

"Lizzy?" Lydia pleaded, her expression hurt, confused and fearful.

Tears in her eyes, Elizabeth hugged her sister before turning on her heel and entering the house.

She stopped at a footman. "Make sure Mr. Wickham and his wife leave the grounds of Pemberley immediately."

Chapter Thirty-Six

Darcy watched his wife as she moved about the room. He had woken from his nap quarter of an hour ago, and he instantly felt the change in her. He had already asked whether everything was well, but she had given him a blinding smile in response, one that did not quite reach her eyes saying everything was well.

He was not fooled with her assertions - she avoided looking into his eyes and her skittish behaviour reminded him of the first weeks of their engagement when she had been uneasy in his company.

He decided that he would have nothing of that. There would be no more barriers or misconceptions between them.

He caught her right hand around the wrist, bringing her closer. "What is the matter?" he asked. Looking up into her eyes, he caught a grimace of pain reflected there before she schooled it with a pleasant expression.

Frowning, he pulled up the long sleeve of her dress. He remembered well that earlier in the day she had worn elbow length gown, and he wondered why she had changed. It was a warm day; she could not be cold.

Looking down at her hand he saw a bruise around her delicate wrist.

"Who did that to you?"

"It is nothing." She tried to cover the bruised place with her other hand. "I must have hit my hand against something."

He turned her hand and saw that the discolouring ran all around her small wrist.

"I am asking you once more. Who did this to you," he spoke, keeping his voice calm. "Because it was not me."

They had made love earlier in the afternoon, and for a moment he had kept her hands above her head, but he was certain that he had not marked her. He was always very careful not to apply too much pressure so that he did not bruise her, even when in passion.

"It is nothing," she repeated. "No harm done." She smiled, trying to remove her hand from his inspection. "I think that it is time for your dinner," she said quickly, in her most animated voice. "The cook prepared fish just as you like it."

He held her arm gently by the elbow, keeping her close to him as he stared steadily into her face till she looked at him. "Who did that to you?" he asked again quietly.

"You are still so weak," she paused, biting down on her lower lip. "You should not worry."

"Do you think that I will worry less being aware that someone has manhandled you in our home, crushing your hand with enough force to leave a bruise and not knowing his name?"

"It does not hurt."

"Elizabeth, I am losing my patience. Tell me at once, or I will find out the truth from someone else."

As he gazed into her face he could see her resolve faltering. Tears were forming in her eyes.

"He gripped my hand only after a short moment, before Colonel Fitzwilliam came to stop him," she confessed at last. "It did not hurt, only later did I notice the bruise."

"Who?" he asked, trying to keep his voice calm and not frighten her. He could not imagine anyone in his right mind who would dare to physically harm his wife in his own home.

"Wickham," she whispered.

"Wickham? What was Wickham doing here?!" he cried angrily.

"I should not have told you," she choked, tears running down her cheeks.

He realized that he was scaring her, even though she had done nothing wrong and was the victim.

"Forgive me," he murmured gently, pulling her to him, so she climbed on the bed next to him. "Now tell me everything," he said, arranging her against him with her head on his shoulder, her legs draped over his, his arm supporting her back. "What happened?" he coaxed her, kissing her bruised wrist.

She took one long, deep breath before she started to speak in a rushed voice. "After I woke from my nap, Colonel Fitzwilliam came to talk with me. He told me that Wickham was here waiting in front of the manor with my youngest sister Lydia. At first I did not believe him, but when I reached the vestibule, I saw that is was true. They were there and Wickham demanded to see you but the butler would not let him inside. They were on their way back from Gretna Green. I slapped Wickham for what he did to my sister and it was then that he grabbed my hand. Wickham insisted on seeing you, but I ordered the servants to make sure that Mrs. and Mr. Wickham left the grounds of Pemberley. Colonel Fitzwilliam saw their marriage license and says that they are indeed married." She finished her tale with a sob, hiding her face in her hands.

Darcy fought the temptation to mount his horse that very moment and go after the bastard. He could not believe that Wickham had dared to come to his house, threaten his wife, then hurt her. What is more, he had obviously talked Lydia into eloping. He had not succeeded with Georgiana, so he had gone after the second best -Elizabeth's youngest sister. It was low behaviour even for him.

Wrapping his arms around a crying Elizabeth, he whispered. "All will be well love. I will take care of everything."

She pushed from him abruptly, shaking her head. "I cannot allow you to do that! They are gone; I told them to go away. Georgiana knows nothing about it."

"Do not cry," he dried her cheeks with his fingers. "He is not worth your tears, your nerves or your worry. Go wash your face, and then ask Colonel Fitzwilliam to come to me."

He kissed her wet, salty lips repeatedly, the fury building inside his chest at the sight of the red blotches on the delicate skin of her neck and chest. He could well imagine how shaken she must have been after her encounter with Wickham.

At last, after many hugs and reassurance, she acquiesced. After washing her face, she went to find his cousin.

***

"You know," Richard said without preamble as he entered the room a few minutes later.

Darcy nodded. "I noticed the bruise on her wrist and questioned her. She tried to evade the answer, but in the end she told me all."

"Your wife was adamant that I was not to tell you," his cousin said, bringing a chair to sit beside the bed. "I tried to convince her that you would learn sooner or later, but she said that she did want you to worry."

"First, thank you for protecting her," Darcy spoke earnestly. "She told me that you stopped him after he grabbed her hand."

"I would never have guessed that Wickham would try to manhandle her. If I had known, I would have kept her a safe distance away from him."

Darcy clenched his fists. "I would like to break his neck with my bare hands."

"You are not the only one who wished to do so, I assure you. A small crowd of menservants gathered around Wickham and had I not been there to stop his assault on Mrs. Darcy they were quite ready to protect her."

"Perhaps that would be better," Darcy murmured.

"My thoughts exactly. We might have disposed of Wickham forever."

Darcy ran his hands through his hair. "Will you help me? I will be unfit to travel for some time yet and I need someone to talk with Wickham."

"Naturally, I will do it," Colonel agreed without hesitation. "I am guessing that your intention is to help Wickham now that he is your brother."

Darcy shrugged. "Elizabeth will be worried about her sister if I do nothing."

"I do not think that your wife expects you to do anything. She made herself perfectly clear where her priorities and loyalty lay," Colonel interjected. "And you know Wickham. He is a scoundrel and a leech. The more you do for him, the more money you give him, the more he will want. If you pay his debts now, in a year he will accumulate twice as much, then expect you to pay him off yet again. It is a waste of money. It is exactly what he wants you to do."

"You are right, and I know well how Wickham operates, but I feel sorry for that poor girl, not to mention that Elizabeth is heartbroken over her sister's fate. Lydia is even younger than Georgiana and she is a victim. Wickham went after her because of me—tis the only reason for this marriage. I have to do something for her."

Colonel Fitzwilliam was silent for a moment, frowning. "I have an idea..."

"I am listening."

"The girl is ruined for life and that we cannot change. I am thinking that we may convince Wickham to allow her to live separately from him, return to her mother perhaps, or settle her is some small cottage somewhere in the country far away from the society. Her reputation would be damaged, but she would have a better life than to be left with him."

"That is a good solution, very good indeed," Darcy smiled. "Elizabeth will be pleased with it. We only have to find Wickham."

"Oh, I am certain that he is staying somewhere close, Lambton most likely, so that we could find him easily. He is not stupid and he knows that you care too much for Elizabeth to do nothing for Lydia."

"Will you go and talk with him then?"

"Tomorrow, first thing in the morning."

"Thank you, Richard; I am truly grateful for this." Darcy extended his hand to his cousin in gratitude. "And for everything you have done for us."

"You are most welcome cousin; you know that you are like a brother to me—much more so than Henry. It is a shame but Henry and I have never quite understood one another."

"It is not my business but..." Darcy paused, looking up at the other man. "I thought that there was a possibility for us to be brothers in name as well – brothers-in-law at the very least."

Colonel Fitzwilliam stood up from the chair, and walked to the window. His hands were clasped behind him in a military manner. "I talked with Jane today as you must have guessed and it is complicated, difficult. She is fond of Bingley, but I am certain she does not love him the way a woman should when she is about to marry. She is not in love with him nor is she attracted to him."

"You are not giving up hope then?"

"Me?" Colonel Fitzwilliam pointed to himself. "Never! I will never surrender. Perhaps I should take my example from Wickham."

"What is your meaning?" Darcy frowned. "I do not like the sound of that." He eyed him warily.

The other man shrugged. "Seduction and elopement does not seem such a bad idea to me."

Darcy's eyes widened. "I have not heard that and I do not know anything about it."

"Oh, come on Darcy, we both know that being in my shoes you would not hesitate to do the same." His cousin challenged.

Darcy hung his head. "Why does my wife have so many unmarried sisters?"

Colonel Fitzwilliam chuckled. "Everyone has their burdens, I suppose."

***

As autumn came to Pemberley, all the guests had left and Darcy and Elizabeth were alone once more. Georgiana had accepted Lady Eleanor's invitation to spend a few weeks in Bath with her aunt and uncle.

Colonel Fitzwilliam had found Wickham with little difficulty because, exactly as they had predicted, he had stayed in Lambton. The cad was offered ten thousand pounds on condition of allowing Lydia to be separated from him. Stupid girl that she was, Lydia had refused stating that she would not abandon her husband. His cousin was convinced that they would hear from Wickham again in the future as he was not the man to walk away from the prospect of such rich connections. They assumed that he hoped for more, still believeing that keeping Lydia with him would eventually be his pass to an easy living.

Elizabeth was aware of everything what had transpired, but she did not try to find Wickham again. Darcy knew that she suffered because of her sister's most unfortunate marriage, but as Colonel Fitzwilliam had once said, she made herself perfectly clear where her priorities and loyalty lay.

As far as his health was concerned Darcy recovered rapidly under Elizabeth's constant care. And the only reminder of his illness was that he tired easily and needed much more sleep than before.

At the end of October Elizabeth told him that she had early symptoms of being with child. He was exceedingly happy upon hearing the news. He wondered what the baby would look like, whether it would be more like him or Elizabeth, and whether it would be a girl or a boy. He would not mind a girl in the least as the thought of a tiny girl with her mother's eyes and bouncing curls pleased him very much.

They calculated that the child should come at the beginning of May, not later than the fifteenth.

As November turned into December they were convinced of her condition, as was the rest of Pemberley. They made no official announcement, but everyone seemed to know that a new Darcy was on the way though Elizabeth was not yet showing.

Darcy believed that there had never been a more loved Mistress of Pemberley than his Elizabeth, including his own mother. He did not know how she was able to have such easy relationship with everyone, from kitchen maids and stable boys, to the parson's wife. He admired her for that and was even slightly envious of her ability to effortlessly interact with people.

She was very popular among the tenants, the servants and neighbours, much more than he. It was most noticeable when they were together in the company of others. For example, after Sunday's service, people did not address him anymore and talked only with her, telling her about their problems, mentioning the burning issues concerning the community. It was obvious that such matters, like improving the road leading to Lambton, was his concern not hers, but somehow it was Elizabeth who heard about it first.

Christmas came and went, spent happily with only the three of them, not counting the little person in Elizabeth's belly. A day after New Year the bad news came. Anne de Bourgh had died, despite Lady Catherine's every attempt to save her life. For years the entire family had tried to convince Lady Catherine that Anne's coughing was much more serious than a passing cold. But Darcy's aunt always knew better and was not one to listen to the counsel of others. She had only seen the seriousness of her daughter's state when Anne started to cough blood.

Darcy felt sad to hear about his cousin's life ending so prematurely, even though Anne had been indifferent to him. And he was quite surprised how moved with Anne's death Elizabeth proved to be. She cried for an entire afternoon after hearing the news.

He felt guilty that he could not attend the funeral, but there were several reasons for that. Firstly, Elizabeth did not want him to travel so far in the dreadful cold weather of an English winter after his recent illness. Secondly, he wanted to give Richard the chance to become the Master of Rosings Park and was determined to play the role of the ungrateful nephew as long as necessary. Thirdly, he did not wish to leave Elizabeth alone now that it was clearly evident that she was with child. In her fourth month, her condition was now visible to everyone and he had no intention of leaving her alone.

As the harsh winter had come to Pemberley Elizabeth began to grow, getting bigger with each day. Having no experience with pregnant women, Darcy was not sure whether his wife's progress was natural. From the sixth month on she was quite heavy with child. The bulge of her belly seemed to almost swallow her small form. He began to think that the child was abnormally big, but when he shared his fears with the doctor, he learned that everything was perfectly natural. She walked, or rather waddled, the short distance from the stuffed armchair chair to a sofa.

The doctor told her that she needed to walk more because it would make her stronger when her time came and was good for the baby. She listened to his advice and, wrapped in her fur coat, walked around the frozen lake every day. Darcy accompanied her, fearing that she might fall on the slippery ground. There was no enthusiasm in her as far as walking was concerned and he never told her that from a very active person she had become a lazy one. She slept late in the morning, never leaving her room before ten, then napped in the afternoon, and by nine she was in bed again.

She ate all the time. He could swear that every time he looked at her she was either sleeping or eating. She began to keep food in their private sitting room, and more than once he was awakened in the middle of the night to the sound of her sucking on the bones of a cold chicken leg. For someone who had barely nibbled at her food before that was quite a change.

He could hardly understand how one person could eat so much. Only once, the first and the last time, he dared to voice his opinion on the subject. It was aimed as a playful remark, but she seemed to have lost all sense of humour. She declared that she had been feeding his child and if he could not stand looking at her, she might very well leave his sight forever.

Her body began to change, not only her midsection. Her bosom was twice as big, green veins marking the milky flesh, nipples turned from pink to dark red. Her hips rounded, becoming wider, and she had gained more flesh all over. Her face filled, making her eyes not as large as before, her collarbones stopped protruding.

Another result of her condition was that as much as she wanted food she wanted him. Gone was shy and innocent Lizzy of the first months of their marriage, blushing furiously when he touched her intimately and turning her eyes away from his naked body in embarrassment.

She became aggressive, boldly reaching to the front of his breeches so he would have no doubt what she wanted from him. At the beginning he felt blessed with her increased appetite for lovemaking. That was something new, as in the past she had been happy with two or three times a week routine which usually was barely enough for him. Now the situation had changed drastically; in the morning, in the evening, in the middle of the day and in the middle of the night, she demanded his attention, reaching her pleasure quickly and falling asleep more than once before he finished.

After a few weeks of such a treatment he began to get fatigued, and tried to discreetly avoid her, finding excuses that he had to leave early in the morning, or write letters late in the evening. She did not take the hint though and more than once went to search for him. When he feigned reluctance, she simply lowered herself to her knees, making use of her capable little hands and soft lips, looking up at him with those big, shining eyes. He never turned her down - he did not wish to hurt her feelings, and to be truthful he was afraid of weeping. He did not deal well with tears.

Darcy did not look with anticipation to spring because he was terrified to even think about the birth. He prayed to God silently every day, as he touched her constantly kicking stomach, to make it as easy for her as possible and to allow her and the baby to survive. He now understood perfectly his father's reaction to his mother's death. If anything happened to Elizabeth and the child, he would die too; there would be no life for him without them.

Chapter Thirty-Seven

Darcy finished sealing the letter to his solicitor in London and placed it on the small heap of the correspondence waiting to be sent.

It was late March and the weather had much improved during the last two weeks. Interrupting his work, even though he had a few more letters he needed to write, he walked to the large window to look at the vast expense of the newly greening grass.

His heart clenched with both joy and fear when he saw two female figures emerging from the park. As his wife and sister made their slow progress towards the house, he could see how slowly Elizabeth walked, supported heavily on Georgiana's arm.

Lately he had begun to have nightmares, dreaming that something would go terribly wrong during the birth. He woke several times a week in a cold sweat, his heart pounding, only to find Elizabeth sleeping safely next to him. With a sigh and heavy heart, he returned to his desk to start another letter, but found he could not focus on writing.

Elizabeth was currently displeased with him as he refused her the opportunity to attend Jane's wedding to Bingley. The event was to take place in two weeks and Darcy was of opinion that three days travel would be dangerous for his very pregnant wife. Moreover, an unavoidable reunion with Mrs. Bennet was not something that she needed right now. He was more than certain that her mother would not miss the opportunity to say something very upsetting and he felt that the additional stress should be avoided at all cost because of Elizabeth's delicate condition. A light knock on the door of his study announced Elizabeth's arrival.

Darcy stood up to greet her and as she opened the door he could first see the heavy bulge of her belly appearing before the rest of her.

"Have you and Georgiana had a nice walk?" he asked, making his way to her as she stopped in the middle of the room.

She smiled at him. "Yes, thank you. It is so nice to stroll without the burden of coat, boots and a hat."

"I am glad." Darcy leaned down to kiss her cheek, his hand wondering over her midsection.

"Feel." She covered his hand with hers, guiding it down so he could touch the spot where the baby was kicking.

"Can I see?" he asked.

She nodded with a smile and they walked a few steps to sit down on a sofa. Comfortably settled, Elizabeth lifted the skirt of her dress to show her belly covered with loose undergarments. She untied the petticoats from under her bosom and lowered them, exposing the naked skin.

Darcy's hand ran over the round expense of her stomach. Settling his hand close to Elizabeth's navel, he felt a foot pushing against his touch. As if the baby felt his hand, it pushed harder, so when he took it away he could still see the small lump.

"He is terribly strong," he murmured, tracing the shape of the protrusion with his finger.

"He?" she asked, looking down to see what he was seeing. "How do you know it is a boy?"

"I think that a girl would be smaller and this is quite a foot," he explained, disappointed that the lump began to disappear. "I have big feet too."

She rolled her eyes, righting her undergarments and the dress as she covered herself. "Perhaps it is a girl with very big feet."

"No, it is not," he insisted. "Your feet are small, and our daughter, if we are blessed with one, will have pretty little feet as well."

Snuggling close to him she asked, "Have you thought about what we discussed?"

He stiffened instantly. "Elizabeth, I have not changed my mind. It is unthinkable for you to travel so late in your confinement."

"Nonsense, the baby will not come for six weeks; that is plenty of time to make such a short trip."

"The baby may very well come in four weeks; I counted too."

She pushed away from him, crossing her arms over her belly. "I want to go to the wedding. I want to see Jane and my younger sisters."

"Elizabeth, be reasonable."

"No," she huffed, lifting herself with much effort. "You are being obstinate about it with no good reason."

"My love, I beg you to understand my concern. I..."

"No!" Elizabeth narrowed her eyes at him. "I do not understand! I want to attend Jane's wedding!"

Running his hand over his face, he continued, "That is out of question. We can invite them to come here for their honeymoon."

She said nothing to this, simply lifting her chin in defiance. Turning to escape the room, she moved as fast as her large belly would allow.

With a slight pounding in his head, signalling the beginnings of a headache, Darcy returned to his desk. He had not even managed to finish one sentence of a new letter when Georgiana barged into the room completely out of breath.

"Brother, come!" she exclaimed, her eyes wide.

Fear clenched his heart as he stood up. "Elizabeth?"

His sister nodded. "She was with me in the music room when she began to have pains."

As Darcy ran into the music room, he saw Elizabeth bent in half, one hand gripping the back of the armchair, the other clenching her stomach. Her face was twisted with pain.

"Fitzwilliam," she breathed upon seeing him.

While he hovered over her, she spoke in quick desperate breaths. "I think that it is time to get Mrs. Harris."

"But it is too early," Darcy proclaimed, his hands shaking. "At least four weeks too early."

"She moaned, bending farther down. "I cannot help it. Send for the midwife!"

"I will see to that," Georgiana said, fleeing from the room.

As soon as the pain eased, Darcy picked Elizabeth up in his arms and with the utmost care carried her through the house to their rooms. Her eyes were closed, her face peaceful, but as he reached their bedroom she began to moan again, palming her stomach. After placing her on the bed, he stood staring down at her as though not knowing what to do.

"Can you put the pillows behind my back?" she rasped.

"Of course, yes, of course," Darcy murmured, helping her to settle more comfortably.

Darcy was watching the large bay window, searching for some sign that the midwife had come. He glanced back at his wife and wiped his sweaty palms against his trousers. Eternity seemed to pass before he spied a carriage coming down the drive in front of the manor. Soon after there was a knock at the door and a round, tall, robust woman entered.

Mrs. Harris was reputed to be the best midwife in the northern part of the Derbyshire and fortunately she lived in Lambton. She glanced at Elizabeth, sitting against the pillows in the middle of the bed, her legs apart, panting heavily. Then the heavy set woman turned and her eyes rested upon a very pale, wide eyed Darcy.

"Mr. Darcy will leave us alone," the woman announced, moving to Elizabeth's side and lifting her skirts.

"I wish to stay with my wife," Darcy replied bravely.

Not bothering to even look at him, the midwife repeated, "Mr. Darcy, you will leave. I have to attend to your wife and I need no fainting father hovering over my back."

"I have no intentions of..." Darcy started in an offended voice, but Mrs. Harris interrupted him sharply, turning her head to glare at him. "Do not argue with me, Sir. I helped you into this world, your buttocks being the first thing that saw the light of the day, and if you wish a row with me, I will leave you to deliver this baby yourself."

"Fitzwilliam, leave please," Elizabeth panted.

Darcy exited the room, closing the door. He sank into a nearby chair, cradling his head in his hands. He could not remember a time when there was so much fear building inside of him. Their baby was coming too early; would it survive? Would it be able to live on its own outside Elizabeth's body? Why was this happening to them? Had there not been enough anguish in their lives this past year?

Lost in his thoughts, he did not notice Mrs. Harris standing in front of him. Only when she spoke did he lift his head to look at her. "You will not become a father today, Mr. Darcy," she announced.

Standing to his feet, he mumbled, "I will not? But she is... she is in pain."

"It happens to some women, those early pains, which are not true labour. She must stay in bed for the next few days, but you will have to wait several weeks yet before the baby is born."

"She is well then?" he asked, wanting more confirmation.

"As well as she can be."

"Thank you," he breathed. Immense relief washed over him.

The midwife assured him that she would come again before the evening to check on Mrs. Darcy because she had to return to Lambton to see to the wife of the blacksmith who was about to deliver her fourth baby. As the midwife left, Darcy entered the bedroom and saw that Elizabeth looked much calmer, with less distress written on her face.

"You must be quite pleased," she said archly as she considered him.

He shook his head, sitting down next to her. "I do not comprehend..."

"Now it is certain that I cannot attend Jane's wedding to Mr. Bingley," she explained.

Placing both hands on her belly, he said. "You gave us quite a scare, Son." He kissed the top of the hard bulge, before burying his face in Elizabeth's neck and kissing her. "I love you and I do not know what I would do if anything happened to you."

Combing her fingers through his hair, she gave it a light tug just as he liked. "We are fine. Mrs. Harris claims that such early pains are perfectly normal and happen quite frequently."

Darcy pulled back to look at her. "I will grow completely grey before this baby comes."

"I think that I can see a few already." Her tone was playful.

"You must feel better if you are teasing me."

"Come here," Elizabeth whispered, patting the place beside her.

Darcy lay down next to her, his head on her shoulder, one hand draped over her belly. He breathed a heavy sigh of relief. She was safe and sound in his arms—for now at least.

***

It was a late afternoon when Elizabeth awoke from her nap. The baby was kicking her ribs again and she could not sleep when it was so active. Moreover, she needed to use the chamber pot badly. Having dealt with that necessity she returned to bed.

Situating herself comfortably, she palmed her stomach. Fitzwilliam thought that the baby was a boy, but she knew that he would be just as pleased with a girl. Nevertheless, she preferred a boy. After all, it was her duty as Mrs. Darcy to produce an heir for Pemberley.

With her earlier pains now completely gone, she was thankful to God that the baby would not be born early. Her husband had been terrified earlier today; she had never seen him so scared. Now she worried how he would deal with the situation when her time came in a few weeks. Mrs. Harris might have been quite right about him fainting.

Glancing about the room, she wondered where he had gone. He had stayed by her side, holding her hand till she had fallen asleep earlier that day. Perhaps, she reasoned, he has gone to finish his letters. After all she could not expect him to sit by her side for the entire day. As soon as the thought was finished, his handsome face appeared in the open door.

"How are you feeling?"Darcy asked tentatively.

She gave him a blinding smile. "Very well, thank you."

He made his way to the bed, his steps careful. "I need to tell you something, but you must promise that you will not become overexcited."

"Has something happened?" Worry instantly tugged at her heart.

"No, no, it is nothing very disturbing—at least I hope that it is not. It is, however, unexpected."

She rolled her eyes, becoming impatient. "Can you simply tell me what is happening?"

"Yes, of course." He nodded, before turning his head in the direction of the door. "Your sister is here to see you."

With a frown, Elizabeth observed as Jane entered the room, her face flushed with embarrassment.

"Jane?" she whispered almost in unbelief.

"Lizzy!" her older sister cried, rushing to the bed where they fell into each other's embrace.

"What are you doing here?" Elizabeth began. "You are supposed to be preparing to wed Mr. Bingley."

Jane pulled away. "That will not happen."

"You broke the engagement?"

Jane bit her lip, before explaining, "I eloped with Colonel Fitzwilliam five days ago. We are just now returning from Gretna Green."

Elizabeth's eyes widened as she stared at her sister for a long moment, her mouth open, not saying a word.

"Are you very disappointed in me, Lizzy?" Jane enquired.

"No..." Elizabeth began, her voice unsure. "But what about Mr. Bingley?"

Jane lowered her eyes. "I must confess that I feel more relieved than guilty. I wish him all the best, but I think that what happened is better for the both of us. Although I am quite certain that Mr. Bingley does not share my opinion at this very moment."

"Where are you going to live?" Elizabeth asked. "When Lady Catherine hears about this..." she started but Jane interrupted her.

"Lady Catherine has already signed the documents stating that Richard is the owner of Rosings Park. She is moving to Bath," Jane explained. "My husband says that it is too painful for her to stay any longer in the place where her daughter was born and spent her childhood."

"Will she not change her mind about giving the estate to Colonel Fitzwilliam once she learns he is married to you?" Elizabeth fretted. "Lady Catherine hates me and you are my sister."

Jane shook her head. "Richard claims she is a different woman now, so grief stricken that she cares little about the world or the people around her."

Elizabeth was silent for a moment before taking her sister's hand in hers. "I am truly happy for you Jane; it is all very surprising but I am pleased if you are."

Jane squeezed her hand in return, speaking with great emotion. "Thank you, Elizabeth. You know that your approval is of the utmost importance to me."

"Colonel Fitzwilliam is a good man and at least you will not have Caroline Bingley for a sister.

Jane laughed. "That is very convenient indeed." Her expression sobered as she placed her hand on her sister's belly. "Now, tell me how you are feeling. Mr. Darcy told us that you were in pain earlier today."

***

Darcy entered the bedchamber late in the evening fully expecting to find his wife sleeping soundly. Thankfully the pains had not returned and on her second visit Mrs. Harris assured them that it had been only a false alarm. Instead he found the bed empty.

"Elizabeth?" he asked softly, thinking that she must be in the dressing room.

"I am here." Her voice came from the balcony.

"What are you doing out here?" he asked, stepping out next to her. "You will catch a cold."

"I will not; the night is quite warm, and I have this," she answered, wrapping a woollen blanket tighter around her body.

"Feeling well?" he asked, touching the bulge of their baby.

"Yes, but I cannot sleep."

He smiled. "Kicking again?"

"It likes to sleep during the day and become active in the evening."

Cupping her cheek, he ventured, "It was quite a day, was it not?"

"I still cannot believe that my sister is now married to your cousin."

"I am pleased for them, but worried for Bingley. It must have been quite a blow to him."

"Yes, I feel so sorry for him. He was such a good friend to us and helped me so much during your illness."

"Nevertheless, I would do the same if I was in Richard's shoes and you were engaged to another."

"Would you capture me and carry me away?" she asked, looking up at him with warmth in her eyes.

"Always love."

Taking Elizabeth in his arms, he kissed her tenderly under the star lit night. And as he held her to his heart, he was thankful that he had had the foresight to marry for love instead of following his peers and entering a marriage where there was neither affection nor a clear understanding of mind.

"Come love, let us return to bed. The cock will crow soon enough announcing yet another day."

They walked back inside, closing the French doors behind them.

Epilogue

Thomas George Darcy was born on May 10th 1813. He announced his arrival with a set of strong lungs, putting everyone on notice that the new heir to Pemberley had arrived. Nevertheless, his father's joy at the birth of a healthy son, with his mother's beautiful eyes, was short lived. After the strenuous birth Mrs. Darcy developed a fever which held her in its grip for three days.

Even though she overcame the illness and in the space of a month returned to good health, her husband swore that Thomas would be their last child. He would never again put her through such suffering or risk losing her forever. He was of opinion that his son would benefit more from having a mother than from having a sibling or two.

Despite his resolution, he did not take a separate bedroom, and only applied every precaution he knew to prevent another conception. As a result of his actions, around the time when Thomas was learning to sit up by himself, Elizabeth gave him the news that she was again with child. It was then, he was convinced , that the grey hair appeared more markedly at his temples.

The second pregnancy mirrored the first with the only difference being that when the pains came about six weeks early, they were not false. Another boy was delivered, much smaller than his brother, but healthy and breathing well on his own. They named him John Edward.

Mrs. Darcy lost a lot of blood, additionally once again developing a fever. For almost a week the entire estate of Pemberley prayed for her recovery. Her return to health this time was very slow. But most upsetting was that, according to both doctor and the midwife, the birth was so difficult that she would not be able to have any more children.

In contrast to his wife, Darcy was relieved with the news, though he never admitted it aloud to anyone. Seeing how dangerous each birth had been, he silently thanked the God for this development. He felt relieved that he could enjoy his wife without the threat of another pregnancy. And though Elizabeth wished for a daughter, he believed they should be grateful to be blessed with two strong, healthy boys—even more so, as they would have their mother well and living.

By the time John was one and Thomas two, Mrs. Darcy had recovered from her melancholy, and devoted herself completely to raising their sons. Contrary to the practice of many of the women in her social circle, she never left her children to the sole care of a nursemaid. It was her face they saw every morning, and it was their father who put them to bed every evening. When Darcy was busy with estate matters the children were with their mother. And when Elizabeth was occupied with her duties, visiting tenants, or calling on neighbours, Darcy or Georgiana kept a close eye on them. Practically the only time the boys were with their nursemaid was when both of their parents and their aunt had social functions or were not at home.

Such an approach to child rearing raised a lot of eyebrows, and more than one person criticized it. Those voices of disapproval died down once the boys began to grow into fine young men. In fact, the entirety of Derbyshire admired how decent, honourable, polite and handsome Thomas and John Darcy were.

Colonel Fitzwilliam and Jane moved to Rosings Park. Lady Catherine never acknowledged her nephew's marriage; nor did she make any attempt to disrupt their happiness. She remained indifferent, lost in her grief, living alone in Bath for the rest of her life.

Mr. Bingley terminated the lease of Netherfield Park and on the invitation of the Darcys, he came to spend time at Pemberley after being solemnly assured that Colonel Fitzwilliam and his wife were not there, nor did they intend to visit.

After six months spent sleeping late and drowning his sorrow in drink inside Pemberley's library, Bingley began to return to his old self. Darcy convinced him it would be good to buy an estate in Derbyshire, only twenty miles from Pemberley. The constant admiring glances and blushes from Georgiana Darcy did a great deal to heal his bruised ego and they fell in love and were married on her twentieth birthday.

Elizabeth maintained a close relationship with Jane, though mainly through letters as the sisters saw each other rarely. Elizabeth and Darcy made a point to travel to Kent once a year as it was easier than inviting the Fitzwilliams to Pemberley. The Bingleys and their children were frequent guests and he had made it perfectly clear that he had no wish to see Jane or her husband ever again. His wish was, nonetheless, not to be granted. Years later, his eldest son, while staying for a weekend at Pemberley, met a beautiful blonde girl

strolling in the park. He fell instantly in love and was adamant about courting her, eventually asking for her hand. He did not mind in the least that her

name was Elizabeth Fitzwilliam—the only child of Colonel and Mrs. Fitzwilliam of Rosings Park in Kent. This explains how, nearly thirty years after they had parted, the former Miss Jane Bennet and her first love, Mr. Charles Bingley, ended up having a civil conversation while they attended their children's wedding.

As for the two unmarried Bennet sisters, they were more than eager to leave Purvis Lodge and their mother's company. Mary accepted Jane's invitation to stay at Rosings Park and eventually she married the new parson at Hunsford. Kitty spent a few months at Pemberley, but when she received an invitation to stay with the Gardiners in London, she chose the hustle and bustle of town over the peacefulness of the country. There she met her uncle's business partner, a wealthy widower with three young children and they married soon after.

As for Lydia, she ceased contact with her sisters and for nearly two years there was no news from her. Just when Elizabeth lost any hope of ever seeing her again, she showed up at Pemberley one night with a little girl hiding behind her skirts. The child was small, no more than four, as well as undernourished and dressed in mismatched, thin clothes. However, she was strikingly beautiful and anyone who had ever seen Wickham had no doubt that she was his. She had violet-blue eyes, pale skin and black hair.

Lydia asked to stay for the night before continuing her journey. Elizabeth tried to gain more information, but her sister said only that she did not know where her husband was and that her little girl, Emma, was almost five. The next day, as Elizabeth entered the bedroom assigned to her sister, she found it empty. Lydia had left early that morning without a word of explanation or a simple goodbye. A few hours later, the maid who was cleaning the room found the little girl sitting in one of the wardrobes.

Elizabeth's heart broke when she learned that little Emma had been abandoned by both of her parents and the Darcys decided to take her in. For Elizabeth she was the daughter she could not have, while for Darcy, helping Emma eased his guilt over doing so little to help Lydia when she eloped with Wickham.

The beginning of Emma's life at Pemberley was difficult. She kept Elizabeth on the verge of tears with her behaviour which reflected the mistreatment she had suffered in her short life. Given Georgiana's old childhood bed, it was brought from the attic to the nursery and placed next to the boys' beds. Elizabeth planned to give her a separate room when she was older, but for now she thought that having company might be better. Even though they put her to bed every night in the same manner as the boys, covering her with a blanket and kissing her forehead, in the morning the bed would be empty and she would be curled under it, holding the blanket tightly. They tried to explain to her that she did not have to hide under the bed, but the child repeated this routine for the first two weeks. The boys must have taken it for an invitation to play, because one day Elizabeth entered the nursery to find all three children asleep on the floor, each under their respective beds.

Emma spoke not a word for the first year she was at Pemberley and Elizabeth had begun to believe that she was mute. The boys bonded quickly with her though, treating her as a sister and including her in their daily activities. Elizabeth noticed that Emma had no difficulty in communicating with her cousins, using her hands and facial expressions, even though she was still not speaking. She spoke her very first words when Darcy took her for a pony ride—thank you.

Despite the unhappy beginning of her life, Emma grew into a beautiful, kind-hearted girl, never showing any of the bad traits of her father or mother's character. She married surprisingly well to a good man with a large fortune. One who did not mind the fact that his bride's mother, Lydia, was still a courtesan, famous among the leading peers in London's elite circles, having had many prominent lovers over the years.

Emma was always most grateful to her aunt and uncle for taking her in when no one wanted her. She considered Darcy and Elizabeth her parents and Thomas and John, her brothers. When John, as the second son, was looking for his place in life, she convinced her husband to admit him to his ship building company. In time John became his partner, earning quite a fortune for himself which allowed him to live a very comfortable life. His fortune was not too far beneath that of his elder brother, Thomas, who took his rightful place as the Master of Pemberley.

Mrs. Bennet alienated herself from her children, as well as from the rest of her family both in London and Meryton. Her daughters avoided her and she never met all her grandchildren, though she had ten.

As her sons and daughter got older and left for school, Elizabeth began to feel restless not knowing what to do with her long days. She returned to a habit from her youth, writing short stories about fairies. After reading them, her husband encouraged her to send the manuscript to a publisher in London. They were published under a pseudonym and only her closest friends and family knew that Elizabeth Darcy was the author. The stories turned out to be an instant success among children, as well as their parents, and became the standard for children's literature for many generations.

The Darcys kept a close friendship with the Gardiners their entire life, always grateful for everything that they had done in bringing them together.

The End

Made in the USA
Lexington, KY
10 October 2011